Anna Zaires

♠ Mozaika Publications ♠

Published by Mozaika Publications, an imprint of Mozaika LLC.
www.mozaikallc.com

Cover by Najla Qamber Designs
www.najlaqamberdesigns.com

e-ISBN: 978-1-63142-349-9
Print ISBN-13: 978-1-63142-350-5

PART 1

CHAPTER 1
HENDERSON

"What are you doing?"

Bonnie's anxious voice startles me out of my planning, and I look up, shoving the folder I was studying into a stack of files on my desk as I prepare to answer with a plausible lie.

Except my wife of twenty-one years is not looking at me.

She's staring at the computer behind me, where a photograph of a beautiful chestnut-haired bride smiling up at her handsome groom takes up most of the screen.

Fuck. I thought I'd closed that tab. My neck muscles spasm with tension, the bile returning to burn up my throat as I see Bonnie begin to shake.

"Why do you have his picture?" Her voice turns shrill as her eyes swing to me, accusing. "Why do you have that monster's picture on your screen?"

"Bonnie… It's not what you think." I stand up, but she's already backing away, shaking her head, her long earrings flapping around her skinny face.

"You promised. You told me we'll be safe."

"And we will be," I say, but it's too late.

She's already gone.

Back to the refuge of her bed, her pills, her mindless reality TV.

Back to where the kids and I can never reach her.

Sinking back into my chair, I roll my head from side to side, releasing the worst of the agonizing tightness as I pull out the folder again. The name inside stares at me, each letter taunting me, stoking the bitter fires of rage.

Peter Sokolov.

I'm the last person remaining on his list. The only one he hasn't killed yet for what happened in that shitty village in Dagestan. One mistake, one careless order given, and this is the result. For years, he's hunted me and my family, torturing our friends and loved ones in an effort to get to me, starring in my children's nightmares, destroying our lives in every way.

And now, thanks to his buddy Esguerra's pull with our government, he's allowed to roam free. To marry his pretty, chestnut-haired doctor and live in the United States as if all's forgiven and forgotten.

As if his promise not to kill me is something I'm supposed to believe.

My gaze falls on the rest of the names in the folder.

Julian Esguerra.

Lucas Kent.

Yan and Ilya Ivanov.
Anton Rezov.
Sokolov's allies—monsters, all of them.
They must pay for what they've done.
Like Sokolov, they must be neutralized.
Then and only then will we be truly safe.

CHAPTER 2
SARA

I wake up with the startling realization that I'm married.

Married to Peter Garin, a.k.a. Sokolov.

The man who killed George Cobakis, my first husband, after breaking into my house and torturing me.

My stalker.

My kidnapper.

The love of my life.

My mind jumps to last night, and heat spreads throughout my body—a mixture of embarrassment and arousal. He punished me yesterday. Punished me for nearly standing him up at the altar.

He took me brutally, and in the process, he made me admit it.

Made me confess that I love him—*all* of him, the dark parts included.

That I need that darkness... need it directed at me, so I can overcome the shame and guilt of knowing I fell for a monster.

Opening my eyes, I stare at the bland white ceiling. We're still in my small apartment, but I'm guessing we'll move soon. And then what? Children? Walks in the park and dinners with my parents?

Am I really about to build a life with the man who threatened to kill everyone at our wedding if I didn't show up?

He must be making breakfast because I smell delicious scents coming from the kitchen. It's something both sweet and savory, and my stomach growls as I sit up, wincing at the soreness in my hamstrings.

If we're going to be fucking in exotic positions a lot, I might have to take up yoga.

Shaking my head at the ridiculous thought, I go to shower and brush my teeth, and by the time I come out, dressed in a robe, I hear Peter's deep, softly accented voice calling me.

Or more precisely, calling his "ptichka."

"I'm here," I say, walking into the kitchen—only to find myself swept up in incredibly strong arms and kissed so thoroughly that I lose my breath.

"Yes, you are," my husband murmurs when he finally sets me back on my feet. "You're here, and you're not going anywhere." His large hands rest possessively on my waist, his gray eyes gleaming like silver in his stubble-darkened face. Though he's dressed in a T-shirt and jeans, he must not have shaved yet, because that stubble looks deliciously rough and scratchy, making me wonder what it would be like to have him rub it all over my skin.

Impulsively, I lift my hand to his chiseled jaw. It's just as scratchy as I imagined, and I grin as he closes his eyes and rubs his face against my palm, like a big tomcat marking his territory.

"It's Sunday," I tell him, lowering my hand when he opens his eyes. "So yes, I'm not going anywhere. What's for breakfast?"

He grins and steps back, releasing me. "Ricotta pancakes. You hungry?"

"I could definitely eat," I admit, and watch his metallic eyes brighten with pleasure.

I sit down as he grabs plates for both of us and sets them on the table. Though he only came back for me last Tuesday, he's already completely at home in my tiny kitchen, his movements as smooth and confident as if he's been living here for months.

Watching him, I again get the unsettling sensation that a dangerous predator has invaded my small apartment. Partially, it's his size—he's at least a head taller than I am, his shoulders impossibly broad, his elite soldier's body packed with hard muscle. But it's also something about *him*, something more than the tattoos that decorate his left arm or the faint scar that bisects his eyebrow.

It's something intrinsic, a kind of ruthlessness that's there even when he smiles.

"How are you feeling, ptichka?" he asks, joining me at the table, and I look down at my plate, knowing why he's concerned.

"Fine." I don't want to think about yesterday, about how Agent Ryson's visit had literally made me sick. I'd already been anxious about the wedding, but it wasn't until the FBI agent slapped me in the face with Peter's crimes that I lost the contents of my stomach—and nearly stood Peter up.

"No ill effects from last night?" he clarifies, and I look up, my face heating as I realize he's referring to our sex life.

"No." My voice is choked. "I'm fine."

"Good," he murmurs, his gaze hot and dark, and I hide my intensifying blush by reaching for a ricotta pancake.

"Here, my love." He expertly plates two pancakes for me and pushes a bottle of maple syrup my way. "Do you want anything else? Maybe some fruit?"

"Sure," I say and watch as he walks over to the fridge to take out and wash some berries.

My domesticated assassin. Is this what our life together will always be like?

"What do you want to do today?" I ask when he returns to the table, and he shrugs, his sculpted lips curved in a smile.

"It's up to you, ptichka. I was thinking we could go out, enjoy the beautiful day."

"So… a walk in the park? Really?"

He frowns. "Why not?"

"No reason. I'm game." I focus on my pancakes so I don't start giggling hysterically.

He wouldn't understand.

We eat quickly—I'm hungry, and the ricotta pancakes (*sirniki*, he calls them) are to die for—and then we head out to the park. Peter is driving, and when we're halfway there, I notice a black SUV following us.

"Is that Danny again?" I ask, glancing back.

Ever since Peter's return, the Feds have left us alone, and Peter is much too calm about the tail for it to be anyone but the bodyguard/driver he hired.

To my surprise, Peter shakes his head. "Danny is off today. It's a couple of other guys from that crew."

Ah. I turn around in my seat to study the SUV. The windows are tinted, so I can't see in. Frowning, I look back at Peter. "You think we still need all that security?"

He shrugs. "I hope not. But better safe than sorry."

"And this car?" I look around the luxurious Mercedes sedan Peter bought last week. "Is it extra secure somehow?" I rap my knuckles on the window. "This seems really thick."

His expression doesn't change. "Yes. The glass is bulletproof."

"Oh. Wow."

He glances at me, a faint smile appearing on his lips. "Don't worry, ptichka. I have no reason to think we'll get shot at. This is just a precaution, that's all."

"Right." Just a precaution—like the weapons he had inside his jacket at our wedding. Or the bodyguard/driver who's there to pick me up when Peter can't. Because normal suburban couples always have bodyguards and bulletproof cars.

"Tell me about the houses you found," I say, shoving aside the unease generated by the thought of all those security measures. Given his former profession and the kinds of enemies he's made, Peter's paranoia makes perfect sense, and I'm not about to object to whatever precautions he deems necessary.

Like he said, better safe than sorry.

"I'm going to show you the listings in a second," he says, and I realize we're already at our destination.

He expertly parks the car and walks around to open the door for me. I place my hand in his, letting him help me out, and I'm not the least bit surprised when he uses the opportunity to draw me to him for a kiss.

His lips are soft and gentle as they touch mine, his breath flavored with maple syrup. There is no urgency in this kiss, no darkness—just tenderness and desire. Yet when he lifts his head, my pulse is just as fast as if he'd ravished me, my skin warm and tingling where his palm cradles my cheek.

"I love you," he murmurs, gazing down at me, and I beam up at him, my unease replaced by a light, buoyant sensation.

"I love you too." The words come even easier today—because they're true. I do love Peter.

I love him even though he still terrifies me.

He grins and leads me to a bench. "Here." He pulls me down to sit and takes out his phone, swiping across the screen a few times before handing it to me. "These are the listings I've found," he says, looking at me with a warm silver gaze. "Let me know which houses you like, and we can go see them."

I flip through the pictures as the buoyant feeling intensifies.

Is this what true happiness feels like?

"Let's walk and talk," I tell him when I'm done looking through the photos, and he gladly agrees, clasping my hand in a firm grip as we wander through the park and discuss the pros and cons of the different houses.

"You don't think four bedrooms is too small?" he asks, gazing down at me with a questioning smile, and I shake my head.

"Why would I think that?"

"Well…" He stops and faces me. "Have you considered how many kids you'd like to have?"

My stomach dives. Here it is—the topic we've been avoiding since Cyprus, when Peter admitted he was trying to impregnate me and I crashed a car trying to escape. I was expecting it to come up at some point—we haven't been using condoms since Peter's return and he outright told my parents he'd like us to start a family soon. Still, my heart pounds in my chest, and my palm grows sweaty in Peter's grasp as I try to imagine what it would be like to have a child with him.

With the merciless killer who obsessively loves me.

Taking a breath, I reach deep for my courage. Peter is no longer a criminal, no longer a fugitive, and I'm his wife, not his captive. He gave up his vengeance so we could have this—a real life together.

Walks in the park, children, and all.

"I've been picturing three," I say steadily, holding his gaze. "But I think I could also be happy with one. What about you?"

A tender smile blooms on his darkly handsome face. "Definitely at least two—assuming all goes well with the first." He places his big palm on my stomach. "Do you think there's a chance...?"

I laugh, stepping away. "Are you kidding me? It's way too soon to tell. You came back less than a week ago. If I knew I was pregnant, that would be problematic."

"Very," he agrees, catching my hand and squeezing it possessively. We resume walking, and he gives me a sidelong glance. "I take it you're okay with this?"

"With a baby now, you mean?"

He nods, and I take a deep breath, looking ahead at a group of skateboarding teens. "I guess. I'd still like to wait a little, but I know this means a lot to you."

He doesn't answer, and when I look at him, I see that his expression has darkened, his jaw tight as he stares straight ahead. The buoyant feeling evaporates as I realize I've inadvertently reminded him of the tragedy in his past.

"I'm sorry." I raise our clasped hands to press his fist against my chest. "I didn't mean to remind you of your family."

His gaze meets mine, and some of the raw agony in it recedes. "It's okay, ptichka." His voice is husky as he lifts our joined hands higher to drop a tender kiss on my knuckles. "You don't have to walk on eggshells around me. Pasha and Tamila will always live in my memories, but *you* are my family now."

My heart squeezes into an aching ball. He's right. I *am* his family—and he is mine. Because the wedding happened so fast, I didn't have a chance to truly think about that, to articulate that reality in my mind.

We're married.

Truly married.

I can no longer think of George as my husband because Peter holds that title now—just as he can't think of Tamila as his wife.

"And you're right," he continues as I process that realization. "Family is important to me. I want us to have a child, and I want it soon. However…" He hesitates, then says quietly, "If you want to wait, I won't force the issue."

I stop and gape at him. "Really? Why not?"

A quicksilver smile flashes across his face. "Do you want me to?"

"No! I just…" I shake my head, pulling my hand out of his grasp. "I don't understand. I thought that was part of it, you know, marriage and all. You forced the wedding, so…"

All traces of humor leave his gaze. "You nearly died, my love. In Cyprus, when you thought that I would force a child on you, you tried to escape and nearly died."

I bite my lip. "That was different. *We* were different."

"Yes. But childbirth in general can be dangerous. Even with all the medical advances today, a woman risks her health, if not her life. And if anything happened to you because I insisted…" He stops, his jaw clenching as he looks away.

I stare at him, my heart beating heavily in my chest. The odds of anything serious happening to me in childbirth are very low, and my first instinct as a doctor is to tell him that, to reassure him. But at the last second, I think better of it.

"So you would wait?" I ask carefully instead.

Peter turns back to face me, his gaze somber. "Do you want to wait, my love?"

Now it's my turn to look away. Do I? Up until this moment, I'd assumed that Peter's return and the rushed wedding meant that a child was imminent in our future. I'd resigned myself to the thought, even embraced it on some level.

If nothing else, my parents could have the grandchildren they've been wanting—a positive I hadn't considered until our dinner the other night.

"Sara?" Peter prompts, and I look up to meet his gaze.

Here it is.

My chance to delay it.

To do the right thing, the smart thing.

To have a child when I'm sure that we can make it, that Peter can live this kind of life.

All I have to do is say yes, use the choice he gave me, but my mouth refuses to form the word. Instead, as I hold his gaze, seeing the tension there, I hear myself say, "No."

"No?"

"No, I don't want to wait," I clarify, shutting down the rational voice screaming in my mind as I watch a bright, joyous smile curve his lips.

Maybe this is the wrong decision, but at this moment, it doesn't feel that way. Peter was right when he said that life is short. It *is* short and uncertain, full of pitfalls. I've always lived it cautiously, planning for the future on the assumption that there would be one, but if there's anything I've learned over the past couple of years, it's that there are no guarantees.

There's just today, just now.

Just us, together and in love.

We spend another hour in the park, then go grocery shopping together, stocking up on food for the week. Peter buys enough to feed ten people, and when I question him about that, he informs me that he intends to invite my parents for dinner this Friday—and to pack me lunch to take to work each day.

When we come home, he disappears into the kitchen, and I go on my computer to deal with the emailed congratulations and gift cards—a popular choice for the majority of the guests at our wedding, given that no one had time to shop for an actual gift. I print out all the gift cards, sort them into categories, apply the codes to specific retailers as needed, and email back thank-yous. The whole process takes less than forty minutes—yet another perk of our simple, speedy wedding.

With George, we spent two weekends in a row on this task.

I'm about to shut down the computer when I see another email in my inbox—this one from an unknown sender but also with the subject of "Congratulations."

I open it, expecting another gift card, but inside is just a short message.

Congratulations on a beautiful wedding. If you ever need to reach us, you can use this email address.

With best wishes,

Yan

I blink, staring at the email. I have no idea how Peter's former teammate got my email, or why he decided to write to me, but I add his email address to my contacts, just in case.

Done with the gifts, I follow the delicious smells into the kitchen, where Peter is preparing lunch.

Maybe it's too soon to tell, but I'm feeling optimistic.

This marriage thing is going to work out.

The two of us will make sure it does.

CHAPTER 3
PETER

As we eat lunch, I barely taste my food, all my attention on Sara as she tells me about the wedding gifts and Yan's strange email. Her hazel eyes look almost green as she animatedly gestures with her fork, her skin like pale cream in the bright sunlight streaming through the kitchen window. In a casual blue sundress, with her chestnut hair in loose waves around her slender shoulders, she's every dream of mine come to life, and my chest tightens at the recollection of what it was like to be without her all those months.

I'm never letting her go again.

She's mine, until death do us part.

"Why do you think he decided to give me his contact info? Do you think he just wants to keep in touch?" she asks, spearing a piece of cucumber in her Russian-style salad, and I force myself to focus on the conversation instead of how much I'd like to spread her out on the table and feast on her rather than the food I've prepared.

"I have no idea," I answer, and it's true. Yan Ivanov took over our assassination business after I left, so I can't imagine he'd want me back. For months before that, there was tension between us, and I suspect if I hadn't voluntarily stepped down as team leader, he would've done his best to take my place.

Then again, he doesn't think civilian life is for me; he stated as much at our wedding. So maybe he expects me to return and is keeping an eye on the situation just in case.

With Yan, one never knows.

"Well, I hope they come visit us," Sara says. "The guys, I mean. I didn't get a chance to talk to them at the wedding, and I feel bad about that."

I raise my eyebrows. "Really? *That* is what you feel bad about?"

She drops her gaze to her salad bowl. "And nearly standing you up, obviously."

The metal edges of the fork handle cut into my palm, and I realize I'm squeezing the utensil too hard. I'm no longer mad at my ptichka, though some of the hurt still lingers. I understand how difficult it was for her to admit she loves me, to embrace me fully after everything I've done. She needed me to leave her no choice, and I obliged, threatening her friends to make her show up at our wedding.

No, the source of my anger is not Sara, but the man who tried to manipulate her into bailing on our wedding.

Agent Ryson.

The fact that he dared to show up like that fills me with blistering fury. I leave Henderson alone, they leave me and Sara alone—that was the deal. No more FBI surveillance, no harassment, just a clean slate so we can lead peaceful lives.

He threatened Sara, too. Accused her of conspiring with me to kill her husband. I have no idea what he said to her, exactly, but it must've been bad to make her react so strongly.

Under any other circumstances, he would've already been rotting with the worms, but I'm supposed to be a law-abiding citizen now. I can't go around killing FBI agents—not without giving up the life I've fought for, the civilian life that Sara needs. So as tempting as it is, Ryson lives—for now, at least. Later on, when enough time has passed, he might meet with an unfortunate accident or an overly aggressive mugger, à la Sara's patient's stepfather... but that's a thought for another day.

Today I have Sara all to myself, and I intend to enjoy it.

"Don't worry, my love," I say when my new wife continues to eat quietly, avoiding my gaze. "It's over. It's in the past—as are whatever other mistakes we've made. Let's just focus on the present and the future... live our lives without always looking back."

She looks up, her eyes uncertain. "Do you really think we can?"

"Yes," I tell her firmly, and reaching over, I bring her hand to my lips for a tender kiss.

———————

After we eat lunch, we go see the listings I showed her, and Sara falls in love with one house—a five-bedroom Victorian that was built in the eighties but completely renovated last year. It has a large back yard—for the dog and the kids, she gleefully tells me—and a gorgeous fireplace in the living room. I'm not crazy that it's so close to the neighbors and the yard is completely open, but I figure if we plant some trees and put up a fence, we'll have sufficient privacy.

Either way, it's better than living in Sara's current rental.

Before we leave, I put in an above-market all-cash offer, and the realtor calls us a few minutes later to inform us that the offer has been accepted.

"That's it," I tell Sara when I hang up. "The closing is next week."

Her eyes widen. "Really? Just like that?"

"Why not?"

She laughs. "Oh, I don't know. I suppose because most people don't buy houses as easily as they buy shoes."

I smile and reach out to take her hand. "Most people aren't us."

"No," she agrees wryly, looking up at me. "They're not."

We return home, and I make us dinner—grilled scallops with sweet potato mash and steamed broccolini. As we eat, Sara brings up moving logistics, and I tell her that I'll take care of everything, just as I did with the wedding arrangements.

"All you'll need to do is show up at the new place," I say, pouring her a glass of Pinot Grigio. Then, remembering her inexplicable upset over the sale of her Toyota, I add,

"Unless there's something you want to decide on together? Maybe you want to choose new furniture or decorations?"

She smiles ruefully. "No, I think I'm good. I'm not overly picky about house stuff. If you want to run with it, I'm fine with that."

"To our new place, then." I lift my wine glass and clink it gently against hers. "And a new life."

"To our new life," she echoes softly, and as she sips from her glass, I can't help remembering the time when she tried to drug my wine, early on in our relationship. She'd been so defiant then, so sure that she hated me.

Does she still? In some small way?

My mood darkening, I set my wine down and stand up. Walking around the table, I pull Sara to her feet.

"What are you—" she begins, but I'm already kissing her, tasting the wine on her lips.

Her soft, plush lips that have been driving me to distraction all day.

I've been doing my best to act like a good husband, to do all the normal things with her instead of chaining her to my bed and fucking her all day long like my instincts demand. I've been calm and patient, letting her recover from last night, but I can't do the civilized thing any longer.

I need her.

Right here.

Right now.

Her arms wind around my neck, her slender body arching against me as I bend her over my arm, unable to get enough of the taste and smell of her, of the feel of her delicate tongue stroking against my own. She's fucking delicious, and my cock hardens, my heart thudding furiously in my ribcage as I clear the dishes from the table with one swipe of my arm, heedless of the mess I'm creating.

We need to get new dinnerware anyway.

She gasps as I stretch her out on the table and flip up the skirt of her sundress, exposing pale thighs and a pretty blue thong edged with lace. Unable to control myself, I tear off the scrap of silk and bury my head between her thighs, my tongue dipping hungrily between her folds, my lips closing around her clit on a hard, greedy suck as I drape her legs over my shoulders.

"Peter… Oh God, Peter…" Her hips lift off the table, her hands fisting tightly in my hair, and I feel like my cock will explode in my jeans at the taste of her, at the warm, feminine scent and the feel of her silky flesh under my tongue. I love everything about this, from the way her sharp little nails scratch my skull and her toned thighs squeeze my ears, to the gasping sounds tearing from her throat and the way her slick pussy quivers and contracts under my tongue.

This is paradise, fucking heaven, and I can't believe I went without it—without *her*—for nine agonizing months.

Continuing to feast on her clit, I slip a finger inside and feel her inner walls clench around the intrusion as her hips lift and shimmy, wordlessly begging for more.

"Almost there… just a bit more," I growl into her folds, stroking her from the inside, and as I find the bit of spongy tissue that signifies her G-spot, her whole body arches and she comes with a keening cry, her hands clenching spasmodically in my hair as her pussy pulses around my finger.

By now, my cock is threatening to explode inside my jeans, so I withdraw my finger and flip her over onto her stomach. Then I pull her toward me until she's bent over the table, her dress bunched up around her waist, exposing the firm white globes of her ass and a pussy glistening with her wetness and my saliva. Unable to wait even a second longer, I unzip my jeans and push them down along with my briefs, freeing my aching cock.

"Ready?" I say hoarsely, leaning over her as I guide myself to her entrance, and her breath audibly hitches as I push in without waiting for a reply.

Inside, she's velvety soft and slick, her tender flesh gripping me tightly, sheathing me so perfectly that my balls draw up against my body and a low groan escapes my throat as my fingers dig into her hips.

This is fucking madness, total and utter insanity. After our talk last night, we had sex two more times before falling asleep, and I shouldn't be feeling like this, so desperately hungry for her that I'm on the verge of losing control. But I am that hungry. I'm ravenous for all things Sara. The need to possess her claws at my bones, the dark lust arcing up and down my spine. I feel it burning in my veins, incinerating me from the inside out.

She's my addiction, and I can't get enough.

Releasing her hips, I reach over and grab her elbows, pulling on them to make her arch her back before I slam into her harder, feeling her inner muscles clench around me as I start fucking her in earnest.

She cries out with every punishing thrust, her upper body lifted off the table by my grip on her elbows, and I feel the orgasm boiling up within me, the pleasure rising like a tidal wave. Groaning, I throw back my head, hammering into her faster, and her cries intensify, her pussy tightening around me as her whole body goes stiff. I feel her spasms begin, and then I'm there, my cock jerking in release as her wet flesh pulses around me, milking me, squeezing me until there's nothing left.

Until I collapse over her, pressing her into the table as I breathe heavily, inhaling the heady scent of sex and sweat and her.

My Sara. My wife.

My obsession.

We could spend an eternity together, and that still wouldn't be enough.

CHAPTER 4
HENDERSON

I lie in bed, staring at the ceiling. For the second night, I can't sleep, dark thoughts crawling around my mind as my neck keeps locking up.

The plan I'm formulating is extreme, monstrous even, but I don't see any other choice. I can't strike at Sokolov directly—he and his bride are too well guarded. If I try and miss, there will be hell to pay.

Besides, Sokolov is not the only one I want eliminated.

His allies are just as dangerous… to me, to my family, and to the world at large.

This is really the only way.

He and the others must be made to pay.

CHAPTER 5
SARA

I wake up to the quiet beeping of my alarm. Shutting it off, I roll over onto my back and stretch, feeling both sore and satisfied. After we cleaned up the kitchen and showered, Peter took me one more time before we fell asleep, and then again during the night.

Someone needs to bottle up the man's sex drive and sell it as a drug. They'd make a fortune.

Grinning at the thought, I hop out of bed and run into the shower. I can already smell whatever deliciousness Peter is cooking in the kitchen, and my stomach is more than ready to start the day.

"Morning, ptichka," he greets me when I step into the kitchen after quickly showering and getting dressed for work. On the table are two plates with avocado toast and egg, and on the counter is a lunch bag—I presume for me to take to work.

"Hi." My heartbeat accelerates as I take him in. He's shirtless today, his dark jeans riding low on his hips and the tattoos on his arm gleaming in the morning light. His body is a work of art, with perfectly defined muscles and broad shoulders tapering to a narrow waist. Even the scars on his torso have a kind of violent, dangerous beauty to them—just like the man himself.

"Do you have time to eat?" he asks, and I nod, fighting the urge to lick my lips as his ab muscles flex in front of me.

Maybe Peter is not the only one with an insane libido.

The condition might be contagious.

"I have fifteen minutes," I say huskily, forcing myself to walk over to the table instead of toward him. If I give him a good-morning kiss now, we'll end up right back in bed.

"Good. I'll take you to work this morning," he says, joining me at the table. Picking up his toast, he bites into it, and I do the same with mine, enjoying the zesty lime flavor combined with the savory fried egg and crisp rye bread.

"Is this a busy week for you?" he asks when I'm almost done with my toast, and I nod, patting my lips with a napkin.

"Yes, actually. Really busy. Wendy and Bill—you know, my bosses—just took off for vacation, so I'm seeing some of their patients in addition to my own. Oh, and I'm inducing one of my patients tomorrow afternoon, so I'll probably be home late. Plus, I have some shifts at the clinic in the second half of the week."

"I see." Peter's expression is neutral, but I sense a subtle darkening of his mood. He's not happy about this, and I can't blame him.

I'd also rather spend time with him than go to work.

"Will you be home for dinner tonight?" he asks, and I smile, glad to be able to give him some good news on this front.

"I should be. If there are no emergencies."

"Right." He stands up. "Let me grab a shirt, and I'll drive you to the office."

"Thank you—and thanks for the delicious breakfast," I call out, but he's already gone into the bedroom.

CHAPTER 6
PETER

Sara's office is walking distance from her apartment, so the drive is just a few short minutes. All too soon, I'm pulling up to the curb and handing Sara her lunch, all the while feeling like I'd sooner gnaw my arm off than let her out of the car.

I hate that I won't see her all day long, that I won't be able to touch her or talk to her until evening. It's even harder than last week because we got to spend this Sunday together—and I now know what paradise feels like.

It's what we had back in Japan, only without the bitter animosity—without Sara resenting me for stealing her away from her career and everyone she loves.

It takes all my strength to remain seated and calm as she kisses my cheek and whispers, "Love you. See you soon," before jumping out of the car.

I watch her slim figure disappear into her office building, and then I message the crew to give them their Sara-watching instructions for the day.

If I can't be with her, at least I'll know where she is and what she's doing.

At least I'll be sure she's safe.

I spend the morning transferring the funds for the closing this Thursday and organizing the upcoming move. I plan to have us in the new house by next week, which means there's a lot of work to be done. Though the place has just been renovated and won't require major upgrades, I have to install proper security measures.

Suburbia or not, our house will be a fortress, and no one—least of all Agent Ryson—will be able to accost Sara at home again.

It's mid-afternoon and I'm washing vegetables for dinner when my phone vibrates on the countertop. Pressing on the screen with one semi-dry finger, I skim Sara's text.

So sorry. Just got a call from the clinic. They're completely overrun, and they're begging me to come in tonight. It'll only be until ten or so. Again, I'm so sorry.

The zucchini I was washing snaps in half, and I shove the phone away with my elbow to avoid subjecting it to the same fate.

I should've fucking known. "If no emergencies come up" is code for "an emergency is bound to come up." It was that way before Japan, and even though Sara's current job is less focused on the obstetrics side of OB-GYN, her mindset hasn't changed.

Work still comes first for her, even volunteer work at the clinic.

It takes me a solid twenty minutes to calm down and start thinking rationally. Sara's career is one of the reasons I went through all that trouble with Novak and Esguerra, why I agreed to give up my revenge on Henderson. Being a doctor—helping patients—is important to her; she needs her career as much as she needs to be near her family and friends. I knew this when I stole her away, but it didn't matter to me at the time.

All that mattered was keeping her.

Now that I have her and she's happy, I can't regress to that way of thinking, can't forget what it was like when I was the source of her misery, when every time she looked at me, I saw torment in her eyes.

It's different now. Whatever her remaining reservations, she's finally admitted that she loves me—loves me enough to have my child.

A daughter or a son... like Pasha.

For a moment, it hurts to breathe again, but then the pain passes, leaving a bittersweet ache in its wake. I've been able to think of Pasha like this more and more in recent months, without the rage poisoning the memories. And I know it's all due to her.

My little songbird whom I so badly want to cage again.

Taking a deep breath, I slowly let it out and focus on the calming task of making dinner.

If Sara can't come home tonight, I'll just have to come to her.

CHAPTER 7
SARA

I expect someone from Peter's crew to take me to the clinic, but Peter himself is waiting for me by the curb.

I grin, some of my tiredness fading as his eyes skim over my body before settling hungrily on my face.

"Hi." I walk straight into his embrace and inhale deeply as his strong arms close around me, pressing me tightly against his chest. He smells warm, clean, and distinctly male—a familiar Peter scent I now associate with comfort.

He holds me for a few long moments, then pulls back to gaze down at me. "How was your day, my love?" he asks softly, brushing my hair off my face.

I beam up at him. "Crazy busy, but all better now." I'm ridiculously overjoyed that he came to bring me to the clinic himself.

He grins back at me. "Miss me, did you?"

"I did," I admit as he opens the car door and helps me in. "I really did."

His answering smile makes me want to melt into the seat. "And I missed you, ptichka."

"I'm sorry I have to do this," I say as we pull away from the curb. The car smells of something deliciously spicy, and my stomach rumbles as I say, "I was really looking forward to having a nice dinner at home."

Peter glances at me. "I brought you dinner. It's on the back seat."

"You did?" I turn around in my seat and spot the source of the delicious smell—another lunch bag. "Wow, thank you. You didn't have to, but I really appreciate it." Stretching, I grab the bag and put it on my lap.

I was going to buy some pretzels from a vending machine at the clinic, but this is infinitely better.

"Why *do* you have to do this?" Peter asks, stopping at a red light. His tone is casual, but I'm not fooled.

He was looking forward to our dinner as well.

"I really am sorry," I say, and I mean it. When Lydia, the receptionist at the clinic, called me at lunchtime, I came very close to refusing her pleas—but in the end, the knowledge that a few dozen women would miss out on their cancer screenings and essential prenatal care if I didn't show up won out. "They're short of volunteers today, and I couldn't leave them in the lurch."

He gives me a sidelong look. "Couldn't you?"

I pause in the middle of opening the lunch bag. "No," I say evenly. "I couldn't."

Here it is, what I was afraid of all along. I suspected it was only a matter of time before my long hours would start bothering Peter, and it seems that I was right to worry.

Tensing, I prepare to hear an ultimatum, but Peter just presses on the gas, accelerating smoothly.

"Eat, my love," he says in the same casual tone. "You don't have a lot of time."

I follow his suggestion and dig into the food—a vegetable medley with couscous and roasted chicken. The seasoning reminds me of the delicious lamb kebab Peter made for us back in Japan, and I inhale everything in a matter of minutes.

"Thank you," I say, wiping my mouth with a paper towel he so thoughtfully packed along with the utensils. "That was amazing."

"You're welcome." He turns onto the street where the clinic is and parks right in front of the building. "Come, I'll walk you in."

"Oh, you don't have to—" I stop because he's already walking around the car.

Opening the door for me, he helps me out and shepherds me to the building, as though I might wander off if he doesn't keep a hand on the small of my back.

I expect him to stop when we reach the door, but he comes inside with me.

Confused, I stop and look up at him. "What are you doing?"

"There you are!" Lydia hurries toward me, her broad face relieved. "Thank God. I thought you weren't going to— Oh, hi." She blushes, staring at Peter with what I can only interpret as a full-blown crush.

"Peter was just—" I start, but he smiles and steps forward.

"Peter Garin. We met at our wedding," he says, extending his hand.

The receptionist's eyes go wide, and she clasps his hand, giving it a vigorous shake. "Lydia," she says breathlessly. "Congrats again. It was a beautiful event."

"Thank you." He grins at her, and I can almost sense her swooning on the inside. "You know, Sara just told me you're short on volunteers today. I'm no doctor, obviously, but maybe there's something I can do to help out around here tonight? Maybe you have some files that need sorting, or something that needs fixing? We only have one car for now, and I'd rather not drive back and forth to pick up Sara."

"Oh, of course." Lydia's excitement level visibly quadruples. "Please, there's so much work. And did you say you're handy? Do you by any chance also know something about computers? Because there's this stubborn software program…"

She leads him away, chattering, and I stare in disbelief as my assassin husband disappears around the corner without so much as a look back.

CHAPTER 8
PETER

I help Lydia with her software issue, fix a leaking faucet, and hang up a few decorations in the waiting area while two dozen women—many of them visibly pregnant—watch me in fascination.

As the only doctor here tonight, Sara has a never-ending stream of patients, so I don't bother her. It's enough to know that she's just a couple of rooms away, and I can reach her in a minute if I need to.

Once all the basic tasks are done, I get to work assembling an ultrasound machine that a local hospital donated. I've never worked with medical equipment before, but I've always been good at putting things together—weapons, explosives, communication devices—so it's not long before I figure out what goes where and how to test it to make sure it's working.

"Oh my God, you're a lifesaver, just like your wife," Lydia exclaims when I show it to her. "We've been waiting for a technician to stop by for months, and oh, this is going to be so helpful! Sara is with her last patient now. Do you think you might have time to fix up this one cabinet, too? It's been drooping and—"

"No problem." I follow her to one of the exam rooms and add a few screws to make sure the cabinet in question doesn't fall on anyone's head.

"You are so good at this," the receptionist gushes when I'm finished. "Did you ever work in construction, by any chance? You seem so practiced with that drill and all..."

"I worked on some construction projects as a teen," I say without elaborating. This woman doesn't need to know that the "projects" were forced labor in a youth version of a Siberian *gulag*.

"Oh, I thought so." She beams at me. "Let me check if Sara is done."

"Please." I smile back at her. "I'd like to take my wife home."

The receptionist hurries away, and I stretch my arms, releasing the stiffness in my muscles. It's only been a few days, but I'm getting restless, eager to move and do something physical. After I made dinner, I went for a long run in the park and stopped by a boxing gym to work off some steam, but I need more.

I need a challenge of some kind.

For the first time, I seriously consider what I'm going to do with the rest of my life. Thanks to the Esguerra-Novak double gig, I have enough money for me, Sara, and a dozen kids/grandkids—particularly if we don't get into the habit of buying private planes, specialized weapons, or other expensive props. I don't have to work to support us, and I didn't make any plans beyond getting Sara and binding her to me—partially because I've always enjoyed the downtime between jobs.

Now I'm starting to realize that was because I knew that the time off was temporary, that another challenging, adrenaline-filled mission was in my future. Now there's nothing—just a series of calm, peaceful days stretching out into infinity.

Days where all I'm going to be doing is thinking about Sara and waiting for her to come home.

"Peter?" Sara pokes her head into the room, and a big smile lights her face when she lays her eyes on me. "I'm ready to go home if you are."

"Let's go," I say, and shelve the problem for another day.

I'll think about what to do with my time later.

For now, I've got my ptichka, and she's all I need.

CHAPTER 9
SARA

The next two days fly by in a blur of work. On Tuesday, I stay late in the hospital for a delivery, and Wednesday is another shift at the clinic, where I'm once again the only doctor seeing all the patients.

It's exhausting, but I don't mind because Peter finds a way to be near me both evenings—on Tuesday, by catching up on some emails at the Snacktime Café by the hospital, so I can pop out to see him while waiting for my patient to be ready to deliver, and on Wednesday, by volunteering at the clinic alongside me again.

"Why are you doing this?" I ask him as we're driving to the clinic. "I mean, don't get me wrong, I'm very glad you are—and Lydia is over the moon, for sure. But is this really what you want?"

He glances at me, his eyes gleaming silver. "What I want is you, in my bed twenty-four-seven. Or falling short of that, handcuffed to me at all times. But since I know how much your career means to you, I'll settle for the next best thing."

I stare at him, unsure how to react. With any other man, I'd be convinced that it's a joke, but with Peter, that's not a safe assumption to make. Especially since I understand how he's feeling.

I also miss him fiercely when we're apart.

We arrive at the clinic a minute later, and I go to prepare for a flood of patients while Lydia grabs Peter to move some furniture. From seven until ten, I see women for issues minor and major, and then a familiar name pops up on my chart.

Monica Jackson.

My chest tightens painfully. The eighteen-year-old girl came in last week after a second brutal assault by her stepfather, who got out of prison on a technicality instead of serving out his seven-year sentence for raping her when she was seventeen. I'd helped her that time, giving her some money to lessen her alcoholic mother's financial dependence on the bastard, but there was nothing I could do last week. Monica was terrified that her stepfather would sue for custody of her younger brother and win—or that the child would end up in the foster system.

Her hopeless situation had shaken me so badly I'd cried for a solid hour.

Taking a deep breath, I put on my calmest face and stand up as the girl enters the room. "Monica. How are you?"

"Hi, Dr. Cobakis." Her small face is so radiant I almost don't recognize her. Even the half-healed bruises still visible on her skin don't detract from her glow. "I'm ready to get my IUD."

I blink at her enthusiasm. "Wonderful. I assume you're feeling better?"

She nods, hopping up on the exam table. "Yes, much better. And guess what?"

"What?"

She grins. "He can't bother me anymore. Like, ever. Last week, he was going to work at night, and he got mugged in an alley. They slit his throat, can you believe that?"

"They... what?" I sink back into my chair as my legs fold under me.

Her grin fades, and she gives me a penitent look. "I'm sorry. That sounded mean, didn't it?"

"Um, no. That is…" I shake my head in a futile effort to clear it. "Did you say someone *slit his throat*?"

"Yeah, the muggers or mugger. The police don't know how many there were. His wallet was taken, though, so they were definitely after his money."

"I see." I sound choked, but I can't help it. The memory of the two methheads Peter killed to protect me surfaces so vividly in my mind that I can smell the coppery stench of death and see the puppet-like way they'd crumpled, with the dark pools of blood spreading out from under their prone bodies…

So much blood that their throats must've been slit.

"Dr. Cobakis? Are you okay?"

The girl sounds worried—I must've gone pale.

With effort, I pull myself together and smile reassuringly. "Yes, sorry. Just some bad associations, that's all."

"Oh, I'm sorry. I didn't mean to freak you out. And please understand: I'm not saying I'm happy he's dead. It's just that—"

"You're glad he's out of your life. I get it." I stand up again and, as calmly as I can, hand Monica a plastic-wrapped paper gown. "Please go ahead and change. I'll be right with you."

Leaving the girl to it, I step out, my legs unsteady and my lungs fighting for breath.

Last week, after I learned about Monica's second assault, I didn't just cry.

I also confided in Peter, telling him exactly what happened.

If this is not a macabre coincidence, then Agent Ryson was right.

I'm as much of a monster as Peter. I killed Monica's stepfather by pointing at him the deadliest weapon I know.

My new husband.

CHAPTER 10
SARA

I still can't breathe by the time I get into the car with Peter, the weight of Monica's revelations sitting like an iceberg on my chest.

"What's wrong, ptichka?" he asks as we start driving. "Are you okay?"

I want to laugh hysterically. Am I? Should I be?

Is there a wellness barometer for when you've inadvertently commissioned a hit?

"Sara?" Peter prompts, glancing at me, and though his tone is mildly curious, there's a glimmer of dark knowledge in his gaze.

He must've noticed Monica at the clinic.

Whatever hopes I'd harbored about this being a horrible coincidence evaporate, leaving behind a deepening horror.

Peter committed this murder for me.

His victim's blood is on *my* hands.

There's no point in asking, but I can't help it. I have to hear the words out loud. "Did you do it?"

I expect him to stall or deny it, but he answers without hesitation, his gaze trained on the road ahead. "Yes."

Yes.

There it is. No misunderstanding, no confusion.

He killed a man for me.

Slit his throat, just like he'd done with those methheads.

"Would you rather I'd left the girl in his clutches?" His voice is calm and steady as he glances at me again. "I did it so you wouldn't worry—and so that your patient could have a normal, happy life."

I swallow thickly and look away, staring blindly out the window. What do I say to that?

How could you?

Thank you?

I force myself to look back at his profile. "I thought…" My throat closes, and I have to start again. "I thought you were going to be law-abiding. Isn't that one of the conditions of your deal with the authorities?"

Peter nods, keeping his eyes on the road. "It is—and I *am* law-abiding. I consider what I did as *aiding* the law— as in, the law that's supposed to be protecting girls like Monica from men like her stepfather."

I look away again, my eyes burning as the cold weight on my chest grows.

He doesn't even see what he did as wrong. And why would he? This is what he is, what he does.

Killing is as normal to him as delivering a baby is to me.

"Sara." His deep voice reaches me, and I realize we're already parked. I must've zoned out for the rest of the ride.

Steeling myself, I turn toward him.

He reaches over to clasp my hand. "Ptichka..." His voice is soft, his big hand warm as it engulfs my ice-cold fingers. "Why did you tell me about this if you didn't want my help? Did you really expect me to watch you cry over that *ublyudok* and do nothing?"

I flinch. I can't help it.

This, right here, is the crux of the matter, why Monica's revelations are so crushing.

Because deep inside, I *didn't* expect him to meekly stand by. On some level, I knew what he would do—even before he promised that my patient would be "fine."

I knew and I pretended that I didn't.

Because secretly, I *wanted* this to happen.

I pointed Peter at the problem, and he provided a solution.

Just like that.

"Sara..." He lifts his hand to cradle my cheek, his gaze dark yet warm in the dimly lit interior of the car. "Don't do this, ptichka. Don't beat yourself up. He deserved it; you know he did. Do you honestly believe Monica's the only girl he's ever hurt? Your legal system had a chance to fix the situation, to lock him up for good—and they let him go. You did the world a favor by telling me about him."

I close my eyes, wanting to lean into his palm, to let his deep, soothing voice chase away the horror and the guilt icing me from within.

Not only do I love a killer now, but I've become one myself.

"Don't do this, my love. He's not worth it." His breath warms my face, and then his lips brush against mine in a gentle, coaxing kiss.

A shudder ripples through me in response, a flash of heat igniting underneath the chill encasing me, and all of a sudden, gentleness is not enough.

I don't want to be soothed—I want to be fucked into oblivion.

Opening my eyes, I sink my fingers into his hair, gripping his head, and angle my face to deepen the kiss. My tongue pushes into his mouth, and my nails dig into his skull as I press against him, leaning over the console separating our seats. His breath catches, his hands sliding into my hair to grip it tightly in response, and a low growl rumbles deep in his chest as he responds with his own aggression, his teeth cutting into my lower lip as he kisses me back, harder and deeper, pressing me back toward my seat.

Yes, that's it. My head spins, the heat inside me intensifying to a conflagration. He tastes like violence and male hunger, like punishment and love all mixed together. I can't think under his sensual assault, and I don't want to.

I want this.

I want him.

Somehow, the seat behind my back reclines, and then Peter is on top of me, the car shaking as he tears at my clothes, one hand delving under my blouse while the other reaches for the zipper of my pants. His callused palm is burning hot and rough as it slides across my bare stomach, and my eyes pop open long enough for me to see the car windows fogging up. It's nearly enough to turn me lucid, to make me recall where we are, but then his hand moves lower, his kiss turning even more aggressive, and the maelstrom of need sweeps me away again.

I don't know when or how he gets my pants and underwear down, or at what point I tear off the button on his jeans. All I know is that he's suddenly inside me, so hard and thick it hurts. I cry out, panting as he starts fucking me in earnest, but he doesn't stop, doesn't slow down—and I don't want him to. We go at it like animals, with no restraint or finesse, and when I come, clinging to him and screaming, he's right there with me, in the madness that is our connection.

In the darkness that is our love.

CHAPTER 11
PETER

I'm almost certain some neighbors saw what happened in our car in the parking lot—and I know my crew definitely did—but I don't give a fuck as I lead a shaky Sara to the elevator. She's as disheveled as I've ever seen her, her blouse buttoned crookedly and her hair a hot mess around her flushed face. I'm sure I look similar, and I can't help grinning as we pass by a preppy couple pushing a stroller in the lobby. They give us a scandalized look, and Sara turns away, her cheeks flaming impossibly brighter.

It's so cute. My poor ptichka is embarrassed by our little bout of semi-public sex—though she's the one who initiated it.

"Don't worry. We're moving later this week," I remind her as we enter the elevator, and she presses her forehead against the mirror, her eyes squeezed tightly shut as she bangs a little fist on the glass.

"I can't believe we did that. I just... Oh, God, I'll never live this down."

She sounds so mortified that I want to hug her. So I do exactly that, ignoring her attempts to push me away as I hold her. After a moment, she relaxes, and I stroke her tangled hair until the elevator reaches our floor.

Then I bend down and lift her into my arms to carry her to the apartment.

She doesn't object, just hides her face against my neck as we pass by another neighbor in the hallway. The guy—a boy barely out of his teens, really—grins and gives me a thumbs up as he walks by.

If only the kid knew the whole story.

When we get to the door, I set Sara on her feet to get the keys, and she runs into the apartment as soon as I open it. I'm still taking off my shoes when I hear the shower come on, and by the time I join Sara there, she's already stepping out of the tub, still adorably flushed and embarrassed-looking.

I'm glad to see her like this.

It sure beats the way she looked in the car after she learned about Monica's stepfather's demise.

"Do you think anyone actually saw us?" she asks anxiously, wrapping a towel around herself, and I bite back another grin as I start to undress.

"What do *you* think, ptichka?"

"Well, it's late, and the parking lot is kind of dark, and—oh, shut up!" She slaps me on the arm as I drop my shirt in the laundry basket and start laughing, unable to help myself.

If nobody in this whole apartment complex saw the parked car rocking like a ship in a hurricane, I'll eat my own foot.

She groans, hiding her face in her hands, but then she looks up, suddenly pale. "You don't think we'll get arrested, do you? For public indecency or something like that?"

I stop laughing. "No, my love." I can see the fear and guilt on her face, and I know it's not due to our parking lot shenanigans.

She remembered what preceded it, and she's worried about the fallout.

"Sara…" I take her hands in both of mine. Her palms are cold again, despite the steam from the hot shower still filling the small bathroom. "Ptichka, nothing is going to happen to either one of us. There's nothing tying me to that man's death—nor anyone really investigating it. I know—I had the hackers check. As far as everyone is concerned, an ex-con got mugged in a bad neighborhood, that's all. No cop is going to waste his time digging further—but even if they did, they wouldn't uncover anything. I'm good at what I do… or did."

"I know you are. And that's…" Her slender throat works as she swallows. "That's terrifying."

"Why?" I ask gently, rubbing my thumbs across her palms. "I told you, that part of my life is in the past. We're looking forward to the future, remember? And now your patient can do the same. She's free to live her life without fear. Isn't that what you wanted for her?"

"Of course it is." She pulls her hands away and wraps her arms around herself, looking so forlorn that I almost regret doing this for her.

Maybe it would've been better if I'd come up with some other way to take care of Monica's problem—or at least disposed of the body.

Then again, I wanted Sara's patient to know that her assailant no longer poses a threat. An unexplained disappearance wouldn't have accomplished that. The poor girl would've always been looking over her shoulder, fearing the asshole's return.

This is for the best, I'm sure of that. Now I just need to convince Sara.

"Ptichka—"

"Peter—" she begins simultaneously, so I stop, letting her speak.

She takes a breath and slowly lets it out. "Peter, if we're… to do this for real—if we're to build a normal life together—I need you to promise me something."

"What is it, my love?" I ask, though I can guess.

"I need you to promise me you'll never do this again." Her hazel eyes are intent on my face. "I need to know that if someone happens to upset me, he won't end up in an alley with his throat slit. That if our children have a difficult teacher at school, or are bullied by a classmate, or if someone flips us off as we drive by, that murder is *not* on the table as a solution."

I blink slowly. "I see."

"Can you promise me that?" she presses, clutching the edges of her towel. "I need to know that the people around me are safe—that by being with you, I'm not condemning anyone else to death."

It's my turn to take a deep, calming breath. "My love… I can't promise not to protect you. If someone is trying to hurt you or our children—"

"We go to the authorities, like everyone else." Her chin lifts stubbornly. "That's what the police are for. And in any case, I'm not talking about a clear-cut case of self-defense. Obviously, if we're walking down the street and someone pulls a gun on us, it's a different matter—though disarming or simply wounding that person should still be the preferred solution. I'm talking about murder as a way to deal with people who are *not* posing a mortal threat. You see the difference, don't you?"

I don't, not really. I have no intention of killing random jerks who honk at us or whatever it is Sara is imagining here, but I'm not about to stand by and let some ublyudok make her cry like her heart is breaking.

She's looking at me expectantly, though, and I know she won't let this drop. "All right," I say after a moment of deliberation. "If that's what you want, I promise I won't kill anyone who doesn't pose a threat to us or anyone we care about."

"And you won't torture or beat up or hurt them in any way, right?"

I sigh. "Fine. No physical harm, I promise." There are still a number of levers I can pull if it comes down to it—bribery, blackmail, financial pressure—so I feel comfortable making this promise. Besides, what constitutes a "threat" is open to interpretation as far as I'm concerned.

If some fucking bully assaults our kid in school, he—or his parents—will *not* walk away unscathed.

Sara doesn't look satisfied with my very specific promise, so I reach for her towel and pull it off at the same time as I unzip my jeans.

"Wait—" she starts, but I'm already herding her back into the shower, where I make sure that whatever hypothetical future assholes I might need to deal with are far, far from her mind.

CHAPTER 12
PETER

The next morning, Sara is quiet and a little distant, undoubtedly still dwelling on my solution to her patient's problem. That's not likely to lead anywhere good, so I seek to distract her by bringing up her new hobby: singing with the band.

"When is your next performance?" I ask over breakfast. "I've seen the videos of you on stage, but I'd love to see it in person."

She looks up from her omelet, blinking as if just refocusing on me. "Oh, I actually meant to tell you. Our guitarist, Phil, texted me late last night. He's secured a gig for us tomorrow night, but only if everyone can make it on short notice. Do you think we can move the dinner with my parents to Saturday?"

My first impulse is to say no. I've been counting on having her to myself after the dinner—an event that would likely take two or three hours, max. This performance gig would eat up our entire Friday night, and then we'd still have to get together with her parents over the weekend—which is also when we're going to be settling into our new place.

Then again, I've been dying to see my little songbird on stage, singing her heart out. And this is important to her, so it's important to me.

"Of course," I say calmly and get up to start cleaning up. "We can do dinner with your parents on Saturday. Or better yet, invite them over for a Saturday brunch."

I've always known that living this life means I'll have to share Sara's time and attention, and I can't let my obsession with her ruin this for us.

I can handle this.

It's just something I need to get used to.

———

I finish cleaning up while Sara gets dressed, and then I drive her to work.

"Don't forget: the closing is at six today," I tell her as we pull up in front of her office. "I'll pick you up at 5:30, okay?"

She nods, still not quite meeting my gaze as she reaches for the door handle.

"Sara." I catch her wrist as she opens the door. "Look at me."

She reluctantly obeys, and I reach over with my other hand, tucking an errant strand of glossy chestnut hair behind her ear. "Say it, ptichka. I want to hear the words."

She stares at me, and I feel the rapid pulse in the slender wrist I'm holding. She's fighting herself again, fighting her feelings for me, and I won't stand for it.

"Say it," I demand, my grip tightening, and I see the exact moment she gives up the fight.

Closing her eyes, she inhales deeply, then opens them. "I love you." Her voice is quiet but steady as she looks into my eyes. "I love you, Peter... no matter what."

Something deep within me—a knot of tension I didn't even know was there—relaxes, and I bring her hand up to my lips, kissing the soft skin on each knuckle. "I love you too. I'll see you at 5:30, okay?"

"Okay," she murmurs, and I force myself to let her go.

To let her fly free, if only until tonight.

CHAPTER 13
SARA

True to his word, Peter picks me up at 5:30 sharp, and we drive to the title company's office to sign papers.

"You put the house in my name?" I give Peter a startled look when I see space for only my signature on the documents.

He nods, his lips curving in a smile. "It's for the best, my love. Just in case."

A chill wraps around my spine. "Just in case" could refer to any number of things, but when your husband used to be hunted by law enforcement agencies worldwide and still has ties to the criminal underworld, the words take on a particularly sinister meaning.

I want to probe deeper, but the title agent—a pretty, polished woman in her thirties—is watching us with undisguised curiosity, so I just sign at every X and try not to think about the terrifying possibilities.

Like, say, a SWAT team breaking down our door in the middle of the night because they've uncovered Peter's role in Monica's stepfather's murder.

"All done," the woman says brightly when I hand her the last of the papers. "Congratulations on your new home."

"Thank you." I stand up and shake her hand. "We're very excited."

Peter shakes her hand next, and I can't help but notice the way she looks at him—like a cat eyeing a saucer of cream. He seems oblivious to her interest, but I still feel an ugly stirring of jealousy.

Maybe I should tell Peter that *she* upset me?

I quash the dark joke as soon as it pops up in my mind, but it's too late. I'm back to thinking about everything and feeling sick. All day long, I've been trying to convince myself that what happened was a one-off and that Peter will keep his promise not to hurt anyone else, but every time I come close to believing it, I remember what he threatened to do at our wedding if I stood him up.

Murder—or the threat of it—will always be a part of his arsenal, and nobody around me is truly safe. I might as well be walking around with a live grenade.

Peter escorts me out, and we drive home, where the table is already set with candles and a bottle of champagne is chilling in a bucket of ice while delicious smells waft from the oven.

"To our new home," he toasts after pouring us each a glass, and I knock back the fizzy drink, trying not to think about puppet-like bodies in dark alleys and spreading pools of blood.

About the live grenade who's always at my side.

CHAPTER 14
PETER

The movers aren't due until noon, so after I drop Sara off at work on Friday, I go for a long run with a weighted backpack to imitate the training I used to do with my guys. I need the hard exercise to work off some of the restlessness I've been feeling—and to take my mind off how much I miss my workaholic wife.

Ending my run in a quiet, nearly empty park, I strip off my sweat-soaked T-shirt and start on a set of calisthenics, using the eighty-pound backpack to add difficulty to basic one-arm push-ups and pull-ups on a nearby tree.

I'm almost finished when I see a teenage boy running toward me, his T-shirt flapping around his skinny body. For one heart-stopping moment, he looks exactly like my friend Andrey, the one who gave me all of my tattoos at Camp Larko.

The illusion dissolves as the runner gets closer, but I still can't look away.

The kid is sprinting like the hounds of hell are chasing him, his eyes wild and his arms pumping desperately at his sides. A few seconds later, I see why.

Four older, bigger boys—young men, really—are running after him, yelling out insults as they go.

It's none of my fucking business, but I can't help it.

As soon as the Andrey lookalike sprints past me, I unclip my backpack from around my waist and toss it casually on the ground. Then, just as his pursuers are about to barrel past me, I step into their path, extending my arms on both sides.

They screech to a halt, just barely avoiding crashing into me.

"What the fuck, man?" the biggest one snarls. "Move!"

He tries to shove me aside—a major mistake on his part. My well-honed instincts kick in, and a moment later, the guy is sprawled on his ass, groaning, as his three comrades back away, hands raised defensively.

"Scram," I tell them, and they do, pausing only to grab their fallen friend and drag him away.

I'm bending down to retrieve my backpack when I spot movement out of the corner of my eye.

It's the kid I helped, his skinny chest heaving as he stares at me. "How did you do that?" There's awe and envy in his voice.

"Do what?" Picking up my backpack, I stuff my discarded T-shirt into it.

"Take him down like that."

I shrug, putting on the backpack and securing the straps around my waist. "Just some basic self-defense training."

"No, dude." The kid's blue eyes are huge—and eerily like Andrey's. "That was something else. Were you in the Army? And are you doing a workout with that?" He points at my backpack.

"Something like that, and yes." I turn to leave, but the boy is not done with me.

"Can you teach me? How to fight, I mean?"

I pretend not to hear and start jogging.

He's not deterred. Catching up to me, he jogs at my side. "Can you teach me? Please?"

I pick up my pace. "I'm not in the business of training kids."

"I'll pay you." He's breathless from the run but somehow manages to keep up with me. "Here." He sticks his hand into his pocket and returns with a pair of twenties. "They were going to take it anyway, so you might as well have it."

I'm about to refuse when an idea comes to me. Stopping next to a bench, I eye the kid speculatively. "You want to learn? Really?"

"Yes." He all but bounces in excitement. "I want to know how to defend myself. I mean, I took a little karate when I was younger, but it didn't really—"

"How old are you?" I interrupt.

"Sixteen. Well, almost. My birthday is next month."

"And who were those guys chasing you?"

The boy flushes. "My older brother's friends. They're all pledging to a fraternity, and it's some kind of a ritual for them. You know, grab money from a nerd."

I almost roll my eyes at the ridiculousness of it all. Am I really considering this?

"Please, sir." The kid shifts from foot to foot. "My dad always says I need to stand up for myself, but I don't know how. And the way you just stopped them… I would kill to be able to do that."

The kid has no idea what he's saying, but for some reason—maybe because I'm still thinking of Andrey and how he always got picked on at our hellish camp before the sadistic guard boiled him alive—I extend my hand and say, "Give me your cell."

The kid eagerly pulls out his phone and hands it to me. I program in my number and give it back to him.

"Call me this weekend, and we'll set up a time. What's your name, by the way?"

"Aiden, sir. Aiden Walt." He hesitates, then decides to be brave. "And you are?"

"Peter Garin," I say and resume running, leaving the teen standing by the bench.

CHAPTER 15

SARA

As has been his habit all week, Peter picks me up after work, only instead of us going home or to the clinic, we drive to the bar where my band is performing tonight.

"Thank you so much for this," I say between bites of the chicken pasta he brought for me to eat in the car. "Seriously, this is delicious."

"You're welcome." His silver gaze is warm as he glances at me before turning his attention back to the road. "I'm glad you like it."

"I can't believe you had time to cook today. Weren't the movers supposed to come?"

He grins. "Oh, didn't I tell you? They came—and tonight we're going to sleep at the new place."

"What?" I almost choke on my pasta. "Are you serious?"

He nods. "I hired four guys, and they packed and moved everything in record time. I've already unpacked all the necessities, including everything for the kitchen and the bedroom, so it's just a matter of dealing with a few more boxes over the weekend. And buying some new things, of course—but I figured we could do that together."

"You are amazing," I say, and I mean every word. His relentless, obsessive drive—that nearly superhuman ability to overcome insurmountable odds in pursuit of his goal—used to terrify me, but now that I'm no longer fighting to escape him, I see it for the asset that it is.

The same formidable force of will that Peter used to make me fall in love with him is now smoothing all the minor bumps in our peaceful suburban life—a life that's possible only because Peter has performed a virtual miracle and gotten himself off the Most Wanted lists.

If I didn't know better, I'd think him a wizard, bending fate and reality to his will.

"So, I've decided to open a training studio," he says casually as I resume eating. "I'll start scoping out a place next week."

I pause mid-bite, staring at him in disbelief. "Really?"

"Yeah. I met this kid in the park today, and he begged me for some fighting lessons. So that gave me the idea, and the more I think about it, the more I like it. I'm thinking self-defense classes for women and teens, boot camp programs for hardcore athletes, weapons training for bodyguards, and so on. I have some experience with training others, having done it with my guys when I was first putting together the team, so it might be fun."

"That is an *excellent* idea." I can't hide the excitement in my voice. "That will be such a perfect thing for you to do."

He shoots me a wry glance. "Better than assassinations?"

I laugh because he's read my mind. "Yes, much better." I've been worried about what he'd do here, whether he'd miss his adrenaline-filled former profession, and this settles my mind quite a bit.

With the training studio to occupy his days and provide a new challenge, my assassin husband might actually adjust to our calm, civilian life.

Feeling lighter than I have since Monica's visit, I finish my pasta just as we pull up to the bar where I'm performing tonight.

The light feeling evaporates as soon as we step inside. The bar is huge, loud, and crowded, with most of the patrons already drunk, and I can feel Peter's growing tension as we make our way to the backstage area, where the other band members are getting ready.

"Hey, there they are, the newlyweds! So glad you could make it." Phil pulls me into a big hug, and my husband's face turns to stone, his hand starting to curl into a fist.

Shit. I've forgotten about Peter's extreme possessiveness.

I push my bandmate away and swiftly grab Peter's arm. The steely muscle flexes under my fingers, and I know I was right to worry.

My grenade was about to explode.

"Where are Simon and Rory?" I ask, rubbing my hands over Peter's bicep, like I'm just enjoying touching all that lethal muscle—which I would be, if I weren't so concerned for Phil. "Are they ready to go?"

"They're changing over there." Phil jerks his head to the right. "You should go change, too. We've got your outfit prepped. And don't worry, I'll give him back to you when you're done." He grins at Peter, who still looks like he wants to hammer nails into him. Slowly.

"Okay. I'll be quick." I give Peter's bicep a warning squeeze and reluctantly head into the changing area.

Our guitarist better be unharmed when I return.

CHAPTER 16
PETER

"So," Phil says, his good-natured expression evaporating as soon as Sara is out of sight. "Jealous bastard, aren't you?"

I stare at him, unblinking. "You have no idea."

If he ever hugs Sara again, it'll be the last thing he does. This place already has me on edge—with all the drunks crowded together out there, it's the perfect place for some assassin to strike—and the mere thought of this beer-bellied asshole's paws on Sara has my fingers itching to break his chubby neck.

He stares back at me, then bursts out laughing. "Oh, man, you should see the look on your face. I never knew that whole killer stare was a real thing."

I force myself to blink, lessening said "killer stare" as he continues, happily oblivious to how true his observation was. "Sorry, man. Didn't mean to poach on your territory. We've all just known Sara for a while, and she's like a sister to us. Well, not really, because we're not related and she *is* smoking hot, but you know what I mean. And honestly, we didn't even know she was into men. Not saying we thought she was batting for the other team—just not into dating, being a widow and all. Though I guess she was secretly dating you and…" He shakes his head. "Damn, I can't believe we didn't know."

"Yes, well, now you do." I should probably be more gracious, given his transparent attempt at male bonding, but I'm still barely restraining myself from killing him over that hug—and all the other times he's undoubtedly hit on my "smoking hot" wife.

She wasn't my wife at the time, but she was *mine*.

Fortunately, Sara reappears before my patience is tested further. She's wearing a white halter-top dress that reminds me of Marilyn Monroe in the famous skirt-blowing scene. On another woman, it might've looked simply flirty, but on Sara, with her dancer's posture, it's as elegant as it is sexy.

"Thought it was appropriate," Phil says as I stare at her, my mouth watering with the urge to nibble on the soft skin exposed by the dress's open neckline. "You know, since she's a new bride and all."

I tear my eyes away from her delicate collarbones. "What?"

"The white dress," the guitarist says, grinning. "I chose it. Like a continuation of your wedding and all."

"Ah." I turn back to watch Sara as she stops to talk to their drummer, Simon.

How bad would it be if I stole her away right now? Just picked her up and carried her out of here, then kept her in my bed until we both couldn't walk?

I want her singing for me, and only me, in this dress.

And in any other dress, come to think of it.

"Man, you have it bad," Phil says, and I glance at him, irritated. The idiot is shaking his head and grinning, like he can't see that I'm about to literally break his neck.

"Phil, hey!" A blond woman rounds the corner, and I realize it's Sara's friend from the hospital, Marsha.

Spotting me, she freezes for a second, then hesitantly approaches us.

"Hi, Marsha." I smile at her as gently as I can. No need to scare the woman further; she already has all sorts of suspicions about me. "I didn't know you'd be here."

"Yeah, well…" Her gaze darts to Phil. "Can I talk to you?"

"Sure." He looks back at me. "Excuse me."

I return my attention to Sara as Marsha all but drags the guitarist away. My ptichka is now talking to the redheaded guy, Rory, and I don't like the way that muscle-bound peacock is looking at her.

I start heading over there, but Sara ends the conversation and sticks her head out to the stage area. "They're ready for us," she yells over her shoulder, and I quietly exit the backstage area to join the crowd in the bar.

My ptichka's performance is about to begin, and I don't want to miss it.

71

To my amazement, the rowdy crowd quiets down as soon as Sara steps out onto the stage. And when she opens her mouth, I see why. She's as phenomenal up there as any pop star, her voice strong and pure as she belts out the lyrics she's composed. I've heard her practice this in Japan, but I listen as raptly as everyone in the bar.

It's impossible not to.

The song is both evocative and upbeat, an unusual mixture of country, R&B, and recent pop hits—all combined with Sara's unique spin.

She's more than good.

She's amazing.

Our eyes meet, and my heart expands in my chest, until it feels like it can't be contained. It's surreal, how badly I need her, how I crave her with every cell of my body. The primitive instinct awakens in me again, the urge to throw her over my shoulder and drag her off to my lair.

I want her far from everyone's eyes, so I can devour her all on my own.

One song, three, five, fifteen—before I know it, it's been two hours. They keep calling her back, demanding an encore, and she keeps giving in—until finally, it's all over.

I catch her as she steps off the stage. Literally grab and lift her, pressing her against my chest.

"Newlywed's privilege," I growl at her rabid fans, and as she hides her face, blushing and laughing, I do what I've been dying to do all evening.

I carry her off, to enjoy all on my own.

CHAPTER 17
PETER

I restrain myself long enough to get us home, though each time Sara shifts in her seat and I catch a glimpse of her bare thigh under that flirty white skirt, I'm tempted to pull off the road.

The only thing that stops me is that I don't want another quickie in the car. I need her in my bed, where I can feast on her delicious body all night long. Where I can show her that she'll always be mine, no matter how many men salivate over her.

It helps that she's talking nonstop, still riding the high from her performance. She's telling me all about how Phil's guitar needed a last-minute tune-up and how Simon almost didn't make it because he has an article deadline. Focusing on her words keeps me from reaching under her skirt and trailing my hand up her smooth, shapely thigh before delving under the lacy thong she put on this morning and stroking her soft, silky—

"Can you believe Marsha is going out with Phil now?" Sara says, and I realize I've stopped listening, lost in the heated fantasy.

"She is?" I do my best to refocus on her words. "When did that happen?"

"Rory told me they hooked up the night of our wedding. Isn't that funny? Marsha was apparently too drunk to drive after the ceremony, and Phil volunteered to bring her home. And the rest, as they say, is history."

"That's great," I say, forcing myself to keep my eyes on the road instead of devouring Sara with my gaze. "Good for them."

And I mean it, too. Maybe the flamboyant nurse will keep the guitarist occupied, and he'll stop slobbering over Sara every chance he gets. And in turn, maybe he'll keep Marsha distracted enough to stay out of our business.

Sara had told her a bit too much during my absence, and though Marsha doesn't know for sure that I'm the man who stalked Sara and killed her first husband, she strongly suspects it.

"Yeah, I hope it works out for them," Sara says. "They both deserve a good partner."

I nod noncommittally and risk another glance at Sara. She's looking at me with a smile, and then she kills me by casually laying her hand on my thigh.

My cock, already semi-erect from the X-rated images in my mind, snaps to full attention. The touch of her slender fingers heats my skin even through the thick material of my jeans. It's as if a live wire is lying on my thigh, sending jolts of electricity straight to my groin. My heart rate spikes violently, and my jaws clench as the road ahead blurs for a dangerous second.

"Sara." I all but growl her name as my hands tighten convulsively on the wheel. "Ptichka, if you don't move your hand right now…"

Her breath audibly hitches, and she yanks her hand away, having finally realized what she's doing. It doesn't help, though. I can still feel her touch. It's branded into my skin, my mind… my heart. Maybe one day it won't feel like this, with her casual affection slaying me each time, but for now, we're still too new, too raw. Not long ago, she'd feared and hated me. I'd been a monster in her eyes. And maybe I still am—but now she loves me.

She knows she needs me, dark parts and all.

When we pull up in front of our new house, I pause to make sure nothing sets off my well-honed sense of danger. Nothing does—not that it should. The place is now as secure as possible, with cutting-edge technology monitoring everything and my crew positioned in strategic locations throughout the neighborhood.

I won't chance enemies from my past intruding on our peaceful present.

"Wow," Sara exclaims as I help her out of the car. Her head swivels from side to side, her eyes wide in amazement. "Where did all these trees come from? And that fence? When did you have time to do all this?"

I spare a glance at what she's talking about. I indeed had a tall fence put up, and I planted trees all around the property to provide privacy and obscure the line of sight for any potential snipers.

"Yesterday," I tell her, placing a hand on her lower back to shepherd her to the entrance.

She can marvel at our new place tomorrow; tonight, all her time belongs to me.

We've barely cleared the doorway when my restraint snaps like a twig in a hailstorm.

Shutting the door with my foot, I flip on the hallway light and back her up against the wall, my hands going to the bottom of her dress. Hiking up her skirt, I find her lacy thong damp and her pussy soft and slick underneath it.

Fuck, yes. Performing must've excited her in more ways than one.

"Peter." Her eyes go wide as she clutches at my biceps. "Wait, let's first—ahh..." Her words end on a moan as I penetrate her with two fingers, reveling in the slippery, silky tightness.

"Tell me you want this," I demand, pumping my fingers in and out of her, letting the rough tip of my thumb graze over her hooded clit with every stroke. "Tell me you want *me*."

Her eyes look increasingly glazed, her pupils dilating more each second. "I do. You know I do." She sounds breathless, her inner muscles tightening and her hips undulating in a rhythm that tells me she's on the verge. "Please, Peter..."

I pull my fingers out and lift my hand to her face. "Suck them." I push the fingers between her plush lips. "Get them nice and wet, you understand?"

Her eyes widen again, but she obeys, her agile tongue swirling around my fingers as I thrust them into her mouth. It feels amazing, making me imagine that tongue on my cock. Wanting more, I push my fingers deeper and feel her throat convulse in a gagging reflex, coating them with more saliva.

Fuck. If I don't get inside her, I'll explode.

Unzipping my jeans with my free hand, I pull my fingers out of her mouth and push them back into her pussy, letting her slickness mix with the saliva as I resume finger-fucking her, wanting that glazed look back in her eyes.

It doesn't take long—within thirty seconds, she's breathing fast, her pale skin beautifully flushed. Her gaze is still locked on mine, but her eyes turn hazy and unseeing, her mouth opening as her nails dig into my biceps and her thigh muscles quiver like a string.

I wait until I'm sure she's coming, and then I pull my fingers out again—only to lift her by her toned thighs and spear her with my aching cock. Her wordless O transforms into a loud gasp, her legs wrapping tightly around my hips as I penetrate her all the way in one ruthless thrust. I can feel her inner muscles pulsing and contracting as I settle deep within her, and it takes all my willpower not to give in to the powerful urge to come.

She's not getting off this easy.

Not tonight.

Somehow, I'm able to hang on until her spasms ease and her body slackens against mine, her lids closing as a blissed-out glow appears on her face. Lowering my head, I kiss her parted lips and move the hand that finger-fucked her from her thigh to the tempting crevice between her ass cheeks.

She's so relaxed and caught up in my kiss that there's minimal resistance as I press one slick finger against her tight back opening and carefully work it in. I'm already inside her to the first knuckle when her eyes fly open and her body stiffens, her inner muscles clamping on my cock and finger as her legs tighten around my hips.

"Let me in, ptichka," I murmur against her lips. "You know you want this."

Not that she has much choice. I'm holding her up with my free hand and the weight of my body. With her legs wrapped around my hips and my cock buried deep inside her, there's no way she can escape or control the depth of penetration of either of her orifices.

She's completely at my mercy, and that's exactly what I want.

I haven't taken her ass since our wedding night, but I haven't stopped thinking about it—about how those perfect round globes had felt pressed against my balls and the look of ecstasy-edged agony on her face. I had hurt her, I know, and something about that had been perversely right, uniquely satisfying.

As much as I adore her, I still want to punish her sometimes, to see fear fight with arousal in her pretty eyes.

Raising my head, I see those eyes reflect exactly that as she stares up at me. "I…" Her breath is quickening again. "I don't know if—"

I swallow her next words with another kiss and resume working my finger into her tight opening as I lift her higher with my free hand, moving her on my cock. She whimpers against my lips, and I feel my cock rub against the finger through the thin wall separating her two orifices.

My breathing speeds up, my balls drawing up tighter, and whatever restraint I still possessed vanishes. Deepening the kiss, I surge higher into her and simultaneously push a second finger into her ass. She stiffens, her nails digging deeper into my arms and her inner muscles clenching in resistance, but it's futile. I'm already inside her, so deep that she'll never get me out.

There'll be no escape for her.

Not now. Not ever.

Everything within me is screaming for me to fuck her, to drive into her over and over until I erupt and the unbearable tension fades, but there's something else I want as well. Breathing heavily, I lift my head and capture her gaze as she looks up at me dazedly, her face flushed and her lids heavy with arousal.

"Tell me what you need," I command thickly, and her breath hisses between her teeth as I push my fingers deeper into her ass, stretching it, preparing it. "I want to hear you say it."

"I don't..." She moans, her eyes squeezing shut as I scissor my fingers, stretching her further. "I don't know."

"Yes, you do. Look at me."

Her eyes obediently flutter open, and her delicate tongue peeks out to dampen her lower lip.

"Tell me, Sara. Tell me what you really need."

"I…" Her breathing quickens further as I begin to grind into her, making sure to press on her clit with every movement. "It's… this. Peter, I need this. I need you inside me. I need you to"—she gasps as I thrust deeper into her— "take me and…"

"And what?" I prompt, my spine tingling as I feel her inner muscles tighten.

"To fuck me." She's panting now, her gaze turning hazy and unfocused. "To… to hurt me."

"Yes." My voice comes out hoarse. "That's right. And you are mine. Mine to fuck, to hurt, to do anything I want with. Aren't you, my love?"

She nods, her eyes refocusing on mine. "Yes. Always."

Always. The word pierces my chest, bringing with it a mix of warm tenderness and violent satisfaction. I love that she understands it now. Admits it.

We are meant for each other. I've known it from the beginning—and now she knows it too.

Dipping my head, I reclaim her lips, keeping the kiss soft and gentle even as I pull my fingers out of her and hook both hands under her thighs, spreading her legs wider as I lift her higher. My cock slips out of her pussy and presses against her back entrance.

Her breath hitches on a gasp, but I'm already lowering her onto my stiff cock, using the force of gravity and the slickness of her natural lubrication to aid my penetration. If I hadn't stretched her with my fingers, it would've been impossible, but as is, the ring of muscle gives in to the unyielding pressure and I slide into her tight channel, feeling her insides squeeze me in a frantic effort to resist the invasion.

"Peter..." She's trembling as I lift my head, meeting her gaze once more. "Peter, please..."

"Yes," I promise huskily. "I will please you, ptichka. I will give you what you need... everything you need."

And holding her gaze, I begin to move, taking her to where pain edges into pleasure and love and hate collide.

To that beautiful place where she's mine and mine alone.

CHAPTER 18
HENDERSON

I study the new set of photos on my screen as I rub the knotted muscles in my neck, trying to ignore my growing headache.

Reaching out to the FBI worked, and it didn't take much prodding, either. Agent Ryson was only too glad to resume his investigation into Sokolov for me.

I'm not holding my breath that he'll uncover anything, but that's not the point of it, anyway. I just need an investigation to exist, even if it's more of a personal vendetta by a disgruntled agent.

Opening the folder on my desk, I study the blueprints inside. The plan is beginning to take shape, slowly but surely. Now I just need to find the right people to execute it.

The sounds of automatic gunfire reach my ears, exacerbating the painful throbbing in my temples. Shoving the folder aside, I stand up and walk into the living room.

"Jimmy."

My fifteen-year-old son doesn't react.

I repeat his name louder.

"What?" he snaps without tearing his gaze away from the screen.

"Lower the volume on that fucking game," I say as calmly as I can.

He flips me the bird.

My headache morphs into a blazing migraine, my neck spasming with fresh pain as icy rage spreads through my veins.

Outwardly calm, I walk over to the couch and snatch the controller from my son's hands.

"Hey!" He jumps up, trying to grab it back, and the back of my hand crashes into his face, knocking him off his feet.

"I told you to turn down that fucking game," I say as he stares up at me, cradling his jaw.

And dropping the controller on the floor, I walk back into my office.

CHAPTER 19
SARA

I wake up Saturday morning with the knowledge that Peter and I have been married for a week—and that we just spent the first night in our new house.

I didn't have a chance to look at everything last night, so I take in the bedroom now. It's bright and spacious, with the walls painted a soothing, pale blue-gray and the recessed ceiling at least twelve feet high above our king-sized oak-frame bed.

It's pretty and modern, and I have a sudden wifely urge to buy plants to put in every corner.

Grinning, I stretch, then wince at the inner soreness. After that brutal claiming in the hallway, Peter carried me upstairs and took me again in the shower, then one more time in this bed.

One of these days, we'll need to talk about what a normal, healthy amount of sex is. Men aren't supposed to fuck their wives every night like they just got out of prison.

I picture that discussion and shake my head. Who am I kidding? Soreness or not, I don't mind his desire for me one bit. Peter's intense sexuality is a part of him, as unapologetically fierce as his love for me. It accepts no boundaries, adheres to no restraints. And I want him like that: savage yet tender, lethal but perversely sweet.

I'm done pretending that I'm anything but crazy over him, as wrong as that might be.

Delicious breakfast smells are already seeping in from under the closed door, so I take a quick shower in our new, luxurious bathroom, throw on a T-shirt and a pair of yoga pants, and hurry downstairs, my stomach rumbling.

My husband is standing by the restaurant-grade stainless-steel stove, flipping pancakes, and I stop, saliva pooling in my mouth at the sight. Dressed in a well-worn pair of jeans and nothing else, he's all wide shoulders and lean, hard muscles, the tattoos decorating his left arm flexing with every movement of his powerful biceps. His thick, dark hair is deliciously mussed, as if inviting my fingers to touch it, and his tan skin gleams in the bright morning light.

Turning, he faces me with a sensuous smile. "There she is, my little songbird. How are you feeling?"

I lick my lips, unable to take my eyes off the broad expanse of his chest. "Hungry."

"Uh-huh, I thought so." He grins. "Unfortunately, ptichka, you slept so late that it's now brunch time. Your parents are getting here in twenty minutes, so you'll have to wait."

I glance up at the clock and realize he's right. "This is all your fault," I tell him, crossing my arms over my chest. "You kept me up *really late*."

"I know. Poor darling. Come here." He comes toward me, eyes gleaming darkly, and I back away.

"Nuh-uh. We don't have time."

He reaches for me. "We always have time."

"The pancakes—"

His warm lips close over mine, his tongue invading the recesses of my mouth, and my fingers find their way into his silky hair as my head falls back into the cradle of his palms. His breath is honey-flavored—he must've been sampling those pancakes—and I can't help but blink dazedly when he finally lifts his head, staring down at me without a hint of playfulness.

"I can't fucking wait until we're alone again," he mutters, then dips his head, claiming my mouth with a fiercer, harder kiss, one that leaves no doubt of his ultimate intent.

He's going to take me again.

The moment my parents leave, I'll be back in his bed.

The doorbell rings just as he comes up for air again. "Fuck." Breathing hard, he lets go of me. "They're early again."

I smooth my hair with an unsteady hand, painfully cognizant of my kiss-swollen lips. "You better get dressed. I'll go greet them."

"Hold on." He strides over to the stove and flips the pancakes from the pan onto a serving dish. "So they don't burn," he explains before heading out of the kitchen.

I sneak a peek in a mirror on my way to the door. I definitely look like I've just been ravished, but there's no helping it.

I smooth my hair again and open the door to greet my parents.

They insist on a tour of the house first, so we go from room to room while Peter sets the table. As I show everything to my parents, I'm once again amazed at how much my husband accomplished yesterday. Though a few boxes are still sitting discreetly in some corners and the furniture is minimal at best, everything is organized and neat... almost unnaturally so.

"I can't believe you're so settled already," Mom says, voicing my thoughts. "I thought your closing was Thursday?"

"It was," I say. "But Peter has a way of getting things done."

"No kidding," Dad mutters, opening a linen closet and finding the towels already inside, neatly folded. "He's a machine, that husband of yours."

I reach over to squeeze Dad's weathered forearm. "Yes, and that's a good thing."

My parents aren't exactly on board with our relationship yet, but I'm hoping that as they spend more time with Peter, they'll come around. Our first dinner together went relatively well last week, thanks largely to Peter being surprisingly open about his past and his feelings for me. It also helped that he told them straight out that he wants to start a family, tantalizing my parents with the promise of grandchildren they'd all but given up hope of seeing.

With my dad having turned eighty-eight and my mom just nine years younger, their grandparently biological clock is getting increasingly loud.

Though my dad's arthritis is acting up and he's using a walker today, he insists on braving the stairs to see the whole house. We finish the tour in our bedroom, where I'm surprised to find the bed made. Peter must've done it when he went upstairs to get dressed.

After they view the room, Dad goes to use the restroom while Mom checks out our walk-in closet.

"So what do you think?" I ask when she comes out.

She regards me seriously. "It's a beautiful house, honey."

"But?" I prompt when she doesn't go on.

She sighs and walks over to sit down on the bed. "Your dad and I are still worried about you, that's all."

"Mom—" I start in an exasperated tone, but she holds up her hand and pats the bed next to her.

I walk over to sit down next to her, and she says in a low voice, "Agent Ryson came up to your father in the park yesterday morning. I don't know what he told him, but your dad's blood pressure was through the roof all day. I tried to pry, but he wouldn't tell me anything other than that he's worried for you."

I stare at her, an icy vise squeezing my heart. Why was the FBI agent there? What did he tell my dad? If it's anything like what Ryson had accosted me with on my wedding day, it's a wonder Dad didn't have another heart attack right then and there.

Could the FBI know something about Monica's stepfather?

My lungs cease functioning as the thought flits through my mind. I must've visibly paled too, because Mom frowns and reaches over to clasp my hand. "Are you okay, honey?"

"Yes, I…" I force myself to resume breathing. "I'm fine." My voice is a bit too high-pitched, so I throw in a smile to make it more convincing. "Sorry, I'm just worried about Dad. How's his blood pressure today?"

Mom sighs and lets go of my hand. "Better. Not perfect, but better. I do wish he'd tell me what Agent Ryson said, though."

"Right." I manage to sound almost normal. "I'll ask Dad about it today."

"I think it's better if you don't." Glancing at the bathroom door, she lowers her voice further. "Whatever it was, it was obviously stressful, and I don't want him dwelling on it."

"You got it, Mom," I say and get up to smile at Dad as he comes out of the bathroom. "Now let's go sample those pancakes."

———

As we eat, I observe Peter interacting with my parents. Though I know he'd much rather be alone with me, he's again polite and respectful… downright kind in his manner. Going up and down the stairs seems to have aggravated my dad's arthritis, so Peter helps him with his walker—and does it so casually and deftly that my dad forgets to take offense.

At first, my parents are wary and reserved, but as the meal goes on, they seem to warm up to Peter—even my dad, despite whatever Ryson must've told him. It helps that Peter takes charge of the conversation, barraging my parents with questions about how they met and what I was like as a child instead of waiting for them to pry into his murky past.

"Sara was such a perfect baby, you wouldn't believe," Mom tells Peter, beaming at me. "Slept all through the night, ate when she was supposed to, almost never cried. And never got sick, either, though she was born small— just under six pounds. We were so terrified—because of our age, you know—but she quickly put all our fears to rest. It was like she knew we weren't the typical young parents who could take the strain, and she made sure everything would go by the book. That's silly, obviously—she was just a baby—but that's the impression everyone had."

"I could believe that," Peter says, regarding me with such warmth that I blush and have to look away.

Besides steering the conversation to my parents' favorite topics, Peter shows his attentiveness in a variety of little ways. Mom gets her chamomile tea without asking, and Dad's pancakes are served with a fresh bowl of fruit and whipped cream in addition to the homemade strawberry jam. I don't know where Peter sniffed out this specific preference of my dad, but my parents clearly appreciate it.

"You're an excellent cook," Mom tells him, and he gives her a big, warm smile, his eyes crinkling in genuine pleasure.

Watching him like this, I begin to wonder whether Peter is really doing this just for me. Is it possible that some part of him craves this too? That because he's never had parents of his own, he's enjoying being a part of our family? Because if he's pretending, he's doing a great job.

I, for one, am convinced that he's starting to like my parents—and that despite everything, they might eventually like him back.

As we're wrapping up the meal, my parents finally get around to questioning us—about work and all sorts of typical parent stuff.

"So have you decided what you're going to be doing?" Mom asks Peter, and he nods, telling them all about the training studio he's planning to start.

"I like that idea," Dad declares. "Seems like a solid fit, with your background and all."

Peter smiles at his approval. "I thought so. In any case, it's something to do for now, when Sara is at work."

There's no trace of resentment in his voice, but I still can't help a pang of unease as he gets up and starts clearing off the table. He's bothered by my hours, I can tell. After all the months apart, the evenings and weekends we get to spend together are not enough—for either one of us.

Maybe this new training business will make things better, giving him something to focus on that's not me, and as we settle into our married life, we won't miss each other as intensely. If not, then sooner or later, something will have to give—and it'll have to be on my side.

Peter has sacrificed everything to make me happy, and I can do no less for him.

As my parents leave, I debate telling Peter about Ryson's visit to my dad, but I decide against it. He was already upset to learn that the FBI agent had interfered with our wedding. If he knew that Ryson is continuing to harass my family, he might do something about it—and that's the last thing I want.

Promise or not, Peter will do whatever it takes to protect me, and I don't need another man's death on my conscience.

PART II

CHAPTER 20
SARA

*O*ver the next month, we settle into our new home and continue with the routine we've fallen into during our first week of marriage. Though Danny and the rest of Peter's security team are always around, Peter drives me to and from work himself, and he volunteers with me at the clinic. In between, he works on setting up his new business and gathering clients—a venture in which he's having great success.

I sneak out of my office one afternoon, when I have a couple of appointment cancellations, and have Danny drive me to the park that Peter has chosen as his outdoor training grounds. And then I watch, grinning, as he puts five teenage boys through their paces, making them sprint, jump over benches, climb trees, and attempt to punch him in the face.

None of them succeed, of course, but they look like they're having fun trying.

I know how they feel because I asked him to teach me a few moves last Sunday, and we spent the morning in his gym, practicing some basic self-defense. It was like fighting a mountain, and the only move I mastered was lifting my legs to become a dead weight when he'd grab me from behind—to pull my attacker off-balance, supposedly. Needless to say, all that grabbing ended in us having sex the moment we got home, and I'm still far from being able to defend myself—not that I need to, with Peter and the bodyguards always around.

He spots me a minute later, and a radiant smile lights his face before he turns back and barks out the next set of instructions at the boys. Then he comes toward me, leaving his students to grunt and pant as they attempt to do a pull-up on a tree.

It's a hot August day, and he's shirtless, dressed only in a pair of camouflage pants and combat boots. I watch, mouth dry, as he comes toward me with a loping stride, his muscled torso glowing with a hint of perspiration.

"What are you doing here, ptichka?" he asks, stopping in front of me, and I jump at him, looping my arms around his neck. He catches me, twirling me around as I kiss him unabashedly, and by the time he puts me down, we're both breathing heavily while his students hoot and wolf-whistle in the background.

"Back to it," he barks over his shoulder, his hands still on my waist, and they instantly obey, resuming their attempts at pull-ups.

"A real drill sergeant, are we?" I grin up at him, reaching up to smooth his thick hair into some semblance of order. It's getting long on the sides as well as the top, and harder to control. I like the messy look, so I don't say anything, but we'll probably need to get him in for a haircut soon.

"You bet," he murmurs, dipping his head to kiss me again, and I laugh, pushing him away before we start making out for real. It's happened in public way too often; Peter has no shame when it comes to me.

In part, it's because we keep feeling like we don't get enough time together. My current job has more predictable hours, but I still have a few pregnant patients—and my bosses have extended their vacation, so I've been seeing all of their patients this month as well.

They asked me to cover for them, and I couldn't say no.

"Yes, you could," Peter said when I explained that I have to be on call for yet another weekend because Wendy's patient is about to deliver. "You could definitely say no. What's the worst that would happen? They'd fire you?"

"Well, yes," I began, then stopped with a sigh. "I know, I know. We have money, and I technically don't have to work."

"That's right." His gaze was intent on my face, and I looked away, not ready to go there yet. Logically, I know he's right—we're multimillionaires, thanks to his recent adventures—but I've worked too hard to become a doctor to simply give it up.

"You could still volunteer at the clinic," he said, and once again, he had a point. I've thought about that several times, about how nice it would be if I could cuddle with him every morning instead of getting up with the alarm and racing off to work. As frustrating as my captivity in Japan was, we were always together there—something I didn't appreciate at the time, given my anger with Peter, but now recall with perverse longing.

"It's not the same," I told him. "I wouldn't get to deliver babies at the clinic."

It's true, and he let the matter drop, but I know we'll return to it again.

It's inevitable, given our mutual obsession.

And it is an obsession. I can't deny that. I thought I loved George, at least in the beginning, but my feelings for him were a pale shadow of the way I feel about his killer. I'd never missed George this way when we were apart, never longed to come home to him with this kind of intensity. Our lives were more or less separate, and I thought that's the way things were supposed to be, that all marriages—all relationships—were like that.

There's no separation of any kind with Peter. Not even close. It's like an invisible thread binds us together, even when we're physically apart. He's constantly in my thoughts, and I often catch myself physically aching for him, as if my body is addicted to his touch.

It doesn't help that when we *are* together, he showers me with attention and pampers me until I feel like a spoiled pet. Massages, foot rubs, brushing my hair—he does it all when we have time. And that's not even counting the sex.

Oh God, the sex.

Ever since our wedding night, when I admitted to Peter—and to myself—that I need a certain degree of force from him in order to cope with our nontraditional relationship, he's had zero compunction about unleashing his inner monster in the bedroom. Though there are plenty of times when he's sweet and tender, more often than not, he takes me with unbridled hunger, leaving me sore and aching in the morning. No part of my body is off limits to him, and I frequently find myself tied up on my knees, with my mouth stuffed full of cock and my ass burning from his rough claiming.

He may be my husband now, but he's still my tormentor.

The key part, though, is "my." To my relief, sex with me is where Peter seems to channel his darker impulses. As far as I'm aware, he's kept his word about not hurting anyone else, and as the weeks march on, I find myself less worried when we're around my family and friends. My parents are slowly warming up to him, and my bandmates seem to like him—which surprises me, since Marsha is now seriously dating Phil and she's *not* a Peter fan.

Or at least I assume that's why I've barely seen her since the wedding.

"Marsha never seems to come out with us lately," I tell Phil when we're all grabbing a drink after a Friday night performance. "You guys are still together, right?"

He flushes, clearly uncomfortable. "Yeah, but she's been, um… really busy."

I nod and pick up my drink. "Right, okay."

It's ridiculous to feel hurt by my friend's abandonment. After all, I'd avoided her for a bit after learning that she'd been helping the FBI keep tabs on me. And in any case, I can't blame her for being cautious. Any sane person would want to stay away from a man she suspects of being a conscienceless assassin who'd once tortured her friend and killed her husband.

"What is she busy with?" Peter asks, coming up behind me to knead my shoulders. His tone is light and casual, but I can feel the tension in his strong fingers as he massages my knotted muscles. "Is she working more shifts?"

"Something like that," Phil mumbles, then motions to the bartender. "A round of tequila shots, man. The best you got."

The tequila burns my throat as we down the shots, and the slight awkwardness dissipates as Rory and Simon launch into an animated discussion of the pros and cons of natural blondes. Phil joins in, but Peter stays quiet, observing them with a vaguely amused expression, and when I excuse myself to go to the bathroom, I hear him order a round of vodka.

"None for me?" I ask, seeing only four shot glasses upon return, and my husband grins at me.

"Afraid not, ptichka. I need you awake and conscious in my bed tonight."

He accompanies the words with a squeeze of my knee, and the guys guffaw as I fight a blush. Peter is completely unapologetic about his desire for me, using every opportunity he gets to touch me and otherwise lay claim to me—in private or in public. My bandmates are convinced we fuck like rabbits all the time, and it's true.

My husband has the stamina of a teenage boy on Viagra.

Still laughing, the guys down the vodka, and Peter immediately orders another round. I eye him with some confusion—I've never seen him drink so heavily—but I figure he's just letting off a little steam after a long week.

Two more rounds of vodka shots later, though, I realize something else is going on. For one thing, I'm pretty sure Peter spilled his last shot on the floor. My bandmates were too drunk to notice, but I'm only lightly buzzed and I saw him tip the glass to the side right before he took the shot with them.

It's as if Peter is deliberately trying to get them plastered.

After another half hour and three more rounds of shots, my suspicion solidifies into certainty. Rory and Simon are now ten sheets to the wind, with Rory singing an Irish ballad and Simon pitching in off-key, while Phil is deep into a philosophical treatise on the randomness of life and reversion to the mean. Peter is acting like he's equally drunk and fully into Phil's ramblings, but to me, it's obvious that my husband is manipulating the conversation—to what end, though, I don't know.

"And so you see, a movie studio CEO could think he has the golden touch with blockbusters, but really, he's just on a winning streak," Phil slurs, and Peter nods, as though it all makes sense. "You think you have it made, but it's just luck, man. Just fucking luck. And then bam! The pendulum swings the other way. Because it's all random and reverts to the fucking mean. We don't get that as humans—we think we have control 'cause we see a pattern—but it's all bullshit. Life is like a rusted-out pendulum in an earthquake, swinging this way and that, sometimes getting stuck on an upswing. And sometimes—sometimes your whole life is on an upswing, until a tremor shakes that rust loose." He shakes his head mournfully, and I decide he's definitely had enough.

I don't know what Peter's agenda is, but alcohol poisoning is no joke.

Leaning over, I touch my husband's hand and pitch my voice low. "Let's go home. I'm getting sleepy."

He turns up his palm and gently squeezes my hand, his eyes completely sober even as his lips curve in a seemingly tipsy smile. "Just a little longer, my love. Phil here has a point."

I frown, confused. "He does?"

"Oh, yeah," Phil slurs. "You just don't see it 'cause you can't see it. You can't even imagine it. No human can, because our minds aren't capable of coming up with truly random patterns. And when algorithms do it for us, we don't believe they're random. Like the random shuffle on your music player? Not random. If it were, you'd sometimes get the same song two, three, four times in a row, and that does not seem random to us. That seems like a song is being deliberately chosen, like there's a purpose behind it, but that's false. It's just math, just programming. And so—"

"So they tweaked the algorithm, removing true randomness to make it seem more random," Peter says, sounding drunkenly serious as he plays with my fingers. "I hear you, man. It's crazy."

Phil bobs his head. "Isn't it? I tell Marsha this all the time, but she doesn't believe it. She doesn't get that sometimes a coincidence is just a coincidence, that something can be simply random. Like take you and Sara. There was some bad guy named Peter in her past, and Marsha thinks it's you, even though the FBI told her—*they outright told her*—that it's not. Like what makes more sense: that you're a wanted killer who for some weird reason is allowed to roam free, or that there might've been two Peters in Sara's life? It's like a song that comes up twice—hard to believe, but genuinely random. I mean, there is that one FBI guy who's still talking to her, but I'm pretty sure he's just hitting on her, the asshole."

I freeze, my hand tensing in Peter's grasp as my husband chuckles and shakes his head, all but oozing male sympathy. "Wow. Asshole indeed. What's the guy's name?"

"Tyson or something like that." Phil hiccups and loudly yawns. "Rhymes with bison."

Shit. My heart hammers in my chest as Peter glances at me, his gaze hard and unreadable. Has he suspected something like this all along? Is that why he's been plying Phil—and by default, Rory and Simon—with alcohol all night?

Did he somehow learn that the agent had approached my father?

I've been trying to forget about that, to stop worrying about the FBI finding out about Monica's stepfather, but every so often, I wake up in a cold sweat from a nightmare where SWAT agents burst through our bedroom door. Officially, there's a deal, but Ryson is clearly on a mission of his own.

What has he been telling Marsha? What has *she* been telling him? My mind spins as Peter orders one final round, then makes our excuses to the guys, leaving them to down the shots on their own as he shepherds me out of the bar and into Danny's car.

My former assassin is law-abiding enough—or smart enough—not to drink and drive.

I wait until we get home before I bring up what Phil told us. "Peter, about the—"

"Why didn't you tell me Ryson was still in the picture?" my husband interrupts, stepping up to me. There's only a faint hint of alcohol on his breath as he leans in, trapping me against the back of the couch with his powerful body.

He's either had even less to drink than I thought, or his metabolism is off the charts.

My throat goes dry and my breathing jacks up as I see the icy hardness in his metallic eyes. This is the Peter who used to terrify me, the man who'd broken into my house and so ruthlessly interrogated me to find George.

The killer who's never known remorse.

"I didn't know he was talking to Marsha," I say when I'm able to sound semi-calm. I know Peter won't hurt me outside of our bedroom games, but it's hard not to be intimidated when he looms over me like this, the heat from his muscular body surrounding me, his nearness both a temptation and a threat.

He might not hurt me, but he will hurt others.

Agent Ryson's life—and possibly Marsha's—is on the line.

"No?" His eyes narrow. "What about your parents? You didn't know he's been sniffing around them either?"

"No, I—" I stop before I make the situation worse by lying. "Okay, I knew he'd talked to my dad a couple of months back, but I figured it was just the one time. Are you saying he's approached them again?" My words are coming too fast, but I can't help it.

I'm terrified both for the agent and of what he might uncover.

Peter stares down at me, then finally steps back, letting me inhale a full breath.

"Earlier today," he says grimly, and it takes me a second to realize he's answering my question. "My crew saw him approach your mother when she was at a mall with Agnes Levinson. One of the guys tailed him when he left, and do you want to guess where the fucker went?"

I swallow. "Where?"

"To the hospital. Where you used to work—and your friend still does."

Of course. That's what gave him the idea to question Phil tonight. Or more accurately, to interrogate him—only with alcohol instead of a designer drug as an aid.

"Do you think he knows? About Moni—" I stop as it occurs to me that it might not be safe to speak so openly.

If the FBI are on to us, the house might be bugged.

"It's fine. I do daily sweeps," Peter says, understanding my concern. "Nobody's listening."

Daily sweeps? There's paranoia, and then there's whatever this is. I know our house has all the security of a military base—I've seen the futuristic tech embedded throughout—but I didn't realize my husband was *that* paranoid.

"And no," he continues while I'm gathering my thoughts. "I don't think he knows anything. My hackers are keeping tabs on the files related to Sonny Pearson, and nobody's accessed them in weeks."

Sonny Pearson? Is that Monica's stepfather's name? My stomach tightens as I stare at Peter, images of dark alleys and pools of blood swimming in front of my eyes. I've mostly put that murder out of my mind, just like all the other awful things Peter's done, but now that I know the man's name, the horror and guilt are fresh again.

"Stop it, ptichka." Peter's tone gentles, and I realize my face must reflect my thoughts. Reaching over, he captures both of my hands in his big palms. "Don't go there again. It's over."

Pulling me toward him, he enfolds me in a soothing hug, and I wrap my arms around his waist, inhaling his familiar scent as my cheek presses into his muscled shoulder. It's perverse to let him comfort me like this, but I can't resist accepting this from him.

It's the only way I can cope with loving someone so ruthless.

As he holds me, patiently stroking my hair, I feel a growing hardness pressing into my stomach, and I know that in a few more moments, he won't be content with simply holding me.

It's tempting to go along with that, to find refuge in the mind-melting pleasure he always gives me, but I need to make sure of something first.

"Peter..." Pulling back, I gaze up at him. "You're not going to do anything to Marsha or Agent Ryson, right?"

He stares down at me, his hands tightening on my sides. "Define 'anything.'"

"Peter, please."

His lips flatten, and he steps back, releasing me. "Fine. Your friend is safe. I won't go near her. Even if she didn't avoid us like the plague, you now know better than to trust her."

"My lips are sealed around her, I promise. And you won't go near Ryson either. Right?" I prompt when Peter neither confirms nor denies my statement.

A muscle ticks in his chiseled jaw. "*He* poses a threat. You know that, Sara. It's no longer just an assignment for him. He wants to bring us down; he's obsessed with it."

"Yes, but we're not doing anything wrong—just living our life. And if we continue doing that, he won't be able to do anything to us. However, if you rise to his bait…"

Peter swears under his breath and turns away, walking over to stand by the window. I follow, knowing that if I don't extract this promise from him, the FBI agent's days are numbered.

"You know this is exactly what he's hoping for," I say when Peter turns to face me, his expression forbidding. "He wants you to violate the terms of your deal. It's killing him that you are here with me, and that we're happy. This"—I reach out to clasp Peter's hand—"is the best revenge you can have. Let him run around sniffing at our heels. He won't find anything because there won't be anything to find."

As I speak, Peter's fingers tighten into a fist in my grasp before slowly relaxing, and his eyes take on a peculiar gleam. "All right," he says huskily as he grips my wrists and moves them lower. "I see your point." He presses my hands to his crotch, where I feel a growing bulge.

I lick my lips as an answering warmth ignites in my core. "So I have your word?" I gently massage his erection through his jeans before sinking down on my knees in front of him. "You won't hurt Ryson in any way?"

He closes his eyes and grasps my shoulders as I unzip his jeans. "Yes, you have my word. He's safe." His voice is strained with need, but I hear the dark note underneath as he adds, "As long as he doesn't try anything else."

CHAPTER 21
HENDERSON

I turn into an alley, shivering at the biting gust of wind. It's unseasonably cold in Budapest this week, reminding me of my brief stint in Vladivostok in the early nineties.

Fuck, I miss those simpler days.

She's waiting for me by the back door, as agreed, her small, boyish figure bundled up in a thick jacket and her short, platinum-blond hair standing up in spikes around her elfin face.

If I didn't know what she really was, it would be easy to believe her cover as a waitress at a trendy bar.

"Mink?" I say as I approach, and she nods.

"Here." I hand her a thick envelope. "US passport and half of the agreed-upon payment."

She takes the envelope and stuffs it into her coat. When she takes her hand out, she's holding a folder. "These are the men you want," she says, handing it to me. Her English is as American-sounding as mine, without so much as a hint of an Eastern European accent. "They're the best, and they'll do anything."

I open the folder and flip through the files inside. Each of the candidates has a rap sheet as long as my targets', and all are elite former military.

Best of all, I see four whose appearance could be sufficiently altered with wigs and makeup.

"All good?" she asks, and I nod, closing the folder.

These were the last puzzle pieces I was missing.

"Are you sure you don't want me to take him out myself?" she asks as I stuff the folder into my own coat. "Because I could, you know."

"No, you couldn't," I say. "He's too well guarded. And even if you managed, that's not the plan. Your job is to make sure he doesn't get taken alive, understand?"

She gives me a mocking salute. "Aye, aye, General. Consider it done."

And pivoting on the heel of her Doc Martens, she opens the door and disappears into the bar.

CHAPTER 22
PETER

I didn't think it was possible to love Sara more, but as the weeks pass and we find our stride as a married couple, my feelings for her both intensify and deepen. I realize now that there was a lot I didn't know about the object of my obsession—our relationship had been so tense that she'd never truly relaxed around me. Now, however, I get to see a different side of her, and I adore every new trait and quirk that I uncover.

My ptichka hates politics but is weirdly fascinated by natural disasters, religiously devouring all the news coverage before sending in a generous donation. She claims to love dogs more than cats, but it's cat videos she's addicted to on YouTube. She thinks *The Big Bang Theory* is the funniest show of all time and makes me watch it with her on the weekends. And best of all, she sings when she's in a great mood—sometimes under her breath, sometimes out loud.

"You should include that in your next performance," I tell her when I catch her humming in the kitchen one Saturday morning. "I like that melody. Very evocative."

She grins up at me. "Really? It's something I just composed. Still need to come up with the words for it."

"You will." I drop a kiss on her smooth forehead. "You always do."

Her music is evolving, just like our relationship. She's more confident in her choices, and it shows in the band's performances, which now consist of original material composed by her—and draw increasingly larger crowds. A month ago, Simon created a YouTube channel for their band, and it's already at fifty thousand subscribers.

"It's only a matter of time before we go really big," Rory tells us giddily after a sizable outdoor venue completely sells out for their Friday night concert. "We're on the verge of breaking out, I just know it."

Phil and Simon are just as excited, wanting to go out to celebrate, but Sara refuses, claiming that she's tired. Concerned, I immediately take her home, so I can tuck her into bed in case she's getting sick.

"I'm fine, really," she tells me in exasperation when I physically pick her up to carry her from the car to the house. "I'm tired, but I can walk. Seriously, it's just been a long week."

Ignoring her protests, I carry her into the house, not setting her down until I get to our bathroom upstairs. Once there, I draw her a hot bath and make sure she's comfortably settled in before I go to the kitchen to make her some echinacea tea.

When I return with the tea, she's already nodding off in the tub, looking so adorably sleepy that I put her in bed as soon as I towel her off, ignoring the predictable hunger that having her naked in my arms generates.

I need to take care of her right now, not fuck her.

She falls asleep immediately, without so much as a sip of the tea, even though it's only ten p.m. and we don't normally go to bed until eleven at the earliest. I feel her forehead to make sure she's not running a fever, then grab my laptop and settle in a lounge chair by the bed, figuring I'll do some work as I keep an eye on her. There's a surprising amount of paperwork that goes along with running a legitimate business like my training studio and generally managing a fortune.

I'm glad about that. Not the paperwork—nobody likes *that*—but that I'm able to keep busy. Training civilians in the basics of self-defense is a far cry from the adrenaline-fueled missions of my past, but it helps occupy my days and takes the edge off my constant longing for Sara. Though her bosses are now back, she still works too much, and it takes all my willpower not to pressure her to cut back and spend more time with me.

As is, outside of work, we do everything together, from running errands to volunteering at the women's clinic to hanging out with her family and friends. Whenever she has an appointment cancellation, she drops by my training studio to practice some of the self-defense moves I've taught her, and I often swing by her office around lunch, in case she has time to grab a bite with me. I've even scheduled our dental cleanings to take place at the same dentist's office at the same time, so we can be together for the drive.

It may seem like too much to most people, but it's barely enough for me.

After an hour, I check on Sara. Still no fever, and she's sleeping peacefully, if a bit too deeply. Maybe she *is* just tired.

Yawning, I put my laptop away and take a quick shower before getting into bed as well. Pulling her to me, I inhale deeply, drawing in her sweet scent, and then I let myself drift off, reveling in the feel of her in my embrace.

CHAPTER 23
SARA

I'm still strangely tired when I wake up the next morning, and the breakfast smells wafting from the kitchen downstairs make me nauseated instead of awakening my appetite as usual. Bleary-eyed, I stumble to the bathroom, and as I'm brushing my teeth, it dawns on me that today is Saturday.

As in, four days after my period was due to start.

The surge of adrenaline chases away all remaining grogginess. Heart racing, I rush back to the bedroom and pull out my phone, frantically counting the days on the calendar to make sure I didn't make a mistake.

Nope.

I'm definitely late, and this time, I can't blame it on stress.

I've stocked up on home pregnancy tests since our discussion about children, so I rush back to the bathroom to take one. Except I've already peed, and I can't squeeze out so much as a drop of urine.

Silently cursing my lack of foresight, I stuff the completely dry test back in the box, put it back in the drawer, and go get dressed.

I'll have to wait until after breakfast to take the test.

———————————

"Your parents are almost here," Peter informs me when I get downstairs, and I recall with a jolt that they're coming over for brunch today.

"Did I oversleep again?" I glance at the clock. "Oh, wow, yeah."

It's 11:27 a.m.—exactly three minutes before my parents are due to arrive.

"You must've been really worn out," Peter says, garnishing a fluffy-looking quiche with a sprig of parsley. "How are you feeling this morning, ptichka?"

I hesitate, then give him a bright smile. "Fine. Just needed to catch up on my sleep, that's all."

Given how much my husband wants a baby, it's better if I know for sure before I tell him. If this is a false alarm, I'd hate for him to be disappointed.

He doesn't look like he completely believes me, but the doorbell rings before he can say anything. I hurry to the door to greet my parents, and by the time we get to the dining room, Peter has already set the table.

"Oh, wow," Mom says when she tries a bite of the quiche. "Peter, I have to say, I've been to five-star restaurants that aren't as amazing."

He gives her a warm smile, and my dad grunts approvingly as he bites into his own portion. My parents are still somewhat wary of Peter, but he's slowly winning them over by being a model son-in-law. With George, when we'd get busy, we'd sometimes go a month or more without seeing my parents, but Peter makes sure we meet with them at least once a week. He's also been cutting their grass and taking care of technological and handyman-type tasks around their house, all the while making my parents feel like they're doing it all by themselves and he's just lending an occasional hand.

"You have a real gift for this," I told him a couple of weeks ago. "Is winning over hostile in-laws something they teach in assassin school?"

Peter nodded placidly. "In-laws, explosives, high-caliber weapons—all must be handled with care. Besides, I like your parents. They created *you*."

I grinned at him then, feeling incandescently happy. I don't know what I imagined when I pictured our life as a married couple, but so far, everything about it has exceeded my expectations. The darkness of our shared past still hovers in the background, but the future now looks so bright that it almost doesn't matter.

We've achieved the impossible: a normal, happy life together.

After we finish brunch—which I choke down despite persistent low-grade nausea—I take Mom upstairs to show her a stylish coat that I bought online. Dad stays downstairs, settling in our living room to watch the news on our big-screen TV while Peter clears away the dishes.

Mom approves the coat immediately—she loves fashionable things—and I'm about to excuse myself to finally take the test when Dad's tense voice floats upstairs.

"Lorna, Sara, come here. You need to take a look at this."

My phone buzzes at the same time, and so does my mom's.

Exchanging worried looks, we simultaneously pull out our phones.

On my screen is a notification from CNN.

Suspected terrorist act at FBI field office in Chicago, it reads. *Casualties unknown.*

CHAPTER 24
SARA

My heart is pounding and the quiche is like a rock in my stomach by the time we get downstairs. Peter and my dad are in the living room, staring at the TV screen—which is showing a sizable building up in flames.

The same building where Ryson had interrogated me so many times.

Mom covers her mouth, her face starkly pale as we watch helicopters circle the burning building. Below, firefighters and paramedics are frantically working to rescue survivors and load the injured onto stretchers.

It looks like a scene out of a movie, except it's happening right now, less than an hour's drive away.

"While the authorities haven't made any official statements, early indications suggest that a sophisticated, powerful explosive went off inside the building," the female newscaster says in a grave tone. "As of now, all airports and government offices nationwide are on high alert, and air traffic in the Chicago region has been grounded."

The image on TV flips to show SWAT-like figures rushing into O'Hare with bomb-sniffing dogs, all but mowing down the terrified travelers in their way.

"Chicago residents are advised to stay off the roads to clear the way for emergency vehicles," the newscaster continues. "Anyone with information about this terrible event can call the number below." A 1-800 number appears in a bold font on the bottom of the screen. "As of now, three people are confirmed dead and fifteen injured. We'll keep you posted as we learn more." She pauses, hand to her ear, then says, "This just in: Seven people are now confirmed dead, and the explosion appears to have originated on the third floor of the building."

Third floor?

That's where Ryson's office is.

Could he have been there?

Is he among the dead?

I'm not fully cognizant of swaying on my feet, but I must have, because suddenly, Peter is there, his powerful arm looping around my back. "Here, sit down, ptichka," he murmurs, guiding me to the couch. "You look like you're about to faint."

I blink up at him, struck by how calm he appears as he sits beside me. Other than some tension in his jaw, nothing about Peter's expression suggests that anything unusual is going on. Then again, I'm sure he's seen worse.

Maybe even done worse.

An awful thought nibbles at the back of my mind, but I shove it away, not wanting to so much as verbalize it to myself.

I'm not going there, not even for a second.

"I can't believe this," Dad says, his voice shaking, and I turn to see him sitting next to me, his face as pale as Mom's as he stares at the TV. "The FBI building of all places. How could they have gotten past all that security?"

How indeed?

The dark thought flickers back to life, but I determinedly stamp it out. This horrible tragedy has nothing to do with me or Peter.

"Are you okay, Dad?" I ask, reaching over to touch his arm.

This can't be good for his faulty heart.

He nods, his eyes still glued to the screen. "Thank God it's a Saturday. Can you imagine how many people would've died if today was a weekday?"

I look back at the TV, where firefighters are battling the flames and victims are being carried away on stretchers—a lot fewer victims than I would've expected from an explosion of this size. Of course, some people might've been blown apart, with their remains yet to be discovered, but I suspect Dad is right, and there were fewer people because it's the weekend.

"Maybe the bomb went off late. Or early," Mom says unsteadily as she sinks into a stuffed chair next to the couch. "I'm sure the animals who did this wanted to kill as many as possible."

"I'm not so sure," Peter says, and I turn to see him regarding the screen with a thoughtful expression. "Whoever's behind this clearly knew what they were doing."

I swallow thickly, my stomach beginning to churn around the boulder-like weight of the quiche inside. I don't want to think about the people who did this, because that way lie those dark, awful thoughts, the ones I don't even want to acknowledge.

"Excuse me," I mutter, standing up. The nausea that's tormented me all morning is getting worse by the second. "I'll be right back."

Naturally, Peter comes after me, catching me right before I reach the bathroom downstairs.

"You okay, my love?"

I nod, swallowing. Saliva is pooling unpleasantly in my mouth, and the churning in my stomach is reaching washing-machine speeds. "Just need the restroom," I manage to say, and stepping around him, I dive for the open door.

I barely have time to slam it shut and kneel over the toilet before I lose the contents of my stomach.

Of course, it was too much to hope that Peter would hear the retching noises and slink away like most normal husbands would. I'm still heaving into the bowl when I feel his strong hands gathering my hair to hold it away from my face, and as soon as I lift my head, he helps me up and hands me a glass of water to rinse my mouth.

I'm pathetically grateful for his support as I bend over the sink and grab a toothbrush with trembling fingers. My legs feel like they belong to a jellyfish, and my T-shirt is sticking to my sweaty back.

I brush my teeth twice, then wash my face while Peter flushes the toilet and wipes the lid with a paper towel, looking concerned but not the least bit grossed out.

"Come, my love, let's get you to bed," he says when I'm done. "You're clearly not well."

"I'm fine now," I protest as he lifts me up to hold me against his chest. "Really, I feel better."

"Uh-huh." He carries me out of the bathroom and past my parents in the living room, who stare at us with round eyes. "You're either severely upset or sick, and you need to be resting."

"What happened?" Mom hurries after us as Peter heads for the stairs. "Is Sara sick?"

Peter nods grimly. "Yes, she—"

"May be pregnant," I blurt out, then mentally curse myself as both Peter and my mom freeze in place with identical looks of shock on their faces.

This is not how I planned to share the news.

Well, possible news. I still haven't taken the damn test.

Mom recovers first. "Pregnant? Oh, Sara!"

"I don't know for certain yet," I say quickly as tears—presumably of joy—appear in her eyes. "It's just that my period is a few days late and—"

"You're pregnant?" Peter's voice is strained, and when I look up, I see the strangest expression on his face.

Bewilderment mixed with something very much like panic.

Is he actually freaked out by this?

Wasn't this what he wanted all along?

"It's a possibility," I say carefully. "If you put me down, I'll go pee on a stick and let you know."

Still looking shell-shocked, my husband slowly lowers me to my feet.

"Okay, good." Extricating myself from his hold, I step back, grateful that my legs seem to have recovered. "Now give me a few minutes."

"Chuck!" Mom yells, rushing to the living room as I head upstairs, with Peter on my heels. "Did you hear this? Our Sara might be pregnant!"

I wince, cursing myself yet again for blurting this out so impulsively, and with such bad timing. I can still hear the TV blaring with the latest developments in the deadly attack, and here I am, distracting everyone with something as mundane as a potential baby.

Mine and Peter's baby.

My heart skips a beat as my husband follows me into the bathroom upstairs and takes out the pregnancy test box from the drawer. "Here you go, my love," he says, handing it to me. His voice is still rough, but he seems to be recovering from the shock. "Do your thing."

I walk over to the toilet and stop, looking at him expectantly.

"A little privacy, please?" I say wryly when he shows no sign of moving.

He stares at me, unblinking, then turns around. "Go ahead. I'm not going to look."

I roll my eyes but decide it's not worth arguing over. Boundaries are not my husband's strong suit in the best of times, and right now, he's probably worried I might faint as I pee.

I do my business on the stick, then set it on some clean toilet paper on the counter and wash my hands as Peter stares at the test like he's trying to hypnotize it.

"It looks like a plus," he says in a choked voice as I wipe my hands on the towel. "Wait—no, it's definitely a plus. Sara, does that mean…?"

My heart swan-dives in my chest as I look at the test—where a small but unmistakable plus sign is now showing. "I think so." I lift my gaze to Peter's face. "I'll do a blood test in my office to make sure, but—"

"You're pregnant."

It's a statement, not a question, but I still nod, instinctively knowing he needs the confirmation. "About five weeks along if my calculations are correct."

For a moment, my husband shows zero reaction, his metallic gaze shuttered as he stares at me. But just as I'm starting to worry that he's changed his mind about wanting a child, he steps forward and grabs me in a huge hug.

"A baby," he mutters against my hair, his powerful body all but trembling as he holds me against him, his embrace tight enough to squeeze the air from my lungs. "We're having a baby."

"You are?" My mom's voice is shrill with excitement, and Peter releases me, letting me see my seventy-nine-year-old parent bouncing in the doorway like an overeager kid.

She must've come up just a second ago.

I start to reply, but before I can say a word, Mom runs out of the bathroom, yelling at the top of her voice, "Chuck, it's positive! The test is positive! They're having a baby!"

Her excitement must be contagious because I find myself grinning as I look up at Peter, who's staring at me with yet another peculiar expression.

"Are you okay?" I ask, reaching up to stroke his bristly jaw. "You *are* pleased about this, right?"

He captures my hand, pressing it against his cheek. "Are *you*?" His voice is low and husky, his gaze inexplicably worried. "Are you pleased, my love? Is this what you want?"

"I—yes." I take a deep breath. "It is."

And it's true. I want this baby. I want it so badly I can taste it. I hadn't admitted it to myself before, but when my period had come as usual for the past three months, I'd felt more than a little pang of disappointment.

Somewhere along our twisted journey, this baby has gone from being my worst nightmare to my most fervent wish.

"So no regrets?" Peter confirms. "No fear or hesitation?"

"No." I hold his gaze without flinching. "None."

And as a slow, incandescent smile breaks across his handsome face, I rise up on tiptoes and kiss him, overcome by a surge of love for this dark, complicated man.

For the father of my child.

CHAPTER 25
PETER

By the time we come downstairs, Sara's parents have already found the bottle of Cristal I've been keeping in the refrigerator for a special occasion.

"Here, let me," I say, noticing that Chuck is struggling to open it. Taking the bottle from him, I pop the cork and pour three glasses—one for everyone but Sara. For her, I take out a bottle of Perrier and pour some sparkling water into a champagne glass.

My ptichka won't be able to have alcohol for the duration of her pregnancy and while she's breastfeeding.

Breastfeeding our baby.

My ribcage tightens again, and my heartbeat skyrockets. I still can't believe that this is real, that what I've wanted for so long is finally happening.

Sara willingly having my child.

The two of us as a real family.

My happiness is so absolute it's terrifying. I can't remember ever feeling like this before: overjoyed and deeply uneasy at the same time. All I want to do is grab Sara and lock her in a fortress, or barring that, wrap her in a padded safety suit and carry her with me everywhere, lest she and the baby get hurt in any way.

"To our first grandchild," Lorna says, lifting her champagne glass, and I force myself to smile as I clink my glass against hers, then Chuck's, then Sara's. All three of them are grinning and laughing, completely caught up in the joy of the occasion. I should be too, but for some reason, I can't let go of the worry that hangs over me like a malignant cloud.

Something feels off, but I can't put my finger on what it is.

Someone's phone dings with a notification, and Chuck puts down his champagne before reaching into his pocket to glance at the screen. "Twelve dead now." He looks up, the smile gone from his face. "What a shame we had to find out about our grandson on such a dark day."

"Could be a granddaughter," Lorna says, but she sounds somber too.

Maybe this is it. Maybe this is what's bothering me.

It *is* a dark day—for Ryson and his colleagues, at least. For me, it's potentially a cause for celebration. If Ryson's been blown to pieces, he'll be out of our hair for good. It does worry me that Sara and her parents are upset, though.

Stress is not good for pregnancy.

"Come, ptichka. Have a seat." I carefully steer her to a chair by the kitchen table, and then I go into the living room, where the newscaster is loudly speculating on which terrorist organization may have been behind the attack. I look at the images of the burning building for a second, then power off the TV.

I don't need Sara listening to this in her condition.

I return to find Sara's parents in the foyer, getting ready to go. "Are you coming tomorrow as well?" Lorna asks Sara as she picks up her bag. "I was thinking the two of us could have some tea while Peter helps your dad set up that new receiver."

"Yes, of course," Sara says, grinning. "You know I'll be there, Mom."

"Good." She pecks Sara's cheek. "Now get some rest, honey, okay?"

"Will do," Sara says dutifully, and I nod, smiling, as Lorna pointedly catches my gaze. She doesn't believe her daughter for a second, but she knows me well enough to realize that I will make sure said resting happens.

"See you tomorrow," Chuck says to me gruffly, and to my surprise, he pats my shoulder as he shuffles toward the exit.

"Have a safe drive home," I say, and then I'm baffled again when Sara's mother gives me a brief but warm hug before following her husband out.

I wait until the door closes behind them before turning to Sara. "Did they just—"

"Officially accept you as part of our family?" She beams at me. "Why yes, I believe they did. Congratulations, baby daddy."

My heart squeezes into a tiny dot before expanding to fill my entire chest cavity. "I love you," I say thickly, pulling her toward me. "You can't even imagine how much."

And as she winds her slender arms around my neck, I kiss her, tasting the softness of her lips—and the love that she now gives back freely.

CHAPTER 26
SARA

After my parents leave, Peter and I drive to my office, where I draw a vial of blood. A few minutes later, we have the official confirmation.

I'm five weeks pregnant.

I'm also ravenous, since I threw up the only food I've eaten today. "I don't think I can wait until we get home," I tell Peter, so he stops by a small pizzeria on the way.

I've never been to this place before, and I'm pleased to discover that though we're the only customers right now, their pizza is the real deal, as good as anything I've had in fancier places. The only fly in the ointment is that the TV is on, showing the aftermath of the attack, and the owner—a plump, middle-aged man who speaks with a strong Italian accent—keeps talking to us about it as we eat by the counter.

"Such an awful, awful event," he says gloomily, kneading a ball of dough in front of us. "What is the world coming to? First 9/11, then the Boston Marathon, now this. At least it's the FBI they targeted this time, not innocent citizens, you know? Not that those agents are guilty, but you know what I mean. If you have some kind of beef with America, makes way more sense to target them or the CIA or something else having to do with the government."

I nod noncommittally as I stuff my face with the delicious pizza, and that's all the encouragement the man needs to keep going.

"They say the explosive was something unusual, something really advanced," he says, rolling the dough with practiced movements. "I wonder what it is and how those terrorists got their hands on it. Sounds more like something Russia or China would have, or even our own military. I bet all the conspiracy theorists are going to come out in full force, claiming it's an inside job or what-not."

I bite into another slice, letting the man ramble on as I sneak a glance at Peter. I expect him to be calmly eating as well, but to my surprise, he's frowning, his slice untouched in front of him as he stares intently at the TV.

"What is it?" I ask quietly as the owner turns away to get more flour. "Is anything the matter?"

He tears his gaze away from the TV and gives me a rueful smile. "Not really. Just old instincts nagging at me, that's all."

I want to question him further, but the owner is back to rolling the dough in front of us and speculating on who might be behind the explosion.

"Thank you very much. This was delicious," I tell the man when I can't eat another bite, and Peter swiftly pays our bill and hustles me out of the place. Despite his denials, my husband is clearly worried about something—I can see it in the tense way he grips the wheel as we drive home—and the dark kernel of suspicion I'd suppressed returns, making my stomach roil anew.

Could it be?

What are the odds that this is all a terrible coincidence?

I fight the doubt for as long as I can, but finally, I can't take it anymore.

The moment we're inside the house, I turn to face my husband. "Peter... I need to ask you something."

Even to my own ears, my voice sounds strange.

He immediately gives me his full attention. "What is it, ptichka?" He clasps my shoulders. "Are you feeling okay?"

I nod, swallowing as I stare up at him. My heart is tap-dancing in my chest, and I'm starting to feel sick again.

Maybe that pizza was a mistake.

Maybe bringing this up is a bigger mistake.

"What is it, my love?" Gently, he guides me to a loveseat by the entrance. "Here, sit down. You look pale."

"No, I'm fine," I say, but I sit anyway, because it's easier to comply than to argue. He sits next to me and clasps my hands in both of his, massaging my palms with his thumbs as though I need soothing.

And maybe I do.

It all depends on how he answers my next question.

"Peter…" I reach for my courage. "I need to know. Did you—" I draw in a breath. "Did you have anything to do with what happened today? With that… explosion?"

He turns into a statue, neither blinking nor reacting for the next few moments. Finally, he says tonelessly, "No." Releasing my hands, he stands up, and without saying another word, he walks back to the entrance to remove his shoes.

I stare after him, feeling both awful and awfully relieved.

I believe him.

He has never deceived me, has never denied his culpability in any crime.

My husband might be a killer, but he's not a liar.

"I'm sorry," I say when he walks by without looking at me. "Peter, I'm really sorry, but I had to ask. The third floor is where Ryson's office is and—" I stop because he disappears into the kitchen.

I take a breath, then walk over to the door to remove my shoes as well. I feel terrible that I asked—that I even entertained the idea in the first place. Not only is this attack a truly heinous act, but it's also something that would've jeopardized our life together—something Peter has fought hard for.

Something he's given up his vengeance for.

I'm fully prepared to grovel when I enter the kitchen, but Peter is nowhere to be found. I go around the house, looking for him, and it's not until I peek into the guest room's walk-in closet that I find him.

He's crouched over a laptop, his fingers flying over the keyboard with record speed.

Frowning, I kneel next to him and peer at the screen. He's typing up an email, but it's in Russian and the interface of the program he's using is unlike anything I've ever seen.

"What are you doing?" I ask cautiously. "Peter... why are you in here?"

"Hold on," he says without looking up. "Let me finish."

I shut up and watch him type. It takes him another couple of minutes, and then he shuts the laptop and taps at the wall in the closet.

It glides to the side, revealing another closet-sized space.

A space filled to the brim with military-grade weapons, including several rocket launchers and grenades... as well as spare laptops.

Speechless, I watch as Peter places his laptop on a shelf and taps another wall, causing the original wall to slide back into place, covering the opening.

I finally find my tongue. "Is that—"

"A hidden weapons locker? Yes." He stands and extends a hand to help me up. "But don't worry, my love." His eyes gleam with chilly amusement as I clasp his hand and rise to my feet. "I'm not planning to use it to commit any terrorist acts."

I wince and release his hand. "I know. I'm sorry. I shouldn't have—"

"No, you should've." He smooths my hair back from my face, the gesture as tender as ever even as his gaze remains that of a stranger. "I always want you to come to me if you have any doubts. Besides, you and that pizzeria owner have helped me realize something."

I blink up at him. "What's that?"

"That I need to look into what happened. Something about this stinks to high heaven."

"What do you mean?"

"I don't know yet." He drops his hand and steps back. "I just contacted our hackers, though, so I'll have more information soon."

He turns and walks out of the closet. I hurry after him, catching up right before he leaves the guest room.

"So you're not mad?" I ask breathlessly, stepping in front of him to block the doorway. "That I asked you?"

His lips twist. "Mad? No, ptichka. Why would I be?"

"Well, because you're innocent, and I pretty much accused you. I really am sorry; I shouldn't have even considered that—"

"Why shouldn't you have?" He cocks his head. "It wouldn't have been the worst thing I've done."

My stomach tightens. "I know, but—"

"It was a logical assumption on your part. A sophisticated explosive, a difficult target, and a motive on my end. In fact, I'm surprised you believe me."

I'm pretty sure he's mocking me with that last bit, but I deserve it. "What can I do to make it up to you?" I ask instead of apologizing again. "How can I make this better?"

His eyebrows rise, and his eyes gleam with sudden interest. "What did you have in mind?"

My pulse picks up, and a warm flush covers my body as he gives me a decidedly heated once-over. Sex wasn't what

I had in mind, but if that's what he wants, I'm more than happy to oblige.

"This," I murmur, and holding his gaze, I begin to strip.

CHAPTER 27
PETER

After we make love, Sara falls asleep in the guest room, and I leave her there to nap. I did my best to be gentle during sex, but I must've worn her out regardless.

Either that, or she just needs the extra rest and I have to be more diligent in making sure she takes it easy over the next eight months.

The anxiety-tinged joy fills my chest again, crowding out the remnants of hurt. It doesn't make sense to be upset at Sara's question; if anything, I should be glad she trusts me enough to ask me outright instead of letting such suspicions fester.

I also can't blame her for having the suspicions in the first place. I would've never done something as blatant and showy as blowing up the FBI building, but I have been quietly planning to eliminate Ryson—who had continued to sniff around after I made my conditional promise to Sara.

If he'd left us alone, he would've been safe, but he hadn't—and I felt perfectly justified in what I was going to do to him.

Will still do to him if he survives.

My unease intensifies again, but this time, the worry is more concrete. I don't believe in coincidences, and all of this feels too coincidental. I didn't tell Sara this, but I have already located a list of the dead and injured, and Ryson is among the latter, having been taken to the hospital in critical condition.

If I didn't know better, I'd think someone did me a favor.

After a half hour, I check on Sara. She's still sleeping, so I make my way back to the guest room closet and take out a few weapons. I stash them strategically throughout the house and carry a few down to the garage, where I hide them in a special compartment in our bulletproof car.

Just in case.

Paranoia appeased, I open my laptop and begin answering emails from my trainees as I wait for my ptichka to wake up.

———

"Oh my God," Sara says the next morning, her gaze glued to the TV. "Peter, Ryson *was* there. They've just identified the victims of the explosion, and he's listed as being in critical condition. Can you believe that?"

I nod noncommittally. "I heard about that earlier. That's really unfortunate for him."

According to my sources, he's got third- and fourth-degree burns over most of his body. I almost feel bad for the fucker. I would've taken him out in a much more humane manner—most likely via a drug-induced heart attack, so it would've looked like he'd died from natural causes.

"What a terrible tragedy," Sara says, her gaze still locked on the screen. "I hope he recovers."

"Mm-hmm." There's no need to upset her by disagreeing. "Do you want anything to eat, or do you still feel nauseated, my love?" All she's had so far this morning is a piece of dry toast, though I've made her favorite omelet and pancakes.

She turns toward me. "I'm good for now, thank you. The nausea is almost gone, but I think I'll just eat at my parents' while you do your thing with Dad's receiver."

"Okay, sure. Ready to go then?"

She stands up and comes over. "Yep. Let's go."

I take a different route to my in-laws' house and make sure that my guys sweep the area ahead of our arrival. The hackers are still investigating the explosion, but my danger meter is pinging nonstop.

Maybe Sara and I should get out of town, go on our honeymoon now, instead of around the holidays as we originally planned. It could be an early babymoon, or whatever those things are called.

Sara's parents greet us warmly, and her mom goes into her usual hostess mode, offering us tea, crackers, fruit, and everything else under the sun. I politely decline—I had a big breakfast—but Sara goes to town on her mom's offerings while I set up Chuck's new receiver.

"You need to plug that in here," he says, pointing at the audio wire, and I nod, thanking him as though I didn't already know that.

Sara's dad needs this to be a team project, and I'm happy to oblige.

I'm almost done testing the surround sound when my phone vibrates in my pocket. Pulling it out, I glance at the screen—and ice invades my veins.

SWAT on the way, a text from my crew states. *Three minutes out.*

CHAPTER 28
SARA

I hear it right before Peter bursts into the kitchen, where Mom and I are discussing potential nursery themes.

The unmistakable roar of helicopter blades.

"Let's go." He picks me up before I can blink. "Excuse us," he says to my stunned mother, and holding me tightly against his chest, he steps around her, heading for the door.

I grip his shirt spasmodically. "Peter, what—"

"No time." He yanks open the door and backs out, holding me—only to freeze in place as a huge black van screeches onto our street and figures in SWAT gear pour out, face shields down and assault rifles aimed at us.

My brain feels like it's suddenly turned to sludge.

I can't process this.

Can't even begin to.

Slowly and very deliberately, Peter lowers me to my feet and steps in front of me, shielding me with his body. "Don't shoot." His tone is oddly calm as he raises his hands above his head. "There's no need for violence. I'll come with you."

My tongue somehow untangles itself. "Wait!" I lurch forward on unsteady legs. "There was a deal. You can't—"

"Back up, ma'am!" the front-most agent barks, and I freeze as several weapons swing in my direction.

"I said there's no need for this." Peter's voice sharpens as he steps up, putting me behind him again. "I'm not resisting. Nobody has to get hurt, you understand?"

"What's going on here?" Dad demands from behind me, and I realize with a surge of panic that my parents came out of the house.

"Get back in." My voice shakes as I risk a glance behind me. "Dad, please get Mom back in."

The chopper is now almost directly overhead, its roar drowning out my words.

"On your knees!" someone shouts, and I look back to see my husband obeying, his movements as slow and deliberate as before.

He doesn't want to make them nervous, I realize with nauseating fear. They know what he's capable of, and even though he's unarmed, they're terrified to be confronting him.

"Peter Garin, you are hereby charged with federal employee assassination, destruction of government property, use of explosives, and conspiracy to commit murder," the agent who spoke earlier shouts over the chopper noise. He edges toward Peter with handcuffs as his colleagues hold their assault rifles pointed at my husband's face. "You have the right to—"

His helmet explodes before he gets the next word out, and all hell breaks loose.

CHAPTER 29
PETER

I'm moving before I fully register the crack of the sniper's rifle.

It's instinctive, purely automatic.

I have only one agenda.

Survive long enough to protect Sara and the baby.

As always in such situations, my thoughts are clear and sharp.

Sniper at five o'clock, identity unknown.

One agent dead. The rest about to open fire.

Nine opponents in front of me. Sara and her parents behind me.

I seize the M4 from the agent whose brains I'm wearing, and throw myself sideways as I spray his colleagues with bullets, aiming at where I know the gaps in their armor are likely to be.

I need to draw their fire away from Sara, to have them focus on me as the sole threat.

Out of the corner of my eye, I see Sara's parents dragging her inside the house. She's screaming something, but it's impossible to hear over the helicopter noise and the *rat-tat-tat* of automatic gunfire.

The ground next to me explodes with bullets, but I keep moving, keep squeezing the trigger. Their armor protects them, but it also slows them down, buying me precious seconds. Even when I don't kill them, my bullets knock them down and out.

Five enemies left now.

All the weapons I prepared are in our car, with only a Glock strapped to my leg, so when my borrowed gun clicks empty, I throw it aside and dive behind two fallen agents, grabbing one's weapon on the way.

Fire punches at my left arm, but I ignore it.

I can still hold the gun, so the wound can't be that bad.

The SWAT van is now just a dozen feet away, so I throw myself toward it, both for cover and because that's as far from the house as I can manage. As I hit the ground, I squeeze off another few rounds and get lucky with my angle, catching two agents underneath their face shields.

Fire bites at my right calf, but the adrenaline keeps me moving.

More bullets pepper the ground around me, though I'm now behind the car.

The chopper.

Flopping onto my back, I squeeze off a round in its direction, and a rotor blade explodes, causing it to tilt sharply in the air. I fire again, and it swerves away, disappearing behind the trees a couple of blocks over.

Without pausing, I roll under the van and come out on the other side, facing the three remaining agents.

Only there are two of them in front of me.

One is running toward the house.

CHAPTER 30
SARA

Everything happens in a flash. One moment, I'm standing behind Peter as the agent is about to cuff him, and the next, there's a thunderous *crack* and the man's helmet explodes, blood and brains spraying all over as Peter springs into action, snatching the dead man's gun.

"Sara, get in!" Mom grabs my arm, yanking me backward as deafening gunfire erupts, mixing with the roar of the chopper.

"No, you go in!" I yell, twisting out of her hold. I can't leave Peter out here. "Get inside now!"

"Your baby!" Dad shouts over the noise, grabbing my wrist as I'm about to lunge forward. "You're pregnant, remember?"

The reminder is like a bucket of ice water thrown in my face.

I'd forgotten about the tiny life inside me, the child Peter wants so badly.

"Get inside, Sara. Now!" Mom yanks on my other wrist, and this time, I obey, stumbling into the house as the street turns into a war zone.

"We have to... get away... from the windows," Dad wheezes, bending over in the foyer. "The bullets, they—"

"It's okay, Dad. Just breathe." I grab his elbow as he starts to collapse, but he's too heavy for me to hold and I just manage to soften his fall.

"Where are your pills?" My voice rises in panic as his face begins to turn blue. "Mom, where's his medication?"

"The k-kitchen." She sounds like she's going into shock. "T-top cabinet on the right."

"Okay, be right back." The living room window explodes as I sprint past it, but I barely register the fragments of glass peppering my skin.

I have to get Dad's medicine.

I can't think about Peter right now, can't focus on the toxic terror squeezing my chest.

He'll make it.

He has to.

Opening the cabinet, I grab Dad's nitroglycerin pills and a bottle of aspirin, then sprint back as the noise of the chopper fades away and the gunfire stops.

Mom is kneeling over Dad's unconscious body, her face a mask of terror as she looks at me. "He's not breathing. Sara, he's not breathing."

I'm already on my knees, pushing on Dad's chest as I count under my breath, then bend over to breathe into his mouth.

His chest rises with the air I give him, then falls and remains unmoving.

Fighting my growing panic, I begin the chest compressions again.

One, two, three, four—

The door flies open, and two wrestling men tumble in.

It's a SWAT agent and a blood-covered Peter.

CHAPTER 31
PETER

I fire before the agents do, squeezing off two rounds that hit them right under their face shields. Fueled by adrenaline, I jump to my feet, only vaguely aware of the burning pain in my arm and calf.

I have to stop the fleeing agent.

I can't let him hole up with Sara and her family inside.

Putting on a burst of speed, I catch up with him by the entrance and tackle him as he spins around, ready to fire. The weapon clatters across the porch, and we crash into the door, pushing it open with our momentum.

I only have a split second to take in the scene inside, but it's enough for me to angle to the right and avoid tumbling into a kneeling Sara and her parents.

We crash into the couch instead and roll across the floor together, struggling for the Glock tucked into his belt. I land on top of him and yank the weapon out, but he rams his elbow into my injured arm, knocking the gun out of my hand.

Ignoring the blaze of pain, I snatch his knife and jam it into the gap between his armor. He gasps like a landed fish, and I stab him again, then twice more.

His body goes slack underneath me.

"Peter!" Sara's voice reaches through the roar of my heartbeat, and I look up, taking in her white, tear-streaked face. She's pressing on her father's chest in the unmistakable rhythm of CPR, her mother kneeling next to her.

I crawl off the dead man and push up to my feet. The room spins around me in a sickening circle, and when I glance down, I see that my right leg is covered with blood—and more blood is dripping down my left arm.

Of course. The gunshot wounds.

Pushing away the growing dizziness, I start toward Sara and her parents. "What happened? Did he get shot?" I don't see any blood on Chuck, but—

Sara shakes her head. "Cardiac arrest." Bending over, she pinches his nose shut and blows into his mouth, then resumes pushing on his chest.

Fuck. I take in the pill bottles lying unopened on the floor, and my chest tightens.

It's Sara's worst nightmare, and I brought it upon her.

"You two need to go." Lorna's hoarse voice sounds like that of a ghost, and when I glance at her, I see that she resembles one, her face like bleached parchment paper. "Before they send in the—"

A bullet shatters the wall above us, and I instinctively leap in front of Sara and her mother, shielding them with my body.

My left side explodes in pain, the massive force of the hit throwing me forward as I shove them both behind the couch. My vision flashes white, the pain ricocheting through my nerve endings as another bullet whines by my ear.

No. Fuck, no.

With my last remaining strength, I throw myself to the side, drawing the fire of the shooter away from Sara and her mother. Another bullet punches into the floor next to my knee, sending shards of wood flying everywhere, and through graying vision, I see an armor-clad figure swaying in the doorway, clutching a handgun.

It's one of the SWAT agents I shot.

Dazed and injured but alive.

His face shield is missing, revealing mottled skin and wild eyes. "Die, you motherfucker," he hisses, and aiming at my head, he squeezes the trigger.

CHAPTER 32
SARA

I land painfully on my side, my head banging into the side of the couch as another shot rings out and a warm, metallic spray hits my face and neck.

"Peter!" Terrified for him, I scramble to my knees, wiping the blood out of my eyes—and then I see it.

Mom sprawled on the floor, her face splattered with blood.

Or rather, most of her face.

Part of her cheek and skull is missing, leaving a bloody hole where a cheekbone used to be.

My mind shuts down, a wall of numbness sliding into place as a third shot rings out.

I look at my husband, on his back and bleeding, then at the agent in the doorway, his face twisted with hatred as he aims at Peter's head.

My gaze falls on the gun Peter dropped while wrestling with the other agent.

It's three feet away.

I reach for it and pick it up. It's cold and heavy in my hand, adding to the icy numbness in my heart.

My parents are dead.

Peter is about to be murdered.

I aim and squeeze the trigger a split second before the agent fires.

My bullet misses, but the gunshot startles him, causing his shot to go wild.

He spins toward me, and I fire again.

It hits him in the middle of his vest, throwing him back.

Without any hesitation, I walk over to him and lift my gun again.

"Don't—" he chokes out, gasping for breath, and I squeeze the trigger.

His face explodes into bits of blood and bone. It's like a hyper-realistic video game, complete with smell, taste, and surround sound. Fascinated, I drop the gun and reach out to see if it feels as real—

"Sara." Peter's strained voice reaches me as though through water. "Look at me."

Blinking, I focus on his prone body, and some of my numbness dissipates as I see the amount of blood pooling at his side.

He's hurt.

Badly.

A surge of terror clears the remaining haze from my brain, and I sink to my knees, frantically pulling at his shirt. I have to staunch the flow of blood, to see if the bullet—

"Ptichka, stop." He catches my wrist with startling strength, his eyes boring into mine. "There's no time. You have to hand me the gun. Put it in my hand. You didn't do this, you understand? And then you need to walk away. Get as far away from me as—"

"No." I twist out of his hold. "I'm not leaving you."

He needs a hospital, but there's zero chance the agents will take him there after this massacre. They'll kill him on the spot for killing so many of their own.

Innocent or guilty, they won't care.

"Ptichka, you must—"

"Get up." Jumping to my feet, I grab his uninjured arm, tugging on it with all my strength. "We need to go, now."

I can't lose him.

I won't lose him.

A grimace twists Peter's face as he attempts to sit up and fails. "My love, you need to—"

"Now!" I bark, yanking at his arm, and something about my tone seems to get through.

Jaws clenched, he struggles to a sitting position, and I crouch to loop my arm around his torso. He's impossibly heavy, his large body all hard, solid muscle. My back and legs scream in protest, but I somehow manage to stand up, supporting most of his weight.

"The car," he grits out hoarsely. "We have to get to the car."

The car.

Just outside, parked on the side of the road.

We can do it.

We have to do it.

I take a step toward the door, and suddenly, most of Peter's weight is gone. Glancing over, I see he's somehow standing on his own, though his face is gray underneath the smears of blood and grime.

"The car. Come on," I urge as we step outside. "Almost there. Just a little more."

In the distance, I hear the wail of sirens and the roar of another helicopter.

They're coming for us.

Coming to take Peter from me, just like they took my parents.

"The keys. They're in my pocket," Peter rasps, and I thank heavens for small mercies as I recall that keys in close proximity is all our fancy Mercedes needs to unlock and start.

Opening the passenger door, I all but stuff Peter inside, then sprint around to the driver's side. My heart is pounding in a sickening rhythm, and my hands tremble as I start the car, pull out onto the street, and slam on the gas.

"Where do I go?" I ask frantically as we screech around the corner onto the main road. The sounds of the helicopter and the sirens are getting louder; it's only a matter of time before they find us missing and send a pursuit.

No response.

I risk a glance at Peter. He's half-slumped in his seat, his face colorless and his eyes closed as he holds a bunch of blood-soaked paper towels against his side.

Oh no. Oh, please, no.

"Peter." I shake his knee.

Still nothing.

"Peter, please. I need you to tell me where to go."

He groans as I shake him harder, and his eyes open blearily. "Cabin near Horicon Marsh. Get on I-294 toward 94, then take 41 and 33, turn right on Palmatory and go four miles. Dirt road on the left."

Oh thank God.

I take a sharp right toward the highway and floor the gas as he fades out again. He's losing too much blood, but I can't do anything until I get him to safety.

He's as good as dead if they catch us.

My mind spins like a dreidel on steroids as I tear down the highway. I can't think about my parents or the enormity of what just happened, so I focus on the whys.

Why did they come for him?

Why did someone shoot that agent when Peter was about to surrender?

I believed my husband when he said he had nothing to do with the attack on the FBI, but is it possible he lied to me? Would they have come to arrest him like that if there was no evidence linking him to the bombing?

Logic says no, but I can't bring myself to buy into it. Peter has done terrible things, but he's no terrorist.

Morality aside, when he kills, he does it with precision and discretion.

So why? Why would they think he's involved? And who shot at that agent? Had someone from Peter's crew been that stupid? If so, why didn't they help us further?

If they were willing to kill a SWAT agent, why leave Peter to fight the rest of them on his own?

None of it makes any sense, but dwelling on it is keeping me from hyperventilating at the wheel. I can't think about our infinitesimal odds of survival, or that Peter might be bleeding to death.

Or that the tiny life inside me now has two fugitives for parents.

"Slow down." Peter's hoarse whisper reaches me as I zoom around a Toyota going eighty in the fast lane. "Don't draw attention by speeding. Where's your phone?"

My pulse leaps in joy as I lift my foot off the gas.

Talking is good.

Talking is very good.

"No phone," I answer, some of my relief fading as I glance over to find him conscious but even more pale. "I forgot my bag at—"

"Good. That means they can't track us that way."

Shit. That hadn't even occurred to me.

"What about your phone?"

He grimaces, shifting in his seat as he reaches for more paper towels from a roll tucked into the side of the door. "Untraceable."

"Okay." My mind races. "What else? Should we ditch the car? Is there anyone we can call for help? Your bodyguards? Can they—"

"No." He closes his eyes again, pressing the fresh towels to his side. "Too high profile for them. Won't go against FBI."

Right. That makes sense. Peter's new crew are not criminals; they're paid to protect us from the dangerous people in Peter's past, not help us escape the authorities.

Which means they couldn't have been behind that shot.

"Peter..." I glance over, but he's out again, his head lolling to the side.

Ice coats my insides. "Peter, wake up. You need to tell me what to do next."

No response, just the frantic hammering of my pulse in my ears.

I reach over to shake his knee, but he doesn't react, and I see that he's no longer holding the paper towels, his hand slack at his side.

My ribcage feels like it's shrunk to the size of a child's, crushing all the organs inside.

This can't be happening.

It can't end like this.

"Peter." My voice cracks. "Peter, please... I need you. You can't do this to me."

He can't die and abandon me. Not after fighting so hard for us.

Not after making me love him.

"Wake up, Peter." I shake his knee harder. "Please wake up."

But he doesn't.

He's too far gone.

CHAPTER 33
SARA

*F*eeling like the car walls are closing in on me, I grab his wrist and search for a pulse.

It's there.

Weak and erratic but there.

A sob of relief bursts from my throat, and the road in front of me blurs.

He's still alive.

Passed out but alive.

With a herculean effort, I pull myself together. I can't fall to pieces, not while there's still a sliver of hope.

First things first. I need to treat Peter's wound. It can't wait any longer. Then the car. I have to assume they're looking for it, and it's only a matter of time before we're spotted on the road. That means I need to find us another ride.

The question is how.

If Peter were conscious, he could probably steal one for us, but I don't possess such a skill set. I need to come up with some other solution, something that won't slow us down too much.

An exit sign appears ahead, and I realize we're almost to Advocate Lutheran hospital.

My heart skips a beat, then races faster. Maybe I should bring him in. Right now, before the authorities know we're here.

Before more SWAT agents show up and shoot him dead for killing so many of their own, all the while claiming self-defense.

They'd have to treat him at the ER if I brought him in. They'd have to save him. And when the cops arrive, they won't be able to kill him with all those witnesses around. They'll have to let him recover before carting him away.

Before locking him up in Guantanamo or some other dark hole for the rest of his life.

Even if he's found innocent in the bombing, they'll never let him out—and sooner or later, they'll take their revenge.

If I bring Peter in, I'll never see him again. But if I don't, he'll bleed to death.

Even now, it might be too late. I might lose him like I just lost my parents.

Choking down the suffocating fear, I switch into the exit lane and pull off the highway, heading toward the hospital. When I get there, I find a parking spot under a tree, between an SUV and a van.

"We should be well hidden here." My voice shakes as I turn to Peter. "Now I'm going to look at your wounds, okay?"

He doesn't respond, but I don't expect him to.

Reaching over his lap, I lower his seat to a reclining position. Then I lift his shirt and examine the gunshot wound on his side.

There is an exit hole, and given its location, there's a good chance the bullet missed vital organs. If I disinfect the wound and stop the bleeding, he might make it without a hospital.

Holding my breath, I swiftly examine the rest of him. I find a gun strapped to his left ankle, but it's not an injury, so I ignore it. I then discover that a bullet grazed his left arm and another went through his right calf.

Both wounds are still bleeding, but neither appears to be life-threatening.

I exhale, trembling as I squeeze his limp hand in relief.

I know what to do now.

I just need a little luck on our side.

Leaning over him, I smooth back his blood-crusted hair. "Hang in there, darling, please. I'll be right back, I promise. Just hang in there for me."

I can do this.

I have to do this.

Pulling back, I sit up straight and flip down the mirror to look at myself. As expected, I'm just as much of a mess as Peter, my face pale and tear-streaked, with smears of blood and bits of gore all over my skin and clothes.

Good thing the staff in the ER have seen worse.

"Be back in a few," I whisper, giving his hand one last squeeze, and jumping out of the car, I run across the parking lot to the ER entrance.

Nobody pays me any attention as I walk in, and I keep my head down, angling my face away from the cameras in the corners. As far as I know, my picture isn't on the news yet, but it's best not to risk it.

Inside is the usual ER pandemonium, with several new arrivals mobbing the admitting nurse, demanding to be seen *right now*, and a half-dozen nurses and doctors clustered around two patients strapped to gurneys, with one screaming about the bloody mess that is his leg, and the other in the midst of what appears to be a major seizure.

At the back is a staff-only entrance. The nurses wheel the screaming patient there, and I follow them in, pretending I'm with him. One nurse tries to shoo me away, but someone yells for her, and she disappears down the hall, forgetting all about me.

I follow the gurney without anyone else noticing me, and when we pass by a supply closet, I step in and close the door behind me.

At the back are folded-up scrubs, linens, bandages, medication samples, and first-aid supplies. I quickly change out of my clothes and into nurse's scrubs, wipe as much blood as I can off my face with a pillowcase, and stuff whatever I deem useful into a bag I fashion out of a sheet. Then I cover my haul with more bunched-up linens and head out, pretending I'm carrying soiled sheets to be washed.

No one says anything as I reenter the ER reception area and head to the exit, making sure the bundle in my arms is blocking my face from the cameras blinking in the corners.

Getting back to the car, I find Peter still unconscious.

"All good, I'm here now," I say as I place the bundle of supplies at his feet. "Everything will be okay."

He can't hear me, but that doesn't matter.

It's myself I'm trying to convince.

He's too heavy for me to undress properly, so I push up his sleeve and cut apart the leg of his jeans to get to those wounds. Among my pilfered supplies are mild soap and a saline solution, and I mix them with water to wash away all the blood and dirt near his wounds. Contrary to popular wisdom, it's a bad idea to use strong antiseptics to clean wounds; rubbing alcohol and such are likely to damage tissue and slow the healing process.

When I'm satisfied that the wounds are sufficiently clean and no bullet fragments remain inside, I stitch up and bandage them, starting with the wound at his side. As I work, I thank the powers that be for my residency stint in the ER and all the gunshot victims I'd treated there.

Still, my hands are shaking by the time I'm done, and I realize the adrenaline high is beginning to wear off.

That's not good.

There's still a lot that needs to get done before I crash.

"I have to step away for a few more minutes, okay? So just hang in there for me, darling," I whisper, stroking Peter's face. Leaning in, I press a gentle kiss to his hard jaw and pull away, telling myself that all I need now is a little luck.

A little luck and a lot of balls.

My legs are unsteady as I head toward the ER again. This is the least sure part of my plan, one that relies on too many exogenous factors. By now, our faces might be splashed all over the news, the manhunt kicking into full gear. All it would take is one nosy stranger, and a police/FBI swarm will descend upon us.

Maybe this is a mistake.

Maybe I should just get back in the car and drive, praying that by some miracle, no one has put out an APB on our vehicle.

I'm about to turn back and do exactly that when a blue older-model Toyota screeches into the parking lot, stopping right by the entrance. "Help!" an elderly woman shouts, opening the door, and I rush over to her, helping her get her semi-conscious husband out.

By the looks of him, he's just had a stroke.

Two nurses run out of the ER to help, and I unobtrusively step away, letting them usher in the patient and his frantic wife. The car is left unattended, the driver's door open, and when I peek inside, I see the keys in the ignition.

Bingo.

The ER staff usually send out someone to move the vehicle in such situations, but if they come out and find it gone, they'll most likely assume it has already been moved by someone.

It won't occur to them to report the car stolen until the patient's wife returns and can't find it.

I feel terrible as I slide behind the wheel and drive the Toyota toward our car. I can only imagine how stressed out the poor woman will be when she has to deal with a stolen car on top of her husband's stroke. But there's no choice—not with Peter's life on the line.

I park the Toyota directly across from our Mercedes, jump out, and hurry over to our car. Opening the passenger door, I look my husband over, wondering how I'm going to move two hundred pounds of unconscious male from one car to another.

Oh well, here goes nothing.

Grabbing his ankles, I pull with all my might.

He moves an inch. Maybe.

Fuck.

I put my entire back into it, digging my heels into the asphalt.

Another three inches.

Maybe I should forget this stupid idea and just drive our car. The stroke victim's wife will be happy when she finds her Toyota in the parking lot and—

My husband lets out a low groan.

My pulse leaps into overdrive. "Peter." I scramble into the car, leaning over him. "Peter, darling, please wake up."

He mumbles something incoherent, his head turning to the side.

"Please, I need you." I shake him gently. "Please wake up."

His eyes open, unfocused.

"That's it, darling." My breath hitches in joyous relief. "You can do it. Look at me."

He blinks, his gaze slowly focusing in on me. "Sara? What—"

"We're in a hospital parking lot," I say quickly. "I procured us a car, but I can't move you without your help. Can you walk over there for me?"

His jaw tightens, but he nods.

"Good, let's do it. Come on." I bring the seat up to a sitting position and help him out of the car. He's unsteady on his feet, leaning heavily on my shoulders, but somehow, we make it across the row.

His face is greenish white by the time I help him into the car, but he's clinging to consciousness with every shred of his iron will. "The weapons," he rasps, plopping heavily onto the passenger seat. "Under the back seat. Get them."

We have weapons?

I'm not nearly as surprised as I should be.

Leaving Peter in the Toyota, I sprint back and try to raise the back seat of the Mercedes. It takes some ingenuity, but I finally get it open—and gape at the arsenal inside.

In addition to handguns and assault rifles, there are grenades and what looks like a rocket launcher.

There's no way I'll be able to carry all this across the parking row without someone spotting me and raising an alarm.

Then an idea comes to me.

Grabbing the first-aid supplies, I run back and put them onto the back seat of the Toyota, then yank the sheets out from underneath them and hurry back to the Mercedes. The weapons are heavy, so I have to make three separate trips, but I get everything over to the Toyota—wrapped in sheets.

"All done," I tell Peter as I slide behind the wheel, panting from the exertion, but there's no answer.

He's passed out again.

I lean over and make his seat flat again, both so he can rest and so that he won't be visible in the windows.

Then, taking a deep breath, I pull out of the parking spot and head for the cabin.

CHAPTER 34
SARA

Remembering Peter's admonition about speeding, I drive carefully, obeying every traffic rule and speed limit. Peter's phone is locked and I can't wake him, so I use a combination of road signs and my own vague knowledge of the area to get us to the dirt road he mentioned.

I don't think about my parents or the man I killed so ruthlessly. I can't—not while I need to hold it together. Instead, I focus on getting us to our destination without stopping. By the time we turn into the woods, my bladder is on the verge of exploding, so I pull off onto the shoulder and go behind a tree, camping style. The elderly lady kept a little bottle of hand sanitizer in the car, and I use it before I resume driving, trying not to think about what will happen once we actually get to the cabin.

Despite my best efforts, dangerous questions swirl in my head.

What will we do if Peter's wounds get infected?

Will there be food and water at the cabin?

And worst of all, how long until we're found?

Because we will be found. I can't fool myself into believing otherwise. We've been lucky so far, but we're no match for the FBI. Or at least *I'm* no match. Peter had managed to avoid capture for years with the help of his underworld connections.

I've never regretted not having criminals in my social circle before, but I do now. None of my friends or acquaintances can help us—not without getting in trouble with the law themselves. In fact, other than my husband, the only people I know who have the right skills and contacts are his Russian former teammates, and they're nowhere near—

Wait a minute.

I do have Yan's email.

That's how he congratulated me on our wedding.

My pulse jumps again, the excitement sizzling through my veins before I remember one important fact.

I have no way to send an email other than using Peter's phone, and for that, I need my husband to regain consciousness and put in his password.

I glance over at him, my chest tightening at the gray pallor of his face. He needs to be in a hospital, with an IV providing antibiotics and replenishing fluids, not being jolted about on a pothole-filled road.

If he dies, it'll be on me.

It'll be because I chose to hide him from the authorities instead of bringing him to the hospital.

A "Private Property" sign looms ahead, with a fence on each side and a wooden gate blocking the road. It must be our destination, unless I made a wrong turn earlier.

I stop the car and get out to open the gate. Except a chain with a lock holds it in place. I yank on the rusty lock, unable to believe that after everything, we could be thwarted by something so stupid.

Trying to contain my frustration, I come back to the car and attempt to shake Peter awake. Maybe he has a key stashed somewhere I don't know about.

He doesn't react, no matter how I beg and plead with him, and when I feel his forehead, I find it hot and clammy.

My stomach twists painfully.

A fever so early doesn't bode well.

Hands shaking, I pat him all over, hoping against hope that he has a key hidden in one of the pockets. But there's nothing other than his phone and the gun strapped to his ankle.

Exhausted, I sink to the ground by the passenger side of the car.

It's hopeless.

I don't know how to do this.

What was I thinking, playing at being a fugitive? Peter is the one with the knowledge and the skills, not me. I can't even get through a stupid gate. If he were in my place, he'd probably pick the lock or shoot it off or blow it up or—

Of course, that's it.

I need to think outside my straight-and-narrow box.

Jumping up, I put a seatbelt on Peter and sprint back to the driver's seat.

Sliding behind the wheel, I back the car up until we're some fifty yards from the gate, and then I floor the gas.

The Toyota rips forward.

We hit the gate at sixty miles an hour, knocking the aged wood off its hinges.

The windshield cracks from a piece of the gate slamming into it, but none of the airbags activate, and I press on the brake, grinning triumphantly as we continue down the road at a more moderate speed.

Sara, 1. Stupid gate, 0.

I glance over to check on Peter, and my elation fades as I see a fresh blood stain spreading over his shirt at his side.

His stitches must've torn, either from the encounter with the gate or the rough drive in general.

I need to get us to that cabin, so I can treat him pronto.

The drive there seems to take forever, though realistically, I know it can't be much more than a mile.

Finally, I see it.

A wooden cabin surrounded by trees.

Shaking with relief, I pull up to the front and run up to the cabin.

Surprise, surprise.

The front door is locked.

This time, though, I'm prepared. Grabbing a big rock, I walk up to a window and whack it as hard as I can. It shatters, shards of glass flying everywhere, and I use the rock to clear away the sharpest edges of the remaining glass. Then I climb inside, ignoring the blood trickling down my arms.

I'll deal with my own injuries later. Right now, my priority is Peter.

Walking over to the front door, I unlock it and step out, racking my brain for how I'm going to move him inside. It would be amazing if he woke up again and used that impossible force of will to actually walk over, but I'm not holding my breath given his earlier lack of responsiveness. Maybe I can roll him onto the sheet and then pull that in, or—

My gaze falls on an ancient wheelbarrow. It's leaning against the house next to a rusty axe.

Must be there to haul chopped wood.

I walk over and pick up the handles, then test the wheelbarrow by rolling it back and forth. The wheels creak but seem functional.

I push it over to the car and turn it so that the handles are propped inside the open door, on the floor. Then I grab Peter's ankles and dig my heels into the ground, pulling with all my strength.

He moves a couple of inches.

Gritting my teeth, I pull again.

Then again.

And again.

When he's halfway over the wheelbarrow, I go around to the driver's side and push him farther onto it, my heart aching as he moans from the pain. "Just a little more, darling," I promise softly, and with one last shove, I roll him into the wheelbarrow.

Step one accomplished.

Now I have to wheel him into the house and get him onto a bed.

CHAPTER 35
PETER

*M*y world is fire and pain, mixed with a gentle voice and soothing hands. The agony is unrelenting, but when that voice is near and those cool, tender fingers stroke my burning brow, I can forget it all.

I can just focus on her.

And it is her. Sara, my ptichka. I know it even in the depths of my delirium. Whatever is happening to me, she's there, touching me, speaking to me, feeding me sips of water. Often, she's asking me things, her melodious voice filled with desperation and pleading, but I can't answer her, can't do anything but turn my head toward that voice and accept the fleeting comfort offered by her touch.

She gives up after a while, her tone changing to one of resignation, and I like that more, though not as much as when she's crooning to me, her voice as soft and gentle as the kisses she presses to my cracked and burning lips.

They make me feel good, those kisses—at least until I sink into the darkness and the demons come, wrapping their tentacles around my chest, stabbing me with their scalding pokers. My side, my arm, my calf—they're pitiless as they savage me, burning my flesh to the bone.

Pasha is there too, his skull half-missing, his brain grotesque underneath the glossy waves of his dark hair. "Papa!" he shouts, bouncing on me, driving the hot pokers deeper, stabbing me through to the heart.

"Please, Peter, stay with me," Sara's voice begs, and I latch on to it, fighting the demons in the darkness, struggling against their hold.

More kisses come. Her lips are cool and wet, oddly salty. Like tears. All those tears I've made her shed. But why is she crying again? I don't want that. I want to soak in her caring, to imbibe her love, not her tears. She'd fought against me, but now she's mine. Mine to take care of and protect. Except I can't do anything but burn, the fire eating away at me, consuming me, blanketing my mind with the pain.

"Please, my darling. Tell me the password. I need to unlock your phone."

The words should make sense, but they don't, the sounds bouncing off my brain like sunlight off a lake.

"Papa, do you want to see my truck?" Pasha is back to jumping on me, his little feet like a wrecking ball slamming into my side. "Do you, Papa? Do you?"

I open my mouth to reply, but the demon tentacles wrap around my neck, choking me with a lasso of fire.

"Please, darling…" Tender hands smooth over my face and throat, cooling the burn inside. "Please, I need you to give me the password, so I can reach out for help."

"Papa. Papa. Play with me."

"The password, Peter, please. It's our only chance."

"Don't leave, Papa."

"Please, darling. I need you. *Our baby* needs you."

"Please, Papa. I would be good. I promise, Papa. I would be good."

The agony is unbearable. It feels like I'm cracking in half, the burning tentacles turning into whips as I fall deeper into the darkness.

"Stay with me, Peter. Please, darling…" The salty wetness is back on my lips, the voice pulling me up, shielding me from the demons. "I love you, and I can't do this without you. Please… I can't lose you too."

Something dances on the tip of my tongue, something important that I need to remember. Something my ptichka needs.

Four numbers float up in my consciousness, and I seize them with effort.

It's a birthday.

My friend Andrey's birthday.

We'd always celebrated it at that awful camp.

"Zero six one five," I whisper—or I try to. My tongue doesn't want to obey. I try again, with the last of my strength. "Nol' shest' ahdeen pyat'. Ptichka, passvord den' rozhden'ye Andreya."

CHAPTER 36
SARA

Shaking, I stand up as Peter lapses into feverish Russian, mumbling unfamiliar words interspersed with his son's name, as he's been doing for hours. Despite my best efforts, his condition is rapidly deteriorating, and I know that if I don't get stronger antibiotics into his system, he won't make it.

The penicillin I stole from the hospital can only do so much.

The wooden walls sway around me as I walk over to the sink and return with a cool, wet towel—the only thing that seems to help him. Sitting down on the edge of the bed, I smooth it over his face, neck, and chest, wiping away the sticky sweat. My arm trembles from exhaustion, my eyes burning from tears, but I don't stop.

I can't—not while there's still a sliver of hope.

My whole body aches, my back spasming from the strain of transferring Peter from the wheelbarrow onto this bed. It's past midnight, and the only thing I've eaten is the lone can of chicken noodle soup I found in a cupboard an hour ago. I tried to feed it to him, but I could only get him to swallow two sips. So I choked down the rest. Not for myself, but for the baby.

Peter's child needs the nutrients.

The soup wasn't a lot of calories, but it gave me a little energy—enough that I again tried to coax Peter into giving me the password.

I failed, same as the prior twenty times, but Peter seemed to at least understand me on this attempt. He muttered "ptichka" and said something about a password with a thick Russian accent. Or maybe he even said it in Russian. For all I know, it's the same word in both languages.

My vision blurs again with tears. It was a mistake to come here. I shouldn't have taken this risk. Even in a sterile hospital setting, gunshot wounds are prone to complications, and given how much blood Peter has lost and where I had to treat him, infection was all but inevitable.

If I'd brought him to the hospital, he would've lost his freedom, but he might've lived.

"I'm sorry," I whisper, pressing my lips to his burning forehead. His body is fighting the infection and killing itself in the process. "I'm so sorry for this. For everything."

And I am. I'm sorry for not admitting my love for him sooner, for resisting his love for so long. It seemed important at the time, not to give in to my feelings for

George's killer. It seemed moral and right. But now I see my resistance for what it was.

Cowardice.

I'd been afraid to fall for Peter, terrified to give in and love him. Petrified that if I let him into my heart, I would lose him.

Like I lost George to the bottle.

Like I knew I'd inevitably lose my parents.

More tears stream down my face, burning my throat on the way. That's one worry I no longer need to have.

They're dead.

The worst has come to pass.

I still can't wrap my mind around what happened, can't process the horror of seeing Mom's brains blown out in front of me—and then squeezing the trigger myself. I'd felt no hesitation, no regret as I killed the agent who'd shot Mom—just that terrible numbness. It's as if someone had taken over my body, someone ruthless and cold... and powerful.

God, it had felt so powerful.

Is that how it is for Peter? When he kills, does he turn off the part of himself that makes him human, embracing that rush of power? I'd always wondered how someone with such a deep capacity for love and caring could steal a life without remorse, but I understand it now.

We're all monsters under the surface. Some of us just never get the chance to discover it.

His cracked lips move, and I reach for a bowl of water. Dipping a clean towel in, I drizzle the liquid over his mouth, careful to squeeze it out drop by drop so he doesn't choke. The fever raging through his body is dehydrating him, killing him before my eyes, and there's nothing I can do.

Even if I wanted to take him to the hospital, he wouldn't survive a return trip on that bumpy dirt road—and without being able to access his phone, I can't call or email for help from here. Nor can I drive somewhere to do so.

I can't leave Peter alone for hours when he's this sick.

He's mumbling again, his head tossing from side to side in agitation as he repeats a phrase in Russian. It sounds like what he was saying before, when I thought he might've understood me.

"Nol' shest' ahdeen pyat'. Den' rozhden'ye Andreya, ptichka." His hoarse voice is barely audible. "Nol' shest' ahdeen pyat'."

Leaning over him, I press my forehead to his. "What does that mean, darling?" I whisper, squeezing my eyes against a fresh influx of tears. "What are you trying to tell me?"

There's something vaguely familiar about that phrase, or at least the individual words. Do I know them? I strain to recall what Peter's teammates taught me in Japan. *Spasibo*—that's "thank you" in Russian. *Vkusno*—that means "delicious." Ilya also told me how to say the names of certain foods, and Anton started teaching me the alphabet and how to count to ten—

I sit up, electrified. That's it! That's why some of those words seem familiar.

They're numbers in Russian.

"Peter, darling, is that the password?" My voice shakes as I lean over him again, smoothing back his sweat-dampened hair. "Are you telling how to unlock your phone in Russian?"

He doesn't seem to hear me, his agitation easing as he sinks deeper into unconsciousness. Dragging in a calming breath, I try to recall the specific words he said and how the count to ten goes in Russian. There is an almost musical rhythm to it, if I recall correctly. *Ahdeen, dva, tree,* something, something, something…

Okay, then. So *ahdeen* is one, and I'm pretty sure Peter said that.

It was the third word after something that sounded like "null" and "jest."

I rack my brain, trying to remember how Anton pronounced the rest of the numbers. *Ahdeen, dva, tree…* was it *chet*-something? *pet*-something?…

No, five was *pyat'*—which is what Peter said as the last word.

I try to suppress my excitement, but my heart is racing uncontrollably. I still don't know two of the numbers, but I can venture a guess as to one of them.

Some Russian words are similar to English, which means the one that sounds like "null" could mean "zero."

Okay, then. Zero, unknown, one, five—that's three out of four. I can brute-force guess the unknown number… if Peter's phone doesn't lock me out for too many incorrect attempts, that is.

Jumping up, I grab the phone, and as I start inputting the zero, all ten numbers come to me.

Ahdeen, dva, tree, chetyre, pyat', shest', sem', vosem', devyat', desyat'.

I can almost hear Anton's voice reciting them to me.

Holding my breath, I follow the zero by six, one, and five.

CHAPTER 37
HENDERSON

*M*y hand sweeps out, knocking off the porcelain horses dotting the shelf—Bonnie's idiotic collectibles that she insists on lugging with us all over the world. They shatter with a satisfying crash, but it's not enough to quell the rage burning inside me.

Not yet located.

The words on my computer screen taunt me, rubbing me raw from within.

Manhunt ongoing but fugitive not yet located, the email from my CIA contact states.

How the fuck is that possible?

How could they have gotten away?

According to the SWAT agents who survived the gunfight, Sokolov had been shot at least twice—and there's footage showing his wife stealing some supplies from a hospital, so he had to have been hurt badly enough for them to risk stopping there. Yet there's no trace of the two of them anywhere—nor of the car that she stole at that same hospital, though the police think they might be able to track it before long.

Incompetent bastards. It wasn't supposed to happen this way. Sokolov should've been killed during the arrest.

That sniper bitch, Mink, was paid well to ensure it.

If Sokolov makes it out of the country, it's only a matter of time before he figures out what happened and comes after me and my family—and I can't let that happen.

He has to be killed during capture, but for that, he has to be found first.

Rolling my neck from side to side to relieve the pinching pain, I compose an answering email to my contact.

It's time they expanded the net by calling in Interpol and all the rest.

CHAPTER 38
SARA

I pace around the cabin on unsteady legs, glancing out the broken window every five seconds. It's pitch black outside, the silence interrupted only by the usual forest noises.

Still, I keep looking, keep listening for police helicopters.

It's now been almost sixteen hours since I stole the car from the hospital. By now, its owner would've found it missing and reported it to the police. If they've discovered our Mercedes in the parking lot—and I would be shocked if they haven't—every law enforcement officer in the area must now be looking for the blue Toyota and the fugitives in it.

It's only a matter of time before they find our cabin.

If Yan doesn't get here soon, it will have all been for nothing.

I look at the phone again, rereading his email for the fifteenth time. I should conserve the battery, but I can't help myself. The three little words on the screen are the only thing keeping me going.

On our way.

That's all Yan had replied when I sent him an email detailing the situation and our location. He clearly knows what's happening because he'd answered in under a minute.

On our way. That's it. No specifics, not even a rough ETA. I have no idea if he'll be here in minutes or hours or days.

For all I know, we're looking at weeks.

It had been another agonizing choice when I'd unlocked the phone: call 911 to get Peter the medical attention he so badly needs, or reach out to Yan and continue this fugitive madness. In the end, I went with my instinct—and when I looked at the phone's browser after getting Yan's reply, I was glad that I did.

Our faces are now all over the news, both mine and Peter's. Every media outlet, minor and major, is dissecting our lives online, the articles constantly updating with new details about our wedding and speculations about our relationship. In some, I'm cast as a brainwashed victim; in others, I'm complicit from the beginning. When it comes to Peter, however, there's no ambiguity.

In every story, he's the villain.

"She told me he killed her first husband," Marsha is quoted as saying in *The Chicago Tribune*. "That he tortured and stalked her before kidnapping her. She was gone for months, and when she came back, she was completely messed up. He must've done a real number on her, brainwashed her somehow. Because when he showed up again, she married him. Like, within days. She denied it was him—he changed his last name somehow—but they couldn't fool me. I always suspected the truth."

My bandmates had also been interviewed. "He just popped up out of nowhere," *The New York Times* quotes Phil as saying. "For months, we all knew her as this shy, reserved widow, and then suddenly, she's marrying this mysterious Russian. She said they'd been dating in secret, but I've always thought there was more to that story. And he was so possessive of her. Like, dangerously possessive. You could tell he'd kill anyone who dared look at her a moment too long. He just had that lethal aura about him."

I read through these articles, looking for mention of any specific evidence linking Peter to the bombing, but there's nothing—nor is there anything about his real background and motivations.

Some news outlets claim that he's a Russian spy, and that the bombing was Putin's unofficial response to the sanctions. Others speculate that Peter is an assassin for the Russian mafia, and that the bombing had to do with an ongoing investigation. George is mentioned too, as a brave journalist whose story about the Russian mob resulted in his murder.

There's nothing about the small village of Daryevo or Peter's family, not a single word about the terrible error that led to their deaths.

A few articles talk about my parents' deaths and their neighbors' reactions to the shootout, but I can't bring myself to read those. Each time I try, my throat closes up, and my heart starts beating in an irregular rhythm. The horror and the grief are too powerful, too fresh—as is the stomach-twisting guilt.

I failed my parents, failed to shield them from the darkness I brought into their lives, and I can't face that yet, any more than I can imagine a world without them in it.

It's easier to push it all down, to lock it up tight and focus on surviving moment to moment—to worry about the one person I love who is still alive.

Stopping my pacing, I sit on the edge of Peter's bed and feel his forehead. He's still burning up, his body battling the infection that's causing the wound in his side to look red and inflamed.

I change his bandages, then crush the next dose of penicillin into powder and carefully feed it to him with spoonfuls of water. He's almost totally unresponsive, but I manage to get most of the medicine down his throat. It's not enough—he needs much stronger stuff—but it's the best I can do for now.

"Hang in there, darling," I whisper, running a damp towel over his face to cool him down. "Help is coming. Just hang in there, and all will be well."

It has to be.

I can't bear to think otherwise.

———————

I'm nodding off next to Peter when the front door opens with a loud creak.

The adrenaline blast is so strong I'm on my feet before I can even process the sound. "Wha—"

"It's just us," Ilya says, stepping through the doorway with Yan. "We have to go. Now."

I realize I'm panting, one hand pressed to my wildly hammering heart. "You're here. You came."

Yan is already standing over Peter. "Help me," he orders his twin brother, and Ilya hurries over. Together, they lift Peter off the bed and swiftly carry him out of the cabin.

My brain belatedly switches on, and I grab the first-aid supplies, then run after them.

Outside is a dark-colored SUV with its headlights off but its motor running. "Get in the back with him," Yan tells me as he and Ilya deposit Peter in the backseat, then go around to the front.

I scramble to obey. "There are some weapons in the Toyota," I say breathlessly as Yan gets behind the wheel. "Should we get them or—"

"No time," Ilya says as Yan slams on the gas, and the car rips forward. "If we don't make it out of US airspace before eight a.m., they're going to shoot down our plane."

I suck in a sharp breath and shut up, focusing on protecting Peter from the worst of the jolting. He's lying in the back seat with his head on my lap, and with every pothole we hit at full speed, I'm terrified that he'll fly off the seat and tear his stitches.

At first, I have no idea how Yan can see well enough to drive without headlights, but after a few minutes, my eyes adjust and I begin to make out the shapes of trees and bushes in the faint light of the crescent moon flickering through the clouds.

"Where's the plane?" I ask when we finally turn onto a paved road and the teeth-rattling torture ceases. "How far is it from here?"

"Not far," Ilya says, glancing back at me as Yan turns on the headlights—probably to blend better with the few cars that are out at this time. "Just a little longer, that's all."

"Okay, good." Peter is feverishly mumbling something again, and I wouldn't be surprised if at least some of his stitches got torn. "Do you think we'll be able to—"

"Quiet." Yan's order is knife sharp. "I can't miss this turn."

I fall silent again, letting him concentrate on getting us to our destination. Before long, we turn off on another dirt road, and Yan switches off the headlights as we embark on another bone-rattling adventure.

I keep Peter as still as I can while stroking his sweaty hair. It seems to soothe him, and it helps keep me calm as well. As relieved as I am that we're no longer alone, I know we're not out of the woods yet—literally or figuratively. The tension in the car is palpable, the adrenaline thick in the air.

"*Zdes*," Ilya says suddenly, and Yan takes a sharp right, nearly sending me flying. I manage to catch Peter's shoulders, but he still groans in agony as his injured leg hits the seat in the front.

"Is he okay?" Ilya asks gruffly, glancing back. The sky is beginning to lighten with the first hints of dawn, and his shaved skull gleams in the twilight-like darkness, its pale smoothness marred only by the intricate pattern of his tattoos.

"Depends on your definition," I answer, keeping my voice low. I don't want to distract Yan again. "He needs a hospital. Badly."

"What about you?" Ilya's deep voice softens. "I heard what happened to your—"

"I'm fine." My tone is harsher than I intended, but I can't go there right now, can't poke at that dark well of grief and despair. I can feel it bubbling under the surface, but as long as I don't touch it, don't open it, I can keep myself from drowning in it.

Ilya studies me for a moment longer, then turns back to face the front window. I hope he's not offended, but even if he is, I can't gather enough energy to care. Now that I'm no longer in charge of getting us to safety, I can feel myself starting to unravel, thread by agonizing thread, and it takes all my willpower to hold the fraying ends together.

I have to stay strong.

If not for myself, then for Peter and our baby.

We bump along for ten more minutes before we turn onto another paved road and I see a decent-sized plane standing a dozen yards away.

"This is the airport?" I look around, taking in the forest surrounding the narrow strip of asphalt that seems to end not too far in the distance.

"More of an illegal airstrip," Yan says, hopping out of the car. "Ilya, help me get him out."

I move out of their way as they lift Peter out of the car and carry him onto the plane. Grabbing the first-aid supplies, I hurry after them, expecting to see Anton, Peter's friend and their teammate, inside.

To my surprise, instead of Anton's bearded face, I'm confronted with the hard features of Lucas Kent—the arms dealer whose home I stayed at in Cyprus. He's standing inside the luxurious cabin, arms crossed over his broad chest.

"Hello," I say warily, and he nods at me, his square jaw tight. He must still be upset with me for persuading his wife, Yulia, to help me escape.

That, or he's just worried about this operation.

"We have less than two hours before my guy's shift is over," he says to the twins, confirming that it's at least partially the latter. "Place him here"—he nods toward a cream-colored leather couch—"and we go."

The twins do as Kent says, and he disappears into the pilot's cabin. A minute later, the engines start with a roar, and I sit down next to Peter on the couch as the plane begins rolling. Yan and Ilya each take a seat at the front, and I look out the window, holding my breath as the plane speeds up.

With an airstrip this short, it'll take a hell of a pilot to clear the trees ahead as we lift off.

Apparently, Kent *is* a hell of a pilot because we clear those trees without any issues. I can hear the powerful engines revving up as we climb at a steep angle, and a wave of relief rolls over me as I realize we're in the air.

Not over the border yet, but at least up in the air.

As soon as the plane levels off, I inspect Peter's wounds. There's some fresh bleeding around his calf, but the stitches in his side and arm have held, though the side continues to look angry and inflamed. I feed him another dose of crushed-up penicillin with water and put on fresh bandages.

It might be my imagination, but he feels a little cooler to the touch by the time I'm done, and his face looks more relaxed. It's more like he's sleeping rather than out of his mind with the fever.

I wipe a damp towel over his face and neck to cool him down more, then kiss his stubble-roughened cheek and walk over to where the twins are sitting.

"How's he doing?" Ilya asks, getting up. "Will he make it until we get to the hospital?"

I swallow a lump in my throat. "I think so. That is… yes, he will." I hadn't let myself think that he wouldn't, not really, but the awful possibility had been there, gnawing at my chest and burning a hole in my stomach.

"He's a tough bastard," Yan says, his green eyes gleaming as he lounges in his seat, looking like a corporate shark in his perfectly tailored dress pants and pinstriped shirt. "It'll take more than a few bullets to kill him."

I laugh shakily, then feel wetness on my face.

Am I crying?

Wiping away the errant moisture, I turn away, embarrassed, just as a big paw descends on my shoulder, squeezing lightly.

"It's okay," Ilya says gruffly when I turn back to face him. "You did well, *kroshka*. He'll make it, thanks to you."

"And you," I say huskily. I have no idea what he just called me, but it sounded more like an endearment than an insult. "If you hadn't come…"

"Yeah, you would've been fucked," Yan says matter-of-factly. "They're really ramping up the hunt for the two of you."

I nod, suppressing a shudder. "I figured as much when I saw the news. I can't even begin to thank you for—"

"So don't." Yan stands up. "We don't need your thanks."

I smile, feeling a bit awkward. "That's very nice of you, but I still really appreciate it. I know what a huge risk this is…"

Yan grins sardonically. "Do you? Are you now an expert on life on the run?"

"No, but I'm learning more about it every day," I say evenly. "So thank you. I'm grateful that you came, and I'm sure when Peter wakes up, he'll be too." I have no idea what Yan's deal is, but I have a nagging suspicion that he's toying with me, like a cat with a mouse.

Pushing that unsettling image away, I turn to Ilya. "Where's Anton?" I ask. "Is he okay?"

"He's in Hong Kong on some business," Ilya answers. "Wouldn't have gotten here in time. We got lucky that Kent was in Mexico with us, and that he had a plane. Otherwise…" He shrugs his massive shoulders.

"Right." I bite the inside of my cheek. "I need to thank him too."

"I wouldn't," Yan says dryly. "He's not your biggest fan."

"Oh." So the arms dealer *is* holding a grudge about my escape—or at least his wife's involvement in it. "I guess I should apologize to him first."

"Why?" Yan looks coolly amused as he leans against the side of his seat. "Because you saw an opportunity and took it? He would've done the same in your shoes."

"Yes, well, still." I turn toward the pilot's cabin, but Ilya steps in front of me, blocking my way.

"You don't need to do this," he says, his expression kind. "This is between him and Peter."

"Okay..." I didn't realize there was a specific protocol to these things. "I guess I'll leave it to them, then."

I turn to go back to Peter's couch, but then I remember something important. "Where exactly are we going?" I ask, facing the twins again.

"To the clinic in Switzerland," Yan says. "To get this one"—he nods at Peter—"on his feet. And after that, who knows." He smiles darkly. "The whole world is now your home, Sara Sokolov. Welcome to our kind of life."

PART III

CHAPTER 39
PETER

I wake up with a sense of well-being that belies the pulling discomfort at my side. Soft hands are stroking my hair, and a sweet voice is crooning a soothing melody, making me feel warm and relaxed.

Opening my eyes, I meet Sara's startled gaze. She's sitting on the edge of my bed, holding a comb that she must've been about to use on me.

"You're awake." Her face lights up as she jumps to her feet and leans over me, leaving the comb on the bedside table. "How are you feeling?"

"Fine." My voice comes out raspy, like I haven't used it for a while. My mouth is dry too, as is my throat. Moistening my cracked lips, I ask hoarsely, "What happened? Where are we?"

Beaming, Sara reaches for a glass of water sitting next to the bed. "The clinic in Switzerland. The Ivanov twins got us out."

There's a lot to unpack there, so I suck water through a straw while I sift through my recollections. I remember the bullet ripping through my side and Sara shepherding me into our car, but then things get hazy, more like a jumble of impressions. We must've changed cars at one point, because I have a vague memory of getting into a blue Toyota, but after that, it's pretty much blank. And before the shootout—

"The baby." I grip her wrist, my pulse kicking up. "Ptichka, are you and the baby—"

"We're fine." She puts down the cup of water, smiling brightly. "They checked me over, and we're both perfectly fine."

I exhale in relief, but then I remember something else. "Your parents." My heart cracks in half as her smile disappears. "My love, I'm so sorr—"

"Don't." She pulls away. "I don't want to talk about it."

I watch, chest aching, as she turns away, visibly composing herself. I remember more now, including the agent she shot point blank.

My little songbird, who's dedicated her life to healing, killed a man.

To protect me… and to avenge her mother.

She pulled the trigger not once, but three times.

I can only imagine what's going through her mind right now, with her parents dead and her old life irrevocably lost.

Not to mention the trauma of the shootout and the escape that followed.

How had she gotten us out by herself? I'm sure Yan wasn't waiting outside her parents' house with a plane.

"Sara…" I push up to a sitting position, suppressing a wince as my side protests with pain. "My love, come here."

She rushes over immediately. "What are you doing? Lie down. It's too soon to be moving."

"I'm fine," I say, but I let her push me back flat on the bed. I like her fussing over me, her pretty face animated with worry.

It's better than suppressed grief.

"Tell me what happened after I passed out," I say after she checks my bandages to make sure I've done no damage. "How long have we been here? How did we manage to escape?"

She takes a deep breath. "It's kind of a long story. But essentially, I got us to the cabin you told me about, and then I emailed Yan from your phone. He got Kent involved, and they came for us with a plane—the twins and Kent as the pilot." She takes another breath. "That was two days ago."

Two days ago? I must've been on death's doorstep to be out that long.

Pushing away the implications of Kent's involvement, I concentrate on getting all the facts. "Okay, now tell me the long story," I say, and then I listen, stunned, as my civilian wife details her undercover venture into the hospital and the clever way she procured us a car.

"So yeah," she concludes, "after I figured out what you were saying in Russian and unlocked your phone, I emailed Yan, and the twins came a few hours later. Yan said the two of them were in Mexico when it all happened, working with Kent on some deal, so it was just a matter of grabbing Kent's plane and heading over. Oh, and bribing Kent's air traffic control guy with one and a half million dollars. Yan said you owe him that money."

I owe Yan a lot more than money for this, and he knows it. Kent, too.

Manipulative bastards. I'll have to do some serious favors for them one day.

Noticing my phone on the bedside table, I pick it up and scroll through my emails to see if the hackers came through with any information on the bombing. I need to figure out how this clusterfuck came about.

Unfortunately, there's still nothing, so I put the phone aside and ask Sara, "Where are the twins and Kent? Are they still around?"

"The twins went to Geneva for some business meeting yesterday, and Kent flew home," Sara says. "Anton is flying here from Hong Kong tomorrow, though, so I'm sure you'll see him and the twins then."

That's good; I'll need their help to untangle this mess once I figure out what brought it about. But first, there's something important that I need to know.

"Ptichka…" I lay my hand on her slender knee. "Why did you do this, my love? You could've waited for the authorities to arrive and let me take the blame for that agent. No one would've been the wiser, and you could've gone on with your life, kept your job and—"

"And what?" She jumps up, glaring at me. "Watch you get arrested as you're bleeding to death? Leave you at the mercy of people who are not only convinced that you're a terrorist but who also blame you for the deaths of their colleagues? How could you possibly think I would do that?" Her hands fist at her sides, her entire body rigid with indignation. "You are my husband, the man I love—"

"Also the man who tortured and kidnapped you," I remind her wryly even as tender warmth fills my chest. I hadn't doubted Sara's love, not really, but some part of me must've still thought that she'd embrace the opportunity to free herself—that if it came down to a choice between me and her regular life, she'd want the latter.

Her eyebrows snap together. "Really? We're going there now?"

"No, my love." Suppressing a delighted grin, I pat the bed next to me. I shouldn't find her outrage so adorable, but I can't help it. "Come here."

She doesn't move, just glares at me with arms crossed.

"Okay, then, I'll get up and come to you." I move as if to sit up again, and with a frustrated huff, she plops down on the bed next to me.

"Lie still," she snaps, pushing me down. "You're going to tear those stiches. *Again.*" Despite her sharp tone, her hands are gentle as she leans over me to inspect my bandages, and as I breathe in her sweet, warm scent, my body stirs, reacting to her nearness the same way as always.

"Ptichka." There's a husky note to my voice as I clasp her slim wrist. "My love, look at me."

Her hazel eyes meet mine, and I see her pupils dilate as I cup her skull from the back and pull her face down toward me.

"Wait, you're not yet—"

I swallow her breathless protest with a kiss. Her soft lips part on a gasp, and I invade her mouth, gorging on her addictive taste and feel. It's not the right place or time, but I can't stop myself, the hunger surging through my veins heating my skin to a boil.

She loves me.

She chose me.

She abandoned her life to save me.

It feels like the fever is upon me again, only there's no pain attached. I burn with the need to have her, to feel those gentle hands on my skin. She's mine, now without reservations, and as I guide her hand under the sheets, the last shackles of our dark past fall off, leaving us joined in the present.

Together, no matter what.

CHAPTER 40
HENDERSON

I smile as I read the email that just hit my inbox.

Sokolov's unfortunate escape aside, my plan has worked as intended, especially in regard to his allies. The use of an Esguerra-manufactured explosive in the terrorist attack has opened everyone's eyes to the danger presented by the arms dealer's illegal empire, and the special protection Esguerra had enjoyed courtesy of his quid-pro-quo relationship with the US government is gone. He and all of his associates are now fair game, and a team is already on the way to Lucas Kent's residence in Cyprus.

Even better, Interpol has come through, just as I hoped they would. The Ivanov brothers have been spotted in Geneva, which means Sokolov might not be far. In fact, my contact is tracking down a rumor about a secretive clinic in the Swiss Alps that specializes in patients on the wrong side of the law.

If all goes well, most of my problems will be over soon.

In a few hours, Kent, Sokolov, and two of Sokolov's Russian assassin friends will be dead, and before long, the authorities will get the remaining assassin, Anton Rezov. Then it'll just be a matter of dismantling Esguerra's criminal organization and getting the kingpin himself.

Once that's done, these monsters' reign of terror will be over, and my family and I will be truly safe.

CHAPTER 41
SARA

Smiling, I stride down the hallway, my lips swollen and tingling from the blowjob I just gave Peter. I suppose I should've expected something like this, given my husband's superhuman libido, but he still caught me by surprise.

In my mind, bed-bound patients and sex don't mix.

Not that Peter is a typical patient. From the moment we brought him in and hooked him up to an IV, he's been exceeding all expectations—mine and the clinic staff's. It's like all of his iron will has been redirected toward healing. Within hours of our arrival, his fever had broken, and if the doctors hadn't sedated him to promote rest and recovery, he would've regained consciousness then.

A nurse passing me in the hallway smiles and says hello, and I respond with the same.

I like the staff here. They're nice, even though their patients are some of the worst criminals known to mankind. Not that I have a lot of room to judge.

I'm now a criminal myself.

I shot a man in cold blood.

I haven't been able to process that yet, just as I haven't been able to think about my parents—or what it means that we're fugitives, our pictures all over the news. I've been focusing on the positives instead, rejoicing that we're both here, alive and free.

That I still have Peter and our baby.

It helps to take it moment by moment, to move from one task to another. When I stay busy, I don't notice the fraying of those dangerous edges, or the growing pressure of grief. I'm even able to smile, though a part of me remains numb inside.

It's almost like when I pulled that trigger, I killed something within me.

By taking a life, I lost a piece of myself.

"Hello, Dr. Sokolov," Dr. Jart says as I walk into his office. "How's your husband?"

"Better." I smile at the older man. "Much better."

His bushy gray eyebrows rise. "Oh? He's awake?"

"Definitely. Though I might've… worn him out. When I left, he was sleeping again."

"He'll be doing that a lot," Dr. Jart says. "His body needs sleep for healing." He stands up and walks around his desk. "But I'm sure you know that."

"I do," I admit, watching as he takes out a huge book from his bookshelf. With his grouchy exterior, he reminds me a little of my boss Bill, though personality-wise, Dr. Jart is much friendlier.

I had briefly met the doctor last year, when I'd spent two weeks here after the car crash. When he came in to check on Peter's wounds the other day, he recognized me and we got to talking. Upon learning that I'm an OB-GYN, he invited me to assist with a patient in labor—which I did gladly, once I made sure Peter was stable and resting.

Anything to take my mind off the events of the past few days.

"How's María doing?" I ask, referring to said patient—the teenage mistress of a Mexican drug lord who'd given birth to twins yesterday. "Did she go home already?"

"She's recovering nicely, but no." Dr. Jart sighs. "Gomez wants her to stay here for at least a week, and since he's paying…" He shrugs, walking back to his desk.

"I see." Unlike a traditional hospital that relies on insurance payments and adheres to strict guidelines in regard to the length of stay, this clinic caters to the ultra-wealthy of the underworld, and it's the patients—or whichever wealthy criminal the patients are affiliated with—who decide when they're sufficiently healed.

"So, Dr. Sokolov…" The doctor sits down and regards me with piercing dark eyes. "The reason I asked you to come by is I wanted to discuss something with you."

"Sure. What is it?" I ask, sitting down across from the doctor. I hope they have another patient for me to assist with while Peter is sleeping.

I need to stay busy to keep my mind off things.

"Would you consider joining us here?" Dr. Jart asks. "I don't know what your plans are with Mr. Sokolov, given the"—he clears his throat—"circumstances, but we could really use a female doctor with your specialty on staff. As you know, our obstetrician—Dr. Ludwig—is excellent, but he's a man, and some of our patients, especially those from more traditional cultures, are a bit… uncomfortable with that fact."

"Oh." I stare at the doctor. "Thank you. I… don't know what to say."

A job offer—especially one largely predicated on my gender—was definitely not what I expected. But then again, why should I be surprised? There's no political correctness in this new, lawless world of mine, where violence is part of business and women are seen as extensions of the powerful men they belong to.

"I'm sure you'll need to consult with Mr. Sokolov," Dr. Jart says when I don't say anything else. "If this is something that interests you, of course."

"Right." Suppressing my inner feminist, I focus on the actual opportunity—which does seem interesting. The loss of my career is something I've been avoiding thinking about as well, but I know I won't be able to do that forever. This way, I could still be a doctor—assuming Peter's okay with us staying nearby.

For all I know, he's planning for us to hide out in Asia again.

"Just think about it for now," Dr. Jart says. "You don't have to give us an answer right away—or even anytime soon. We understand that the situation"—he clears his throat again—"is volatile at the moment, so take as long as you need to decide."

"Thank you." I get up and shake his hand. "I appreciate that." I wonder how often he extends job offers to suspected terrorists who are on the run from the law. He doesn't seem entirely comfortable with "the situation," but he's not deterred by it either.

Personnel files at this place must make for some interesting reading.

———————

After the meeting, I stop by the café downstairs to grab a snack. By the time I return to Peter's room, he's awake and looking for me.

"Where were you?" he asks, pushing up to a sitting position—with noticeably less effort this time. His healing speed is remarkable—either that, or his pain tolerance is off the charts. He didn't even wince, though the movement must've pulled at the stitches in his side.

I'm tempted to urge him to lie back down regardless, but I refrain. He seems much more alert now, his gray eyes sharply intent as he stares at me, and I know it won't be long before he's back to his usual self.

"I was talking to one of the doctors," I tell him, walking over to perch on the edge of his bed. "He offered me a job."

Peter's eyebrows pull together. "Here? At this place?"

"Yes. Apparently, they need a woman obstetrician." Picking up his hand, I rub my thumb over the calluses on his broad palm. "What do you think? We'd obviously have to stay in the area, and I don't know how safe it is."

No job is worth endangering our freedom.

Peter is silent for a moment, mulling it over. "It's not the worst idea," he finally says. "First, though, we need to figure out exactly how this happened."

"You mean why they think you're responsible for the bombing?"

He nods grimly, and I take a breath to combat the tightening in my chest. I've been pondering that myself, and if Peter is innocent—which I believe he is—there's only one logical conclusion.

"Someone must've framed you," I say. "Maybe even someone within the FBI."

"Yes." His expression doesn't change. He must've already thought of this himself. "The question is who and why." He reaches for his phone, like he did before, and I watch him scroll through his emails at a rapid clip.

"Maybe the Feds don't have any real suspects, so they decided to use you as a scapegoat," I suggest as he opens one email. "It was probably some terrorist organization behind the explosion, but they decided to pin it on you instead. Someone besides Ryson could've been upset with the deal you'd made, so when the opportunity arose—" I stop because Peter's face turns into granite.

"What is it?" I ask when he keeps reading without saying anything, his posture tensing more each second. My own neck muscles are locked tight, my heart racing as if I'm about to launch into a sprint.

Whatever's in that email is not good. I can tell by his expression.

He lifts his eyes to meet my gaze. "Do you remember when I told you about the retired general, the one in charge of the Daryevo operation?" His voice holds a lethal softness. "The one I promised to leave alone in exchange for amnesty and immunity?"

"Yes, of course," I say as my stomach tightens. "Henderson, right?"

"Right." His nostrils flare. "Fucking Wally Henderson III."

I suck in a breath. "Is he the one behind this?"

"It appears that way." A muscle ticks in Peter's jaw. "Before they came for me, I asked our hackers to look into the explosion because something about it just didn't smell right. And they finally came through with the results."

"They said Henderson framed you? But how? Why? How could he have known this tragedy would happen?"

They came for Peter less than twenty-four hours after the attack. Even someone with Henderson's connections would need time to manufacture evidence strong enough to send a SWAT team into a quiet suburban neighborhood. Even if Henderson had embarked on the task as soon as he learned about the explosion, it should've taken days, if not weeks, to—

"Because he made it happen." Peter's expression is savage. "The fucker is the one who set the bomb."

My jaw falls open. "What?"

"A man matching my description was caught on camera entering the building as part of a janitor crew the day before the explosion." Peter's voice is hard enough to break stone. "And my fingerprints were found on one of the surviving door handles from the third floor, where the bomb had been placed. As for the explosive itself, it was a very unique one, one that's pretty much undetectable—which is how my doppelgänger was able to carry it through security in a lunchbox. Do you know who has access to that kind of explosive?"

I stare at him, bewildered. "I... no."

"The US military. They source it directly from the arms dealer who manufactures it—Julian Esguerra."

My heart rate kicks up again. "The same one who'd brokered the deal for you? The guy you did that favor for?"

"The very same." Peter's mouth twists. "So you see how they could think that I'm the one responsible, right? The US military buys up every batch of the explosive that Esguerra manufactures, and he has a waiting list a mile long in case they stop. However, someone who knows the arms dealer personally *could* obtain a pound or so. Hell, you probably wouldn't even need that much. It's powerful shit—like a nuclear bomb, just not radioactive."

Oh God. I now recall Peter talking about this with Kent when we had dinner together in Cyprus. Something about Uncle Sam and manufacturing constraints for an undetectable explosive. Was that the explosive in question?

"So why..." I gather my racing thoughts. "Why do you think it was Henderson behind this? Could it have been someone else—say, Esguerra himself? You said he wanted you dead at some point, and he has the connections to make this happen, right? Or maybe it could've been some other enemy of yours?"

"Because this has CIA pawprints all over it," Peter says grimly. "The janitor who looks like me, my fingerprints at the scene, my connection with Ryson and the bomb being planted on his floor—it's all classic tradecraft. They've been doing this kind of shit since the Cold War. And guess who's rumored to have been an undercover operative in his youth?"

"Right, Henderson." I remember Peter telling me this at some point. "But doesn't Esguerra also have some CIA connections? Couldn't he have—"

"No." Peter's jaw is tight. "Aside from the fact that he could've already killed me in a thousand different ways if he'd truly wanted to, he had no reason to fuck up a mutually beneficial relationship with the US government. Right now, the authorities believe he's complicit in the bombing, and they're about to go after him as well."

"Oh, that's... that's not good at all." From what I know, Esguerra had been all but untouchable until now.

"No, it's not," Peter says darkly. "Which is why I need to speak to Yan right now. Because the other members of that janitor crew? Their descriptions match Anton, Yan, and Ilya, right down to the tattoos on one's skull."

CHAPTER 42
PETER

I reread the email from the hackers for the third time, all the while compulsively checking the clock on my phone. Three hours ago, I called Yan to share what I've learned, but he didn't pick up. I left him a voicemail to call me back, then texted and emailed him for good measure before doing the same with his brother.

Neither twin has gotten back to me yet—and neither has Anton.

I check the clock again. It's 11:33 p.m.—only two minutes later than the last time I looked. Sara is asleep next to me, her chestnut waves spread over my pillow, and as much as I want to join her in peaceful slumber, I can't bring myself to close my eyes.

My instincts are on high alert again.

Careful not to wake Sara, I push up to a sitting position and swing my legs to the floor. Slowly and carefully, I stand up, ignoring the pulling pain at my side and the ache in my calf. The room spins around me as I take the first step, but my legs are able to support me.

Good.

I can't afford to be flat on my back if something goes down.

At my request, a couple of guns have been delivered to my room, so I walk over to the closet to inspect them. It's nothing fancy—just an M16 and a couple of Glocks—but it's better than nothing.

I check each weapon and load it, then take out a pair of pants from the closet and pull them on under my hospital gown, careful not to dislodge the bandage on my leg. My heart is beating too fast from the exertion, and I'm sweating like a hog, but I throw off the hospital gown and pull on a loose sweater, followed by a pair of socks and boots.

"Peter?" Sara's sleepy voice reaches me as I'm strapping one of the Glocks to my left ankle. "What are you doing?"

I look up from where I'm crouched. "Just getting dressed, ptichka. Don't worry."

"What?" Sara sits up, the drowsiness evaporating from her voice as she takes in my appearance. "Why are you getting dressed? You need to be in bed, resting, not—"

"I think we need to leave." I stand up slowly, breathing through the pain. "Something doesn't feel right."

Sara turns into a statue on the bed. "You think we're not safe here?"

"I don't think we're safe anywhere right now," I say as I sling the M16 over my shoulder and stuff the other Glock into my waistband. "However, it worries me that I haven't heard from Yan or the others."

"You haven't?" She pads across the room with bare feet and stops in front of me, the color of her face matching the white T-shirt she's wearing in place of pajamas. "Could they just be busy?"

"Anything is possible." For all I know, the twins are in the middle of a hit, and Anton is having reception issues on the plane. "In our situation, though, better safe than sorry."

"But where will we go? Three days ago, you were out of your mind with the fever. You need to be in a hospital, healing—"

"I'm fine now," I interrupt. Framing her delicate face with my palm, I say in a softer tone, "Don't worry, my love. You did your part, and now it's time for me to do mine."

And as she stares up at me with huge, scared eyes, I drop a kiss on her tempting lips, then reach into the closet to take out her clothes.

CHAPTER 43

SARA

I get dressed while Peter tries reaching Anton and the twins again. My hands are cold from stress, my fingers clumsy, and it takes two attempts to tie the shoelaces on my sneakers.

"Anything?" I ask when I'm done, and Peter shakes his head, his face dark.

"Nothing. I'm going to try Kent, see if he's heard anything."

"Oh, that's a good idea." I chew on my lip as he punches in some number and waits, phone pressed to his ear.

"It's Peter," he says tersely. "Have you—wait, what?"

He listens in tense silence as Kent fills him in on whatever's happened, and when he lowers the phone, I take a step back at his expression.

"Interpol raided Yulia's restaurants. All of them," he says tightly. "Lucas barely managed to get Yulia out before they came to his house in Cyprus. Now they're on their way to Esguerra's compound in Colombia—the only place that may be semi-safe for them."

"Oh, God." I feel a sudden wave of nausea. "Do you think Yan and the others...?"

"They might've already been taken, yes. Either way, we don't have a minute to waste."

Gripping my hand, he leads me out of the room, his strides as strong and sure as if he hadn't been on the verge of dying mere days ago.

I have to jog to keep up with the pace he sets as we hurry down the corridor and into the staircase. "No elevator?" I ask, panting as we briskly head down, and he shakes his head, tightening his hold on my hand.

"Too easy to get trapped."

I want to remind him of his wounds and beg him to take it easy, but now is not the time. If the authorities have gone so far as to come after Kent—Esguerra's right-hand man and thus another untouchable—Peter is right about the clinic not being safe.

All the usual rules of engagement are out the window.

"Where are we going?" I ask, mostly to distract myself from growing nausea. The so-called morning sickness has been striking at random times of the day and night, and all the jostling from going down the stairs isn't helping.

"A safe house," Peter says without looking at me, and I realize his face is unusually pale, his temples covered with beads of sweat from the exertion.

He's not as recovered as he's pretending.

It takes all my willpower to bite back a plea for him to stop and rest. Instead, I pick up my pace, so he doesn't have to exert any effort to tow me along. "You're not going to tell me where it is?"

"No." His gaze cuts toward the ceiling corner, and I see a faint red light glowing there.

Of course. Cameras.

I should've known better than to ask.

We go down the rest of the way in silence, and Peter stops when we reach the door to the lobby. Slowly, he opens it a fraction and waits, peering through the crack.

"All clear," he murmurs after a minute, and I exhale a shaking breath as we step out.

"Mr. Sokolov," the blond receptionist says in surprise as we pass by her desk. "Are you leaving already?"

"Yes. I will settle the bill later."

She starts to say something else, but we're already exiting the building into a courtyard that serves as the parking lot. It's freezing but beautiful out here, with the white glow of moonlight outlining the snow-covered peaks of the Swiss Alps surrounding us. I barely notice any of it, though, as Peter leads me into the parking lot.

My stomach is now in full-blown revolt, and I have to swallow repeatedly to avoid throwing up.

Suddenly, he stops and crouches between two cars, yanking me down with him.

"Someone's coming," he whispers, reaching for his M16, and a second later, a black SUV screeches to a stop in front of the clinic.

CHAPTER 44
PETER

I expect Interpol agents to jump out of the car, but instead, I see a man dressed all in black.

"Anton!" I stand up and wave, letting him see me. He spins around, relief breaking out on his bearded face.

"Get in!" he shouts, jabbing his thumb at the car. "We have to go."

Sara is already on her feet next to me, and I grab her hand as I half run, half limp toward Anton's SUV. My calf burns like hell, and I feel like I tore some stitches in my side, but none of that matters.

Anton doesn't panic easily, and he looks more than a little on edge.

He jumps back in behind the wheel as we reach the car, and I throw myself into the back seat, gritting my teeth against a wave of pain. Sara climbs in beside me, and we peel out of the parking lot before she even closes the door.

"Yan and Ilya?" I ask when the worst of the pain subsides, and Anton gives me a grim look in the rearview mirror.

"Interpol crashed their meeting in Geneva. I haven't heard from them since."

"Fuck." I close my eyes, feeling sick to my stomach. My body is still on the fritz, weak and shaky—definitely not in any kind of shape to take on a slew of armed agents if they come for us next.

Opening my eyes, I glance over at Sara and find her taking slow, deep breaths, her delicate profile a greenish shade of white.

"You okay, ptichka?" I murmur, and she gives a short nod.

"Morning sickness," she says in a barely audible whisper, and I squeeze her hand, my chest tightening with a mixture of fury and guilt.

My Sara is pregnant. This is the time in her life when stress is most toxic. She should be resting in the comfort of our home, being coddled by me and her family—not running from the authorities, having witnessed her parents' deaths.

I never should've agreed to spare Henderson's life. That ublyudok needed to pay—and this time, he will.

I'm going to tear him apart, piece by bloody piece.

First, though, we need to get out of this alive.

"I tried getting in touch with you," I tell Anton as he turns onto the road leading toward the private airport reserved for the clinic's patients. "Did you dump your phone?"

He nods. "I had just landed and was on the phone with Yan when Interpol stormed their meeting place. So I destroyed it, just in case."

"Good." Our phones are untraceable, the signal bouncing off satellites all over the world, but it's best not to risk it. "Any chance they got away?"

"Anything is possible," he says, but it doesn't sound like he believes it.

"Anton…" Sara's voice is strained. "I'm so sorry, but can you stop the car?"

"Pull over," I tell him, and he swerves off the road, hitting the brakes. The car is still moving when Sara opens the door and leans out, heaving. I wrap one arm around her slim waist and gather her hair in my other hand, holding it away from her face as she vomits.

"So sorry," she murmurs when she's done, and I hand her a water bottle from the case on the floor.

"Nothing to be sorry about," I say as Anton gets back on the road. "This is perfectly natural."

I keep my voice calm, as if I'm not the least bit bothered by seeing my wife puke her guts out on the side of the road while we're running for our lives. As if rage isn't like acid in my veins, tinting my vision a bloody shade of red.

"Are you sick, Sara?" Anton asks, and I realize he doesn't know about the baby yet. And why would he? We've just found out ourselves.

"We're expecting," I say, and despite my best efforts, I don't sound anything but tense.

If something happens to Sara or the baby because of this, I'll never forgive myself.

"Oh." Anton seems at a loss for words. "That's… Congratulations."

"Thanks," I mutter, and then I hear it.

A wail of sirens in the distance.

Fuck.

"Step on it," I tell Anton, but he's already flooring the gas, his face tense.

I turn to Sara. "Put on your seatbelt."

She scrambles to obey, her hazel eyes dark in her colorless face as I check my weapons.

The sirens are coming from behind us—from the direction of the clinic—which means my intuition was right.

They came for us.

The roar of a helicopter soon joins the sirens, and Anton speeds up further, taking a steep curve in the road at a hair-raising speed.

"Slow the fuck down," I bark as Sara convulsively grabs my hand. "We can't crash, you understand?"

If it were just me and Anton, I'd risk it, but not with Sara here.

Not when she'd nearly died in a crash on a road much like this one.

Anton lets up on the accelerator a bit, and I bring Sara's hand up to my lips. "It's going to be okay, ptichka," I murmur, kissing her knuckles. "We just need to get to the plane."

"They might already be waiting for us there," Anton says. "Since they knew about the clinic, they might know about the airstrip too."

"The clinic is on the map, but the airstrip is not," I say, squeezing Sara's hand reassuringly when I feel it tense in my grip. "They'd need to get its location from the staff."

Or so I'm hoping.

Because we *could* be heading into an ambush.

Anton doesn't respond, just floors the gas again as we reach a straighter stretch of road. We're just a few minutes from the airstrip now, but the chopper's roar is growing louder by the second, drowning out the adrenaline-fueled hammering of my heartbeat.

Finally, I see its headlights pop up behind us as we take another sharp turn.

"Get down," I bark at Sara, pushing her flat on the seat, and then I open the window and lean out, ignoring the sharp pulling pain in my side as I aim my M16 at the chopper.

It swerves behind the trees before I can open fire.

I wait, not wanting to waste my bullets.

A second later, the chopper pops up again, and I fire off a round.

It fires back, then swerves away again.

Fuck. We're almost at the airstrip now.

I wait until the chopper appears again, and then I open fire, squeezing the trigger until my gun clicks empty and the chopper falls back in an effort to avoid my bullets.

Ducking back into the car, I swiftly reload, then lean out the window again.

This time, though, the chopper hangs back.

That's not good.

We can't take off with these fuckers shooting at us.

The car turns sharply, and when I glance at the front, I see we're already on the airstrip, heading full speed for the plane.

"RPG's inside," Anton yells, slamming on the brakes. "I'm making a run for it."

We screech to a halt a dozen yards from the plane, and I grit my teeth as my side slams into the sharp metal edge of the car window.

If we survive this, Sara will be upset that I fucked up my stitches.

Anton jumps out of the car, sprinting for the plane, and I provide cover fire as the chopper approaches. The sirens are getting louder too; they must be right on our heels.

"Get on the plane, now!" I shout at Sara, and out of the corner of my eye, I see her scramble to obey.

My M16 clicks empty, but there's no time to reload, so I grab the Glock from my waistband as the chopper swerves away, then comes back, spraying the car with bullets. The glass around me explodes, the shards biting into my face and neck. Gripping the Glock, I push my door open and tumble out, rolling away from the car as I shoot back.

I need them to focus on me, not the plane or Sara.

Bullets hit the ground all around me, sending bits of asphalt flying at my eyes. I can smell the gunpowder, feel the burn of lead as it whooshes by.

This is it.

I won't make it.

My gun clicks empty just as a black van barrels onto the airstrip, screeching to a stop next to our car.

CHAPTER 45
SARA

I'm already by the plane when I see the black van.

Interpol.

They've caught up to us.

"Anton!" I shout over the gunfire and the chopper noise as he reappears in the plane's doorway with a rocket launcher propped up on his shoulder. "They're—"

Boom!

The flash of the explosion burns my retinas, the sound so deafening my eardrums nearly explode. The sky seems to turn into a ball of fire, and burning bits of metal rain down.

Holy fuck.

Anton shot down the chopper.

My stunned gaze falls on the van, and I see two familiar figures jump out.

"Yan! Ilya!" I've never been this glad to see them—especially when they bend down to drape Peter's arms over their shoulders and sprint together for the plane.

"Hurry!" Anton yells, and I hear the sirens getting louder. "We have to go now."

He disappears back inside the plane, and I rush after him, with the twins and Peter on my heels.

The police cars appear just as our wheels lift off the ground.

"So they were pursuing you, not us?" I clarify with Yan as I wipe the dirt and blood off Peter's face before removing a few shards of glass embedded in his skin. I feel bizarrely calm, as if I'm performing a routine Pap smear instead of treating my husband's injuries after a harrowing escape.

I'm either getting used to life on the run, or I'm still in shock and the adrenaline crash is about to hit me.

"Yeah, and we barely made it," Yan says from the seat next to the couch where Peter is stretched out. "The chopper was flying ahead to trap us, but then you must've drawn their attention." As he speaks, he holds up a mirror to apply an antibiotic salve to his ear, where a bullet grazed it, leaving an ugly gash.

"Glad we could serve as your accidental decoy," Peter says as I raise his shirt to inspect the bandage at his side. His color is still off, but he's conscious—and apparently feeling well enough for sarcasm.

"Hey, it was a team effort," Ilya says, a grin splitting his broad face as he lounges in his seat—somehow completely unhurt. "Couldn't have gone better if we'd planned it."

I shake my head, trying not to think about what it felt like to run for the plane while Peter was pinned down by the chopper's fire. It's a miracle that he survived—that we *all* survived and got away.

My hands start to tremble as I unwrap Peter's bandage, and I realize it *is* hitting me.

Peter could've been shot again.

He could've been killed, his skull destroyed by a bullet just like—

No, stop.

"Where are we heading now?" I ask to distract myself from the memories threatening to invade my mind. I can't dive into that dark well, can't focus on what happened to my parents or could've happened to Peter.

I'm not ready to face that yet.

"That's a good question," Yan says, putting down the salve to pick up his phone. "Let me see if our Turkish contact has come through." He swipes across his screen a few times and grimaces. "Fuck."

"What?" Peter tries to sit up, but I push him back.

"Lie still," I say, glaring at him. "I'm not done yet."

"Our air traffic control guy is in jail," Yan says as Peter obeys, letting me clean around his torn stitches. "Someone's sniffed out his extracurricular income."

"So Turkey's out." Peter doesn't sound surprised. "What about Latvia?"

"Let me see." Yan punches in a number, then begins speaking in Russian.

Whatever the person on the other line is saying must not be good because Yan's frown deepens with each moment.

"What is it?" Ilya asks when Yan hangs up. "What did that bastard tell you?"

"Apparently, every airport in Europe is on the lookout for our plane," Yan says. "That includes private airstrips as well. Interpol has put a ridiculous price on our heads, and all four of our faces are splashed all over the news as the suspects behind the FBI bombing. I wouldn't trust anyone right now; they're as likely to turn us in as to help us."

"Fuck." Peter tries to sit up again, and this time, I let him. The shock-induced calm has completely worn off, and I'm cognizant of a terrible weariness combined with chest-crushing anxiety.

We might've escaped, but we're far from safe.

"If Europe is out of the question, our best bet is Venezuela," Peter says as I tape a fresh bandage to his side on autopilot. "Do we have enough fuel to get there?"

"Let me check with Anton," Yan says, getting up from his seat. He disappears into the pilot's cabin, then reappears a minute later. "Yes, but barely," he reports. "If anything goes wrong, we're fucked."

"I say we go for it," Ilya says, scratching his tattooed skull. "At least it'll be warm there."

"Give me your phone," Peter says to Yan. "I'll reach out to Esteban. In the meantime, tell Anton to set course for Venezuela. One way or another, we're landing there."

CHAPTER 46
PETER

Esteban, the greedy little fucker, demands no less than three million euros to make the appropriate arrangements, but we don't have any room to argue.

If we don't land at his little airport, we're fucked.

Finally, all the logistics are ironed out, and I make my way over to Sara's seat. It's big enough for two men, and she looks tiny curled up in it with her knees drawn up to her chest as she stares out the plane's window.

"Ptichka." I sink to my haunches in front of her, ignoring the pulling pain in my calf and side as I rest my hands on her ankles. "My love, are you okay?"

She focuses on me, blinking. "What are you doing? You should be lying down."

"I'm fine," I say, but she's already on her feet, pulling me up and toward the couch. Sighing, I let her—because I do feel like shit.

"Lie down with me," I say as I stretch out on the couch. "I want to hold you."

She frowns. "But your side—"

"Don't worry about it." I pull her down until she has no choice but to stretch out beside me. Rolling onto my uninjured side, I spoon her from the back, inhaling the delicate perfume of her hair as Ilya and Yan pointedly turn away in their seats, giving us a modicum of privacy.

She's rigid at first, undoubtedly worried about bumping into one of my injuries, but after a minute, some of the stiffness leaves her muscles. And that's when I feel it.

An almost imperceptible trembling in her body.

She's shaking all over.

My chest squeezes in agonized sympathy. My little songbird is not physically injured—that was the first thing I made sure of when we got on the plane—but that doesn't mean she got off scot-free.

What she's just been through is enough to give PTSD to a seasoned soldier, much less a civilian woman.

A *pregnant* civilian woman.

"How are you feeling, my love?" I ask softly, placing my hand on her belly. Maybe it's my imagination, but it feels flatter than usual, as if she's lost some weight. And maybe she has.

Between the unpredictable morning sickness and all the stress, she might not be eating properly.

"I'm fine," she murmurs, even as her breath hitches on a betraying quiver. "It's just…"

"The adrenaline aftermath, I know." I keep my voice low and soothing as I move my hand from her stomach to stroke her hip. "It'll pass."

She draws in a deeper breath. "I know. It'll be fine."

"It will be," I promise. "We'll get to our safe house, and everything will be just fine."

It's the first time I've outright lied to her, and judging by the renewed stiffness of her body, my ptichka knows it.

Because it won't be fine.

Nothing can undo what has been done and bring back Sara's parents.

All I can do is seek vengeance—and that, I'll do.

Henderson will pray for death long before I'm done with him.

CHAPTER 47
HENDERSON

Escaped again.

Fury mixes with growing fear in my chest as I read the latest email from my contact.

They escaped, all of them, right from under Interpol's nose.

Another minute, and Sokolov and his Russian friends would've been surrounded. Interpol could've gotten all four of them at once. Instead, they're now in the air, on their way to fuck knows where.

And that's not to mention Kent's successful escape to Esguerra's compound in the Amazon jungle, which even the Colombian government considers impenetrable.

If they all have a chance to regroup, I'm fucked— because by now, they're bound to have figured out what went down and how.

Taking a breath to control a surge of panic, I begin composing an email to my CIA contact.

There's still time to intercept Sokolov's plane.

We just have to reach out to all the airports worldwide and get them to crack down on all air traffic control officers who might be even remotely amenable to taking bribes.

CHAPTER 48

SARA

I must've drifted off in Peter's embrace because I wake up to the low murmur of voices speaking Russian. Opening my eyes, I see my husband in a seat with a computer on his lap and the twins standing next to him. He's pointing to something on the screen and talking in his native language.

"What's going on?" I ask, sitting up. I feel groggy, as if I've been out for hours. And for all I know, I have been.

It's a long flight from Switzerland to Venezuela.

The men glance in my direction. "Just trying to figure out where the sniper was hiding," Yan says at the same time as Peter says, "Nothing, my love. Don't worry about it."

"A sniper?" A fresh spike of adrenaline sends me to my feet. "What sniper?" Then it dawns on me. "Oh, you mean whoever shot at the agent arresting you, causing all of them to panic and start shooting? I was wondering about that. I initially thought it might've been someone trying to help you, but they weren't, were they? They were trying to cause trouble."

Peter glares at Yan—did he think I need to be protected from this?—before turning to face me. "That's right," he says evenly. "Henderson must've hired the sniper to make sure I was killed during arrest. I'm guessing the plan was to frame me, then use the authorities to take me down, along with everyone who's ever helped me—and to do so in a very public way, so nothing could be hidden from the media. If I'd been arrested, I might've been able to convince the authorities of my innocence by finding the real culprits, and then everything could've gone back to the way it was—and Henderson would've been in real trouble."

"But if he had the sniper there, why not just shoot you instead of killing the SWAT agent?" I ask, suppressing a shudder as the image of Peter's head exploding flits through my mind. "If that sniper was in position—"

"Well, for one thing, the angle wasn't optimal to get me," Peter says. "Or at least that's what we've determined based on my recollections of the event. To get that shot, he must've been lying on the roof of the three-story house on the neighboring block. Remember, the white one, with the gray roof?"

I nod, and he continues. "Well, I was closer to our house, so the roof must've been shielding me, at least partially. But more importantly, if I *had been* shot by an unknown sniper, it would've raised all sorts of suspicions about who's really behind the attack, and I'm guessing that's the last thing Henderson wanted. But with the agent getting shot, it was almost certain that the cops would assume it was someone in cahoots with me, and I would be killed in the resulting shootout anyway."

"And you very nearly were." I can't hold back a shudder this time. "You came so close to dying..."

Peter's lips curve in a cold smile. "Yes, but unfortunately for Henderson, I didn't quite get there."

I stare at him, the fine hairs on the back of my neck rising at the dark promise in his voice. I haven't forgotten this side of him, but it had been easy not to think about it when we were going about our suburban life. The Peter I'd agreed to marry hadn't been all that different from the vengeful assassin who'd invaded my home to murder George, but it had been possible to pretend that he was— that he was no longer capable of the terrible things he'd done to avenge Tamila and his son.

Except he is.

He always will be.

And now he has one more reason to go after Henderson.

"How are you going to do it?" I ask, and even I'm surprised at how conversational I sound. "Do you have a plan in place already?"

Because Henderson *will* die for this. I know that as surely as I know that Peter loves me. My lethal husband will make his enemy pay tenfold, and as wrong as it is, I can't muster up an ounce of moral outrage at the thought.

The recently awakened monster within me *wants* Henderson to suffer, to know pain and devastating loss.

Peter's icy smile doesn't waver. "Don't worry about the particulars, my love. Suffice it to say, he won't get away with this."

"I know he won't," I say softly, holding my husband's gaze. "You won't let him."

And getting up, I go to the bathroom to freshen up, cognizant of Peter's eyes tracking me as I walk through the cabin.

CHAPTER 49
PETER

*P*eople process trauma in different ways. Some fall apart and never pull themselves together. Others find a core of strength that gets them through the days. I've always known that Sara was of the latter persuasion, but I've never appreciated her inner steel more than I do now as I watch the bathroom door close behind her slender figure.

She's a warrior, my little bird—as strong in her own way as any trained soldier.

"So do you still think she's all sweetness and light?" Yan says in Russian as I look away from the door and meet his coolly amused gaze. "Because from where I'm standing, your perfect little doctor seems to have developed quite a thirst for blood."

"Shut it, Yan," Ilya snaps before I can respond. "Now's not the time."

Under any other circumstances, I'd already have my hands around Yan's throat, but Ilya is right.

We're about to start our descent, and there's no time for bullshit.

"I'm going to do a last-minute check on the situation on the ground," I tell Ilya, pointedly ignoring Yan. "Esteban promised we'll be all set, but you know how much I trust that weasel."

"Right." Ilya snatches Yan's phone from his brother's pocket and hands it to me. "Good idea."

I punch in the number of a Venezuelan police chief I've had on my payroll for the past three years and wait for the call to connect. If all is well, Santiago will be clueless as to why I'm calling. If not...

"Hola?" he answers.

"It's Peter Sokolov."

There's a moment of tense silence; then he hisses into the phone, "Why the fuck are you calling me? It's too late; there's nothing I can do. They're all over that dinky airport. I told you, I can't do anything when the whole department—"

I hang up before he finishes and look up to meet two sets of identical green eyes.

"Looks like Esteban's airstrip is a no-go," I say evenly. "Any other ideas?"

CHAPTER 50

SARA

I return to find Peter and the twins clustered around the entrance to the cockpit. All three men are on their feet, gesticulating with jabbing motions as they argue in Russian with Anton.

My stomach dives. "What's wrong? Did something happen?"

"Our Venezuelan contact sold us out," Ilya says over his shoulder. "Or maybe he was caught—we don't know for sure. Either way, the police are waiting for us to land, which means we need to stretch our fuel supplies and get to another—"

"There's no stretching the fuel, Anton told you that." Yan's voice is hard and sharp. "I say we chance it with the police. If our fuel runs out, that's certain death, but with the cops—"

"We have seven percent left," Peter says. "That's enough to get us to some other airport nearby."

"Where they'll be waiting for us anyway," Yan says. "We're already on their radar, and if we miscalculate even a tiny bit…"

"It's better than walking into a certain trap," Ilya says. "I say we land somewhere else. Like some private airstrip, or a highway, or maybe even—" He stops abruptly and rushes over to the laptop Peter was on earlier.

"What is it?" I ask, my heart hammering.

"Colombia." His deep voice is incongruously excited. "We're not far from Esguerra's Amazon compound, and he has an airstrip inside…"

"You're kidding, right?" Yan crosses his arms. "There's no way our fuel would last that far—and that's assuming Esguerra would even want to help. He's eyeballs deep in his own shit right now."

"Yes, but it's all the same shit, don't you see?" Ilya's thick fingers fly over the keyboard. "We're the reason he's under attack. So—"

"So he'll gladly save the police the trouble and shoot us down himself," Yan says. "Either way, I don't see how we'd have enough—"

"I'll rerun the fuel numbers with Anton," Peter says and disappears into the cockpit.

I stare after him, my nausea returning as I process the fact that there are no good options for us.

Even if we don't run out of fuel on the way to Esguerra's compound, the arms dealer is unlikely to welcome us.

"We *may* have enough to get to Esguerra's place," Peter says, reappearing in the doorway. "It all depends on the speed and direction of the wind. Right now, we've got a strong tailwind. If it stays as is, we'll make it."

"The wind? That's what we're betting on?"

Nobody responds to Yan's rhetorical question, so he walks over to the couch and plops down, muttering what sounds like Russian curses under his breath.

"I just reached out to Kent," Ilya says, looking up from the computer. "He's at Esguerra's compound right now. Maybe he can convince him to let us crash with them for a bit."

"There's no time for that," Peter says. "By the time they hash it over, we'll be out of fuel. I'm going to call Esguerra directly. He has to let us land. It's our only chance."

CHAPTER 51
PETER

The Colombian arms dealer picks up on the third ring.

"Trouble in paradise?" he says silkily.

"On your end too, I imagine," I answer calmly. The last thing I want is for Esguerra to sniff out any hint of desperation. "I think we can help each other."

He laughs derisively. "Yeah, sure."

"Do *you* know who's behind this shit show?"

"I have a pretty good idea. The former general, right? The fucker you didn't kill because you wanted to play house in the suburbs?"

Fuck. Of course he would know this already. Information is as much Esguerra's stock in trade as the weapons he produces.

I change my tactics. "Listen, I'm sorry this has spilled over to you and your business. But the only way to fix this is to expose Henderson and what he's done. And I know exactly how to do that."

"Really? Isn't this the guy you've been hunting unsuccessfully for three years?"

I ignore the mockery in his tone. "Yes—which means no one knows as much about him as my team and I. It will take you months, if not years, to gather all the data that we have on his friends and relatives, and to go through all the hiding spots we've found and eliminated. Face it: You need me to fix this clusterfuck of a situation quickly, before you lose even more money. How much are all the raids at your factories costing you? Ten million a day? More?"

I was just guessing about the raids, but judging by the silence on the phone, I've struck a nerve.

"Julian, listen to me," I continue as Sara and the twins stare at me intently. "I can take down Henderson, and I can do it quickly. All I need is a place to lay low for a bit and some of your resources, and I'll prove that you had nothing to do with the explosion. By this time next month, you'll be back in Uncle Sam's good graces, and we'll be out of your hair for good. Or you can try to deal with it on your own, and put up with every law enforcement agency coming after—"

"Fuck you and your team." There's no mistaking the fury in Esguerra's voice. "You're the reason for this whole fucking mess. And you know what? I bet if I hand over you and the other 'terrorists' on your team to Uncle Sam, that'll go a long way toward mending that relationship."

"Will it? Are you sure?" It's my turn to sound coolly mocking. "A dangerous explosive—*your* explosive—was deployed on US soil against *the FBI*. Every agency is involved in this, every bureaucrat from high to low. Do you really think all will be forgiven and forgotten if you turn over your co-conspirators? Because that's what they'll believe, you know—that you're just ratting out your cohorts. Unless you expose Henderson for what he is and clear your name quickly, you're just as fucked as we are."

There's another long, tense silence on the line. Then Esguerra says harshly, "Fine. I can give you a place to lay low. I have a contact in Sudan. Once you get there—"

"Sudan won't work," I interrupt. "I have a different place in mind."

"Oh?"

"Your compound. We'll be there in an hour."

And before he can reply, I hang up.

CHAPTER 52
SARA

I watch, stomach in knots, as Peter calmly pockets the phone and walks back to the pilot's cabin—presumably to inform Anton that we're going to Esguerra's compound, regardless of the arms dealer's feelings on the matter.

"You know he'll just shoot us down on approach," Yan says when Peter reappears a minute later. "And that's if our fuel lasts that long."

"It will," Ilya says confidently. "And he won't. You heard Peter: Esguerra needs us to sort out this mess quickly."

"Yeah, sure," Yan mutters and heads over to the bathroom in the back of the plane.

My legs don't feel entirely steady as I walk over to the couch and sit down.

Is this how we'll die?

Not by a bullet, but in a plane crash?

The couch dips beside me, and a big, warm hand covers my knee. "It'll be all right, ptichka," Peter murmurs, raising his other hand to brush back my hair. His fingers graze my jaw, the touch so tender it makes me want to cry.

"How do you know?" I whisper, then chide myself for acting like a needy child.

Of course he doesn't know.

He's just saying it to make me feel better.

"Because I know Julian," he says softly. He hasn't shaved in days, and the dark stubble accentuates the unhealthy pallor of his skin. Nonetheless, he still somehow radiates his usual strength and self-assurance. I know it's most likely a façade, but I can't help but feel reassured as he presses his lips to my forehead, then wraps one powerful arm around my shoulders, tucking me against his uninjured side.

"You should be resting," I murmur after a minute. As strong as my husband is, he's not invincible. It was only days ago that he was at death's door. But when I attempt to pull away, he holds me tighter, and I give up with a sigh, laying my head on his shoulder.

It's not worth fighting over.

After all, this may be our last hour together.

CHAPTER 53
PETER

The tailwind weakens just as we're about to begin our descent. I learn about it via a terse announcement from Anton.

Excusing myself, I carefully extricate myself from Sara's embrace and head over to speak to him, grateful that he had the foresight to speak Russian.

My ptichka is worried enough as is.

Ilya and Yan are already inside the cockpit, with Yan crouched next to Anton, holding a computer.

"How much are we going to fall short by?" I ask without preamble.

"Not much," Anton says. "If the wind speed doesn't drop more, we might have enough for a hard landing—or we might not. It depends on how well this plane runs on fumes."

"Are there any landing strips closer?" Ilya asks. "A wide road would do as well."

"I can't find anything like that on the map," Yan says, and I see him zooming in on a heavily forested region on Google Maps. "We're right on the edge of the jungle; there's nothing but trees, rivers, and narrow dirt roads."

I bite back a vicious curse.

This is bad.

Really fucking bad.

If it were just us, I wouldn't worry as much—people have been known to survive plane crashes—but even a hard landing could be too much for Sara and the baby.

"What's going on?" she says from behind me, and I turn to find her staring worriedly at the controls. "Did something happen?"

Nobody answers. Even Yan has no sarcastic remarks.

"Nothing, ptichka. We're just getting ready to land," I say evenly, and taking her hand, I lead her out of the cabin.

CHAPTER 54
SARA

My insides feel like leaves in a winter storm as Peter guides me to my seat and straps me in, tightening the seatbelt across my lap until it's almost hard to breathe. Then he limps over to the couch and pulls off the cushions. Bringing them over, he dumps them in front of me, then opens an overhead bin and pulls down a duffel bag.

"What are you doing?" My voice starts to shake. "Peter, what are you doing?"

He doesn't reply, just pulls out a long rope and a knife. Grabbing one of the cushions, he ties it to the back of the seat in front of me, exactly where my head would hit if I assumed the classical plane-crash position and something were to push me forward.

Then he takes the other cushion and stuffs it to the left of me, between my seat and the window. It's wedged tightly in there, so he doesn't need to use the rope to hold it in place.

"Are we crashing?" It's a stupid question, as it's obvious what's happening, but I can't help myself. I want him to lie to me again, to tell me that what he's doing is nothing more than a silly precaution.

"No, we're landing," he says as if reading my mind, and then he straps the third cushion to my right by tying it to me.

I was wrong.

I don't want him to lie.

I want him to tell me the truth, so I can properly freak out.

The plane's nose dips, and my stomach follows suit as I feel the sudden change in cabin pressure.

"Peter." My voice is surprisingly steady. "Please, sit."

"In a moment," he says and disappears in the back as Yan and Ilya come out of the pilot's cabin and take their own seats.

A few seconds later, Peter reappears with a few pillows. Ignoring my protests, he ties them all around me, with one small one going on the top of my head. By the time he's done, I resemble a human marshmallow.

Then and only then does he take the seat next to me.

"Take some of these pillows for yourself," I beg, but he just tightens his seatbelt. "Please, Peter. Or at least give a couple of them to your teammates. Why should I have them all? Please, listen to me…"

"Don't listen to her, Peter," Ilya says gruffly from the other row. "We're going to be fine."

"But—"

"Relax, Sara," Yan says coolly. "My brother's right. Besides, padding can only do so much."

Peter barks something sharp in Russian—probably an admonishment for needlessly scaring me—and I feel my ears pop as our descent accelerates.

"Seven minutes to landing," Anton announces over the intercom, and Peter reaches across the table between our seats, his hand burrowing through the mound of pillows to clasp mine. His grip is as strong as usual, but his fingers are cold as they wrap around my palm.

"Six minutes," Ilya says as the plane tilts to the left, enabling me to catch a glimpse of the green forest below.

In the distance, I spot a large cleared area with a smattering of small buildings near a bigger white one, but then the plane tilts to the right and all I see is the sky.

A sputtering sound interrupts the steady drone of engines. It sounds like a giant clearing his throat.

I stop breathing, my eyes snapping to Peter's.

His face is white, his jaw set in a brutal line, but his grip on my hand remains steady and reassuring.

The engines resume their droning, and I suck in a much-needed breath. Cold sweat is gathering under my armpits, and all the pillows make me feel like I'm suffocating.

"Five minutes," Ilya says hoarsely. "Just a little longer, and he'll be able to deploy the landing gear without fucking up our descent trajectory."

The engines cough again, then resume working.

The plane tilts to the right again, and I force myself to glance out the window.

The cluster of buildings—Esguerra's compound, presumably—is almost directly underneath us now, and I see that the white building is a stately mansion. I also notice what looks like prison guard towers at the edge of the cleared area.

"Four minutes," Ilya says, and I spot our destination: a paved runway some distance from the mansion, with a thick patch of forest surrounding it on both sides.

The engines cough again.

"Three minutes," Ilya says, his voice strained as the landing gear starts to unfold with a screech.

With one last sputter, the engines go silent, and the screeching stops.

We just ran out of fuel.

"Ptichka." Peter's voice is eerily calm as my terrified gaze meets his. "I love you. Now brace yourself."

CHAPTER 55
SARA

I've always thought that planes with malfunctioning engines fall out of the sky, like birds that had been shot. But as I stare at Peter in paralyzed terror, I don't feel a sharp drop.

Somehow, we're still gliding forward as we descend.

"Sara." His voice sharpens. "Bend over and hug your knees. Now."

My frozen limbs somehow comply, and out of the corner of my eye, I see him assume the same position.

Oh God.

It's happening.

It's real.

We're crashing.

We're about to die.

My rapid breathing is tornado loud in my ears, my right hand slippery with sweat as I push it through the mound of pillows to touch Peter's arm.

I need to feel him.

Need to know that we're connected to the end.

Then his big hand wraps around my palm again, and for a fraction of a second, it's all I need. The flare of joy is as intense as the panic consuming me, the surge of love so strong it overcomes the fear of impending death.

"I love you," I whisper, turning my head to meet his silver gaze. "I'll always love you, Peter… in this world and beyond."

The initial impact is like landing on a bucking bronco. The plane hits the ground so hard it bounces twice, each jolt rougher than the next. The belt across my lap is the only thing that keeps me from flying off the seat, and my left shoulder slams into the couch cushion as the plane tips violently to one side before leveling off.

The landing gear must not have deployed all the way, I realize as the agonizing screech of metal dragging over pavement reaches my ears over the deafening pounding of my pulse. And then miraculously, we're slowing down.

We're on the ground and slowing down.

The realization sinks in slowly, and it's not until we've stopped that I comprehend it fully.

We survived.

We ran out of fuel, but we still landed.

Breathing raggedly, I sit up and open my eyes—I must've squeezed them shut during the landing—and I see Peter already sitting upright, his stubble-shadowed face creased with a worried frown as he frees his hand from my white-knuckled grip.

Unbuckling his seatbelt, he stands up and swiftly rids me of the pillows before patting me down from head to toe.

"Are you all right?" he asks fiercely, and when I nod, I find myself pulled into his embrace and held so tightly that I can't breathe. Not that I need to. This, right here, is all that I need. His warmth seeps into my frozen body, his comforting scent surrounds me, and with my ear pressed against his powerful chest, I hear his heart beating in tune with mine.

We made it.

We're together, and we're alive.

CHAPTER 56
PETER

If I had my way, I'd hold Sara forever, feeling her warmth and breathing in her scent, but there's still our unwilling host to deal with.

Reluctantly, I release her and step back. Ilya and Yan are already by the door, opening it and lowering the ladder, and I walk over to help them.

Sure enough, outside are enough armed guards to take down a platoon. They've surrounded our plane, and behind them are at least twenty SUVs with reinforcements, with a dozen more pulling up as I look.

"Stay here until I come for you," I tell Sara over my shoulder, and then I step out into the humid heat of the jungle, fully prepared to be shot on the spot.

Just because Esguerra let us land doesn't mean he'll let us live. He might've just wanted our plane undamaged.

No bullets come at me, but I know better than to relax as I go down the steps, the adrenaline helping me conceal the limp.

"I'm unarmed," I call out as the nearest guards raise their M16s. They must be new; I don't recognize any of their faces from my time in Esguerra's employ. "Tell your boss that I'm here to see him."

"Are you now?" Esguerra says, stepping out from behind a cluster of guards. "What a coincidence. Because I could've sworn your plane just happened to crash here… as if you ran out of fuel."

"Yes, well, shit happens. Fuel leak last minute and all that."

He tsk-tsks in false sympathy. "Should fire your maintenance guy. Fuel leaks are dangerous."

"Aren't they, though?" My grin is as sharp as the knife I've concealed in my boot. Despite what I said, I'm never completely unarmed. "But all is well that ends well. We're here now, so why don't we shelve the whys for later and focus on what matters—finding Henderson and unfucking up this situation as quickly as possible."

Esguerra's eyes narrow to blue slivers, and for a moment, I'm sure he's going to kill me. But business sense must prevail because he just says coolly, "All right. You have two weeks to fix this mess. Diego will show you and your team to your lodgings."

He turns to leave, and I allow myself to exhale the breath I've been holding.

We're far from safe, but we've just bought ourselves some time.

PART IV

CHAPTER 57
HENDERSON

"Faster," I bark at Jimmy as he drags the suitcase into the car, his expression one of petulant teenage boredom. Bonnie and Amber, my eighteen-year-old daughter, are already inside the vehicle, waiting tensely.

Unlike my stupid son, they understand the seriousness of this. They know that if Sokolov and his cohorts find us, we'll all suffer fates worse than death.

Defeat is a bitter tang on my tongue as I get in the car and slam the door shut. According to my sources, Sokolov is now at Esguerra's compound as well, which means my enemies are not only regrouping but teaming up.

We have to run again.

We have to hide.

At least until I figure out another way to get at them.

CHAPTER 58
SARA

I wake up to the startling sounds of a baby crying, combined with women's voices trying to calm it down.

Opening my eyes, I sit up, willing my brain to start functioning so I can figure out where I am. And as I look around the plain room, with its white walls and gray carpet, it comes to me.

We're in Colombia, on the arms dealer's compound.

More specifically, we're in the house that Diego—a young guard Peter apparently knows from before—brought us to yesterday. I suspect our host gave it to us because of me. Yan, Ilya, and Anton went to stay with the guards in the barracks, but Esguerra must've figured it might be weird for a married couple to bunk with a bunch of guys.

I'm glad about that; I like the privacy. Not to mention, the house itself is nice—clean and modern, if minimally furnished. I've even found some clothes in the closet, and they look to be close to my size—a helpful development, as my own clothes currently consist of just the jeans and sweater I arrived in.

"Wasn't this Kent's residence? Where is he staying?" Peter asked as we pulled up, and Diego explained that Lucas and Yulia Kent are in the main house with the Esguerras—something about extra security and convenience for business meetings.

The crying seems to be coming from the outside, so I get up and throw on a robe that I found in the closet yesterday. Then I walk over to peek out the bedroom window through the closed blinds.

Two dark-haired young women are crouched over a baby lying on a blanket on the green lawn in front of the house. They're changing the child's diaper, and the baby is wailing like it's the worst thing in the world.

Who are they?

And where is Peter?

Judging by the bright sun outside, it's already morning—which, given that I passed out just a few short hours after our arrival yesterday, means that I slept for something like sixteen hours.

My body must've needed the rest after all the stress.

Automatically, my hand goes to my stomach. It's still flat, with no sign of the life growing inside, but I know it's there. I feel it.

A baby of my own.

In a few months, I'll be changing diapers too.

Assuming we're still alive, that is.

My chest tightening, I step back from the window. For a moment, I'd almost forgotten the precarious nature of our circumstances—and what brought us here.

The roar of the helicopter amid the gunfire, pushing on Dad's chest in a futile effort to restart his heart, Mom's face with a chunk of it missing—

Gasping, I sink to my knees, my heart racing as cold sweat coats my body. For a second, it was as if I'd been transported back in time, the flashback so vivid that I'd smelled the metallic stench of blood and felt the warm spray on my face.

Oh God.

I can't do this.

I can't go there.

Shaking, I get to my feet and stumble into the adjoining bathroom, where I turn the shower to the hottest setting and step in, letting the scalding water burn away the ice inside me.

One day, I'll be able to think about my parents, but not yet.

Not for a long, long time.

———

The doorbell rings just as I'm entering the living room, wearing a pair of jean shorts and a T-shirt that I found in the closet. They fit me surprisingly well. Given what Peter said about this being Kent's house before, I'm guessing all the women's clothes here are Yulia's.

Hopefully, she won't mind if I borrow them.

The doorbell rings again.

"Peter?" I call out, looking around, but there's no response. He must be out of the house.

Taking a breath, I walk over to the front door and open it.

Outside are the two young women I saw earlier, with the baby now sleeping in a stroller. They look to be in their early twenties and are dressed in sundresses and casual sandals. One is petite and strikingly pretty, with a thick, glossy curtain of waist-length hair and a slim, athletic build, while the other one is round-cheeked, with a bright smile and curvy figure. To my shock, both of them look familiar.

Where have I seen them before?

"Hi," the petite girl says, studying me with a peculiar expression. Her eyes are huge and dark in her delicately featured face. "You must be Peter's wife. I'm Nora Esguerra."

The name rings a bell, too—beyond the now-familiar "Esguerra."

"And I'm Rosa Martinez," the other girl says with a faint Spanish accent. Like Nora, she's staring at me like I'm some kind of exotic animal, and I realize that *her* name is familiar as well.

We've definitely met. But where?

"Hi," I say slowly as a memory nibbles at the back of my mind. It's something from years ago, something having to do with my hospital... "I'm Sara Cobakis—that is, Sokolov." Or Garin, or whatever identity Peter's going to have us assume next.

"And you're a doctor, right?" Nora cocks her head. "I don't know if you remember, but—"

"You were a patient of mine!" I exclaim as it comes to me. My gaze falls on Rosa, and my shock intensifies. "You *both* were."

I remember it now. It was years ago, not long after George's accident. I'd been called into the ER to treat two young women who had been assaulted at a nightclub. One of them—Rosa—had been raped, while the other one—Nora—had suffered a miscarriage in the process of trying to defend her friend.

Nora's husband had been there too, a stunningly handsome man who'd looked like he was on the verge of murdering everyone but his young wife.

Had that been Julian Esguerra?

Have I already met the man I've heard so much about?

Nora's lips curve in a smile. "You have a good memory. I'm sure you've had thousands of patients over the years."

"I… yes, but…" Realizing I'm keeping them outside like some door-to-door salesmen, I step back and open the door wide. "Please, come in. You must be hot standing there."

"Thank you," Nora says, walking in, and Rosa follows, pushing the stroller in front of her.

"Is that your child?" I ask Rosa, but she smiles and shakes her head.

"She's Nora's."

"Oh, yes, this is Lizzie." Nora pushes back the hood of the stroller and leans over to pick up the sleeping baby. Cradling her gently against one shoulder, she beams at me. "She's five months old."

"Congratulations," I say softly. I remember how devastated she'd looked in the hospital, how worried for her friend. And Rosa... It's hard to believe the battered girl I'd treated that night is the bright-eyed woman standing in front of me. If not for Nora's presence, it might've taken me longer to recognize her; half of Rosa's face had been swollen and crusted with blood when I last saw her.

"Thank you." Nora's smile dims slightly, then comes back in full force. "She's our world—which is why I told Julian we must give you shelter, no matter how pissed he is about the Henderson situation."

I blink at her. "What?"

Rosa not-so-subtly kicks Nora's foot and says something in rapid-fire Spanish.

"I'm sure she knows about Henderson," Nora says, frowning at her friend before looking back at me. "You do know about Henderson, right?"

"Yes, of course," I say. "I'm just confused as to what your daughter has to do with giving us shelter."

"Oh, that." Nora looks relieved. "Peter didn't tell you?" At my blank look, she explains, "Your husband did a huge favor for us in recent months—one that may have saved Lizzie from the clutches of a very evil man."

"And you," Rosa reminds her, and Nora nods.

"Right, and me. And Julian's life too, though he doesn't want to acknowledge that part."

"Oh, I see." This must've been the favor that Peter had mentioned—the one that ultimately got him the amnesty deal. I want to ask a million questions about that and everything else, but first, I need to stop being such a bad hostess. "Would you like something to eat or drink?" I offer. "I think Peter stocked the fridge yesterday…"

"I'm fine, thank you," Nora says and walks over to sit down on the couch.

"A glass of water for me, please," Rosa says when I look at her.

Grateful to have something to do, I go into the kitchen and fill two glasses with filtered water from the refrigerator—one for myself and one for Rosa. Like the rest of the house, the kitchen is clean and modern, if not overly fancy. I can definitely picture Lucas Kent being at home here; the minimalist aesthetic seems like something that would appeal to him.

"So, how did you and Peter meet?" Nora asks when I return to the living room and hand Rosa her glass of water. She's now on the couch next to Nora, and Lizzie is back in the stroller, still sleeping peacefully.

She must've worn herself out with all that crying earlier.

"It's kind of a long story," I say in response to Nora's question as I sit down on a chair across from them. "What about you and your husband? And what brought you to Chicago that time? Are you originally from the area?"

I'm not sure I want to go into the particulars of my first meeting with Peter. As nice as these young women seem, I can't forget that they're on the side of our host—a man who is, if not precisely Peter's enemy, certainly not his friend.

"My parents live in Oak Lawn," Nora says. "So yes, I'm originally from the Chicago area. And you're from Homer Glen, right?"

"Yes. Wow, what a coincidence." Oak Lawn is less than an hour's drive from Homer Glen.

Esguerra's wife and I were practically neighbors.

Nora smiles. "I know, right? So crazy. As to how Julian and I met, it was at a Chicago nightclub. He was in the area on some business, and I was out with a friend, celebrating my eighteenth birthday. A few weeks later, he kidnapped me and—"

I nearly spit out the water I've started sipping. "He *what*?"

"It's not as bad as it sounds," Nora says, then grins, shaking her head. "Oh, what am I saying? It is as bad as it sounds. But we're happy now, so that's all that matters. How about you? How did you happen to meet Peter?"

"Yes, how did you?" Rosa echoes, and I sense something more than simple curiosity in her intent stare.

I stare back. Something else is tugging at the back of my brain, something big... And then it comes to me.

Of course.

How could I have forgotten?

Turning to face Nora, I say evenly, "You already know how we met. Or at least you should... because you're the one who gave Peter his list."

CHAPTER 59
PETER

It's amazing what one night of solid sleep can do. My side still hurts when I move, and my calf and arm ache dully, but I feel infinitely more recovered as I take a seat across the table from Kent and Esguerra.

Ilya, Yan, and Anton join me on my side, and I smile as a plump middle-aged woman brings in a platter of cut-up fruit and cookies.

This is an improvement from the way Esguerra used to hold business meetings in this office. There was no food back then as far as I recall.

"Thank you, Ana," I say as she places the platter in the middle of the oval table, and the housekeeper beams back at me, pleased to be remembered. I didn't have a lot of interactions with her when I worked for Esguerra, but I have a good memory for names.

"Welcome back, Señor Sokolov," she says with a noticeable Spanish accent. "It's good to see you again."

"Likewise," I say, and she leaves the room.

My smile disappears as I turn my attention to the two men sitting across from me. Neither one looks particularly pleased to be here, and with good reason.

According to our hackers, there was a raid on Esguerra's offices in Hong Kong last night.

Oblivious to the tension in the room, Ilya reaches for a cookie. "This is good shit," he says after biting into it, and Anton follows suit, grabbing a cookie and a bunch of grapes for himself.

Esguerra eyes them coldly, then turns to me. "So, Henderson."

"Right." I push a thick folder across the table to him. "This is everything we have on the bastard. I'll email you the files as well, in case your people want to analyze the data patterns."

"I assume you've already done that?" Kent asks, and I nod.

"About a dozen times."

"And?" Kent prompts.

I shrug. "Nothing conclusive for now. But I do have some ideas."

And as Esguerra leans forward, I suppress the remnants of my conscience and go over what I want to do.

If Henderson thought we were at war before, he was wrong.

This is war—and long before we're done, he'll fold and beg for mercy.

CHAPTER 60
SARA

At my accusing words, Nora flinches but doesn't look away. "So you do know about the list. When I first read your name in the papers, I wondered if that's what brought you two together."

"You mean if you're the reason he broke into my home to torture the location of my now-deceased first husband out of me?" I ask sardonically, and Nora winces again.

"Is that what happened? I hoped that maybe Peter spared you, or at least..." She drops her gaze. "Never mind that."

"She wanted to contact you, you know," Rosa says, leaning forward. "When we first realized who you were, Nora wanted to reach out to you and warn you about Peter."

I stare at Esguerra's wife. "You did?" It wouldn't have helped George—Peter would've eventually tracked him down anyway—but maybe if I'd had advance warning, I wouldn't have been caught off-guard in my kitchen that night.

Maybe I would've agreed to go into hiding, like the Feds wanted me to, and Peter would've found some other way to get to George.

Maybe my tormentor and I would've never met.

My chest contracts at the thought, and to my shock, I realize I don't want that.

Even after everything that's happened, everything I've lost, if I had a time machine and could magically rewrite history, I wouldn't.

I'd choose my here and now with Peter over any life that doesn't have him in it.

"Yes, but I didn't do it." Nora looks up, her gaze somber. "I'm sorry, Sara. I saw your husband's name on the list as I was sending it to Peter, and when we were in the hospital, I thought something about your nametag seemed familiar, but I didn't put two and two together until later. And when I did…" She inhales. "Well, it doesn't matter now."

"It does matter," Rosa says, her brown eyes gleaming. "She didn't do it because her husband stopped her."

"Rosa—" Nora begins, but her friend places a hand on her knee.

"No, let me finish." She faces me squarely. "If you're going to blame anyone, Sara, it should be me. I told Señor Esguerra what Nora was planning, and he made sure that she wouldn't go through with it."

I blink. "You did? Why?"

I don't really begrudge the lack of warning—they were obviously under no obligation to do me any favors—but I don't understand why Rosa would interfere either way.

"Because Peter Sokolov is a dangerous man." Her gaze is unwavering. "Maybe as dangerous as Señor Esguerra himself. And after everything Nora had been through, the last thing she needed was for him to come after her and Señor Esguerra for interfering. Your husband was obsessed with that list; he would've mowed down anyone who stood in the way of his vengeance."

"Yes, I know," I say dryly. "I was there."

It's Rosa's turn to look away.

"So how did you end up married to him?" Nora asks, regarding me with a solemn stare. If not for those big, dark eyes of hers, with her petite stature and baby-smooth skin, she could be mistaken for a teenager. But her gaze betrays her.

It's the gaze of a woman—one who's known more than her fair share of suffering.

She said her husband kidnapped her when she was eighteen. What had that been like for her? I was twenty-eight when Peter came into my life, and I've had trouble coping with the emotional complexities of our twisted relationship. How had this girl done it at such a young age?

How had she been able to survive a man who, by all indications, is devil incarnate?

"I imagine the same way you ended up married to *your* husband," I say as she keeps looking at me, waiting for my answer. "I started off hating Peter, and then, over time, it just... shifted. After he got George's location out of me,

Peter killed him and disappeared, but then he came back for me."

I could tell her the whole messy tale, but I don't need to. She understands; I see it in her eyes.

"I'm sorry, Sara, for my role in your misfortune," she says softly. "I hope one day you'll forgive me. And for what it's worth, sometimes you have to plunge into the darkness to find the brightest light. That's what *I* had to do, at least."

I smile, about to tell her that there's nothing to forgive, when the baby begins to fuss. Rosa jumps up and runs over to the stroller, clearly glad to have something to do, and Nora rises to her feet as well.

"We should get going, let you get settled in," she says as Rosa picks up the baby and quiets her cries by rocking her back and forth. "If you need anything—anything at all— we're just a short walk away, over at the main house."

"Thank you. You've been more than generous," I tell her, and I mean it. It's only now sinking in that *she* convinced her husband to give us shelter; her remark had been so offhand that it had nearly slipped past me.

Who knows if Esguerra would've let us land if not for her?

We might owe our lives to this young woman.

"It was nice seeing you again, Sara," Rosa says, beaming at me brightly as she hands the now-calm Lizzie to Nora, and I smile back, even as my gaze is drawn to the baby.

"Would you like to hold her?" Nora asks softly, and I nod, an almost electric tingle running through me as I reach for her daughter.

She's soft and warm, like a little bundle of heated pillows, and as I settle her against my shoulder, the way I saw Nora do it, she turns her head and stares up at me with huge blue eyes.

"She's beautiful," I whisper reverently—and she is. Her tiny head is covered with dark, silky-looking hair, and her smooth, delicate skin is a gorgeous shade of pale gold. All babies are supposed to be cute, but this one… She's going to be a heartbreaker, I can tell.

What is my child going to look like?

Will he or she have Peter's features?

"She likes you," Nora says. "Look how she's staring at you. She's mesmerized."

I tear my gaze away from the little creature in my arms to focus on her mother. "Your daughter is amazing," I tell Nora sincerely, and she smiles.

"Julian and I think so, but we're biased."

"I think so as well," Rosa says, grinning. "But I'm probably biased, too."

"Do you have any children of your own?" I ask her, and she shakes her head, her smile fading.

"No, unfortunately not." She comes up to me and reaches for the baby. "Come here, Lizzie, sweetie. You want to come to Aunt Rosa, don't you?"

I'm not quite ready to give up the baby, but I have no choice. Lizzie goes into Rosa's arms with a happy gurgle, and right away, the spot where I held her pressed against me feels cold and empty, my chest hollow in some strange new way.

This must be what it feels like to want a child—truly want one. I've handled babies before and enjoyed it, but I've never felt anything remotely like this.

Maybe it's because I'm pregnant. Nature is preparing me to be a mother, releasing the hormones to make sure I welcome the child when it comes.

My hand goes to my stomach on autopilot as I watch Rosa carefully place the baby into her stroller, and when I look up, Nora's eyes are trained on me in wide-eyed comprehension.

"How far along are you?" she asks quietly, and Rosa gasps, spinning around to stare at me.

"You're pregnant?"

I bite my lip. It's still too early to be telling everyone, but there's no point in lying. "Yes," I admit. "Six weeks along."

"Wow, congratulations," Rosa exclaims, staring at my stomach.

"Yes, congratulations," Nora echoes with a warm smile. "I'm so happy for you and Peter."

"Thank you," I say, smiling back.

My old life is gone, but maybe this is the start of a new one, complete with new friendships.

Maybe over time, I'll regain some of what was lost.

CHAPTER 61
PETER

I approach the house just as the front door swings open and a small, dark-haired woman backs out with a stroller, saying, "—and while Dr. Goldberg is no OB-GYN, he does have an ultrasound machine. Julian ordered it for me when I was pregnant. So he can definitely take a look, make sure you and the baby are fine." She turns and stops short. "Oh, hello, Peter."

"Hi, Nora," I say. Then I see her friend, the young maid from the house, standing behind her in the doorway, with Sara at her side. "Hello, Rosa," I greet the maid before turning my attention to the only person who matters to me. "Ptichka, are you okay?"

Sara nods. "I'm perfectly fine. Nora was just telling me about their resident doctor, in case I want to get checked out after everything. But I don't think—"

"That's an excellent idea," I say firmly. "Let's have him check you out today." I remember Goldberg from my time here, and while I'd rather have Sara seen by an obstetrician, Esguerra's trauma surgeon is as brilliant as they come.

"Fine," Sara says. "But he should check you out too."

I shrug. "If you want." When we arrived yesterday, she changed all my bandages and put in some new stitches, and I'm more than confident in her work. But if she'd feel better with another doctor seeing me as well, I don't mind.

Anything to keep my pregnant wife calm and content.

Nora clears her throat, and I realize I completely forgot that she and Rosa are standing there.

"Pardon me," I say, stepping back to let them pass, and as the stroller rolls past me, I catch a glimpse of a tiny face with bright blue eyes.

Lizzie Esguerra.

My chest squeezes with a sudden fierce ache. Fuck, I miss Pasha. After all this time, it still hits me like a wrecking ball, the knowledge that he's gone, that the dimple-cheeked baby who grew into a clever toddler will never go to school, never grow up and have children of his own. Nothing can fill that gaping void, yet as my gaze falls on Sara, I feel the worst of the pain easing, a healing warmth replacing the clawing agony of grief.

I may never hold Pasha again, but I will hold my child with Sara. I can picture it already. If it's a girl, she'll be sweet and graceful, like a little ballerina, and if it's a boy... Well, he won't be Pasha, but I will love him just as much.

"Thank you again," Sara calls out, waving at Nora and Rosa as they head down the road to Esguerra's mansion, and they wave back with smiles as I enter the house and close the door behind me.

CHAPTER 62
HENDERSON

I rub my neck as I stare out the window at the icy landscape.

The cabin is as isolated as can be, far out of the way of the hordes of tourists invading Iceland in the hopes of seeing the Northern Lights.

My enemies won't find us here, though I know they're going to do their best to try. For now, my family and I are safe, but I don't delude myself that we can stay here for any measurable length of time.

Soon, we'll have to run again, hide again.

That is, unless I manage to bring down Sokolov and his allies.

My new plan is risky—insane, really—but I don't see any other way. They won't stop coming after me, and eventually, we'll run out of places to hide.

The good news is that I already know the right people to execute this mission—the same team I used for the FBI bombing. They're both unscrupulous and highly skilled, a worthy match for my opponents.

What I need now is to get my hands on the layout of Esguerra's Colombian compound.

Then I can bring the fight to them.

CHAPTER 63

I try to get Peter to rest, but he insists on making breakfast, and I'm too hungry to argue. He's clearly feeling better today, his color back to its normal healthy hue and his movements only slightly stiff.

If I didn't know he'd taken three bullets less than a week ago, I wouldn't have believed it.

As we devour our omelets in the kitchen, I tell him about Nora and Rosa's visit and the fact that I'd met them once, long before I knew him.

"Nora had miscarried?" he says, frowning, and I realize he must not have known about that.

"Yes. I'm guessing you'd left Esguerra's employ by then?"

He nods. "I left right after I rescued him from the terrorist group that had captured him in Tajikistan. Remember how I told you he was pissed that I endangered his wife in the rescue? Well, she definitely wasn't pregnant at the time—or if she was, I didn't know it. I wouldn't have let her talk me into using her as bait if I did."

Right. Because Peter has a soft spot for babies. I saw the look on his face as he glanced at Lizzie, the agony mixed with tender longing. It broke my heart, even as it made me love him all the more.

He'll be a wonderful father, as caring as my own dad had been.

"He's not breathing. Sara, he's not breathing."

I'm already on my knees, pushing on Dad's chest as I count under my breath, then bend over to breathe into his mouth.

His chest rises with the air I give him, then falls and remains unmoving.

Fighting my growing panic, I begin the chest compressions again.

One, two, three, four—

"Sara!"

Gasping, I stare up at Peter in confusion. His face is a mask of worry as he holds me by my upper arms, and we're both on our feet, even though I was sitting and eating a second ago.

"What happened?" I ask hoarsely as he sits down and pulls me onto his lap, wrapping his strong arms around my trembling body. I'm glad he's holding me because I'm not sure I could remain upright on my own. My heart rate is in the supersonic zone, and icy sweat is dripping down my back.

"You went white, and then you started hyperventilating." His voice is strained. "And when I touched you, you began screaming."

"I… what?" My throat is sore as well, I realize as I shakily reach up to touch it.

"I want you to see a therapist." His silver gaze is hard. "As soon as possible."

I shake my head on autopilot. "No, I'm f—"

"You're not fine." His arms tighten around me. "You had a full-on flashback. You weren't here; you were elsewhere. What did you see? Was it your parents? Did you see them die?"

I flinch, the spear of pain like a bullet through my heart. "No," I lie in desperation. I can't talk about this, can't think about it at all. I can feel the dark memories bubbling under the surface, threatening to suck me in. "It's not that. It's just—"

I land painfully on my side, my head banging into the side of the couch as another shot rings out and a warm, metallic spray hits my face and neck.

"Peter!" Terrified for him, I scramble to my knees, wiping the blood out of my eyes—and then I see it.

Mom sprawled on the floor, her face splattered with blood.

Or rather, most of her face.

Part of her cheek and skull is missing, leaving a bloody hole where a cheekbone used to be.

"Sara. Fuck, Sara!"

Peter's face is like a thundercloud as he stares down at me, his eyes narrowed and his big body tense. He must've been shaking me, trying to get me to come out of the flashback, because my skin feels bruised where his fingers had gripped my arms with excessive force.

"I'm sorry," I whisper raggedly. My pulse is in the stratosphere, my throat as raw as if I'd swallowed thorns. I don't understand why this is happening, why all of a sudden, my mind is playing these awful tricks on me.

"No, don't." Releasing my arm, he cradles my cheek, his broad palm warm on my frozen skin. "Don't be sorry, my love. It's not your fault. None of this is your fault."

And as he presses my face against his shoulder, rocking me back and forth, I close my eyes and try my hardest to believe him.

CHAPTER 64
PETER

My guts are in a knot as I watch Goldberg examine Sara. The short, balding man is a trauma surgeon by training, but he seems to know what he's doing—and any doctor is better than none.

Of course, Sara is a doctor herself, but she can't exactly perform her own gynecological exam.

"Well, from what I can see, you and the baby are perfectly fine," he announces when he's done, and I blow out a relieved breath.

Next step: get Sara to a therapist to deal with those terrifying flashbacks.

Spikes of ice still grip my chest when I think about how her face had turned white and blank, as if all life had left her body. And when the hyperventilating and the screaming started… Fuck, I'd give anything to never see her in that state again. I know what PTSD is—I've seen it in many soldiers—and to have my ptichka suffering like that had been more than I could bear.

I need to make her better.

I need to undo the damage I have wrought.

"Now, I'm sure you know this better than I do, but you need to avoid stress as much as possible," Goldberg says to Sara, and she nods, looking every inch the calm, capable doctor herself. And if I hadn't seen her melt down at our kitchen table—twice—less than an hour ago, it would be easy to believe that she's just fine.

That the events of the past week have been just a blip on her emotional radar.

But they're not. They couldn't be. As strong as my ptichka is, she's been through too much for it not to impact her. She'd held it together while we were in survival mode, but now that we're relatively safe, her mind and body are catching up, trying to deal with the extreme trauma.

As far as I know, she hasn't even cried about her parents—or talked about the man she killed.

I'm no shrink, but that can't be healthy. Maybe that's why the flashbacks are hitting her so hard: because she's fighting off her feelings, refusing to think about her grief.

I've seen this in the military, too. Young soldiers, wanting to seem strong, would try to control their feelings to the point that they *lose* control over them entirely. Bottling up that kind of trauma never works; the men would always end up breaking down, or turning to drugs and alcohol to cope. My nightmares after Daryevo aside, I've never had those kinds of issues—but then again, I'm lucky in a way.

I've been in survival mode most of my life.

"Thank you, Dr. Goldberg," Sara says, hopping off the table, and when she goes behind a curtain to put on her clothes, I pull the doctor aside.

"Is she really fine?" I ask in a low voice. "Because she's just lost her parents, and in general, the last few days have been… difficult."

The doctor sighs, peeling off his gloves. "I don't know what to tell you. Physically, she's healthy. Emotionally… well, that's not really my department. You might want to talk to Julian, see if he can bring someone to the estate for her to talk to. I know that a couple of years ago, Nora was going through a rough time, and he had a therapist brought here for her. Maybe he could do the same for your wife?"

I was thinking of getting Sara to see a shrink remotely, but in person would be even better.

"Thanks, I'll talk to him," I tell Goldberg as Sara returns, and he nods, smiling.

"Good luck. And remember: keep it low stress, okay?"

"Thank you. We'll do our best," Sara says, smiling back at him. It's her sweet, warm smile, and for a second, I feel an ugly spike of jealousy. It's illogical—the doctor is a hundred-percent gay—but I can't help it.

I haven't seen that smile from her in days.

Not since she's lost everything because of me.

CHAPTER 65
SARA

Peter is quiet on the way back to our house, his expression closed off. I know he's worried about me, but I wish he'd talk to me, distract me from my thoughts. Instead, he silently holds my hand, and as comforting as his touch is, it's not enough to keep my mind from wandering... from going places I can't have it go.

"So, is Esguerra going to help you get Henderson?" I ask brightly—partially because I'm curious, partially to have something to talk about. "You're going after him, right?"

Peter glances down at me. "Yes—and he will."

"Oh, good. Do you already know how you're going to find him?"

"We have some ideas," he says vaguely, then falls silent again.

Great. He probably doesn't want to talk about it, lest I have another freak-out. Is this how it's going to be with us from now on, with Peter thinking I'm so fragile I might shatter at the least provocation?

The worst part of it is, I'm not sure he's entirely wrong. After what happened at breakfast, my mind feels like a minefield, full of tripwires and hidden dangers. I don't know what's going to trigger me and cause those awful memories to take over. And Peter doesn't even know about the mini flashback I had earlier this morning, before Nora and Rosa's visit.

If he knew, he'd be convinced I'm a basket case.

"How are you feeling?" I ask, deciding to focus on a more innocuous topic. "How's your side doing?"

He smiles at me. "Much better, thank you. Another few days, and I should be good as new."

"Really? You heal remarkably fast."

His smile fades. "I have a thick hide."

Whereas I don't. I'm a fragile fucking flower, falling apart at the seams if he so much as says boo. He didn't say so, but I hear the words anyway.

I all but *feel* his worry for me.

Giving up on conversation, I focus on our surroundings. We're walking past what must be the guards' housing; I see tough-looking men with machine guns going in and out of the dorm-like building. All around us is exotic greenery, and the air is thick and humid, scented with tropical vegetation and a hint of ozone from the clouds gathering on the horizon.

Esguerra's mansion is some distance to the right, the white, two-story building reminding me of a Civil War-era plantation. It's surrounded by pretty landscaping and lush green lawns, as well as a few smaller buildings.

The guard towers I spotted from the plane are visible in the distance, with armed guards on top of them, and I'm sure there are dozens of other, less obvious security measures in place.

Once, seeing all these men with weapons and knowing that I'm on a ruthless criminal's compound would've unnerved me, to say the least. But now it makes me feel safe.

Now the enemy are the people most citizens count on for protection: the law enforcement authorities.

Well, and Henderson—who's using said authorities as his tool of vengeance.

When we get back to the house, Peter prepares our lunch, and we eat—this time, without any meltdowns on my part. He's still quiet during the meal, though, his gaze trained on me with undisguised worry.

"Stop," I groan when I can't take it anymore. "Please, stop looking at me like that. I'm not going to freak out, I promise."

"You can't promise that because the flashbacks aren't something you can control, ptichka," he says quietly. "And the more you try, the worse they may get. Which is why I'm going to talk to Esguerra about getting a therapist here."

"What? Oh, come on. This can wait until—"

"No, it can't." His face is set in implacable lines. "Not with what happened this morning."

"Peter, please. Nothing really happened. You're making a mountain out of a molehill. There's no need to embarrass me in front of Esguerra by asking him to do that. Besides, won't it mean you'll owe him yet another favor? Once you've dealt with Henderson, we can talk about therapy and all that. Until then—"

"Until then, you'll see whoever we can bring here."

Ugh. I shove my empty plate away and get up. It's impossible to sway Peter when he sets his mind on something. I both love and hate that about him—and in this instance, it's definitely the latter.

Why can't he understand that I'm just not ready to deal with the emotional fallout of what happened? That I'd rather risk the occasional flashback than delve into the toxic pool of guilt and horror sloshing around in my mind?

If I could simply erase those memories, I would. Barring that, I just don't want to think about them.

"Ptichka…" He catches my wrist as I'm about to leave the kitchen. His touch burns through me, his fingers binding me like a shackle. "Listen to me, my love. You're hurt, injured—as surely as if you'd caught a bullet. Would you let *my* wounds fester? Or would you do your best to bring about their healing?"

I grit my teeth. "It's not the same thing."

"Isn't it?" His gray eyes are soft as he tucks a strand of hair behind my ear with his free hand. "How is it different?"

Because it is, I want to shout. Because it doesn't matter what I do, or how many therapists I talk to.

Nothing will bring my parents back.

This isn't a bullet wound that will heal with care.

Yet as I stare up at Peter, it occurs to me that I could argue with him for weeks, and it wouldn't change a thing. I can't convince him that I'm fine.

Not with words, at least.

Slowly and deliberately, I lick my lips. Predictably, his gaze falls to my mouth, and his grip on my wrist tightens as I repeat the action, then follow it up with my teeth sinking seductively into my bottom lip.

My goal was to distract him from his worry, but my own heartbeat accelerates as his breathing quickens and his gaze shoots up to meet mine. His pupils are already dilated, turning the silver of his irises to dark steel. I'm acutely aware of the heat emanating from his fingers as he holds my wrist, and the proximity of his tall, strong body makes me want to melt against him, to rub my aching breasts on the broad, hard plane of his chest.

"Ptichka…" His voice is low and thick. "You're playing with fucking fire."

My nipples pinch into tight, hard buds, and liquid heat soaks my panties. Holy fuck, am I turned on. That tone, combined with the hint of violence in the too-tight grip of his fingers on my wrist, does more for me than hours of foreplay. Other than the blow job I gave him in the hospital, we haven't had sex for several days, and my body is desperately craving his possession.

Stepping forward, I rise on tiptoes and press my lips to his, wrapping my free arm around his muscled neck. For a moment, he's stiff, as if taken aback by my aggression, but then his instincts take over, and I find myself backed against the refrigerator, with his hard body pressing into me and his mouth devouring me like there's no tomorrow.

I can feel the bulge of his erection as he grabs my other wrist and stretches my arms above my head, pinning them against the cold steel of the fridge. More heat ripples through my insides, and I moan into his mouth, lifting my leg and hooking it behind his ass, so I can rub my aching, swollen sex against that bulge. I didn't feel comfortable borrowing Yulia's underwear in addition to the clothes, and the jean shorts are rough and scratchy against my bare folds, the sensation uncomfortable yet perversely exciting.

"Fuck me," I breathe as he lifts his head to gaze down at me, his eyes glittering and his jaw tightly clenched. Clasping both of my wrists in one big hand, he unzips his pants, freeing his erection as I beg, "Fuck me *now*."

"Oh, I will. Believe me."

His breathing is heavy, his gaze fierce as he releases my wrists and unzips my shorts, then roughly yanks them down my legs. Shaking with need, I step out of them, and he grips my ass, lifting me up. As I clutch his shoulders, he spreads my thighs wide and lowers me onto his thick cock, spearing me in one hard stroke.

Air whooshes out of my lungs as my legs wrap around his hips and my nails dig into the coiled muscles of his shoulders. Fuck, he's big. My body had somehow forgotten this part. My inner tissues feel painfully stretched, my arousal tempered by the stinging burn of his entry. That is, until he begins to move.

Still holding my gaze, he pulls out and thrusts back in. There's no waiting, no teasing me with shallow thrusts; right away, his rhythm is hard and driving, as merciless as the man himself. And that's exactly what I need. The growing heat and tension lessen the discomfort, my body softening and liquifying, welcoming him deep inside. Each stroke hammers at my G-spot; each time his pelvis slams against mine, it presses on my clit.

My orgasm is as violent as it is sudden. It blasts me long before I'm mentally prepared, the pleasure tearing at me, ripping me apart. Gasping, I cry out his name, my legs tightening around him, but he doesn't stop.

He hammers into me until I come again.

I'm still riding the orgasmic aftershocks when a vein starts throbbing in his sweat-slickened forehead, and his thick cock further swells inside me. With a groan, he thrusts as deeply as he can, and my inner muscles squeeze around his shaft as it jerks and pulses, bathing my insides with his seed.

CHAPTER 66

Breathing heavily, I reluctantly withdraw from Sara's tight, slick pussy and carefully lower her to her feet. She looks just as overwhelmed as I feel, and a sharp pinch of regret chases away the warm afterglow.

I was too rough with her.

Again, I was too fucking rough with her.

I know she likes it that way now, but she's pregnant.

Traumatized and pregnant.

What the fuck was I thinking, losing control like that? I need to be coddling her, keeping her rested and relaxed, not fucking her brains out against the fridge like some out-of-control animal.

She sways on her feet as I release her and step back, and I grip her arm, steadying her as she reaches for a paper towel to mop at the wetness between her legs.

"Ptichka... Are you okay?"

She grins, throwing the balled-up towel in the trash. "Never better. How about you?'

I frown, then remember my injuries. Now that I'm paying attention to it, my side does hurt a bit, but it's nothing I can't handle.

"I'm perfectly fine," I say as a worried look appears on her face and she grabs the hem of my T-shirt—undoubtedly intending to lift it to inspect my bandage. Gently guiding her hands away, I step out of her reach. "Really, I'm okay."

I can't believe she's worried about me when I've just savaged her like this. I know I hurt her—I could feel the extreme tightness of her body when I thrust into her. What if I hurt the baby too?

What if she miscarries, like Nora did that time?

As I stand frozen, processing that horrifying thought, she bends over and picks her shorts up off the floor. Her curvy little ass flashes in the air with the movement, and despite the cum still coating my cock, I feel it twitch with interest.

Fuck, I *am* an animal.

"Sara…" My voice is strained as she faces me. "Are you really okay?"

She blinks. "I told you, never better. Come, let's go clean up." And grabbing my hand, she tugs me to the bathroom.

We shower together—well, Sara showers, and I use the handheld showerhead to strategically wash around my bandages—and then she lies down for a nap, claiming food coma and post-sex drowsiness. I lie down with her and hold her until she falls asleep. Then I quietly get up and leave the house.

I know why she's tired, and it has nothing to do with food or sex. Her body is crashing after the nonstop adrenaline of the past week, and the demands of the growing baby don't help.

The guilt is like a roll of barbed wire in my stomach.

I did this to her.

I'm responsible for all of her misfortune.

If I hadn't been so selfishly obsessed with her, if I'd just let her be, she'd still be home with her parents, living her calm, peaceful life. If I'd walked away after our first meeting, she might've married someone else… someone who could ensure she spends her pregnancy in comfort and safety.

Instead, she's with me on the run, suffering from PTSD-like flashbacks and exhaustion.

"Hey there, Peter," Diego greets me as I walk past him on the road, and I nod curtly, not in the mood for chitchat.

I have one goal right now: to speak with Esguerra.

I need that therapist brought here right away.

Before long, I'm knocking on the door of Esguerra's mansion.

"Is he here?" I ask Ana when she opens the door for me, and the housekeeper nods.

"Yes, please, come in. Would you like something to eat or drink while I go get him?"

"No, thank you. I'm good." I follow Ana into the foyer and lean against the wall, too wound up to sit.

She goes up the wide, curving staircase, and a few minutes later, Esguerra comes down, buttoning his shirt as he walks. His hair is disheveled, and a pissed-off scowl is etched into his face.

I either pulled him from a nap or something involving Nora.

My bet is on the latter.

"What is it?" he barks. "Did Henderson—"

"No, it's nothing like that." I take a breath as his scowl deepens. "It's personal. I need a favor."

He stops in front of me, cold amusement replacing the concern in his gaze. "Really? Food and shelter are not enough for you?"

"Do you know any shrinks?" I ask, refusing to take the bait. "Preferably, someone well-versed in the treatment of PTSD."

He looks taken aback. "For you?"

Remembering Sara's words, I nod coolly. "For me."

I don't want my ptichka to feel embarrassed—not that she should. Needing help to process extreme trauma doesn't make one weak, just normal.

Esguerra studies me with an unreadable expression, then nods. "I may know someone. How soon do you need her here?"

"Today, if possible. Barring that, tomorrow or the next day."

"All right. I'll do my best to get her out here tomorrow."

"Thanks," I say and turn to leave. I know I'll owe him for this, and he will certainly collect, but if it helps Sara, it will be worth it.

I'd do anything to get her well.

"Peter," Esguerra calls out as I'm about to step out of the room. When I turn to face him, he says quietly, "Why don't you and your wife join us for dinner tonight? Nora would love to get to know your Sara better."

"Sure," I say, concealing my surprise. "We'll be here."

"Seven o'clock," he says, then turns away and goes back upstairs.

CHAPTER 67
HENDERSON

My back aches from shoveling snow all day, and Jimmy is pissy as fuck that I made him do it with me, but it had to be done.

We needed to have the driveway clear, so we can get away in a hurry if the need arises.

My plan to get at Sokolov and the others—Operation Air Drop, as I'm calling it—is still missing a crucial component, which is the layout of Esguerra's compound and its security details.

Once we have that, we'll be able to strike, but in the meantime, I have to do everything in my power to keep my wife and children safe.

I have to save them from the monsters hunting us.

CHAPTER 68
SARA

I know it's silly to feel nervous about the dinner after everything we've been through, but I can't help it. For one thing, the only clothes I've found in the closet are shorts and T-shirts, and while Peter has assured me that we don't need to dress up, I'd definitely feel better if I had something like a pretty sundress to put on. Also, after my afternoon nap, my morning sickness has decided to wake up.

It's apparently as jet-lagged as I am.

I've already thrown up once, but I still feel queasy as Peter leads me to the main house. Remembering his insistence on getting me a shrink doesn't help. Did he already talk about it to our host? I hope not, but knowing my husband, he most likely did.

Procrastination is not a concept he's familiar with.

Either way, my stomach churns as Peter knocks on the door. A moment later, it swings open, revealing a middle-aged Hispanic woman. "Señor Sokolov," she says, beaming. "Welcome. And this must be your lovely wife."

I smile and extend my hand. "Hello. I'm Sara."

"Oh, hello." She shakes my hand vigorously. "I'm Ana, Señor Esguerra's housekeeper. Please, come in."

We follow her into the house. Inside, Esguerra's mansion is a stunning mix of traditional and modern décor, with heavy, Baroque-style furniture complemented by gleaming hardwood floors and abstract art on the walls. I recognize a couple of the paintings from an art class I took in college. If they are originals—and I suspect they are—the foyer walls alone are worth millions of dollars.

Ana leads us into a formal dining room, where an oval table is set up with gleaming silverware and gold-rimmed plates. Neither Nora nor her husband is there yet, but I recognize the couple sitting on one side of the table.

Lucas and Yulia Kent.

Their blond heads are bent close together, their hands intertwined on the table as they laugh about something. As we walk in, however, they look up, the smiles disappearing from their faces.

Thick tension pervades the room as Ana disappears, leaving us alone.

Peter is the first to break the silence. "Lucas." He nods coolly at the hard-jawed man. He then turns to Kent's model-like wife. "Yulia. Good to see you."

"Good to see you, too." Her blue eyes cut toward me, her expression reserved. "And you, Sara."

My nausea abruptly intensifies.

Oh, crap. Panicking, I look around for a bathroom, but I don't see one.

"Ptichka…" Peter grips my arm. "What's wrong?"

If I try to speak, I'll vomit. Clamping my hand over my mouth, I twist out of his hold and sprint out of the room, back toward the entrance.

I barely make it outside. The second I bend over the porch railing, my stomach expunges all its contents.

Naturally, Peter follows me out and witnesses the whole thing—and so does Yulia, I see out of the corner of my eye. Mortified, I finish heaving as he holds my hair, and by the time I look up, she's gone.

A second later, however, she returns with a wet paper towel. "Here you go," she murmurs, handing it to me, and I gratefully accept it to wipe my mouth.

Ana comes out next—Yulia must've told her what's happening. Clucking over me, the housekeeper leads me to a bathroom, where she hands me a brand-new toothbrush and a tube of toothpaste.

By the time I've washed my face and thoroughly brushed my teeth, my stomach feels infinitely more settled.

"You okay, my love?" Peter asks as soon as I come out of the bathroom, and I nod, averting my gaze.

"Sorry about that."

"Nothing to be sorry for," he says, catching my hand. "Consider this the official announcement of your pregnancy."

And dropping a kiss on my forehead, he laces his fingers through mine and leads me back to the dining room.

The Esguerras are already there, sitting across from the Kents when we return. I instantly recognize our host: he's indeed the gorgeous man I met in the hospital. His dark hair is longer than it was then, but his strikingly sensual features are the same. Unlike that time, however, he's not radiating grief and rage; he's calm and in control, like a king sitting on his throne.

A cruel, tyrannical king, given what I know about the man.

For the first time, it occurs to me to wonder what happened to the men who had assaulted Nora and her friend. Did Nora's husband kill them?

Scratch that. Of course he killed them.

The only question is how much he made them suffer first.

"There you are," Nora says, looking at me. "Come, sit here." She pats the chair next to her, and I walk over there.

"Julian, this is Sara," she says as I stop next to her. "You might remember her from the hospital in Chicago."

"Of course. It's good to see you again." He looks at me with a piercingly blue gaze, and for the first time, I notice something slightly off about his left eye, as well as a thin scar that goes from his left cheekbone all the way into his eyebrow.

Did someone slice through his eye with a knife, and if so, how did his eye survive?

Unless… is that an artificial eye?

"Thank you. It's good to see you too—and thank you for your hospitality," I say, suppressing my curiosity. It wouldn't do to gawk at our ruthless host.

He gives me a cool nod as I take my seat next to Nora, and Peter sits opposite me, next to Yulia.

"Thank you for the paper towel," I tell Yulia, and she nods noncommittally before looking away. Like her husband, she must still be upset with me over what happened in Cyprus. In hindsight, I feel terrible that I misled her about my relationship with Peter in order to escape. I shouldn't have involved her in my last-ditch effort to avoid falling in love with my tormentor.

I have to get her alone tonight, so I can properly apologize.

"How are you feeling?" Nora asks softly, leaning in, and I smile at her, the worst of my embarrassment fading at the look of concern on her face.

"Much better now, thank you."

"I had pretty bad morning sickness with Lizzie," she confides with a rueful smile. "I was throwing up everywhere, to the point that Julian had taken to carrying one of those airplane vomit bags with us wherever we went."

"I think I may need to do that," I say, and she laughs as Peter watches us with an unreadable expression.

Does he disapprove of my budding friendship with Esguerra's wife? If so, why?

As I ponder that, Ana walks in, wheeling in a cart with bowls of soup.

"I had a special, lighter broth prepared for you," Nora says as Ana puts a clear soup in front of me, rather than the creamy versions I see in front of everyone else. "I figured it might be easier on your stomach. Let me know if you'd rather have the mushroom cream. Rich food was the biggest trigger for me when I was in my first trimester, so I figured it might be for you as well."

"This is perfect, thank you," I say, touched by her thoughtfulness. "I haven't noticed a correlation with different foods for me yet, but I *am* craving something lighter, after... you know."

"Yeah, I figured as much." She grins. "And let me know if any of the smells at the table bother you. Ana will take away whatever it is. Smells was another big thing for me with Lizzie."

"Thank you. You're too kind." I dip my spoon into the soup and bring it to my lips, tasting it cautiously. To my relief, it's as light as Nora promised, with a mushroomy undertone and a hint of miso. "Is your daughter napping?" I ask, swallowing the soup.

"She *was* when I left her upstairs with Rosa a few minutes ago," Nora says. Sighing, she glances at the dining room entrance. "Is it wrong that I already miss her?"

I smile. "Not at all. She seems like a very sweet baby."

Nora rolls her eyes. "I wish. She's a little terror, is what she is. Don't let that cute exterior fool you. She's her father's daughter *all* the way."

Esguerra chooses that moment to look over at us. "What's that, my pet?"

"Nothing." Nora gives him a beatific smile. "Just telling Sara what a perfect angel our daughter is."

He lifts his eyebrows in obvious skepticism, and Nora gives him an exaggeratedly innocent look, rapidly batting her long lashes. His lids lower, his mouth taking on a sensual curve, and a look passes between them, one so intimate and heated that my insides warm.

Feeling like a pervert, I look away—only to meet my husband's storm-colored gaze across the table.

"You're not eating," he quietly observes, and I realize it's not my potential friendship with Nora that worries him.

It's me.

He's watching me like I might throw up—or freak out—at any second.

My mood darkens. So much for reassuring him with sex earlier today.

Dipping my spoon into the soup, I focus on finishing the entire bowl, so I can put his mind at ease on that score, at least. He watches me for a few seconds, then resumes eating his own soup, apparently reassured that I'm not about to starve myself.

Everyone makes quick work of the soup; then the men get into a discussion about some security measures on the compound. I'm only half-listening because Nora is talking my ear off about Chicago clubs and restaurants.

Apparently, we've been to a lot of the same places over the years.

For the second course, Ana brings out a green salad and a delicious-smelling seafood paella. Nora offers to give me plain rice and chicken, but I decline, thanking her for the consideration.

My stomach is behaving, and I really want that paella.

As the meal proceeds, I notice an awkward pattern at the table. Though Nora and Yulia are sitting directly across from one another, they're neither looking at nor talking to each other. In fact, other than thanking Ana and praising her cooking at one point, Yulia has either spoken only to her husband or stayed silent.

Do the Esguerras dislike her for some reason? Come to think of it, when we visited Cyprus, Peter did say something along the lines of Esguerra having "it in for her."

I'll have to ask Peter what happened there.

There's some tension between Peter and Lucas, too, but it's not nearly as pronounced. Maybe Kent's assistance in our rescue negates his culpability in my escape in Peter's eyes, and the two men now consider themselves even.

We're already halfway through the dessert—a delicious homemade tiramisu—when the conversation turns to the topic that brought us all here.

Henderson.

"It's looking like tonight is going to be doable," Esguerra says to Peter. "I'll know for sure in about an hour—your North Carolina guy is being squirrely."

My husband frowns. "Let's offer him more money."

"I did," Kent says. "And I also told him that if he doesn't cooperate, he'll be added to our list. So I'm guessing he'll come through."

"What's happening tonight?" I ask, looking around the table at the men. "Did you already locate Henderson?"

Esguerra and Kent look at Peter, who gives a minute shake of his head—denying them permission to fill me in. My husband then focuses on me. "It's nothing for you to worry about, ptichka," he says softly, reaching across the table to cover my hand. "We haven't found him yet, but we will—and tonight is just a step in that direction."

My teeth clench together, and I yank my hand away.

Here it is again, the assumption that I can't handle anything remotely upsetting.

Before I can say anything, I hear a baby's shrieking cry. It sounds like it's approaching the room. A moment later, a frazzled Rosa walks in, with a screaming Lizzie in her arms.

"So sorry to interrupt, but she won't stop crying," she says. "I've fed and changed her, so I don't know what her problem is."

To my surprise, Esguerra gets up instead of Nora. "I've got it," he says calmly, and walking over to Rosa, he takes the baby from her, handling the child with exquisite gentleness and startling expertise.

His features soften as he gazes down at the small, scrunched-up face, and to my shock, the baby quiets down as he rocks her gently, murmuring something nonsensical in his deep voice. He doesn't seem to care that we're observing him in this tender moment; he's entirely caught up with the tiny creature in his arms.

"See what I mean? Totally daddy's girl," Nora whispers in my ear, and I close my mouth, realizing I'm gaping at her husband like he's just grown a tail.

I did *not* expect to see the powerful arms dealer so hands-on with the baby.

"He's the only one who can handle her when she gets like this," Nora continues softly, and when I glance back at her, I see her watching her husband and child with naked adoration.

She's clearly in love with him.

With a man who kidnapped her when she was barely out of high school.

I suppose I shouldn't be surprised, given my own relationship with Peter, but it's still a bit jarring, observing them like this. A part of me wants to tell her to see a shrink for her Stockholm syndrome, while another, bigger part is cheering for their unorthodox love story.

If *they* can make it work long-term, maybe Peter and I can also.

Maybe a few years from now, we'll all be sitting at a dinner table like this again, only it'll be my baby in Peter's arms.

Our youngest, obviously. Our oldest will be running around on his or her own by then.

I'm so caught up in this daydream that I almost miss my moment with Yulia. She's already excused herself and is stepping out of the dining room when I realize that she's finally heading to the restroom.

"Excuse me, I'll be right back," I tell Nora and Peter, and without waiting for a reply, I get up and hurry after Yulia.

CHAPTER 69

SARA

I catch up with Yulia in the hallway by the bathroom.

"Wait, please," I tell her as she's about to walk in. Realizing what I'm saying, I quickly amend, "I mean, don't wait if you have to go. I'll be out here, waiting until you're done."

She steps away from the bathroom door. "No, please, go ahead. I can go elsewhere. There are plenty of restrooms on this floor."

"What? Oh, no, I'm fine." I laugh, realizing she thinks I urgently need the bathroom. "I just wanted to catch you alone for a minute, to apologize about the whole thing in Cyprus."

Her beautiful face tightens. "There's no need. It's all in the past."

"No, it's not. I caused a rift between Peter and your husband. I'm truly sorry about that—and about giving you the wrong impression about my relationship with Peter. I needed your help to escape, but I should've been more truthful. Peter did kill my first husband, and he waterboarded me, like I told you—but that was early on, before things got complicated with us, too. I mean, I *was* his captive in your house—that's why I was trying to escape—but I was also falling for him by then and—"

Yulia lays a slim hand on my arm. "It's okay, Sara." Her blue gaze softens. "You don't need to go into details. I understand."

"You do?"

She nods. "I'm not an idiot. I know that things can change, and that the ugliest of beginnings can lead to something beautiful over time. As far as using me to escape, I'm sure I would've done the same in your shoes. In fact—" She stops. "Never mind that. I'm just glad you and Peter are in a good place now. I mean… you are, right?" Her gaze falls to my stomach; then she looks up with a silent question.

"Oh. Yes, for sure." I wince internally, recalling how I told her that Peter intended to force a child on me. Covering my stomach with my hand, I say firmly, "This one is very much wanted."

She smiles. "Good. I'm glad to hear it. Now if you'll excuse me…" She glances at the bathroom.

Grinning, I step back, realizing I've been holding her up this whole time. "Thank you," I say as she goes in. "For your help that time and for everything."

"It was my pleasure," she says, and as she closes the door, I head back to the dining room, feeling infinitely more relieved.

———————

When I return, everyone's on their feet, milling around the table with post-dinner drinks, and before long, we're saying our goodbyes.

"Thank you. Everything was wonderful," I tell Nora sincerely, and she grins.

"I can't claim any credit. It was all Ana," she says, and at that moment, her husband calls her name from upstairs.

"Coming!" she yells back, and stepping forward, she gives me a quick hug.

"Stop by anytime, okay?" she says, and I promise to do so.

She heads upstairs, and I turn to Yulia. She and Lucas are staying in the main house, so she's standing in the hallway next to her husband, watching us leave. Impulsively, I come up to her and give her a hug as well.

"Thank you again," I tell her as we separate, and she smiles at me warmly.

"Good luck, Sara. I hope to see you around."

"Oh, you will," I tell her. "Bye, Lucas." I wave at him, smiling, and he gives me a stony look in return.

Okay, so only one of the Kents has forgiven me so far.

"Ready?" Peter asks, looping his arm around my waist, and I nod, leaning in to him as he leads me away.

Back to our temporary home.

CHAPTER 70

"So, what's up with Yulia and the Esguerras?" Sara asks at breakfast the next morning. "At dinner, it seemed as if there was some tension there, and I remember you mentioned something about it in Cyprus."

"Oh, that?" I ladle her some more steel-cut oatmeal with berries. I've started researching optimal nutrition for pregnant women, and I plan to shift Sara's diet toward more healthy foods. "Yes, there's definitely tension—and for a good reason."

She puts down her spoon. "Oh?"

I debate glossing over the whole ugly story, but she hasn't had any flashback episodes this morning or last night, and this has nothing to do with her parents or any of the traumatic events she's been through. So I decide to fill her in, especially since she seemed to be getting chummy with Kent's blond wife last night.

"Do you remember how I told you that Esguerra once had a run-in with a terrorist group and had to be rescued?" I ask. At Sara's nod, I say, "Well, there was a reason they captured him. His plane had been shot down over Uzbekistan, and *that* happened because of some information that Yulia provided to the Ukrainian government."

"What?" Sara's eyes grow huge. "Why would she do that? Was she with Lucas at the time?"

"From what I've heard, they'd had a one-night stand in Moscow right before the crash. As to why, that was her job at the time. She worked as a spy for the Ukrainian government in Moscow."

"Oh, wow, that's…" Sara appears to be struck speechless.

I smile. "Yeah, I know. Kent was on the plane too, by the way. So were nearly fifty of Esguerra's men. Pretty much all of them perished—which is how Esguerra ended up in a hospital in Tashkent, wounded and unprotected."

"Oh, fuck," Sara breathes. "How is she still alive, much less married to Lucas?"

I grin. My little civilian is starting to think the way I do. "Honestly, I'm not sure," I tell her. "I left the estate right after that whole mess went down. But I'm guessing she's alive *because* they're married. I helped him retrieve her from Moscow at one point because he wanted to personally punish her, but I don't know much beyond that. Just that they somehow ended up together and, by all indications, are pretty happy."

Sara shakes her head. "Wow. I just… I have no words." She digs into her oatmeal, and I make quick work of mine before getting up to clear away the dishes.

As I load the dishwasher, I watch her covertly. She seems lost in thought as she sips her tea, but there's no sign of that terrifyingly blank look, no hyperventilating or panic attacks connected to the flashbacks. She did wake up from a nightmare last night, but I made love to her and she fell back asleep.

Maybe yesterday was an anomaly, and my ptichka will be all right, after all. In any case, the therapist is flying in this morning and will be able to see her as early as this afternoon.

Another piece of good news is that last night's operation went off without a hitch. With Esguerra's resources and my detailed files on Henderson, we got everyone we hoped to get—which means we're one step closer to resolving the situation.

If there's any shred of empathy in Henderson, he'll cave.

If not, we'll find him anyway—and he'll die knowing all those deaths are on his conscience.

CHAPTER 71
HENDERSON

I stare at my computer screen, my skin crawling with horror. I expected Sokolov and the others to throw all their resources at finding me, but I didn't expect this. The messages filling my inbox are surreal.

My uncle. My cousins. Bonnie's family. All of our friends.

Gone.

Abducted from their homes, their schools, on their way to work, and from their churches.

With shaking fingers, I click over to CNN and open a web video discussing it.

"It is now believed that last night's series of kidnappings in Asheville, Charleston, and the Washington D.C. area may be connected," the news anchor informs the camera with barely concealed excitement. "So far, no demands have been made, but the police are expecting to hear from the kidnappers at any moment. In total, nineteen citizens have been reported missing, with one of the abductions caught on a security camera."

The video flashes to a grainy footage of two masked figures grabbing Uncle Ian as he's filling up his car at a gas station. The kidnappers' movements are smooth and coordinated—they're clearly professionals who know what they're doing.

"In another twist to the story, it appears that a number of these citizens have suffered abductions and assaults in the recent past," the anchor continues, and the camera flashes to a weeping redhead—my friend Jimmy's wife, Sandra.

Thank God they let her be. It's bad enough my oldest friend—after whom we'd named our son—is in their ruthless clutches.

"Why does this keep happening to us?" Sandra sobs, her mascara running down her freckled face. "Last time, they beat him up and shot him, and he had to retire from the force. And now this? Why? What do they want from us?"

Me. They want me.

Acidic bile churns in my throat.

The cops won't see any demands from the kidnappers because the demands were sent directly to me.

Or rather, to the CIA, where they must've known I still have contacts.

I should've foreseen this and taken some steps to prevent it, but I assumed that everyone Sokolov had interrogated before is safe, since they knew nothing the first time.

I'd been focused on Operation Air Drop, and I underestimated how sociopathic my opponents are.

My neck spasms, the ever-present pain flaring into agony as I pause the video and click over to my inbox, where I read the last email again.

Nineteen hours, nineteen lives, the message received by the CIA reads. *The clock starts at noon EST. Turn yourself in, Wally, or watch them all die, one by one.*

CHAPTER 72
SARA

After breakfast, Peter steps out to catch up on some business with Esguerra and his Russian crew, and I decide to go visit Nora in the main house. For the first time in a week, I don't feel tense or anxious. My stomach is fully settled, and my heart is beating at a normal pace.

I'm humming under my breath as I walk, enjoying the feel of the warm, humid air on my skin. I feel good, almost like I did before all this happened, before my parents—

My mind shuts down, a wall of numbness sliding into place as a third shot rings out.

I look at my husband, on his back and bleeding, then at the agent in the doorway, his face twisted with hatred as he aims at Peter's head.

My gaze falls on the gun that Peter dropped while wrestling with the other agent.

It's three feet away.

I reach for it and pick it up. It's cold and heavy in my hand, adding to the icy numbness in my heart.

My parents are dead.

Peter is about to be murdered.

I aim and squeeze the trigger a split second before the agent fires.

My bullet misses, but the gunshot startles him, causing his shot to go wild.

He spins toward me, and I fire again.

It hits him in the middle of his vest, throwing him back.

Without any hesitation, I walk over to him and lift my gun again.

"Don't—" he chokes out, gasping for breath, and I squeeze the trigger.

His face explodes into bits of blood and bone. It's like a hyper-realistic video game, complete with smell, taste, and—

"Motherfucker! Sara, what happened? What's wrong?"

I snap back to reality, gasping for air. I'm on the ground, curled in a fetal ball, with Lucas Kent crouched over me. His hard features are tense with worry, his pale eyes surveying me from head to toe. Not spotting any obvious injuries, he grips my shoulders and pulls me to my feet.

My knees are weak and I'm shaking all over, my sweat-soaked T-shirt clinging to my body. I'm also so cold that I'm shivering despite the heat of the sun beating down on my skin.

"Are you okay?" Kent asks, holding me by my shoulders. When I nod on autopilot, he lets go of me and demands, "What happened? Did something scare you or hurt you?"

I shake my head, still breathing too fast to speak.

"Okay. Diego!" He waves at the guard passing by—the same one who showed us to the house, I realize dazedly.

"Stay with her," Kent orders when the young man hurries over. "I'm getting Peter."

And before I can object, he takes off at a run.

CHAPTER 73
PETER

"Where's Kent?" Esguerra asks when I walk into the small, modern building that serves as his office. He prefers to conduct business away from the house and family—never mind that Nora is well versed in the ins-and-outs of his illegal empire.

"How should I know?" I reply as I take a seat next to Yan, who's looking at his phone. Ilya and Anton are already here as well, with Ilya happily munching on a cookie from the platter that Ana must've brought in again. "Isn't he staying in the house with you?"

Esguerra frowns. "He was making the rounds with the guards this morning." He glances at one of the many TV monitors lining the walls, then faces us. "Looks like we'll have to fill him in later. I have a call coming up." His gaze swings to me. "Any word from Henderson?"

"No, and I wouldn't expect to hear from him anytime soon. We're still"—I glance at the clock on one of the monitors—"about an hour from the start of the deadline. I'm guessing we'll have to make good on our threat with at least a few bodies before he realizes we're serious."

Esguerra nods. "All right. I've already given our men the instructions on which hostages are to be killed first. Any word from your hackers?"

"Actually, yes," Yan says, looking up from his phone. "They've just tracked down the sniper for us—the one who shot the agent during Peter's arrest."

My hand tightens on the table. "Who is he?"

"*He* is apparently a *she*," Yan says, his eyes on his phone again. "Goes by the name of Mink and is from the Czech Republic. Hold on—the picture is loading now."

"What about our doppelgängers?" Anton asks. "Any word on those fuckers?

Yan doesn't respond, and when I look at him, I see a vein ticking in his temple as he stares at his phone's screen.

"What is it?" Ilya asks, frowning, and his twin wordlessly hands the phone to him.

Ilya's broad face seems to turn into stone. "Her?" He looks up at his brother. "*She* is Mink?"

What the fuck? I snatch the phone from Ilya's hand and examine the picture on the screen.

The woman's face—caught in half-profile by the camera—is young and rather pretty, with delicate features emphasized by the short blond hair standing up in spikes around her pale face. On the side of her neck is a small tattoo of something indiscernible, and her small ear is studded with a dozen piercings.

"Who is she?" I ask, looking up at the twins. "How do you know her?"

Yan's face is tight. "It doesn't matter." He grabs the phone from me. "I'm sending men to capture her—she may know where Henderson is."

"It does matter," Esguerra says as Yan's thumbs tap furiously at the screen. "Who the fuck is she?"

"We met her in Budapest," Ilya says when Yan ignores the question. "She works as a waitress in a bar."

A waitress from Budapest? Why does that sound familiar?

"Did you sleep with her a while back?" Anton blurts out, staring at Yan. "Is she the one Ilya was pouting about when we were in Poland?"

Ilya's massive jaw tightens. "I wasn't pouting. But yes, *he*"—he jerks his thumb at his brother—"fucked her."

Yan slams his phone on the table. "Shut your fucking mouth."

I watch the scene in amazement. Cool, collected Yan is as close to losing control as I've ever seen him.

Ilya's face goes red, and he stands abruptly, sending his chair crashing to the floor.

I leap to my feet as well, knowing a fight is coming—and at that moment, Kent bursts in.

"It's Sara," he says, breathing as if he's run a four-minute mile. "Peter, you need to come with me right away."

CHAPTER 74
PETER

*I*gnoring the nagging pain in my side, I carry Sara back to our house. She's capable of walking—I know, because she told me so in a shaking voice—but I don't give a fuck about that. She's so pale and fragile-looking that I have to hold her, have to feel her slender body pressed against me, so that I know she's physically uninjured.

So that I can pretend she and the baby are all right.

My blood froze at Kent's appearance, and I'm still not recovered fully. It doesn't help that when I sprinted over, my ptichka was even more pale than she is now… even more breakable.

"Here we are," I say soothingly as we approach the house. "We'll get you into a shower right away, okay?" Her clothes are covered with dirt and grass stains, as are her palms, her knees, and half her face.

She doesn't object—either to the shower or to my help undressing—which tells me how terrible she's feeling. Yesterday, she'd been all about convincing me that she's all right.

When I have her naked, I turn on the water and wait for the temperature to adjust. Then I usher her in and strip off my own clothes before joining her under the spray. The water immediately soaks my bandages, but I don't care. I'm pretty sure those things can come off now, and I'll be fine.

"What did you see, my love?" I ask gently as I pour soap into my hand. Despite my worry about her, my cock is hardening, lured by her silky skin and pink-tipped breasts. Ruthlessly, I suppress the urge to do anything but wash her. Sex won't fix this, no matter how much I wish it could.

My ptichka needs to face whatever demons she is fighting.

She needs to let me—and herself—in.

She squeezes her eyes shut and shakes her head. "I can't talk about it. I'm sorry."

Fuck. I feel like putting my fist through the glass wall of the stall, but instead, I begin washing her, focusing on being as gentle as I can.

She doesn't need any more violence.

She's seen too much as is.

Worry, mixed with a healthy dose of guilt, is still devouring me from the inside as I feed Sara lunch. I shouldn't have left her alone for those thirty minutes. I should've been there, done something to prevent this.

Hell, I should've protected her from the trauma in the first place.

To my relief, she seems much more recovered after the shower—to the point that she's again trying to pretend that all is fine, that Kent didn't find her curled up like a wounded child on the grass.

"Why don't we let the therapist rest after her flight?" she says when I inform her that I'm taking her to see the doctor immediately after we eat. "Tomorrow will be soon enough to start the sessions."

"She'll rest after she talks to you." I'm not putting this off—not after what I saw. Esguerra messaged me, wanting me to stop by his office after lunch, but I'm not leaving her alone again.

Henderson and all that shit can wait.

Sara sighs, poking at her kale salad, then looks up. "You do know that I'm not going to magically be cured if I talk to this doctor, right?" Her hazel eyes are troubled. "Therapy doesn't always help in situations such as this."

At least she's finally acknowledging there is a "situation."

Getting up, I walk around the table to her chair. "I know, my love," I say softly, looking down at her upturned face. Placing my hands on her shoulders, I massage them, feeling the tension in the delicate muscles. "It won't be magic, but it'll be a start."

And sinking to my knees beside her chair, I wrap my arms around her and hold her, needing to feel her heartbeat against mine.

Needing to convince myself that I can undo the damage I have done.

CHAPTER 75
SARA

The doctor is a tall woman in her late forties. If Sandra Bullock had played the stylish boss/villain in *The Devil Wears Prada*, she might've looked something like this therapist, right down to the trendy designer glasses.

"Hello," she says, sticking out her slim, perfectly manicured hand. "I'm Dr. Wessex."

"Hi." I shake her hand. "I'm Sara."

We're in another house similar to the one Peter and I are staying in, in a small office with a window facing the road. I can see Peter pacing around outside; Dr. Wessex was adamant that he couldn't be present during my therapy session.

"It's nice to meet you, Sara." She takes a seat behind a glossy table, and I sit down on the reclining chair on the other side. "Your husband has told me a little bit about what brings you to me today, but I'd love to hear about it in your own words."

I shift in my seat. "I'd really rather not talk about it."

She cocks her head. "Why? Is it because it pains you?"

I take a breath as my chest compresses. "No. I mean, yes, of course. I just… don't want to think about it."

"Because your parents were killed?"

I flinch and look away.

"Or because something else happened?" the doctor presses. "Maybe something you have trouble processing?"

My breathing speeds up, and I clench my hands. As my nails dig into my palms, the small pain helps me stay focused on the present.

I can't go there.

I won't go there.

When I remain silent and refuse to look at her, Dr. Wessex sighs and says, "Have you ever heard of Eye Movement Desensitization and Reprocessing, or EMDR?"

I give her a blank stare and shake my head.

"It's a fairly new, nontraditional psychotherapy that I've had great success with over the past year. The idea here is that you'll go through your negative experiences while focusing on an external stimulus. Specifically, I'm going to ask you to track my hand movements with your eyes as you narrate a specific painful memory."

I blink. "What?"

She smiles. "I'm going to do this"—she moves her hand rhythmically from side to side, as if checking my vision—"and you are going to track the movement with your eyes. Here, let's practice."

She resumes the side-to-side movement, and I follow her fingers with my gaze like a cat tracking a laser pointer. I don't see how this is going to help anything, but I'm game to try.

"Okay, good," she says when I have it down. "Now, let's focus on a distressing memory… say, your most recent flashback. What was it that you saw earlier today? What event did you relive? Or if you'd rather not focus on that one, choose something else—or we can start from the beginning."

I'm still tracking her hand movements with my eyes, and it somehow makes it easier to detach from the volcanic pressure building in my chest. I can feel the enormous weight of it, but it's as if it's happening to someone else.

My eyes dart from side to side, following her fingers as I begin speaking. Slowly, haltingly, I go through the events of that day, from the SWAT team showing up to the moment I first pulled the trigger.

It's only there that I stop, unable to say another word because I'm shaking too violently. To my relief, Dr. Wessex doesn't push it. Instead, she tells me to focus on how my body is reacting, and the thoughts I'm having in this moment. And all the while, she's moving her hand back and forth, keeping me focused.

Keeping me distracted from the suffocating pain and grief.

By the time Peter comes inside the house to collect me, I'm so wrung out emotionally and physically that we go straight home, where I promptly fall asleep.

I wake up an hour and a half later to the muffled sound of male voices. Throwing on a robe, I creep up to the window and peek through the closed blinds.

It's Kent, Esguerra, Peter, and Yan. They're standing outside, discussing something.

Holding my breath, I try to make out what they're saying.

"Nothing yet," Kent says, looking disgusted. "Are we sure the message even got to him?"

"Oh, it got to him," Peter says grimly. "The fucker's just too chicken to do anything about it."

Esguerra looks at Yan. "What about your hookup? When is she supposed to get here?"

Yan's jaw tightens visibly, but then he seems to regain control. "Soon," he says without any emotion. "Very soon."

"Good." A terrifying smile curves Esguerra's lips. "Once we have her, it might not matter whether Henderson does the noble thing or not. We'll find the snake bastard anyway."

The men disperse, and I step away from the window, confused yet hopeful.

I still don't know what exactly they're doing, but it sounds like they're making progress with Henderson—and as wrong as it is, I can't wait for the former general to get his due.

CHAPTER 76
HENDERSON

"You are a fucking psycho! You hear me? A psycho!" Bonnie screams, tears and snot running down her face. "Five people we care about are dead, and you don't give a fuck!"

I duck as she throws a glass, and it crashes into the wall behind me, shattering on impact. Each word she flings in my direction is as lethal as her projectiles, and the answering rage combines with my migraine to dapple my vision with specks of red.

I shouldn't have forgotten to refill her medication. She should've been doped up in bed, not going through my emails and watching the fucking news.

A plate whizzes by my ear, and I lose it.

"I do give a fuck!" I roar, rounding the table to grab her bony shoulders. "My cousin Lyle's one of those dead people. But so what? They'll kill all of them regardless. And you and Amber and Jimmy, too. You think I should just present myself to these killers on a silver platter? Is that what I should fucking do?"

I'm shaking her so hard her teeth are rattling in her empty skull, but she refuses to back off.

"Maybe you fucking should!" she screams, her spittle spraying in my face. "We'd all be better off if you were dead!"

Enraged, I shove her away—and she crashes into the fridge just as our daughter enters the kitchen.

"Mom? Dad?" Her wide blue eyes dart from me to Bonnie. "What's going on?"

Fuck. Amber wasn't supposed to see that.

Of my two children, she's the one who's always on my side.

"Nothing, sweetheart," I manage to say calmly. "Your mom just needs her medicine, that's all."

And leaving Bonnie sobbing on the floor, I lead my daughter away, back to her room.

I can't save everyone I care about, but I *will* protect my family.

Even if the ingrates make it fucking hard to do.

I've finally gotten my hands on the layout of Esguerra's Colombian compound, and I'm studying it for Operation Air Drop when it occurs to me that the house is silent.

Too silent.

There are no videogame explosions in the living room, no clattering of dishes in the kitchen despite the fact that it is dinner time.

My blood pressure spiking, I go from room to room.

Nothing.

No one is here.

Our cabin in Iceland is as cold and empty as the snow-covered roads outside.

I run into the garage, and sure enough, the Jeep is missing. Bonnie must've taken it to go into town with the children.

That stupid bitch. I slam my palm against the wall. I told her a million times we can't step a foot out of this place. How could she take such a risk given what's happening with all our friends and relatives? Doesn't she realize my enemies will flay her rib from rib?

Unless... My chest seizes, the air evaporating in my lungs.

She wouldn't.

She couldn't.

She wouldn't fucking dare.

Nonetheless, my legs carry me back inside the house, to her room. I'd looked inside it only briefly, just long enough to see she wasn't there.

So now I step in and look around—and fury nearly boils me alive.

On her nightstand, underneath her TV remote, is a small piece of paper with her handwriting.

We're leaving, it says. *We'd rather take our chances out there than be "safe" in here with you.*

CHAPTER 77

PETER

I step into the interrogation shed, where a young woman sits bound to a chair. Her small face is decorated with bruises, and her lower lip is split, giving her a pouty look. Her gaze, however, is clear and defiant.

No pushover, this pretty sniper. I wonder if Yan gave her those bruises during interrogation, or if they're from the fight she put up during her capture yesterday.

Hearing footsteps, I turn around and see Yan and Ilya entering the room.

"We've just gotten the files on the men whose names she gave us," Ilya says, holding out his phone. "Our doppelgängers have quite a resume. All four are former Delta Force, same unit. They and a few of their buddies got court-martialed fifteen years ago for gang-raping a sixteen-year-old girl in Pakistan. Six of them got arrested, but the others broke them out and they all went on the lam. Since then, they've been doing random jobs here and there, everything from minor assassinations to planting bombs for terrorist organizations."

As he speaks, I scroll through the photos on the screen. They'd clearly had great disguises while impersonating us. The faces looking at me bear very little resemblance to our own; at best, one looks vaguely like me—and even then, his hair is dirty blond.

An idea occurs to me. "Who did their makeup and disguises?" I ask the sniper, coming to stand in front of her chair. "It looks like it was someone very skilled."

She claims not to know where Henderson is hiding, and that chicken-livered ublyudok didn't cave, letting his friends and relatives die in his stead, so we'll need to get to him some other way… maybe through the team he used to plant the explosive.

She's silent for a moment; then she says sullenly, "Me. I did it."

I raise my eyebrows skeptically. "Is that right?"

Her nostrils flare. "Why would I lie? I've already given you all those names. What's one more in the grand scheme of things?"

Her English is as pure as any American's. I wonder when and how a Czech girl learned to speak it so well.

"This will be easy to verify," Yan says, stepping forward to stand next to me. "She can show off her skill on me tonight."

"And on me." Ilya's hands twitch at his sides as he glares at his brother.

Great. They're still at each other's throats over who gets to fuck her.

Pushing my irritation aside, I ask the girl a dozen more questions, and she answers them all, albeit reluctantly. As she's a private contractor with no particular loyalty to anyone, she's wisely decided to cooperate with us in exchange for her life and eventual freedom.

I'm planning to off her anyway—Sara's parents are dead because of her—but for now, I don't mind letting her believe she's going to walk away.

Either way, she's not as useful as I hoped. She said she's only met Henderson in person once, and has no idea where he could be hiding. Nor does she know where our impersonators are, though she's frequently worked with them in the past.

Another dead end, but I'm not losing hope.

We now have more names to track down, and one of them is bound to lead us to our target.

When I get home, I'm relieved to see that Sara is still napping, as she's been doing for the past two afternoons. Though she doesn't want to admit it, the pregnancy and the accompanying morning sickness are taking a heavy toll on her.

And that's not to mention the therapy sessions with Dr. Wessex. Whatever the therapist is putting Sara through seems to be exhausting my ptichka to the point that she passes out as soon as she gets home.

"What kind of treatment is she doing with you?" I asked Sara last night, and she explained about the eye movement and how it's supposed to retrain her brain to process the traumatic memories differently. I'm not sure I understand it fully, but she's only had one minor flashback incident since starting therapy—at least as far as I know.

It's entirely possible she's hiding them from me. She still hasn't cried or talked to me about what happened, so I know it's bottled up inside her, all the grief and pain filling the emptiness left behind by her parents' passing.

The strange part is that I feel some of it too—not just as echoes of her pain, but as my own loss. Over the four months following our wedding, I'd gotten to know Chuck and Lorna, had grown to like and respect both of them. They'd been good people, loving parents, and though they'd had every reason to hate me, they'd slowly been opening up to me, letting me be a part of their lives.

A part of their family—a family that I once again failed to protect.

Quietly, I back out of the bedroom, my chest painfully tight. I don't know if I'll ever forgive myself for what happened, for failing to foresee that the enemy I'd hunted so diligently might not be content to slink out of the shadows and resume his life.

For not anticipating the treasonous form his vengeance might take.

My mood is still dark as I enter the living room and open my laptop to check the encrypted email I used to reach out to Henderson's contact in the CIA. All nineteen of our prisoners are now dead, so I'm not expecting to see anything—I'm checking more out of force of habit.

Which is why a message from an unknown sender catches me completely by surprise.

Opening the email, I read it—then read it again, unable to believe my eyes.

If you want Wally, meet me at Marison Café in London at 9 a.m. on Wednesday. Come alone.

-Bonnie Henderson

CHAPTER 78
SARA

"—Clearly a trap," I hear Ilya say as I exit the bedroom, yawning from my nap. "He's trying to lure you out, that is all."

"Obviously, but we still have to pursue the lead," Kent says as I stop just out of sight in the hallway and peek into the living room.

Peter, Esguerra, Kent, and all three of my husband's Russian teammates are crowded around a laptop on the coffee table, filling the small space with so much testosterone that I can almost taste it. "Lethal masculinity" are the words that come to mind as I view their tall, superbly fit bodies and hard faces.

Lethal, panty-slaying masculinity.

Of course, Peter is far more magnetic than the others, I decide as they continue talking, oblivious to my presence. Kent's blond looks bring to mind a pillaging Viking, and

I sense something decidedly cruel in Esguerra—and, to some extent, in Yan and Anton. Ilya is the only one who seems to have any shred of human kindness in him, and he's definitely not my type—though I can see how many women would find those overly large muscles and skull tattoos a turn-on.

"Are we even sure Peter is the one who's supposed to come alone?" Esguerra says, crouching to peer at the laptop screen. "The email isn't addressed to anyone specific."

My breath catches in my chest, and all thoughts of the men's looks disappear from my mind.

Someone's trying to get Peter to go somewhere alone?

"Our hackers are tracing the email now," Yan says, looking at his phone. "We'll know the IP address it was sent from soon."

Peter waves dismissively. "It won't be a real IP address. Henderson knows how to cover his tracks."

"But what if it's not Henderson?" Esguerra stands up. "What if it *is* his wife?"

Ilya snorts. "Yeah, sure. And if we believe that, he's got a bridge he can—"

"No, Julian is right," Peter interrupts. "Something about this is very un-Henderson-like. If he wanted to lure me out, he'd provide a more believable lead—by posing as, say, his CIA contact or some such. Signing that email with his wife's name is like telling us straight out that it's a trap. You don't need to have worked for the agency to know that it's a tactic least likely to succeed."

"Maybe that's why he's using it," Kent says. "*Because* it's so absurd and unbelievable."

"Or maybe because he's not the one who wrote the email." Esguerra folds his arms across his chest. "I'm telling you, it could be from his wife."

"Why would his wife contact Peter?" Anton asks, scratching at his beard. "We just killed nineteen of their friends and relatives and left the bodies for the cops to find. You think she has a death wish of some kind?"

"Maybe she does," Yan says as I clap my hand over my mouth, suppressing a horrified gasp.

Nineteen people?

They killed *nineteen innocent people* in their quest to get Henderson?

"Think about it," Yan continues, oblivious to the sick hammering of my heartbeat. "We've been after her husband for years. Think of the stress the whole family's been under. Isn't this what we thought might happen when we fucked with those people the first time? Weren't we hoping that someone in Henderson's family—the wife, the daughter, the son—might slip up under pressure and make this kind of mistake?"

"This is more than a mistake," Kent says. "We didn't find her because she contacted her friends out of worry. She reached out to *us*—to the email address that only Henderson and his CIA contact would have."

"Unless she accessed her husband's email and saw the forwarded message from the CIA," Esguerra says. "Then she would have it too."

Still holding my hand over my mouth, I back away, careful not to make a sound.

I understand now why Peter didn't want to tell me any specifics about their plan.

It's not because of my mental state—it's because what they did amounts to mass murder.

CHAPTER 79
PETER

We're in the middle of strategizing how to best approach the situation when Sara walks into the living room.

"There you are," I say, smiling. "How was your nap?"

Her eyes briefly meet mine, then dart away. "It was fine. Hello, everyone." She waves at the men without a smile.

"Let's reconvene tonight," Esguerra says, getting up from the couch. "Eight o'clock, my office."

I glance at Sara, who's slipped past us to the kitchen and is pouring herself a glass of water. I don't want to leave her alone—that's why I called everyone over here.

Discerning my dilemma, Esguerra says, "Sara, Nora was wondering if you'd be able to help her out with Lizzie tonight. Rosa has the evening off."

Sara looks over, her face expressionless. "Sure, I'd be happy to."

Esguerra nods, satisfied, and everyone swiftly clears out, leaving us alone. I'm glad—because I don't like this strange mood Sara's in.

Did something happen while she was napping?

"Ptichka…" I enter the kitchen and stop in front of her. "Did you have another flashback this afternoon?"

She blinks up at me. "What? No, I didn't."

I give her a dubious look. "Are you sure?"

Her delicate jaw tightens. "Yes. I'm fine." Setting her water glass on the counter, she turns away.

Only I'm not about to let her get away with such an obvious lie. Grabbing her arm, I turn her to face me. "Then what is it?" I demand. "What happened?"

She looks up at me, and I see a peculiar blankness in her soft hazel eyes. "Nothing. Nothing happened."

"Sara… don't shut me out."

Something agonizing flickers in her gaze before she veils it with that blankness. "I told you, it's nothing."

"It's not nothing if you're refusing to talk to me. Ptichka…" I release her arm to tuck a wavy strand of hair behind her ear. "Please, my love, tell me what's wrong."

Her face tightens. "Nothing. Just leave it."

Just leave me. I drop my hand, hearing the unspoken words as clearly as if she'd shouted them at me. The email had temporarily distracted me from my dark mood, but now it's back, the knowledge that I've caused all this pressing down on me, suffocating me with its sickening weight.

I did this to Sara.

Her parents are dead because of me.

Her old life is lost because of me.

Because I didn't leave her.

Because I can never leave her.

"Do you hate me?" I ask quietly. "I wouldn't blame you if you did."

She stares at me, her pupils darkening as her breathing speeds up. She doesn't deny it, and why would she?

If not for my obsession with her, her parents would still be alive.

"I should." Her voice is tight. "A normal person would."

The pressure on my chest grows, the pain within becoming more acute. Of course she should. I'm to blame for all of this.

"I'm sorry." The unfamiliar words force themselves through my throat, scraping it raw on the way. "I'm sorry about this, about everything. I failed to protect them… to protect you. I should've anticipated that he would do something like that, but…" I stop, knowing I have no real excuse.

With all the bodyguards and the security measures I'd had in place, I was prepared for my enemies to strike, but not that way.

Sara's eyes widen as I speak, and before I'm done, she begins shaking her head. "What are you talking about?" she exclaims when I fall silent. "That's not what I'm— You think I'm blaming you for my parents' deaths?"

I frown in confusion. "Aren't you?"

"Of course not! If anything, it's me who—" It's her turn to break off, her eyes glittering with painful brightness. Before I can say anything, she continues. "The point is,

Henderson is to blame for what happened, not you. *He* set the explosive, killing all those innocent people so he could frame you for their deaths. *He* sent the SWAT team to my parents' house."

"I know. But he was *my* enemy."

"Yes, and you are *my* husband." Tears are now swimming in her eyes. "*I* fell in love with you. *I* brought you into their lives. *I* pushed for the so-called normal life in the suburbs. If I'd just accepted my feelings for you earlier, we could've lived happily in Japan. And then none of this would've happened, and my parents would still be—"

"Are you seriously trying to say that you're to blame for any of this?" I interrupt incredulously. Capturing her hands in mine, I squeeze them softly. "Sara, ptichka… are you under the impression that you're somehow responsible for what happened?"

Does she not remember how she ended up in Japan in the first place? How I forced myself into her life and stole her?

The tears in her eyes shimmer brighter, and she tries to look away again, but I don't let her. We're going to get to the bottom of this. Now. Today. No matter how hard this is.

Because finally, my ptichka is opening up, talking about what happened.

"Sara…" Releasing her hands, I caress her delicate jaw. "My love, you are not in any way to blame. It's all on me—all of it. From the first moment I saw you, I wanted you, and I let nothing stand in my way… not even your feelings. I was a bastard—and I still am, because even after everything that's happened, I can't bring myself to do the right thing."

Her graceful throat works. "The right thing?"

"Walking away. Letting you go." My mouth twists as I lower my hand. "That's what a good man would do. A man who wanted to repent for his sins. But that's not me. I can't do that. The nine months we were apart nearly destroyed me—and I'd sooner burn in hell for all eternity than spend a lifetime without you."

She flinches, and I again glimpse torment in her gaze before she turns it carefully blank. "You don't have to do that," she says raggedly. "I'm not asking you to leave me. I don't *want* you to leave me. That's the last thing I want—and I definitely don't blame you for what happened with my parents."

"Then what did you mean when you said that you should hate me? That a normal person would hate me?"

Her breathing picks up again, and she steps back, shaking her head as more moisture pools in her eyes. "Forget it." Her voice shakes. "Just forget it."

I stare at her, a new suspicion occurring to me. "When did you wake up?" I ask, going on a hunch.

A visible shudder ripples over her skin, and I know I guessed right.

She did overhear us.

I try to remember what we said, exactly—and wince internally.

The nineteen dead bodies were definitely mentioned.

Stepping closer, I clasp her slender shoulders. "I'm sorry you heard that," I say gently. "For what it's worth, I was counting on Henderson trading himself for at least some of those people."

She swallows. "Yeah, sure."

"Would you rather I did nothing? Do you want him to walk free after what he's done?"

Her chest heaves. "I should." Her voice is strained as she stares up at me. "Not walk free, but be arrested. Pay for his crimes in the normal way."

"And do you want that?" I ask softly. "If you could wave a magic wand and have him go to jail for his crimes, would that satisfy you? Would it be enough considering what he's done? To us, to Tamila and Pasha... to your parents?"

Her breathing quickens more with every word I speak, and I can see her start to tremble. Twisting out of my hold, she moves to walk away, but I catch her wrist and turn her to face me.

"Tell me, Sara." Ruthlessly, I pull her closer. I want to get it all out in the open, to get to the core of what's bothering her. "Is that what you'd want for him? Your normal civilian justice? Or would you want him to suffer? To know true pain and loss?"

The tears spill over, covering her cheeks with wetness. "Stop it," she chokes out, tugging on her wrist. "I don't... I'm not..."

"Not like that?" I refuse to let go. "Are you sure about that, my love? There isn't a part of you that's just a tiny bit glad that your patient's stepfather got his just desserts? That *you* got to pull the trigger on the agent who killed your mother? That though Henderson is still out there, he's already paying for his crimes in flesh and blood?"

The tears flow harder, and I feel her shaking intensify as I say softly, "He deserves it, Sara. You know he does. It's regrettable that others had to die in his stead, but that's how this world works. It's not fair. It's not just. I know—because if there was any fairness in this life, my son would be here with us today. Instead of dying with a toy car clutched in his fist, he'd grow up to drive the real version. He'd go to school and go out on dates. And one day, at some point in the future, he'd meet someone he'd love as much as I love you—someone who'd make him forget about life's brutal lessons."

She's crying now, pounding on my chest and sobbing, and I wrap my arms around her, holding her as the dam finally cracks and she gives in to her pain.

As she faces her grief and loss.

CHAPTER 80
SARA

I cry for what feels like hours, so caught up in my pain that I barely feel it when Peter picks me up and carries me over to the couch in the living room. As he holds me on his lap, gently rocking me back and forth, I grieve for my parents and for the man I killed, for Peter's victims and for Pasha and Tamila. And most of all, I grieve for the woman I had been once, one who couldn't imagine taking a life… or loving a man capable of murder.

It hits me in waves, all the pain and guilt and rage. God, there's so much rage. I didn't know I had it in me. If Henderson were here now, I'd kill him with my bare hands. I'd watch him die and bask in every gruesome moment. Despite all odds, Peter and I had built our dream life together—only to lose it all in a few devastating minutes.

Is that what it had been like for Peter when Pasha and Tamila had been killed? Did he feel like this—like his world had suddenly stopped spinning?

As I cry, I relive it all—all the memories I've fought so hard against. I hear the gunfire and the roar of the chopper, smell the blood and panic in the air. I see my parents die and feel the cold weight of the gun in my hand as I pull the trigger... once, twice, a third time.

I remember what it felt like to see the agent's face explode and to know that I took a human life—that deep inside, I'm capable of all the same things as Peter.

I cry for that and for the knowledge that my child will never know a truly peaceful life, that he or she will grow up in a world colored with shades of darkness. I cry for my dad, who never got to be a grandfather, and for my mom, whose last moments were spent hunched over her husband's dead body.

I cry for them and I rage at fate, and all the while, Peter is there, holding me.

Lending me his strength, so I can fall apart without breaking.

CHAPTER 81
PETER

I wait until Sara's sobs quiet down before I give in to the dark heat brewing in my veins. For a solid hour, I've held her on my lap, feeling her supple body shake and tremble, her shapely ass squirm all over my groin as her soft breasts rubbed against my chest.

It's wrong to crave her this way when I've just witnessed the depths of her suffering, but I can't help it. Her agony has scoured me raw, stripping away the thin gloss of civilization masking my baser urges.

I'm a beast unleashed, and she's my prey.

Savagely, I kiss her, tasting the salt of tears drying on her lips as my hands rip at her clothes, baring her smooth skin. She's passive at first, drained by the emotional storm she's undergone, but before long, her slender arms wrap around me, and she kisses me back, her hands tearing at my clothes with matching ferocity.

My T-shirt lands on the floor, joining the pile of her clothes, and then she's fumbling with the zipper of my jeans as she straddles my lap naked.

"Let me," I order hoarsely when it seems to be taking her forever, but she's already got it, and my cock springs free, swollen and aching, desperate to be buried in her tight, wet heat.

"I love you," she gasps as I plunge deep, and I feel her inner muscles clench around me, squeezing me, welcoming me despite the pain I must be causing.

Just like she's embracing me despite all the suffering I've brought into her life.

I don't deserve her love, her forgiveness, but as I slide my fingers into her hair, holding her still for my devouring kiss, I know that I have it.

That she is truly mine, for better or for worse.

CHAPTER 82

"Are you sure you're going to be okay?" Peter asks for the tenth time as we approach Esguerra's mansion after dinner, and I nod, looking up at his concerned expression.

"Don't worry. I will be just fine."

For the first time in a week and a half, I'm not lying. My eyes feel like I've been rubbing them with sandpaper, and I have a pounding headache from all the crying— not to mention some soreness from our living room lovemaking—but all of that is minor. The worst of the pain—the grief and guilt I'd been unable to face all these days—is lessening, though it may never be fully gone.

Of course, there's still the matter of the nineteen dead hostages, but I'm trying not to think about it. Because what would be the point?

My husband might be a monster, but I can't live without him any more than he can live without me.

"I don't have to go," Peter repeats again. "We can just turn around and go back home."

"You mean back to the house Esguerra's letting us crash in? The same Esguerra whose hospitality is predicated on you helping him get Henderson in a speedy manner?"

Peter lifts his broad shoulders in a shrug, looking unconcerned. "He'll understand if I can't make it to the meeting."

I smile up at him, my chest flooding with glowing warmth. My dark knight—always willing to go into battle on my behalf. "Maybe—but there's no need. I'll be fine. And to be honest, I really want to hang out with Nora and Lizzie."

"All right, my love. If you're sure," he says as we stop by the front door of the mansion. "Call me if you need anything, okay? I won't be far." He points at a small building nearby—must be the office Esguerra was referring to.

"Sounds good. I'll see you soon." Placing my hands on his broad shoulders, I rise up on tiptoes and press my lips to his. I meant it to be a goodbye peck, but he loops one arm around my waist and slides a hand into my hair, holding me still as he deepens the kiss, plundering my mouth as if we hadn't had sex in months, instead of mere hours. My heart rate speeds up, a warmth curling low in my core as his cock hardens against my belly, and for a moment, I'm tempted to agree to his unspoken proposition.

To bail on our commitments tonight, so we can go back to the house and spend the next two hours in bed.

It's only when Peter breaks the kiss to drag in air that my head clears enough to realize we're making out on

Esguerra's front porch—and that the curtain on the nearby window is twitching, as if someone's peeking out.

"Wait…" Breathing heavily, I twist out of his hold and step back. "We can't—we shouldn't here."

He stares at me, his powerful chest rising and falling, and I know that if we weren't in public, he'd be on me already.

"All right," he says gutturally, his big hands flexing at his sides. "But don't stay here too long… Remember, first and foremost, you're mine."

And with that atavistic statement, he turns around and strides away.

If Nora has noticed my red-rimmed, swollen eyes, she's tactful enough not to say anything as I accompany her to Lizzie's room. Instead, she entertains me with a story about a scarlet macaw she'd spotted on her morning run today, and other interesting encounters with the local wildlife.

"It sounds like you love it here," I say, smiling as she bends over the crib to pick up her daughter. The baby makes a disgruntled sound, but then she settles into her mother's arms, laying her tiny head on Nora's slender shoulder.

"I do love it." Nora beams at me as she sits down in a rocking chair, gently patting Lizzie's back. "I have from the beginning."

Chewing on my lower lip, I take a seat on the small sofa next to the chair. Dark curiosity is gnawing at me, but I don't know if I should get that personal with this young woman. "Do you love *everything* about it?" I finally venture.

I'm not talking about the weather or local nature, and I see that Nora understands. Still, my question is vague enough that she could answer it like that if she chooses—I don't want to make her uncomfortable in any way.

Her eyes are dark and thoughtful as she studies me. "No," she says quietly. "Not everything—though I do love *him*."

Of course she does. I saw it at the dinner. And he loves her... though some might say a man like that isn't capable of that depth of feeling.

Before meeting Peter, I would've agreed with them, but like everything else in my life, my views on the topic have shifted and evolved over the past two years.

I now know that ruthless killers can love, and that the heart can lack a moral compass.

"Do you know about their most recent operation?" I ask softly when Nora falls silent. "The one with all the hostages?"

I probably shouldn't go there, but I still can't get the nineteen dead people out of my mind.

Nora nods. "I do. I assume you do, too?"

"Peter wasn't going to tell me, but this afternoon, I overheard them." I swallow. "So yes, now I know."

"Ah. I was wondering about—" She gestures at my eyes and smiles ruefully. "Never mind."

I cock my head, marveling at how calm she looks, how unfazed by it all. "It doesn't bother you?" I ask, unable to help myself. "You don't find this sort of thing... horrifying?

She sighs, shifting the baby to the other shoulder. "I do. Of course I do. I'm not like Julian; I wasn't born to this kind of life."

"So how do you do it then? How do you let it slide?"

"To be honest," she says softly, "I don't know. All I know is that I love him… that I need him like the rainforest needs the sun. My world is darker with him in it, but it's brighter too, richer in so many ways."

I bite the inside of my cheek. I understand her so completely that it's scary. "Do you ever wonder if it's you… if something inside you is wrong and broken?" I ask as the baby starts to fuss. "If maybe normal women wouldn't have… you know?"

She sighs again and shifts Lizzie back to her other shoulder. "It's possible. I know Julian and I— Well, the way we are together is not for everyone, that's for certain." She's about to say more, but Lizzie's fussing is growing in volume, and Nora stands up instead, bouncing the baby to calm her down.

I rise to my feet as well. "May I hold her?"

Nora grins as the baby's fussing escalates to screaming. "Right now? Are you sure?"

"I do need the practice," I say wryly. "And your husband said you could use the help."

"In that case, here you go. This bundle of joy is all yours." She hands over the baby with exaggerated eagerness.

To my surprise, Lizzie immediately stops crying and stares up at me with big blue eyes.

"Why, you little traitor," Nora says to her daughter with mock outrage. "See if you get breastfed tonight."

I laugh, bouncing the baby in my arms, and as she gurgles, her tiny fist reaching for my hair, I feel more of the pressure in my chest easing, the dark clouds lifting long enough to let me glimpse a hint of light.

CHAPTER 83
HENDERSON

Nowhere to be found.

The words rattle around my migraine-ridden brain, the letters twisting on the screen like snakes.

All my contacts are telling me my wife and children are nowhere to be found. It's like they vanished into thin air.

My neck spasms in pain, the agony radiating down my left arm. I want to howl like an animal and down a pack of pills, but I can't.

I need all my wits about me for this.

The odds are high that Sokolov already has them. What else could explain their disappearance? There are no records of them leaving Iceland, no plane tickets issued to anyone matching their description.

They must've been captured and abducted.

Soon, I will get a demand to turn myself over, along with some body parts from my children. Sokolov won't spare them—not after what he's done to the rest of our friends and family.

Not after what happened to his son in that shitty little village.

There's only one thing left to do, one last desperate plan to try.

Picking up the phone, I dial the number on my desk.

"Operation Air Drop is a go," I say when the man on the other end picks up. "Get the team ready. We strike next Saturday, in a week."

CHAPTER 84
PETER

I run again through Plan A with my team, Kent, and Esguerra. Then we go through Plans B, C, D, and E.

Unlike an assassination gig, we're heading in more or less blind. The trap could be sprung from anywhere, take any form Henderson's CIA-trained mind can conjure up. From snipers to MI5 to Interpol, we could be ambushed in a hundred different ways, and we have to be prepared for them all.

We also have to allow for the unlikely possibility that it is *not* a trap, and Bonnie Henderson really did reach out.

Which is why, despite my extreme reluctance to be apart from Sara for any length of time, I'm going to London with my team on Tuesday, the day after tomorrow.

I can't imagine my ptichka will react well to this, but there's no other choice. Kent and Esguerra are going too, to provide backup with their own teams.

We have to find Henderson and finish this.

There's no other choice.

"How do you think Nora will feel about you going in person?" I ask Esguerra as we're wrapping up.

He shrugs, though his expression tightens. "She won't be pleased, but she knows this is important. I can't delegate something this big; growing soft is dangerous in our line of business. Besides, it's the four of you who'll be in most danger. Kent and I will only get involved if all else fails... and unlike yours, our faces are not plastered all over the evening news."

CHAPTER 85
PETER

*O*n Monday night, I prepare all of Sara's favorite foods and open a bottle of sparkling grape juice for dinner. Though it's now been a couple of days since Sara's had any flashbacks, I hate the thought of leaving her alone for so long.

Even with her staying at the Esguerras' house, with Nora and Yulia within shouting distance, I'm going to be worried the entire time I'm away.

"Why do you have to go?" she asks again, her heart-shaped face pinched with stress. Her plate, piled high with her favorite pasta, is sitting in front of her untouched, as is her champagne glass with the sparkling juice. She hasn't eaten all day—not since learning that I'm going to London.

"You know it's almost certainly a trap," she continues as I contemplate how to get her to consume some calories. "He's luring you out, using the email from his wife as bait."

"I know—and we've planned for that," I remind her patiently as I nudge the bowl with freshly baked bread toward her. "It's still a chance to acquire a lead. It's hard to set a trap without leaving traces; somewhere, somehow, he's bound to fuck up."

"But what if he doesn't?" She pushes the bowl away. "What if he succeeds in trapping you?"

"Ptichka…" I sigh. "You know he's just going to keep coming after us. I tried to walk away from this once, and look what happened. If I hadn't taken the deal and given up hunting him—"

"No." Sara's eyes glitter with painful brightness. "Don't even go there. I told you, that's not on you. I know how hard it was for you to make that deal, and no matter the outcome, I'll always be thankful that you tried… that you made that kind of sacrifice for me."

"Then eat. Please." I push the bowl of bread toward her again. "If not for yourself, then for me and our baby."

She blinks, as if only now realizing she hasn't had so much as a bite of anything I've made. Picking up a piece of bread, she obediently bites into it, then forks some pasta into her mouth.

I eye a speck of sauce left behind on her upper lip, and as if reading my mind, she runs her tongue over it, making my body tighten.

Fuck, I want to nibble on those soft, plush lips… to feel them pressed against my balls as she uses that tongue on me.

The surge of lust is so strong it catches me off-guard. My heart rate kicks up, and I go from mild arousal to a full-blown erection in a second. The only thing that stops me from stretching her out on this table is that she's finally eating.

Reluctantly, with an obvious lack of appetite, but eating.

Reining in my lust, I finish my own food, watching her vigilantly the entire time.

She consumes about half of the pasta on her plate before she gives up and declares herself full. I coax her into eating some dessert—a bowl of berries with whipped coconut cream—and then I finally give in to my own hunger.

Leaving the dishes on the table, I pick her up and carry her to our bedroom.

CHAPTER 86

SARA

*P*eter is careful with me tonight, unusually gentle, and for once, the tenderness is exactly what I want. Ever since this morning, when he told me he's leaving for London, I've been paralyzed with fear, so terrified for him that I can scarcely breathe.

He's still not fully healed, though he acts as if the wounds don't matter. Over the past two days, he's resumed training with Anton and the twins, performing feats of strength and endurance that few uninjured athletes could've matched. Despite that, I'm acutely aware that he's not superhuman— that he can bleed and die from bullets, just like anyone.

I spoke to Nora after lunch, while Peter was finalizing the logistics with her husband and the others. She was outwardly calm, but I could tell that she was just as worried, her anxiety running just as deep. She told me some more details of their plan—about how Kent and

Esguerra would be heading up the backup teams, how six dozen of their best-trained guards would be involved in the entire operation. How the men have run through over fifty different simulations, preparing for everything under the sun.

It should've reassured me, but the sucking pit of fear in my stomach has only gotten worse. If nothing else, that conversation had impressed upon me just how dangerous the whole endeavor is—particularly for Peter and his teammates.

As most wanted fugitives, they're heading straight into the lion's den.

Closing my eyes, I try not to think about it, to focus only on Peter's lips trailing sensuously over my back. I'm on my stomach, and he's kissing every vertebra on my spine, his calloused palms sliding over my skin with delicious roughness, caressing and massaging me all over. Each touch of his sculpted lips sends tingly warmth spreading through my body, each stroke of his big hands relaxing and arousing at once.

"You're so sweet," he whispers reverently, raining kisses on the dip of my waist, the curve of my ass, the sensitive underside of my buttocks. "So beautiful all over." His deep, faintly accented voice is like brushed velvet to my ears, adding to the heat building in my veins and the pulsing tension growing in my core.

His fingers slip between my legs, finding my slick opening, and I moan as he penetrates me with two fingers, stretching me, filling me until I throb with need. I'm already so turned on I'm on the verge of coming, and as he curls those fingers inside me, pressing on my G-spot, my body spasms, the release sweeping through me like a warm tidal wave.

I'm still coming down from the high when he rolls me over and covers me with his hard-muscled body. "I love you," he murmurs, looking down at me as he holds himself propped up on one elbow. His free palm curves around my jaw, his thumb softly stroking my cheek, and the tenderness in his metallic gaze melts me all the way down to the bone.

"I love you too," I whisper, my chest aching. "And I always will, my darling... no matter what fate throws our way."

His pupils dilate, his eyes darkening, and when he leans in to claim my mouth, there's a new fierceness in his kiss, a hotter, darker kind of hunger. His hand leaves my face and slips between our bodies, and I feel his cock press against my entrance as he wedges his knees between my legs, parting them wide.

Lifting his head, he captures my gaze with his and then thrusts in, penetrating me all the way in one smooth stroke. I suck in a breath at the sudden fullness, at the heat and pressure of him so deep inside.

"Tell me again," he orders roughly. "I want to hear you say it as I fuck you."

"I love you," I gasp as he withdraws and plunges deep. "I love you so much." He thrusts in even deeper. "I'll always love you." I sound increasingly breathless as his movements pick up pace. "I'll love you forever and ever, for as long as we're both alive."

CHAPTER 87
PETER

All my senses are on high alert as I approach the café where I'm supposed to be meeting Bonnie Henderson. Since the twins haven't killed the captured sniper yet, I've decided to put her skill with disguises to use, and I look nothing like myself. My stomach is like a barrel, and not only am I freckled with reddish-blond hair, but I'm also sporting a receding hairline and a double chin.

If I had a mother, even she wouldn't have recognized me.

Thirty-six of Esguerra's men are positioned all around the restaurant, securing a ten-block radius against snipers and law enforcement officials alike. For now, there doesn't seem to be any unusual activity happening, but that doesn't mean anything—which is why Kent and Esguerra are camped out nearby, each with a backup team in case Henderson pulls a fast one.

And I'm fully expecting him to pull a fast one.

What complicates the situation is that a woman matching Bonnie Henderson's description was spotted walking into the restaurant fifteen minutes earlier. I highly doubt it's her—there's no way Henderson would use his own wife like this—but it does mean I have to get close to the Bonnie lookalike to rule out the small possibility that any of this is for real.

When I'm directly across the street from the café, I stop and make sure my concealed weapons are within easy reach. Through the tiny mic in my ear, my teammates inform me that there's still nothing suspicious going on, so I take a breath and cross the street.

I see her in the café immediately. She's at a small table in the back, facing the door. My disguise works: her gaze slides right past me as I inform the hostess about my reservation using a nasal British accent. They have it ready—Yan's made sure of that—and I follow the hostess to a table that's some dozen feet from where my target is sitting.

I take a seat facing her. Opening the breakfast menu, I surreptitiously study her, searching for clues as to her real identity. The damnedest thing is, she looks just like all the pictures and videos of Henderson's wife that I've studied over the years. Every little thing matches—even the fact that she seems older than in all those pictures, her thin face weary and aged. She's still an attractive woman—I can see why Henderson married her all those years ago—but life on the run has clearly taken its toll.

Or maybe that's what Henderson wanted me to think when he got this CIA agent or whoever to pose as his wife.

The waiter comes over to my table, and I order pancakes and an omelet as I keep studying my target. It's still ten minutes before we're supposed to meet, but the woman seems to be getting antsy, looking at the door, then around the restaurant with increasing nervousness.

Her gaze touches on me once, but without any particular suspicion.

The waiter brings out the pancakes first, and I make a production out of devouring them with gusto, though I scarcely taste them. If this "Bonnie," or whoever else Henderson has planted in the restaurant, is looking for any abnormal behavior, they won't find it at my table.

It's five past nine when she starts getting really nervous. She gets up, as if to leave, then sits down again.

Not very professional for a CIA agent.

My omelet comes out, and as I fork the first bite into my mouth, she gets up, her thin body taut with anxiety. Chewing on her lip, she looks around again, then starts heading for the exit.

Well, that's interesting.

Acting on instinct, I grab her wrist as she passes by my table.

"Bonnie Henderson?" I say, keeping the British accent, and she goes completely stiff, fear twisting her face.

"Let me go," she hisses in a low, terrified tone. "I'm not going back to him. Let me go, or I will fucking scream."

Even more interesting.

"I'm Peter Sokolov," I say with my normal accent, releasing her paper-thin wrist. "You wanted to meet me?"

She freezes again, gaping at me. "But you…"

"It's a disguise," I say calmly. "Please, sit."

She fumbles with the chair across from mine, her hands shaking as she pulls it out. If I were a gentleman, I'd get up and help her, but that's not what I'm here for.

If this really is Henderson's wife—and I'm starting to think it might be—she's going to lead me to her husband one way or another.

The waiter comes over, curious about the sudden addition to my table, and I order two cups of coffee just to get him to leave. Something strange seems to be happening with Bonnie/whoever. Now that she's sitting across the table from me, she looks calmer and more composed—at least if you ignore the fine trembling of her hands.

"You emailed me," I say as soon as the waiter is gone. "Why?"

She takes a deep breath. "Because I had to. This madness has to end."

"I agree." I smile coldly. "How nice of you to hand yourself over like this."

"You misunderstand." She squeezes her hands into a tight ball on the table, hiding the tremors. "I'm not handing myself over. I'm giving you what you want: my husband."

I cock my head. "In exchange for what?"

She lifts her chin. "For you leaving me and my children alone."

Ah. I was beginning to suspect it might be something like that. Still, this doesn't fully make sense. Why betray her husband and expose herself to such danger?

"Why would I accept that bargain when I already have you?" I ask. "Unless you think you're safe because we're meeting in public?"

Her throat bobs as she swallows. "I'm not an idiot. I know what you're capable of."

"And yet you're here. Interesting."

The waiter reappears in that moment, and we both fall silent, waiting for him to pour us coffee and leave.

As soon as he's gone, Bonnie grabs her cup and takes a sip of the scalding-hot liquid. "He won't trade himself for me." Her voice shakes slightly as she sets down the cup. "So you can forget about using me as a bargaining tool. It won't work any better than it did with the hostages."

So she knows about that. This is getting more intriguing by the second.

"What are you proposing then? I promise not to kill you and your children, and you lead me to your husband's hideout?"

"Yes. Well, not exactly." She drags in a breath. "I can't lead you to him outright because I don't know where he is. He would've fled our last hideout as soon as he learned that I ran off with the kids—in case you found us, you see."

"So what *are* you offering? And why did you run off?"

She hesitates, then asks quietly, "Do you know how Wally and I met?"

I try to recall if I've come across the information in the huge file I have on Henderson. "No," I admit after a moment. "I don't."

Her lips press together. "I thought so. No one really knows about that. Wally likes to tell people we met at a bar, but that's not the case. I mean, we got together at a bar, but we met earlier—when I was a brand-new trainee at the agency, and he was its star operative... and my teacher."

I conceal my surprise. I might've initially thought her an agent playing the part of Henderson's wife, but I did not expect Henderson's actual wife to be CIA.

She's way too convincing as a nervous socialite.

"Don't worry, I'm not an agent," she says quickly, as if afraid I'm going to shoot her for that revelation. "I dropped out of the training program after Wally got me pregnant. I ended up miscarrying that child, but I never went back. You see, Wally and I got married, and he left the agency shortly after, wanting to pursue a career in the military so he could have a more stable family life—which meant I had to stay home with the children."

I pick up my cup of coffee. "And you're telling me all this why?"

"Because I want you to understand why I'm here." Her eyes burn into my face as I sip the hot, bitter liquid. "I joined the agency because I'm a patriot, Mr. Sokolov. Because I wanted to protect our country from threats both foreign and domestic... from terrorists who'd blow up a building just because."

The puzzle pieces finally click together.

Of course.

That's what pushed her over the edge.

"When did you find out?" I ask, putting down the coffee.

"That Wally was behind the FBI bombing in Chicago? A few days ago—at the same time as I learned that he let all our friends and relatives die rather than give in to your demands." She sounds almost calm as she says this, but I can see what it's costing her.

However she came across that information, it must've been a painful shock.

"Why come to me, though?" I ask, examining her closely. "Surely, you must hate me for what I've done to you and your family. Why not just turn your husband in to the authorities? I assume the evidence you have is pretty damning."

She nods. "It is—and that's another thing I can offer you. If you keep your side of the bargain, I will do my best to clear your name—of that particular crime, at least. As to why I'm here, talking to you, that's very simple." She draws in a breath. "I'm tired, Mr. Sokolov. I'm exhausted from fearing and hating you, and so are my children. Turning Wally in wouldn't end this nightmare for us; the trial would drag on for years, and all along, you'd be trying to get to him through us. This is the best way—the only way—to bring this to an end. I will never forgive you for what you've done to my family, but I will make this bargain with you." Her voice cracks. "All I want is for this to be over… for my children to resume their normal lives."

She's convincing, I will give her that. So convincing that I'm tempted to believe her. But there is one more thing

I need to know. "When I first spoke to you, you thought I was someone your husband sent. I assume that means he's been looking for you. How is it that he didn't find you already, with all of his connections?"

Her face tightens again. "I have connections of my own, Mr. Sokolov. My husband has never understood that. He thinks his success is due to his own brilliance, but I've been at his side all along, smoothing the way, making friends with all the right people, schmoozing with their wives at all the right—" She stops, as if realizing how pointless her bitter recollections are. "In any case," she continues, "I've been preparing for the past two years, just in case I ended up as a widow with you on our tail. I had documents for myself and the kids, along with money and everything else required to stay hidden on our own. But then this happened."

"And you used your emergency stash to run from your husband instead."

Her mouth thins. "Right. So tell me, Mr. Sokolov, do we have a bargain? If I deliver my husband to you, will you let us be?"

I pick up my coffee again. "You said you don't know where he is."

"I don't—but I know what he values more than anything in the world."

"And that is?"

She gives me a level look. "Our daughter. Amber. She's the only person besides himself that he truly loves."

I have to hide my surprise again. Is this woman actually considering giving us her teenage daughter as a hostage?

Is she fucking insane?

"All right," I say, putting down the cup. If she *is* off her meds, I'm not going to look a gift horse in the mouth. "That does sound like a good plan—and yes, if we succeed in luring him out with your daughter, I will leave you and your children alone." And I mean it, too. Though I'd love to have Henderson suffer with the knowledge that his family is dead, I was never really after his wife and kids.

It's *his* head on a spike that I want.

"In that case, here you go." She takes out a phone and pushes it across the table toward me. "This is all you should need for now, but there's more where that came from—as long as you let me leave here today."

I press "play" on the video on the screen, and a minute in, I realize Henderson's wife is not insane—and that while she's left the agency, the agency's never left her.

CHAPTER 88
SARA

I pace around the Esguerras' dining room, anxiety drilling a hole in my chest. Nora and Yulia are both here, as is the young guard, Diego. He's receiving live updates about the ongoing operation through his headphones, so I know that Peter has just entered the restaurant, braving the likely trap.

"He's talking to her now," Diego says, glancing up from his laptop screen after twenty agonizing minutes, and I rush over to see a blurry image of a man who looks nothing like Peter sitting across from a thin woman.

"This is from a long-range camera," Diego explains. "We don't want to spook them by getting too close."

"But all is still quiet?" Yulia asks, leaning over his shoulder, and he nods.

"Henderson's spooks are either preternaturally good—or there's no one around."

I look over at Nora. Unlike Yulia and me, she's sitting quietly, not asking questions. If not for her death grip on Lizzie's stroller, I'd think she was taking all this in stride.

Turning my attention back to the screen, I see that disguised Peter and the woman are still talking.

"Don't worry," Yulia says to me quietly. "If anyone in the restaurant so much as sneezes wrong, our snipers will get them."

"Yes, I know." A dry smile tugs at my lips. "It's amazing how reassuring having snipers can be."

She smiles back, and we share a moment. When I glance over at Nora, however, she's not looking at either of us.

Of course. With all this, I'd forgotten that she's on the outs with Yulia.

I wonder if she resents the fact that I'm not.

"He's coming out of the restaurant," Diego says suddenly, and my gaze snaps back to the screen.

Sure enough, Peter's already on the street.

Diego falls silent, listening intently to whatever information the London team's relaying to him, and as I watch a big smile creep across his face, my knees go weak with relief.

The email *was* from Henderson's wife.

Peter and the others are safe.

CHAPTER 89
HENDERSON

I'm going over the logistics for our operation on Saturday when a notification pops up on my screen. It's an email from my CIA contact.

Sorry, the subject line reads.

Everything inside me turns to ice as I see the text and the video attachment it's forwarding.

Feeling like I'm about to vomit, I press "play."

My daughter's dirty, tear-streaked face fills the screen. "Daddy," she sobs as the camera zooms out, showing her tied to a chair in a nondescript room with white walls. "Daddy, please help me. They said they'll kill us. Please, Daddy, help!"

The video cuts out, leaving me wheezing for air.

Sokolov has her. He has all of them.

It's now a fact.

Shaking, I read the forwarded text.

You know what I want, it says. *Plaza de Bolivar, Bogotá, 3pm Thursday. Be there or watch her die.*

I expected this, knew it had to be coming, but it still hits me like a punch to the gut.

Amber. My sweet, loyal daughter.

That monster will kill her. He won't spare her, even if I do what he says.

There's no more time to plan the logistics, no chance to work out the kinks.

Operation Air Drop can't wait until Saturday.

It has to happen tonight.

CHAPTER 90
SARA

"Do you think it could still be a trap?" I ask Nora as we're swimming in her Olympic-sized pool an hour later. With the immediate crisis over, Yulia has gone back to her room, tactfully sparing Nora her presence, so it's just the two of us by the mansion's gorgeous lanai.

Well, and Rosa with Lizzie, but they're both napping in the shade.

"Anything's possible, but Julian doesn't think so," Nora replies, flopping over to float on her back. Her body in a bikini is so sleek and athletic, it's hard to believe she had a child only months earlier.

I'm wearing a bikini too—one that I borrowed from Yulia, as we're closer in size despite the height difference. The shorts and T-shirts I've been wearing indeed turned out to be Yulia's. She forgot them at Kent's house when they moved to Cyprus, and she's more than happy that I'm getting some use out of them.

"Let me know if you need anything else," she told me when we spoke about the clothes this morning. "Lucas keeps a suitcase full of my stuff on our plane, just in case, so I'm fully equipped."

Turning my attention back to Nora, I ask, "What about what's happening tomorrow? Does Julian think Henderson will actually show up in Bogotá?"

"That's the hope," she says, turning over to swim with a strong freestyle stroke. I'm a decent swimmer, but I have to strain to keep up with her as she cuts through the water, reaching the side of the pool in no time.

It's clear that she doesn't want to talk about this topic, but I can't bring myself to leave it alone. "What if he doesn't?" I ask when she slows down. "He didn't turn himself over for any of the hostages."

She stops and stands, slicking her wet hair back with both hands. "They weren't his daughter," she says, squinting against the sun as she looks at me. "But either way, even if things don't go according to plan, Julian, Lucas, and Peter will improvise something. This is what they do, and they're good at it."

Though Nora doesn't know what will happen any more than I do, some of the tightness in my chest eases at the reminder about Peter's capabilities.

My husband *is* good at this.

Terrifyingly good.

We swim for another hour, chatting about more pleasant things, like Nora's upcoming art exhibition in

Berlin—apparently, she's a serious painter—and when Lizzie wakes up, demanding food, we go back into the house.

With any luck, it'll all be over by tomorrow.

CHAPTER 91
HENDERSON

"We're going to land right here," I say, raising my voice to be heard over the roar of the engines as I point to a patch of trees on the satellite photo. "Then we're going to make our way over there." I jab my finger at the white building in the middle.

"Got it." Danser pushes back his dirty-blond hair, his face in profile uncannily reminiscent of Sokolov's. "Do you have photos of the targets?"

"Here." I hand over the photo of Esguerra's wife. "We want to capture either this woman or her baby—or preferably both. They're our ticket out of the compound."

Barrett peers at the photo over Danser's shoulder. "She looks kind of little. Should be easy enough."

"This one would work also, but I don't know if she'll be at the main house." I pull out a picture of Sara Sokolov and give it to Danser and his teammates. "And this one"—I show a full-length photo of Kent's wife—"would make a nice bonus, except she might also be anywhere on the compound."

"Oh, fuck. Look at that blond hair and those legs." Kilton snatches the picture from me. "I'd do her for sure."

"I'd do all of them, minus the baby," Russ says, stroking his beard lewdly. "Maybe all three at once."

It takes all my acting skills to conceal my instinctive sneer. I can't afford to antagonize these four assholes, or anyone else on their team. So what if they're dumb enough to think with their dicks? They did a good job planting the explosive at the FBI building, and they're experienced with HALO jumps.

I need them for this.

It's my only chance to save Amber.

Massaging the painful knots in my neck, I look over at the other six men on our military transport plane. "Are you clear on your part in this?"

"They are," Danser says before any of them can answer. "Alpha Team will engage the guards at the northern border at 00:58, and Beta Team will be waiting for you with the helicopter at the extraction point on the southern border."

"What if Esguerra doesn't leave the house to check on the disturbance at the northern border?" Barrett asks. "Do we kill the fucker?"

"No, just wound him," I say. "We want him alive, so he can force Sokolov to make the trade for my family. Otherwise, if the arms dealer's dead, no one will care if we have his wife and kid. Of course, if we get lucky and stumble upon Sokolov's wife, that'll be even better."

"So just to be clear," Kilton says. "We want Esguerra's wife and/or baby as hostages to get out of the compound alive, and also to trade them for your family. But if we happen to come across Sokolov's wife or the hot blonde, we grab them too."

"Right," I say. "With Sokolov's wife as the priority out of those two. If we have her, it won't matter if Esguerra gets killed. Sokolov will make the trade anyway."

"What about Kent?" Russ asks. "What do we do if he's there?"

"If we don't have his wife, then kill him," I say. "But if you get her as a hostage, then don't."

The more leverage I have over my enemies, the better. When I first started planning this mission, the goal was to use the hostages we'd acquire to lure Sokolov and the others into a trap and kill them, but the capture of my family has raised the stakes.

The priority now is saving Amber.

"You don't think Kent might be in Bogotá with Sokolov?" Danser asks, handing the photos back to me.

"I don't know if Sokolov is in Bogotá himself," I say, stuffing them into my jacket. "Just because he told me to be at the plaza tomorrow doesn't mean *he'll* be there. Either way, be prepared for anything. Given how impenetrable the compound borders are, logic dictates that the house itself won't be especially well guarded—but of course, there are no guarantees."

"Well, shit." Russ grins. "This ought to be fun. Are you sure you want to do this with us, old man?"

Ignoring the idiot's jab, I grab my oxygen bottle and start suiting up for the jump. Until that video hit my inbox, I wasn't going to join them on this insanely dangerous mission, but now there's no choice.

Not only is this operation now my only chance to gain leverage over my enemies, but Amber herself might be in the compound. I don't know that for sure, of course; they might be holding her in Bogotá or anywhere else in the world. But given that the indicated meeting place is in Colombia, on Esguerra's turf, there's at least a possibility that they're hiding her on the arms dealer's estate.

If we get lucky, we won't walk away with just the hostages.

We might rescue my daughter, too.

CHAPTER 92
SARA

After Lizzie is fed, Nora gives me a tour of the house. It's as big as it appears on the outside, numbering over a dozen rooms, including a dedicated library, a home theater with an enormous screen, a gym filled with all sorts of equipment, and a sunlit room that serves as her art studio.

The half-finished paintings inside are a striking blend of surrealism and modern expressionism, with familiar shapes and objects, like trees, distorted into something intriguingly sinister. The color palette leans heavily toward reds and blacks, as if everything's consumed by fire.

"You are amazingly talented," I say sincerely, and Nora grins, thanking me. As the tour proceeds, she explains that she started painting as a way to keep herself from going crazy on the private island where Julian kept her when he first kidnapped her.

I want to ask her a million questions about that, but we've already arrived at the room where I'm staying while Peter is away—a beautifully decorated bedroom a couple of doors down from the master suite and adjacent to Yulia's room. Nora excuses herself to take care of some business, and I decide to take a quick nap, since I'm tired.

Being pregnant is a lot like being a kindergartener, it seems.

By the time I wake up, it's dinner time, and I join Nora in the dining room again. Yulia is conspicuously absent, and when I ask Nora where she is, she informs me that Kent's wife has already eaten.

"She's still on the Cyprus schedule," she explains with a tight smile as Ana brings out the food.

I decide not to press her further—it must be awkward to have the woman who nearly killed your husband as a guest under your roof. Instead, as we eat, I ask about Nora's family and how they feel about her marriage to Julian.

"Oh, they're still hoping I wise up and divorce him," she says, cutting into her salmon, and as she entertains me with her dad's tense interactions with her husband, I remember how nice Peter had been to my parents—how he had done his best to allay their concerns about him.

How far he'd gone to make sure they were in my life.

My chest squeezes anew, my eyes prickling with tears, but this time, I don't shy away from the pain. The agony of loss is still fresh, the wound unbearably raw, but I can think about them now, can grieve without losing myself in the horror of their deaths.

I don't realize the tears have escaped until Nora quietly hands me a napkin.

"I'm sorry, Sara," she says somberly. "That was insensitive of me."

"No, I'm..." I attempt a watery smile. "I'm fine, really. It's just that..."

"You just lost them, I know." Her dark eyes hold a grim understanding. Has she lost someone close to her, too?

Before I can ask, Rosa walks into the dining room, carrying Lizzie, and I turn away, surreptitiously wiping away the wetness on my cheeks. I don't want Nora's friend/ nanny to see me like this.

It's bad enough Nora had to witness the waterworks.

Nora excuses herself to go feed the baby again— Lizzie will turn into a screaming monster if she's not fed immediately, she explains apologetically—and I finish my food and go up to my room.

As I pass by Yulia's door, I hear her talking on the phone in Russian. Her voice is warm and tender, as if she's talking to a child or a lover, and for a second, it catches me off-guard. But then I remember the photos of a teenage boy in her house—the one I decided had to be her brother because he looks exactly like her.

Could it be that boy she's talking to?

I'm intensely curious about her story, with the whole spy bit and all, but I don't want to bother her while she's on the phone. Entering my room, I close the door and walk over to the window, looking out at the sun setting over the trees.

I miss Peter.

God, I miss him so much.

Right now, he and the others should be in the air, on their way to the meeting in Bogotá tomorrow. If all goes well, by this time tomorrow night, he'll be with me.

His quest for vengeance will finally be over.

Walking over to a bookshelf, I grab a thriller at random and curl up in an arm chair to read it. Though I woke up from my nap only a couple of hours ago, I'm tired again, and before I get too far into my reading, I find myself nodding off.

Yawning, I take a quick shower and get into bed. And then, predictably, I can't fall asleep.

Getting up, I read some more, then scribble down the words to a melody that's been in the back of my mind all day. It's angry and dark, far from my usual music, but something about it feels right—raw and honest and healing.

Feeling tired again, I return to bed, and this time, I drift off into uneasy slumber.

CHAPTER 93
HENDERSON

Icy air whooshes past my ears, drowning out the terrified roar of my heartbeat as we plummet through the pitch-black sky from thirty thousand feet. The night is on our side; the clouds hide even the faintest glow of moonlight.

My night vision goggles are strapped over my oxygen mask, and I see the four other figures next to me. We freefall for what seems like forever before I feel a violent jolt, and the parachutes above us deploy.

"There," Danser says over the comms as the outlines of the treetops appear below. "That's our landing spot."

It's a forested patch deep inside Esguerra's compound, far from the guard towers at the perimeter. The main danger here are the drones that patrol the air, but thanks to the CIA's latest gadget, I have a solution for that.

When we're right over the tree line, my device detects the approaching drones and automatically syncs with them, allowing my contact at the CIA to control the cameras while we're in range. The drone operators won't see anything but the usual scenery as our parachutes float by.

Since I haven't done high-altitude jumps in two decades, I'm flying tandem with Danser, and his feet touch the ground first, taking the brunt of the impact. Still, my knees nearly buckle as we land, narrowly avoiding getting impaled by a tree branch. As I bend over to catch my breath, Danser unhooks the parachute gear from us both and stuffs it into the bushes.

The rest of the team does the same thing, and by the time they're done, I can almost stand upright.

"Ready?" Danser asks through the comms, and I nod, ignoring the residual weakness in my limbs.

So far, all has gone according to plan, and I won't be the reason we fail.

Quietly, we creep through the darkness, using the trees as a cover. The trickiest part will be the open area around the house, but that's what the distraction at the border is for.

Pausing at the edge of the forested patch, we wait for the Alpha Team's signal. The minutes tick by with torturous slowness, and I feel sweat trickle down my back as I stare at the white building ahead.

Fucking jungle humidity.

It's worse than the dry heat in Iraq.

As we suspected, Esguerra's actual residence doesn't appear to be heavily guarded. And why would it be?

Between the drones and all the security at the borders, the mansion might as well be sitting inside a fortress.

There are only two guards walking in circles around the house, and when they pass near us, Russ and Kilton fire off silenced shots, getting them right in the foreheads.

First obstacle eliminated.

"Engaging now," Alpha Team leader says through the comms, and I hear gunfire in the background.

"Let's give it fifteen minutes, see if anyone comes out," Danser says, and we wait, tensely staring at the house.

There are no signs of movement inside, no lights coming on.

Esguerra's border guards either didn't inform their boss of what's happening, or he doesn't think this requires his presence.

Or, if we're lucky, he's not home at all.

Just to be on the safe side, we wait another twenty minutes, and then Danser motions us forward.

Crouching, we beeline across the wide lawn, using the manicured shrubs on the sides as a cover as we approach the pool area in the back.

All is quiet here too.

"Go on," Danser whispers to me as we stop by the back door. "Do your fucking magic."

Nodding, I pull out the CIA device again. It jumps on the house Wi-Fi and syncs with the cameras and the alarm system, giving my contact access to disable everything.

While he's doing that, I activate a cell signal scrambler, in case anyone tries to call out for help.

"All done," I say quietly when I receive confirmation from my contact. "It's showtime."

CHAPTER 94
SARA

I sleep restlessly, waking up what feels like every half hour. Each time I drift off, anxious dreams about Peter combine with fragments of nightmares about my parents' deaths to jerk me awake. It's on the fifth such wake-up that I stumble to the bathroom, bleary-eyed, and decide to read for a bit to distract my overactive brain.

Throwing on a silk robe that I've borrowed from Nora, I turn on the bedside lamp, grab a book, and curl up in the arm chair, yawning.

With any luck, I won't be up long.

I'm halfway through another chapter when I hear it.

A creaking sound right outside my door.

Startled, I look over and see the door swing open.

A tall, black-clothed figure stands in the doorway—a bearded man I've never seen before. His eyes widen as he sees me, and the assault rifle in his hands flies up, pointing at me.

I react on pure instinct.

With a piercing scream, I throw myself off the chair.

A big body lands on top of me, knocking all air out of my lungs before I can roll away. "Shut it, you bitch," the man growls in my ear as a gloved hand claps over my mouth. The pungent odor of male sweat and stale cigarettes chokes my nostrils, and then he yanks me upright by my hair, his hand over my mouth stifling my yelp of pain.

Terrified, I claw at his gloved hand, struggling with all my might, but just like that time with Peter in my kitchen, there's nothing I can do as he drags me out of the room, his rough grip on my hair nearly tearing it out by the roots. Tears of pain stream down my face as he half-drags, half-carries me down the hallway, my panicked screams muffled by his palm.

He's heading to the master suite, where Nora and the baby are, I realize in horror, and then we're there.

Kicking the door open with one booted foot, he pushes me in. "Got Sokolov's bitch," he announces triumphantly, and I see two more armed men inside.

One is holding a knife to Nora's throat, and the other is reaching into the crib for the sleeping baby.

CHAPTER 95
PETER

We're about to start our descent into Bogotá when Julian gets the news.

"That's odd." He frowns, staring at his phone. "Diego just emailed me that there was a shootout with unknown intruders at the northern edge of the estate. Nobody got hurt, and the intruders disappeared back into the jungle before they could be captured. He sent out a team to look for them, but no luck so far."

I get up, my pulse kicking up as my instincts go on full alert. "Who would try to breach your compound like that? And what would they be doing in the jungle at night?"

"Exactly." His face darkens as he stands up and heads to the pilot's cabin, the phone pressed to his ear. "I'm calling Nora."

I follow him as he covers the distance with long strides, ignoring the questioning looks on my teammates' faces.

"Her phone's going straight to voicemail," he says tensely as we enter the pilot's cabin.

Kent looks up at us.

"There was a shootout at the northern border, and I can't reach Nora at the house," Esguerra informs him tersely. "I'm going to pull up the camera feeds at the house. Can you call Yulia?"

Kent nods, his jaw tightening as he reaches for his phone. "I'm on it."

Fuck. I gave Sara a burner phone before we left, but I wasn't going to call her—it's well past midnight, and I want her to get good sleep. But my danger sense is pinging louder with each second.

Sara's phone goes straight to voicemail too, and when I look over at Kent, I can see by his expression that the same thing is happening with Yulia's.

"The cameras are down. I'm sending the guards over," Esguerra says tightly, and I see the bone-deep fear I'm feeling reflected in his eyes.

Something's wrong at the estate.

Very, very wrong.

"Setting course for the compound," Kent says grimly, and the plane tilts underneath me as the engines rev up with a roar.

CHAPTER 96

"Found this one," a fourth man says, dragging in a struggling, nightgown-clad Rosa. He also has his hand clamped over her mouth, muffling her panicked cries. "Looks like we got lucky. The rest of the house is empty. No sign of Esguerra, Kent, or Sokolov." Like his three comrades, he's heavily armed, with an assault rifle slung over his shoulder and two handguns tucked into his belt.

Whoever these men are, they mean business, and we're completely on our own, I realize with a surge of terror. The guards are nowhere near the house, and with Peter and the others away, nobody's coming to our aid.

The man bending over Lizzie's crib straightens, with the still-sleeping baby clasped in front of him. "No blonde?" he says with obvious disappointment.

"Nope, sorry," Rosa's captor says and spins her around to face him. Her mouth opens for a scream, but before she can make a sound, he smashes his fist into her jaw, upper-cut style, and she crumples to the floor, unconscious.

I freeze, staring in horrified disbelief as blood trickles out of one corner of her mouth.

He hit her so casually, as if she weren't a person.

As if he doesn't care if she lives or dies.

"We'll just have to make do with these two," he continues, nodding toward me and white-faced Nora, whose captor is restraining her by holding one hand over her mouth and pressing the knife to her throat with the other. Like me, she's wearing a thin silk robe, but unlike mine, it's gaping open at the top, revealing the inner curves of her breasts.

Rosa's assailant licks his lips, staring at that golden-skinned V, and my stomach twists with sick horror.

Are they planning to rape us?

Kill us?

"Where's the old man?" Nora's captor asks as I resume my panicked struggles, and I realize something about him looks familiar, as if we've met before.

"He went to check out that small building nearby. Said something about wanting to look for his family," my assailant says, restraining me. "Here, bring me some duct tape. This one's getting feisty," he adds, grunting, as I smash my elbow into his ribcage.

"Just knock the bitch out," the asshole who hit Rosa advises, but he brings over the tape anyway. I only have time to let out one short-lived scream before a rag is shoved into my mouth, and the sticky tape is slapped over it.

"That's better," my captor mutters, grabbing my arms. "Now do her wrists too."

The other man is about to obey when Lizzie wakes up with a cry.

"Shit. Silence that kid," Nora's captor orders as the baby, upset at being held by an unfamiliar man, begins to wail at full volume.

Nora's face turns even whiter, her eyes burning like coals as Rosa's assailant heads over and glues the duct tape across the baby's tiny mouth, muffling her outraged screams.

If looks could kill, he would've been eviscerated on the spot.

"Go find Henderson," Nora's captor says to Rosa's assailant. "We'll meet you both downstairs."

The man obeys, exiting the room as I reel from the revelation.

Henderson?

Of course. *That's* what this is about.

Like a cornered rat, Peter's enemy has gone on the attack.

I'm still digesting the implications when a flash of blond hair in the doorway catches my gaze.

My heartbeat jumps.

I'd forgotten all about Yulia.

They haven't found her, but she *was* in the room next to mine.

I have only a millisecond to process her half-naked appearance—and the gun in her hand—because in the next instant, all hell breaks loose.

Smoothly, without any hesitation, Yulia fires at Nora's captor, getting him in the face.

Then she aims the gun at mine.

Time seems to slow, the moment stretching into eternity. I see the fierce concentration in her blue eyes, feel the sudden tension in the hands gripping my arms from behind, and the little bit I remember from Peter's self-defense training kicks in.

Lifting my legs off the floor, I become dead weight in my captor's hold, causing my head to drop by a foot—and as Yulia's gun spits out the bullet, I feel a warm spray of blood as another person's head explodes above mine.

My butt hits the floor, my tailbone screaming at the impact as my captor's body drops behind me.

Yulia's already moving again, aiming at the man holding Lizzie, but there's no need.

He's already crumpling to the floor, Nora's attacker's knife buried in his throat—and the baby clasped safely in her mother's arms.

Did Nora snatch her daughter as she killed him?

Holy fuck, she's fast.

Fighting off my shock, I scramble to my feet, tearing at the duct tape covering my mouth. "The fourth man," I gasp out. "He's—"

"Dead or knocked out," Yulia says, lowering her gun. "I bashed his brains out in the hallway." Her composure is startling—until I remember that she used to be a spy.

I'm about to bring up Henderson when I spot another flash of movement in the doorway.

"Yulia!" I scream, launching forward, but it's too late.

A black-clad arm snakes around her throat with lighting speed, and a gun presses to her temple.

"Not so fast," the older man says softly, using Yulia as a shield as he steps into the room. "Move a muscle, and she dies."

CHAPTER 97
PETER

"Why are your fucking guards so slow?" I bark at Esguerra as he furiously types on his laptop—presumably issuing orders to said guards. "It's already been two minutes. Do you know what can happen in two minutes? They're in that house, alone, unprotected—"

"I know!" Esguerra roars. A vein pulses in his forehead as he slams the laptop shut and jerks to his feet. "You don't think I fucking know? They're on their way, driving as fast as they can. The two guards on house patrol aren't responding; whoever's messing with the cameras and the cell signal must've already offed them."

Fuck. I want to slam my fist into the wall, but it's too dangerous with all the controls in the pilot's cabin. "Are you sure they're still in the house?"

"I know Nora is," Esguerra snaps. "I have tracking implants in her, remember? As of two seconds ago, she was alive and in our room."

Shit. He's right—I forgot about those trackers for a moment. If Nora is alive, then hopefully, Sara is too—which makes it all the more imperative that the guards hurry.

"It's got to be Henderson," Kent says harshly, his knuckles white on the controls. "That fucking bitch lured us out, so he could attack."

"We don't know that for sure," Yan says, and I realize he's joined us in the cockpit. His green gaze swings to Esguerra. "Couldn't it be some other enemy of yours?"

I almost deck Yan. "It doesn't fucking matter who it is. Sara is there, do you understand? She's inside, with whoever they are."

I can't even begin to think of her with Henderson, a man who's desperate enough to take that kind of risk.

A man who didn't hesitate to attack the very country he'd sworn to protect in order to frame me.

What will he do to Sara if he actually has her in his clutches? Will I get there, only to bury her and our unborn child... just like I buried Pasha and Tamila?

No. I push the paralyzing thought away.

I won't let that happen.

Not again.

"Fly faster," I tell Kent grimly. "And Julian, if your guards don't make it there in time, I'll eviscerate them all, each and every single one."

413

CHAPTER 98
SARA

A million thoughts race through my mind. In a flash, I take in the guns on the dead men and on the floor—all within reach, but none close enough to grab before Henderson plants the bullet in Yulia's brain.

My terrified gaze meets Nora's, and I see the same doomed calculation in her eyes.

Even if we were good enough shots to hit Yulia's captor without killing her, we wouldn't be fast enough.

Not with Henderson's gun pressed to her temple.

"Kick away those guns," he orders, and I hesitate for a second, then numbly obey as Nora does the same.

Not only would we be too slow, but Henderson's not much taller than long-limbed Yulia. With him using her as a shield, even a trained sniper wouldn't make the shot.

My gaze falls on the baby clutched tightly against Nora's chest. Lizzie still has the duct tape across her mouth, and I see her little face turning red as she strains to make muffled cries.

Nora is holding her like she will never let her go—and she won't, I realize, taking in her death grip.

I can no longer count on Esguerra's wife for help—not with the infant daughter she needs to protect.

An idea sprouts in my mind, and before I can think better of it, I look at Henderson and say calmly, "I know where your daughter is."

He jerks, as if shot. Recovering swiftly, he demands, "Where?"

"I can take you there," I say, ignoring the knot of fear in my throat. "We can go right now—if you let the others go."

I don't have a plan, or anything resembling one. I just know I want his gun pointed away from Yulia's head—and as far away from Lizzie and Nora as possible. Even if I didn't know about the crimes he's committed, something about the former general would've made my skin crawl. It's nothing outwardly visible—he's trim and fit, in good shape for a man in his late fifties, and his features, framed by a full head of salt-and-pepper hair, are moderately pleasant.

Despite that, he reeks of decay, of rottenness that lurks deep underneath.

At my offer, his eyes narrow. "Do you think I'm an idiot? All three of you will take me to my daughter—or I'll shoot this one." He jabs the gun at Yulia's temple, causing her to wince.

Damn it.

"You don't need *them*," I try again. "You can use me as a hostage. Your beef is with my husband—and he will do anything for me."

"Well, isn't that sweet," he drawls. "A romance for the ages. Maybe I'll kill you later and make him watch. How does that sound?"

I stare at him without flinching, ignoring the nausea spreading through me.

I'm not going to show this monster any fear.

He won't get that satisfaction.

At my lack of response, annoyance flits across his features. "Fine," he snaps. "Like I said, all three of you are coming with me. You and that one with the baby"—he jerks his chin toward Nora—"will go in front of me. And remember, one wrong move, and this one"—he jabs the gun at Yulia's head again—"gets it. Understand? Now walk toward me."

Swallowing, I step toward the door, and Nora cautiously follows, cradling squirming Lizzie against her chest. Henderson backs out into the hallway, still shielding himself with Yulia, and as soon as we're out of the room, he orders us to go downstairs.

"You *will* lead me to my daughter, understand?" he says darkly as we start toward the stairs. "If you try anything, anything at all, I'm going to shoot every one of you bitches—and Esguerra's demon spawn as well."

Locking my knees to stop them from shaking, I approach the wide, curving staircase. The floor is icy under my bare feet, and my heart feels like it's going to jump out of my throat. I don't know what to do, how to get us out of this situation. Henderson's daughter is safe and sound far away from here—all Peter has is the fake video given to him by Bonnie—but Henderson wouldn't believe me if I told him that. And if he did believe me, he'd probably kill us all.

Whether he realizes it or not, he didn't come here to save his family.

He's here for revenge.

Deep inside, he knows he's already lost, and he came on this suicidal mission to make Peter and the others suffer before he dies.

My hands toy with the knot on my robe tie to keep from shaking as I descend as slowly as I can, with Henderson and Yulia a step behind me. Nora is walking to the right of me, her face carefully blank as she holds Lizzie protectively in front of her.

She'd do anything for her daughter, I know—as would I for the tiny life growing inside me.

A life that won't see the light of day if the man behind me has his way.

We're halfway down the staircase when I see headlights through one of the living room windows and hear the front door burst open, followed by the thumping of boots on the wooden floor.

My heartbeat spikes with equal parts relief and terror.

The guards are here.

Somehow, they've found out we're in trouble—and now Henderson is truly cornered.

Alone, without his team, he stands no real chance of escape.

I hear him curse under his breath above me, and a vague plan forms in my mind.

Continuing to descend at the same slow pace, I pull on my robe tie, untying it, and the cool air washes over my bare skin as the silk robe falls on the stairs behind me—pooling right underneath Yulia's and her captor's feet.

The guards burst into the foyer, and I dive for Nora, pushing her against the railing as it happens.

With Henderson's attention focused on the guards, he and Yulia both slip on the fallen robe—and his shot goes wild as Yulia skids down the stairs on her bottom.

Without hesitation, the guards fire at Henderson, and Nora and I huddle together, shielding Lizzie as we hear him fall.

CHAPTER 99
PETER

It's been a day since we've gotten back, and I still can't stop touching Sara, can't stop holding her. Every other minute, I also fight the urge to inspect her from head to toe—even though Dr. Goldberg has already examined her and pronounced her and the baby healthy.

Cradling her on my lap, I stroke her hair and breathe in her sweet scent, a tremor running through my body each time I think about how close I'd come to losing her... how the guards had found her huddling naked on the stairs an hour before we finally burst in.

She tripped Henderson with her silk robe, saving herself, Nora, and Yulia in the process.

The three of them fought against armed mercenaries and won.

"It's fine. We're fine," she murmurs, lifting her head, and I realize I said the last bit out loud. Her hazel eyes gleam softly as she curves her slender palm over my jaw. "I promise you, other than Yulia's tailbone and poor Rosa's jaw, we're totally okay."

"I know," I mutter. "And it's a fucking miracle." Covering her hand with mine, I close my eyes and inhale deeply, trying to calm the mad pounding of my heart.

Like me, Kent and Esguerra had been going out of their minds by the time we landed, though Diego had already informed us that Henderson was dead and our wives were safe. It hadn't been enough to know it intellectually; the awful fear had stayed with me until the moment I laid eyes on Sara.

Until I could hold her in my arms and feel that she's alive and well.

"You saved everyone, you know," I say thickly, opening my eyes as she withdraws her hand. "Not just on the stairs, but before. Kent told me it was your scream that woke up Yulia in time for her to hide under the bed and then come to your rescue. If not for that—"

"We would've defeated them some other way," Sara interrupts with a calm smile. "I'm certain we would have."

The conviction in her voice is both absurd and admirable. For whatever reason, rather than re-traumatizing her, yesterday's attack seems to have energized my ptichka in some way. I've always known that she's strong and capable, but she herself must not have believed it—until she fought my enemy and won.

"Sometimes, a repeat trauma can be perversely healing," Dr. Wessex told me when I spoke to her this morning, after Sara slept through the night without nightmares and woke up as upbeat as I've ever seen her. "Unlike what happened with her parents, this time, she was able to do something—and nobody close to her got killed or truly hurt."

I don't know if I believe the therapist—it has only been a day, and it could still hit Sara later—but I'm cautiously optimistic about my ptichka's mental state.

My own, I'm less certain about. Last night, I barely slept, battling nightmares and cold sweats.

"I'm not letting you out of my sight ever again," I say—and I'm not joking one bit. "No more overnight missions away from you, no work that keeps us apart for any length of time. And I've already ordered my own set of tracker implants from Esguerra; as soon as they arrive, they're going in."

Sara doesn't blink—I've already told her about Nora's trackers. "All right," she says. "But only if you get them too. I want to know where you are at all times also."

I hold her gaze. "It's a deal."

I'll get anything my ptichka wants—as long as she's content and safe.

———

"Are you upset that you didn't get a chance to kill him?" she asks as we're lying in bed a few hours later. Though we've just had sex, I'm stroking her all over, unable to get enough of the sensory pleasure of touching her, of feeling her warm, silky skin under my palms. "I know it was important to you," she continues as I nuzzle her neck, inhaling the sweet perfume of her hair.

I don't want to think about Henderson right now, but Sara seems determined to talk about every aspect of what happened. And when I recall how difficult it had been for her to discuss her parents' deaths, I can't deny her.

If it helps her process things, I'll tell her all about how I dream about dismembering Henderson cell by cell—about how the mere mention of his name brings back every terrible moment on the plane.

So I do exactly that—I tell her everything, all about how terrified I'd been that we'd be too late… that I would fail to protect her, like I'd failed Pasha and Tamila. I describe the nightmares I had last night and how I still shake when I think about how close I'd come to losing her.

I tell her how much it kills me that I wasn't there to confront my enemy, to keep her and our unborn child safe.

She listens, her head resting on my shoulder and her fingers playing with my hair, and when I'm done, she says quietly, "You did keep us safe. It was the move you taught me—lifting my legs to become dead weight when someone's grabbed you from behind—that helped the three of us defeat those mercenaries. And it was you, Kent, and Esguerra who sent in the guards who killed Henderson."

I squeeze my eyes shut, my arms tightening around her as the scene plays out in my mind as it must've happened, with the silk robe and all. A shudder racks my body, and she hugs me back, holding me, reassuring me with her warmth, her aliveness, her strength.

It takes several deep breaths before I can loosen my suffocating hold on her. Still, I keep my arm around her, holding her close. It'll take me years to recover from that day—decades, even.

That is, assuming I ever recover at all.

"What about his wife?" Sara asks, distracting me from a fantasy where I'm able to travel back in time and strangle Henderson with his own intestines before he gets anywhere near her. "Will you honor your bargain with her?"

My free hand curls into a fist at my side. "The jury is still out on whether she purposefully lured us away, so—"

"No, she didn't," Sara interrupts, lifting her head from my shoulder to look at me. "At least I don't think she did. Henderson really thought we had his daughter; if his wife was in on it, he would've known it was all a ploy. And when those men captured us, they said something about there being no sign of you three—as if they were expecting to find you here, and were surprised they didn't."

"Ah." With effort, I unclench my fingers. "That does change things."

If Bonnie Henderson is truly innocent, I will leave her alone—particularly if she turns over all the evidence on her husband to the FBI, clearing our names.

I want that for Sara. I want to give her back a normal, peaceful life.

Sliding my hand into her hair, I study her heart-shaped face, marveling at its beauty. Her eyes stare into mine, clear and direct, and then she murmurs, "I love you," and leans in for a tender kiss.

My chest expands with a rush of feeling so intense that it drowns out the lingering darkness. "I love you too, ptichka," I say softly, and as our lips touch, I know that no matter what the future holds, we'll conquer it together.

Regardless of how our love was born, it's now strong enough.

EPILOGUE
SARA

Six Years Later

"Papa! Papa!"

I look up from my laptop as my five-year-old barrels through the door, his cheeks pink from the cold and his boots tracking snow everywhere. Not noticing me on the couch, he runs straight to Peter in the kitchen, launching his small body at him at full speed.

Grinning, my husband steps away from the birthday cake and catches him in his powerful arms, lifting him to twirl him above his head.

Charlie's laughing shrieks fill the air, mixing with our dog's excited barking, and my chest squeezes—as it does every time I see that look on Peter's darkly handsome face.

Joy. Such unrestrained joy.

I'll never tire of seeing the two of them together.

My tormentor-turned-lover and our son.

If happiness could be defined in an image, this would be it for me.

"Mom! Charlie threw a snowball at me and Bella," Maya yells, running into the room with snow and ice falling from her jacket. Her little face is outraged, her tiny hands balled into fists. "And Lizzie called him a bad word!"

Laughing, I set aside my laptop and catch my tattletale three-year-old in a hug. "It's okay, my darling," I soothe, stroking her tangled chestnut curls as Toby, our golden retriever, runs over to lick the snow from her coat. "Your brother was just playing. He's got a little crush on Bella, that is all."

"I do not!" Charlie's outraged tone matches his sister's. "She's way too blond and weird, and she barely speaks Russian."

"Hey now," Peter reprimands, setting him down. "That's not nice."

"Bella Kent speaks as much Russian as you do, you doofus," Maya says pompously, her little chin going up as she steps out of my hug. Pushing Toby away, she adds, "And in any case, she's only four. Her vocabulary will grow like yours did. Not everyone is born smart like me."

Peter and I exchange a look. Then, unable to help ourselves, we burst out laughing.

Our birthday girl is on a roll today.

Charlie was two and a half when Maya was born, but this past year, she's started teaching him math and reading—the latter in English, Russian, French, and Japanese. Her mind is like a sponge, and her brilliance is matched only by her ego.

For all her off-the-charts IQ, modesty is a concept her three-year-old brain can't quite grasp.

"I thought you told me you *weren't* a child genius?" Peter said to me in amazement when our daughter took up music composition at age two. "That you became a doctor so young because of your parents, not because you were insanely smart?"

"And that's all true. I don't know where this is coming from," I told him, equally puzzled. "Maybe there's some genius DNA in you."

Not that Charlie, our first child, isn't smart. He's bright and curious and energetic—everything we've ever wanted in a son. He's thriving in his private school here in Switzerland; according to his teachers, he's as clever as they come.

Maya, though, is on an entirely different level.

It would be intimidating if she weren't so stinking cute.

"Go tell the others to come in," I say, catching her by her jacket hood. "It's time for cake."

Her tiny face—a miniature replica of mine—lights up, and she bounces out of the room, with Charlie on her heels. Toby jumps onto the couch to curl up next to me, and I use the quiet minute to review the new song I'm composing before closing my laptop.

With everybody here for Maya's birthday, I won't have time to finish it today.

After Bonnie Henderson helped clear Peter's name, we had the option of returning to the Chicago area and resuming our life there. However, we decided against it. Not only would we be subjected to suspicious looks everywhere we went, thanks to our faces being all over the news after the bombing, but without my parents, there was nothing really tying me to Homer Glen. So instead, we decided to make a new home in the Swiss Alps, near the private clinic where I'd been offered a job while we were on the run.

I started working there full-time, but within a month, Peter and I realized that with the pregnancy tiring me out—and us not wanting to be apart for more than a few hours at a time—it wasn't the best solution. So I opened my own practice on the first floor of our home, where I could set my own hours and see Peter throughout the day. Before long, the clinic began referring their pregnant patients to me, and I became the go-to OB-GYN for women with various ties to the underworld.

It's worked out well—particularly since Peter has decided to put his skills and contacts to a new use: recruiting and training former soldiers to work as mercenaries for organizations like Esguerra's.

It's not exactly the peaceful civilian life we were envisioning, but it's way less dangerous than high-profile assassinations—and much more interesting for Peter than teaching regular citizens basic self-defense. As for me, with my flexible work schedule, I not only have time for Peter and our two children, but also my music.

I no longer perform live or have a YouTube channel— after everything that's happened, Peter's become too paranoid about my safety—but I have the satisfaction of having my songs performed by some of the most popular new stars, who pay me well for ghost-writing them. My darker lyrics are especially popular, with two of my songs topping the charts for weeks.

"Cake! Cake! Cake!" The kids burst in like snow-filled tornadoes, with five-year-old Mateo Esguerra in the lead and Bella, Lizzie, Charlie, and Maya chasing him. Squealing, the children surround Peter, who's ceremoniously setting up three candles, and Toby jumps off the couch and runs over to them, barking his head off in excitement.

The adults come in next. As usual, Julian has one arm draped around Nora, holding her against him as if afraid she might run away. Lucas is more circumspect with Yulia, but given the wet pattern on both of their jackets, it's clear they've been rolling in the snow—and I can only hope it was out of the kids' sight.

Charlie, being an intrepid explorer of all and sundry, has already come upon them "playing doctor" in their gym in Cyprus once.

Either way, I'm pleased they're all here. While Peter and I visit the Esguerras semi-regularly, Yulia's been so busy with her restaurants that I've only seen her twice this year. Luckily, little Bella Kent is not-so-secretly obsessed with our Charlie—who claims to hate her but never passes up a chance to get her attention—so Lucas and Yulia had no choice but to show up for Maya's birthday party.

Their beautiful blond angel of a daughter would've puppy-eyed them to death otherwise.

Walking over, I greet Nora and Yulia with a hug. Then we all gather around the cake next to our children, and as Maya blows out her candles, I meet Peter's gaze and make my own wish.

I want him to torment me like this forever—to love me with all the darkness in his heart.

Thank you for reading! I hope you enjoyed the conclusion of Peter & Sara's story and would consider leaving a review. To learn when I have a new book out, please sign up for my newsletter at www.annazaires.com.

Craving more of these characters? Then don't miss:
- *The Twist Me Trilogy* – Nora & Julian's dark tale, where Peter first appears and gets his list
- *The Capture Me Trilogy* – Lucas & Yulia's breathtaking enemies-to-lovers romance

Ready for my other sizzling stories? Check out:
- *The Mia & Korum Trilogy* – an epic sci-fi romance with the ultimate alpha male
- *The Krinar Captive* – Emily & Zaron's captive romance, set just before the Krinar Invasion

- *The Krinar Exposé* – my scorching hot collaboration with Hettie Ivers, featuring Amy & Vair—and their sex club games
- *The Krinar World stories* – Sci-fi romance stories by other authors, set in the Krinar world

Prefer action, fantasy, and sci-fi? Check out these collaborations with my hubby, Dima Zales:

- *The Girl Who Sees* – the thrilling tale of Sasha Urban, a stage illusionist who discovers unexpected secret powers
- *Mind Dimensions* – the action-packed urban fantasy adventures of Darren, who can stop time and read minds
- *Transcendence* – the mind-blowing technothriller featuring venture capitalist Mike Cohen, whose Brainocyte technology will forever change the world
- *The Last Humans* – the futuristic sci-fi/dystopian story of Theo, who lives in a world where nothing is as it seems
- *The Sorcery Code* – the epic fantasy adventures of sorcerer Blaise and his creation, the beautiful and powerful Gala

Additionally, if you like audiobooks, please visit www.annazaires.com to check out this series and our other books in audio.

And now please turn the page for a little taste of *Twist Me*, *Capture Me*, and *The Krinar Exposé*.

EXCERPT FROM TWIST ME

Kidnapped. Taken to a private island.

I never thought this could happen to me. I never imagined one chance meeting on the eve of my eighteenth birthday could change my life so completely.

Now I belong to him. To Julian. To a man who is as ruthless as he is beautiful—a man whose touch makes me burn. A man whose tenderness I find more devastating than his cruelty.

My captor is an enigma. I don't know who he is or why he took me. There is a darkness inside him—a darkness that scares me even as it draws me in.

My name is Nora Leston, and this is my story.

It's evening now. With every minute that passes, I'm starting to get more and more anxious at the thought of seeing my captor again.

The novel that I've been reading can no longer hold my interest. I put it down and walk in circles around the room.

I am dressed in the clothes Beth had given me earlier. It's not what I would've chosen to wear, but it's better than a bathrobe. A sexy pair of white lacy panties and a matching bra for underwear. A pretty blue sundress that buttons in the front. Everything fits me suspiciously well. Has he been stalking me for a while? Learning everything about me, including my clothing size?

The thought makes me sick.

I am trying not to think about what's to come, but it's impossible. I don't know why I'm so sure he'll come to me tonight. It's possible he has an entire harem of women stashed away on this island, and he visits each one only once a week, like sultans used to do.

Yet somehow I know he'll be here soon. Last night had simply whetted his appetite. I know he's not done with me, not by a long shot.

Finally, the door opens.

He walks in like he owns the place. Which, of course, he does.

I am again struck by his masculine beauty. He could've been a model or a movie star, with a face like his. If there was any fairness in the world, he would've been short or had some other imperfection to offset that face.

But he doesn't. His body is tall and muscular, perfectly proportioned. I remember what it feels like to have him inside me, and I feel an unwelcome jolt of arousal.

He's again wearing jeans and a T-shirt. A gray one this time. He seems to favor simple clothing, and he's smart to do so. His looks don't need any enhancement.

He smiles at me. It's his fallen angel smile—dark and seductive at the same time. "Hello, Nora."

I don't know what to say to him, so I blurt out the first thing that pops into my head. "How long are you going to keep me here?"

He cocks his head slightly to the side. "Here in the room? Or on the island?"

"Both."

"Beth will show you around tomorrow, take you swimming if you'd like," he says, approaching me. "You won't be locked in, unless you do something foolish."

"Such as?" I ask, my heart pounding in my chest as he stops next to me and lifts his hand to stroke my hair.

"Trying to harm Beth or yourself." His voice is soft, his gaze hypnotic as he looks down at me. The way he's touching my hair is oddly relaxing.

I blink, trying to break his spell. "And what about on the island? How long will you keep me here?"

His hand caresses my face, curves around my cheek. I catch myself leaning into his touch, like a cat getting petted, and I immediately stiffen.

His lips curl into a knowing smile. The bastard knows the effect he has on me. "A long time, I hope," he says.

For some reason, I'm not surprised. He wouldn't have bothered bringing me all the way here if he just wanted to fuck me a few times. I'm terrified, but I'm not surprised.

I gather my courage and ask the next logical question. "Why did you kidnap me?"

The smile leaves his face. He doesn't answer, just looks at me with an inscrutable blue gaze.

I begin to shake. "Are you going to kill me?"

"No, Nora, I won't kill you."

His denial reassures me, although he could obviously be lying.

"Are you going to sell me?" I can barely get the words out. "Like to be a prostitute or something?"

"No," he says softly. "Never. You're mine and mine alone."

I feel a tiny bit calmer, but there is one more thing I have to know. "Are you going to hurt me?"

For a moment, he doesn't answer again. Something dark briefly flashes in his eyes. "Probably," he says quietly.

And then he leans down and kisses me, his warm lips soft and gentle on mine.

For a second, I stand there frozen, unresponsive. I believe him. I know he's telling the truth when he says he'll hurt me. There's something in him that scares me—that has scared me from the very beginning.

He's nothing like the boys I've gone on dates with. He's capable of anything.

And I'm completely at his mercy.

I think about trying to fight him again. That would be the normal thing to do in my situation. The brave thing to do.

And yet I don't do it.

I can feel the darkness inside him. There's something wrong with him. His outer beauty hides something monstrous underneath.

I don't want to unleash that darkness. I don't know what will happen if I do.

So I stand still in his embrace and let him kiss me. And when he picks me up again and takes me to bed, I don't try to resist in any way.

Instead, I close my eyes and give in to the sensations.

———————

All three books in the *Twist Me* trilogy are now available. Please visit my website at www.annazaires.com to learn more and to sign up for my new release email list.

EXCERPT FROM CAPTURE ME

He's my enemy... and my assignment.

One night—that's all it should be. One night of raw, primal passion.

When his plane goes down, it should be the end. Instead, it's just the beginning.

I betrayed Lucas Kent, and now he'll make me pay.

He steps into my apartment as soon as the door swings open. No hesitation, no greeting—he just comes in.

Startled, I step back, the short, narrow hallway suddenly stiflingly small. I'd somehow forgotten how big he is, how broad his shoulders are. I'm tall for a woman—tall enough to fake being a model if an assignment calls for it—but he towers a full head above me. With the heavy down jacket he's wearing, he takes up almost the entire hallway.

Still not saying a word, he closes the door behind him and advances toward me. Instinctively, I back away, feeling like cornered prey.

"Hello, Yulia," he murmurs, stopping when we're out of the hallway. His pale gaze is locked on my face. "I wasn't expecting to see you like this."

I swallow, my pulse racing. "I just took a bath." I want to seem calm and confident, but he's got me completely off-balance. "I wasn't expecting visitors."

"No, I can see that." A faint smile appears on his lips, softening the hard line of his mouth. "Yet you let me in. Why?"

"Because I didn't want to continue talking through the door." I take a steadying breath. "Can I offer you some tea?" It's a stupid thing to say, given what he's here for, but I need a few moments to compose myself.

He raises his eyebrows. "Tea? No, thanks."

"Then can I take your jacket?" I can't seem to stop playing the hostess, using politeness to cover my anxiety. "It looks quite warm."

Amusement flickers in his wintry gaze. "Sure." He takes off his down jacket and hands it to me. He's left wearing a black sweater and dark jeans tucked into black winter boots. The jeans hug his legs, revealing muscular thighs and powerful calves, and on his belt, I see a gun sitting in a holster.

Irrationally, my breathing quickens at the sight, and it takes a concerted effort to keep my hands from shaking as I take the jacket and walk over to hang it in my tiny closet. It's not a surprise that he's armed—it would be a shock if he wasn't—but the gun is a stark reminder of who Lucas Kent is.

What he is.

It's no big deal, I tell myself, trying to calm my frayed nerves. I'm used to dangerous men. I was raised among them. This man is not that different. I'll sleep with him, get whatever information I can, and then he'll be out of my life.

Yes, that's it. The sooner I can get it done, the sooner all of this will be over.

Closing the closet door, I paste a practiced smile on my face and turn back to face him, finally ready to resume the role of confident seductress.

Except he's already next to me, having crossed the room without making a sound.

My pulse jumps again, my newfound composure fleeing. He's close enough that I can see the gray striations in his pale blue eyes, close enough that he can touch me.

And a second later, he does touch me.

Lifting his hand, he runs the back of his knuckles over my jaw.

I stare up at him, confused by my body's instant response. My skin warms and my nipples tighten, my breath coming faster. It doesn't make sense for this hard, ruthless stranger to turn me on. His boss is more handsome, more striking, yet it's Kent my body's reacting to. All he's touched thus far is my face. It should be nothing, yet it's intimate somehow.

Intimate and disturbing.

I swallow again. "Mr. Kent—Lucas—are you sure I can't offer you something to drink? Maybe some coffee or—" My words end in a breathless gasp as he reaches for the tie of my robe and tugs on it, as casually as one would unwrap a package.

"No." He watches as the robe falls open, revealing my naked body underneath. "No coffee."

All three books in the *Capture Me* trilogy are now available. If you'd like to find out more, please visit my website at www.annazaires.com.

THE KRINAR EXPOSÉ

What happens in an alien sex club stays in an alien sex club, right?

Well... not if you pen an exposé on the place. And certainly not if you omit the fact that the experiences in the article are your own.

Or if the Krinar you've hooked up with is the club's owner, whose many kinks involve blackmail and mind games.

For a young journalist out to prove herself, it's all about landing the next big story.

Until it becomes all about landing in a possessive alien's penthouse bed.

———————

Tires rolled to a stop a few feet from the curb in front of me, and I craned my neck enough to make out a black stretch limo—not the cab I'd been hoping for. I started to amble on farther down the sidewalk to where a cabbie would be better able to spot me, when I heard the sound of car doors opening.

Sure, rapid footsteps fell smoothly upon the concrete in my direction.

Too smoothly.

Some innate self-preservation instinct made my pulse quicken. I had a mad compulsion to drop my boxes and flee, but I was wearing my practical two-inch heels paired with a very impractical pencil skirt. It was doubtful I'd be able to outrun a K.

A second later, it was too late entirely as I sensed *his* heat at my back—running along the entire length of my body, blocking out any trace of the evening breeze. I froze as the familiar scent of inhuman male perfection assaulted my olfaction, bringing with it the memory of the most carnally gratifying night of my life.

Oh, fuck.

My stomach clenched. My nipples hardened. The rest of my body seemed to have a vivid memory of that night as well, judging by its immediate—and mortifying— Pavlovian response to Vair's mere presence. My inner muscles fluttered in anticipation, slick heat rushing to lubricate my sex.

I reminded my stupid sex that this was the same alien who had just destroyed my career and my life. He was the enemy who had invaded my planet. *An enemy who was possibly about to kill me as well.*

Or worse—turn me over to Krinar authorities.

But when warm, long fingers encircled my right bicep, another jolt of sexual electricity shot through me. And when his other hand latched onto my left hip, it felt oddly reassuring, momentarily calming and centering.

"Get in the car, Amy." The command was accompanied by gentle pressure at my crown as Vair physically maneuvered me into the limousine before I had sense enough to put up a fight.

He followed closely behind, folding his huge form gracefully into the luxuriously upholstered passenger cab and taking the seat across from me. The car began moving while I remained stock still—frozen in place amid a mixture of heart-pounding shock, fear, and anticipation.

The moment Vair was settled and his full attention was fixed upon me where we sat face to face, I blushed. And not just a little flush that could pass for nervousness or be attributed to recent exertion from the heavy boxes I'd carried, either. It was the kind that made my skin feel sun-blistered and my head dizzy. The kind that screamed "guilty" in a court of law.

The sort of blush that broadcast exactly how well I remembered the sensation of him plunging deep inside me and the sound of his masculine groans and grunts as he spent himself in me... in my mouth... across my back, my stomach, my...

I broke eye contact—for fear of passing out—and let my eyes roam about as if investigating my surroundings. But I barely took in any of it. Every cell and fiber of my being was too acutely aware of the god-like alien sitting across from me.

Watching me.

God, he was so much better-looking than my masturbatory sessions had given him credit for. So much bigger. More predatory.

Way more dangerous.

"What are you going to do to me?" My voice betrayed me, emerging too high-pitched and with a slight quiver. Pitiable-sounding. *Damn it.*

He seemed taken aback by my question at first—or perhaps by my tone—as he returned his attention to me, but then a slow, sensuous smile spread across his wide mouth and full lips. "What indeed?" His forefinger brushed absently across those gorgeous lips, and I had to remind myself to focus on his mocking tone—and on finding a way to live through this.

My pulse raced as it hit me. *He was blackmailing me?*

Horror and excitement gripped me at once. If I was right and he intended to blackmail me with the video footage of our night together, then there was a chance the video hadn't been released to the masses yet. And I would do anything to prevent its release. Even if it meant…

Fine. It was inevitable.

"You want me to retract what I wrote in my article," I stated, my voice flat. My career as a journalist would be over, but at least I'd walk away with some shred of dignity if I could keep that sex tape out of circulation.

He frowned. "Of course not. Your exposé was brilliant. And"—his tongue ran casually across his full bottom lip as his gaze swept over me—"enlightening."

The heat that pooled anew in my belly was as untimely as it was unwelcome.

I gave myself a mental shake. "You don't want me to retract what I said?" A sense of dread crept up my spine at the realization that I might not have any bargaining chip at all.

"No." His lips parted in a lazy smile as his dark eyes held mine.

Then his gaze fell to my breasts.

My palms were slick with sweat where they gripped the leather seat beneath me. I swallowed. Breathed. "Why the video footage then?"

He leaned forward, his expression deathly serious as reproving eyes returned to mine. "You didn't call, Amy."

It was as if all the air had suddenly been sucked out of the limo.

"You never came back to my club."

I'd soaked through my panties by "Amy"—in spite of the confusion and mild terror that his abruptly accusatory tone evoked.

"I didn't know you wanted me to." The truth tumbled out defensively, faster than I could process what he'd said as conflicting emotions flared to life within me. "I mean—I didn't mean for anything to happen... with you... that night at the club."

What the hell was I saying?

What was he saying?

A bead of sweat trickled down between my shoulder blades, causing me to shiver in my silk blouse. It was freezing in the limo now.

"I see. You were a victim then?" His tone was earnest, but his eyes appeared amused. Smug.

I felt my anger rising. There was no easy answer to his question. I kept my knees glued together and my sweaty palms planted on the seat in an effort to subvert my shaking.

"I never meant for anything to happen between us that night," I reiterated, my words clear and firm despite the dryness now choking my throat.

He sighed. "Humans complicate the most basic emotions by experiencing them through extraneous social filters." His eyes projected a strange sort of pity— and a measure of quiet disappointment that was somehow unsettling.

I needed water. *I needed out of Vair's limo.*

I needed answers more.

"Is it on the internet already?" I blurted, my heart pounding in my ears.

"Is what on the internet, love?"

"You know what!"

"Answer my question, and I'll answer yours," he countered.

"I'm not a victim."

"Good." He said, with the look of a jungle cat ready to pounce. The face of a starving man intent on his favorite meal. "I don't play well with victims."

The Krinar Exposé is now available. Please visit my website at www.annazaires.com to learn more.

ABOUT THE AUTHOR

Anna Zaires is a *New York Times, USA Today,* and #1 international bestselling author of sci-fi romance and contemporary dark erotic romance. She fell in love with books at the age of five, when her grandmother taught her to read. Since then, she has always lived partially in a fantasy world where the only limits were those of her imagination. Currently residing in Florida, Anna is happily married to Dima Zales (a science fiction and fantasy author) and closely collaborates with him on all their works.

To learn more, please visit www.annazaires.com.

Printed in Great Britain
by Amazon

81006151R00261